JUDITH BROOKER

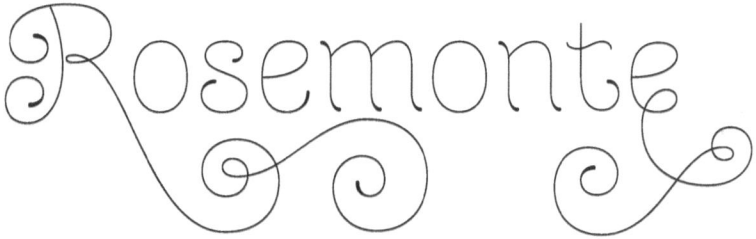

A novel based off of real events

ROSEMONTE

Dedicated to J.P.S.
I miss you too.

Printed in the United States of America

First Edition: July 2014

ISBN 978-0-692-20093-3

Common Day Publishing

9813 Lago Drive

Boynton Beach, Florida 33472

www.JudithBrooker.com

10 9 8 7 6 5 4 3 2 1

A note to the reader

Rosemonte is fiction but it has been loosely based on some of my real life experiences. Details have been changed to protect the identity of guilty or innocent parties. I hope you'll laugh along with Julia as she navigates her way through the hilarious mess that is her life. Please enjoy.

XOXO

Judith Brooker

Chapter 1

As I looked in the mirror I thought, okay good. I mean, what *do* you wear to a job interview for a sales person at a cemetery? Obviously black, that's a no brainer. But I needed to make myself stand out so I chose to wear my super high, jewel-tone Pucci style heels. I felt the geometric kaleidoscope print would make a statement. Looking back, maybe that wasn't my smartest move. I figured crazy shoes, a conservative suit, my long dark hair pulled back into a sleek chignon, in addition to a few tricks up my sleeve. How bad could it be?

On the way to my car I kept thinking I had forgotten something. I had my purse, a pen, and two sample trays featuring an assortment of my baked treats, one sugar free and one regular. A bag packed with a change of clothes because I had to go to work after the interview. A ringing recommendation from, Adam, my best friend who worked for his own family's funeral home, the most lucrative one in town. I knew how to get to the cemetery, so why did I feel so lost?

I was twenty-six, zaftig but not an uggo. For my age I was slightly accomplished. I owned my own home, had my own baking company, and a car that was paid off. On paper I looked good. However, that wasn't reality. My business needed to make more money. Plain and simple, I was barely afloat. Was I ready to quit the bakery and jump into another field that had absolutely nothing to do with baking? I'd graduated culinary school with huge dreams. Dreams of having a fancy pastry shop of my own, or a masterpiece confection that graced the cover of a foodie magazine. Those dreams seemed so far away from where I was in my life. I was tired of working eighteen hour days. I had leather hands from numerous burns at the oven. My life was all work all the time. I needed to make a change. The question was, was this the right one?

As I drove the forty-five minutes from South Philly to Jenkintown, my mind was all over the place. I turned onto Oak Hill Road and continued for a mile or so. My destination was set far back from the street, Rosemonte. My grandfather, who I'd never met, was buried there. He died way before I was born. There was a place saved for my grandmother next to him. I felt strange going there for an interview instead of a funeral.

The tall black wrought iron gates were open but looked like they might slam shut behind me. My Honda chugged up the steep hill to the office, which was like an ancient temple, all stone with heavy double doors. I pulled around to the back of the building and squeezed down the narrow driveway carefully. I didn't want to scrape the sides of my car.

I was there for an interview, nothing more. The clouds were grey and could open at any moment. Did I really feel like carrying an umbrella along with my sample trays? No, but I had my Prada purse and if that got wet I'd really be pissed. Looking at the clock I had to make a decision, which was so hard for me to do. No umbrella. Roll the dice.

I opened my car door and stepped out onto the gravel driveway. Gravel wasn't the best to walk on in four inch heels while carrying two giant cookie trays. Oy, what had I let Adam talk me into? I opened the door and clip-clopped into the office.

A man smiled at me. "Could I be of any assistance, miss?" His blue plastic nametag had Ronald printed on it. Would I have to wear one too? It looked so tacky.

"I'm here to see Bernie Sapowitz." I smiled back as I heaved the trays onto the counter.

Ronald looked kindly at me and said, "I'm Ronnie. Have a seat."

He disappeared into an office. An older man, old enough to be my father, Ronnie wore a class ring from Brandeis as well as a matching lapel pin. The clock in the waiting area confirmed I was right on time.

He reappeared and lead me to a small office. I tried to walk softly, but my heels were making a ruckus. So embarrassing. The entire office was silent, except for my heels.

When we got to the door, Ronnie turned and shook my hand. "Those cookies look good."

I smiled and felt my cheeks start to blush. "Have some. They're for the office. I have a bakery business."

Ronnie announced, "I'm going to brew a fresh pot of coffee." He left me there.

I entered the room, extended my hand and introduced myself. "Hi, I'm Julia. Adam's friend," I said with a bright smile.

The man who didn't get up shook my hand and announced, "Bernie Sapowitz. I run Rosemonte. I do everything around here except own the joint." He was younger than Ronnie, but not by much. He wasn't a good looking man. He had wiry Jewfro hair that was thinning all around. Numerous skin tags dotted the side of his neck, and a dime-sized dark brown spot sat on his cheek.

Bernie waved me to a chair. "Please excuse me, for not getting up. I have knee issues. I'll need replacements, a whole long process that I don't want to do. The recovery is a pain in the ass from what I hear."

T.M.I. I said nothing.

The office had horrible 1970s wood paneling and a table way too big for the room. The six chairs around the table were also too large, and looked like they had seen better days. A musty smell was in the air.

A tall man, even sitting down. Bernie towered over me. I asked, "How tall are you?"

He laughed and replied, "six-four. It's been a long time since anyone has asked me how tall I am."

"I find that hard to believe," I said. I crossed my legs and focused on not shaking my foot because I was nervous. Be cool, I thought to myself.

Bernie asked, "Resume?"

"My what?" I said. Damn. That's what I'd forgotten. Actually, I hadn't forgotten to bring it. I'd forgotten to prepare one. I was such an asshole. Think, think! "I forgot it at home. Can I fax it later today?"

He nodded. "That's okay."

I suddenly felt completely unprepared for the interview. My brain channeled back to when I was in high school, taking business ed. The class taught us how to act on an interview. So far I wasn't remembering much. Probably should've done some research last night, I thought, instead of painting my nails.

Bernie started the interview by asking me a bunch of questions. Some seemed inappropriate; many were none of his business, and a handful had nothing to do with anything. But I found myself answering them because I wanted to make a good impression. If Bernie wanted to know about my boyfriend or lack thereof, I would tell him. He inquired about my family life. Parents, siblings, education, the whole nine yards. I gave honest answers. I told him what I thought he wanted to hear.

"My mother lives in California. We're not that close. I'm an only child. I graduated at the top of my class from culinary school. I really enjoy being my own boss. No steady boyfriend." I sounded like such a spaz. Pull it together!

Next Bernie dove into my relationship with Adam. Now things were getting a little sticky. "Why aren't you dating Adam? He's a fine young man."

Oy vey. "Adam has a girlfriend," I answered.

"I know, but she's a shiksa, and you're a nice Jewish girl."

OMG. What was this, a Jewish dating service? Just as I reached my breaking point there was a knock at the door.

"Who's there, what do you want?" Bernie barked.

I was taken aback. One minute he was acting like a yenta, the next like a grumpy old man.

"It's Matt," called the voice.

"Oh, Matt, come in," Bernie said, his voice back to yenta mode.

Matt opened the door. I immediately thought; watch out, Julia, this guy's a snake. There was something about him I didn't like. Maybe it was his poor posture, or his pleated pants. When he offered his hand for me to shake, it felt like a wet noodle. Gross! He plopped down next to me, giving off a faint odor of Old Spice. Double gross.

Bernie talked shop for a minute. I looked at Matt. Early fifty's, smallish build, full head of mostly gray hair styled like a little boy's. The old-fashioned bowl cut. After the age of six, hardly anyone can pull that off. Matt incessantly nodded his head at Bernie. He was a yes man. There's one in almost every company.

Bernie boasted that Matt was the head of Family Service and the top salesperson month after month.

I asked, "Family Service?"

Bernie nodded at Matt and he went into great detail about the ins and outs of Family Service. He used industry lingo that meant nothing to me: service attendance, Shiva drop-bys, gifting to people, and generally acting like a menche. At this point I was so confused. I thought I was interviewing to sell cemetery plots. Bernie explained that Family Service was the same thing, it just sounded nicer than selling ground. And Family Service counselors sounded better than plot salespeople.

I sat there and tried to look mature as Bernie and Matt talked about how lucrative the cemetery business was. I was money hungry, always have been. From an early age, my father taught to me to save money and work hard. And I did. At the age of eight, I started a loan shark business. My mother would give me lunch money for the week on Sunday night. She didn't pay much attention to me, or what I was doing. I'd pack my own lunch and then lend out money to the kids who forgot their cash. Of course there was interest to be paid. By the end of the year I had earned almost four hundred dollars.

I was born to be an entrepreneur. However, my plan wasn't working. A regular job could pose some difficulties, such as having a boss. I had sales experience selling cookies. Why not try to sell dirt?

"We feel," Bernie said, looking sideways at Matt, "that you'd be a great fit with the family." He called a bunch of people over the speakerphone. One by one, the rest of the sales team, a.k.a. Family Service, appeared in the little office. Suddenly I was surrounded by a motley crew of strangers all staring at me. They looked perplexed, somber, and majorly stressed.

Ronnie sat down next to me. His face still had cookie crumbs on it. His thinning hair was a mixture of blond, gray, and white. His thick walrus moustache looked as if it itched. The glasses he wore made him look like a professor. Glasses made you look smarter. I needed a pair; I needed all the help I could get. Ronnie was covered with spots, I wasn't sure if they were freckles or age spots. He resembled a farm fresh egg from the green market. His shoes were impeccably polished.

After Ronnie got settled he gave me a nod. I took this to be a thank you for the cookies. Not sure what to do, I smiled back. Ronnie gave off a vibe that he meant serious business; he was thorough, almost to the point of being anal retentive.

Next to Ronnie sat Tatyana. A short round woman with a worn face full of sun damage, you could tell she'd been ridden hard and put away wet. Her Russian accent was heavy with sounds that weren't used in English.

"Ronnie, did you make sale last night...yes?" she asked him.

He didn't answer, but raised a finger to his lips to quiet her.

Tatyana wore very tight pants and an equally ill-fitted double knit polyester top. Tons of makeup to cover years of bad skin care. Her blondish mane had wide streaks of brown. Her jewelry was as big as the rest of her. I don't know who she thought she was fooling with that crap. It was pure junk from the shopping channel. She sported blood red nail polish on digits bitten down to the cuticle.

Something about her made me feel at ease. She had a hard and cold exterior, but seemed soft and warm on the inside. In many ways, my exterior did not match my interior either. I was primped and polished for the world to see, but on the inside I was a disheveled mess.

Manny sat next to Tatyana. I ball parked him at mid-fifties. He was dressed in a flashy suit. Pinstripes, a tie in a handsome Windsor knot, matching pocket square folded like a piece of origami. His French cuffs boasted monogrammed initials as well as sterling silver cuff links. His watch sparkled, and his manicured fingernails looked like a hand model's. Everything about him struck me as bold and powerful, but he had the personality of wet sand.

Manny whispered, "Hello." He started to extend his hand but caught an audacious stare from Tatyana. He dropped his hand back into his lap and focused on the notepad in front of him. His posture slumped and hung his head low. He exuded no confidence at all. Wow, who had *his* balls in a jar?

In between Manny and Matt sat Alexis. She was in her late forties, and looked good for her age. Thin, blonde, and dressed extremely sexy for work, she wore knee-high black leather boots, a slim pencil skirt, and a super fitted turtleneck sweater. Her makeup was natural looking. She let out a dainty sneeze, "Achoo." She did not wear a wedding or engagement ring.

Her kind eyes looked at me as if she were trying to send a message. Like run away from this horrible place, or don't take this job, it's a total suckfest. Alexis did not fit in; she stood out from the rest of the group like Marilyn from *The Munsters*.

"This is The Family Service team." Bernie motioned his big banana hands at the group. He introduced me as Julia, Adam's friend. "She'll have the opportunity to work with all of you."

What? I had the job? But we hadn't gone over anything related to the position. I was so confused. The meet and greet had lasted almost two hours. We'd talked about everything except the actual job. How much money was he going to offer me? Benefits, if any, and who paid for them? What was the vacation time like? What kind of interview was this?

Everything happened so freaking fast I felt dizzy. Did Bernie think I had all day to sit and chitchat with him and his staff? I still had cookies and brownies to bake, deliveries to make. I had shit to do!

I heard a car door slam and a giggle that sounded like Peter Griffin from *Family Guy*. I knew that voice. The office door opened and Adam stood in the doorway.

"Hey, Bernie. Did you hire my girl? Make sure you treat her right. Don't be a douche and pull the stunts you do on Manny. No offense, Manny." Adam winked at Manny.

OMG sometimes Adam acted like such a tool. I felt like killing him. How embarrassing! Although he was only three months older than me, most of the time he acted as if he knew everything about everything, and I knew nothing about nothing.

"She has the offer; I'm just waiting for the correct response. Being, YES." Bernie retorted.

"Well? What's it gonna be, kid?" Adam probed.

I said I had to think it over and I would be in touch. I stood up to shake everybody's hand, and told them to enjoy the cookies. Bernie ordered everybody out except me and Matt.

Adam gave me a look. Then he and the Family Service team shuffled out of the room.

Bernie said, "Here's the deal. We're starting a training group in two weeks. I want you in it. The salary's $450.00 a week plus commission. Commission ranges on a scale from five to twelve percent depending on what you sell, plus bonuses. Matt's the top salesman almost every month and he makes a hefty six figures. You have charisma, youth, and beauty on your side. I will do whatever it takes to have you on my team. What's your answer?"

Gulp! I had a lot to think about. "Could I give you an answer tomorrow?" I asked, trying to sound like a seasoned business person. Bernie took a business card from his inside jacket pocket. He wrote his cell number on the back and told me to call me the next morning.

I again shook their hands, not really wanting to touch Matt's sorry excuses for a handshake. But it would be rude to shake Bernie's and not Matt's. I strolled out of the office, saying goodbye to everyone I had met.

Adam grabbed my hand and said, "Come on, coffee time. I want to hear all about it."

Chapter 2

As we walked hand in hand through the parking lot I told him, "You really need to stop biting your nails. What does Da Brat say about it?" Da Brat was my nickname for his girlfriend Joy.

"She doesn't care," he replied.

Duh, of course not, I thought. She doesn't care about her appearance at all, but you clearly do. Adam was all about his looks. Ever since The Notorious B.I.G. came out in the nineties and made it cool for a big guy to be hip, Adam was all about it. He stood six feet two inches and weighed well over three hundred pounds. He spent a fortune on clothes and maintained hair appointments for a cut and color every three weeks. Adam took more time to get ready to go out than most women.

Joy was the opposite, a big tomboy, bordering on butch. I really didn't know why they were together. Adam would never admit it, but I thought it was because she was a trust fund kid. Joy's bank account was replenished every month. She came from a long line of old family money. Her monthly deposits would only get bigger when she got married. That's what really turned Adam on, I figured.

"I know I got to stop. My eyebrow girl told me about some cream you put on your nails to stop the biting, but I doubt it will work. I've been a nail biter forever."

"Your eyebrow girl? Does she do your bikini wax too? Brazilian?" I asked, laughing.

"Whatever. Stop being a hater. Follow me over to Dunkin' Donuts so you can tell me about Bernie and the interview."

Adam knew by the look on my face that I had no time for chitchat, but that didn't stop him from convincing me to join him for just one cup of joe.

I followed Adam's leased Jaguar in my four year old Honda. His car looked fresh from the factory due to an obsession with keeping his automobile immaculate. Adam was a regular customer at the car wash every week. He kept a can of tire spray in the trunk just in case he drove through a dirty puddle. I had a dented bumper, and it had been a month since a car wash other than nature's rain. My car wasn't dirty, but by no means was it clean.

I met Adam when we were in the third grade. He had the hots for me and I thought he was yucky. Our parents enrolled us at the same synagogue so we went to Hebrew school together. I went to his bar mitzvah and he went to my bat mitzvah. We were friendly. Then something happened that bonded us forever.

It happened during the summer before we started high school. It was just another lazy day and I was home alone watching MTV. My parents were due home soon from work. The phone rang. A call that completely changed my life.

A nurse from the local hospital informed me that my family needed to come immediately. My father had just arrived via ambulance. He had suffered an aneurism in his brain and was in a coma.

In the ICU, my family watched and waited in slow motion as my father lay still and lifeless. He never had a chance. He died three days later. We'd never seen it coming. We were totally unprepared.

School was out so no one was around. Most of my friends had already left to go down the Shore. My parents were not avid beach people. Usually they'd give into my whining and we'd go for one long weekend each summer. I was too old to go to day camp and not old enough for a real job. So that summer was me and the TV.

Adam's father helped my mother with the funeral arrangements. Lenny ran a funeral home one, of the biggest in town. He was a makher. You know the type, a pillar of the community, King of the Jews. Death had always been a part of Adam's life. His family had been in the funeral business for seven generations. That summer Adam showed me a different side. He was there for me when I didn't think anyone would understand how I was feeling or what I was experiencing.

My mother let me do whatever I wanted. She gave up on being a mother, and decided to live her life as a free spirit. I had no guidance. Cindy was too busy running off to foreign countries to buy precious gems with her man of the moment. She would go away on trips for "classes." She had more bogus degrees from unaccredited schools than I had shoes.

I had to grow up fast. Whenever I needed help, she'd just cut me a check. Shoving money at a problem was her solution for me. I learned to do the opposite of whatever she told me. Also to save at least half of whatever she gave me.

I parked next to Adam's shiny Jaguar in the Dunkin' Donuts parking lot. He was inside, ordering at the counter. I sauntered up next to him.

"Fly kicks, kid."

"This shows how fab my shoes are, that a straight guy notices them," I said in a snarky tone.

We grabbed our coffees, took the corner booth and sat on opposite sides.

"So, what did you tell Bernie about me? Because I felt like I wasn't on a real job interview. It was more like he was poking around in my life."

Adam laughed and said, "I told him you were pretty and had huge tits."

"You're an asshole! No wonder he didn't take me seriously."

Adam scoffed. "I heard him offer you the job, what's the problem?"

"I don't know if I'm ready to close down my business, that's the problem."

"Come on. You rent space from a pizza shop," he said. "You work your ass off doing everything yourself, from baking to delivery to clean up and sales. How many hours a week are you working, seventy?"

I sighed. "At least."

"Are you making ends meet?"

"Barely," I said, feeling like a loser. I knew exactly how much was in my bank account. My balance had dropped below my safety net of four thousand dollars. I wasn't making ends meet at all.

"Do you have any free time to do anything fun? If you do, do you have any energy?" he asked. What was this, a survey?

"Not much," I admitted.

"When was the last time you went out with the girls? Shopping with Liz? Or on a date? Julia, listen to me, seriously listen. Take this job. You can always go back to baking if you want to. I can give you lots of leads from people planning their funerals. It won't be as bad as you think. Plus, we'll see each other a lot more. Would I ever steer you wrong?"

"No." I said this like a child answering a parent.

"When do you call Bernie? Tomorrow, right? I bet you he calls you tonight. He's a desperate old man," Adam said with a chuckle.

Just as Adam was starting to say something else, his phone buzzed. He checked the text message. It was from Bernie. Adam laughed and showed me the screen. "She's like a young Elizabeth Taylor. How come you're not with her?"

"I don't look like Elizabeth Taylor. My eyes aren't purple!" I shrieked.

"Violet." Adam corrected me. "And in her younger days, she was a hottie!"

"On that note, I gotta go. I have to bake. I need to think about all this." I held my hands up to my head and formed an imaginary cloud of chaos. "Thanks for the coffee. I'll talk to you later." I stood up, grabbed my Prada, and walked towards the door.

Adam waved and called out, "If I didn't think this was good for you, I wouldn't have set it up."

I groaned. "I know."

The drive to the pizza shop seemed short. I looked at the clock on my dashboard: almost two. Even though I knew my clock was set ten minutes fast, where the hell had the day gone? I parked and grabbed my bag of work clothes. I was going to catch a lot of heat for the way I was dressed. Everyone at work usually saw me looking downright shitty. Jeans, old t-shirts, an apron and a ponytail with a pen stuck in it. Make-up free, no fancy shoes.

When I walked in, I was greeted with a myriad of cat calls and hoots from the pizza posse. Mario, the head pizza man, looked extra slimy in a yellowed t-shirt and a face that hadn't been shaved in three days. Angelo the owner was always on the phone shouting in Italian. Tony was tossing a pizza high into the air. He was the only one who was nice to me. Nino, his signature cigarette behind one ear was always leering. Disgusting. I could get used to not having to deal with these hooligans.

The dining room looked shabbier than ever before. The vinyl floor was so sticky I was worried about my shoes. Even though they were cheap, they were extremely unique. The walls sported creations made from wine corks. This was funny because the pizza shop didn't serve wine, so where had all the corks come from? The chairs appeared to have more tears in them than the week before.

When I reached the bathroom; the catcalls finally subsided. I changed my outfit and looked at myself in the mirror. In my work clothes, I looked different than I had this morning. I felt different too. I knew I had a lot to bake and I was already tired.

"Just try," I said out loud.

I went into the kitchen and sat down to make a list of the customers I'd need to tell that I was closing. My orders for the week would be filled, but that would be it. No more baking. I was sad, but excited at the same time. A new adventure, and hopefully a successful one!

❧❀❧

The next morning I phoned Bernie. "Hi. It's Julia."

"Well, hello to you." he said. "Have you made your decision?"

"Yes. I'm in."

"You're making a wise choice. A training class is starting in two weeks."

"Perfect. That gives me time to tie up some loose ends."

"I'm looking forward to seeing you then. I feel you'll be the breakout star of the new group. Don't disappoint me," Bernie warned.

I didn't know how to respond, surprised Bernie had me pegged as a sales force superstar. What experience did I have in cemetery sales? I was used to selling baked goods.

"I'll try my best, Bernie."

"That's all I want to hear." Click.

The next week was hard. Many of the shop owners I'd sold to looked disappointed when I told them about closing. They wished me luck in the future. A lot of them told me if I opened up again to please call them, I was welcome to sell anytime. That made me happy. Angelo didn't seem pleased when I told him I was leaving. Angelo wouldn't miss me, just my rent money.

After the first week of closing the business I had time to do some odds and ends, as well as relax for a day or two, before I started the cemetery sales training class. My friend Liz went with me for a mini spa day. It was nice to see her and catch up over Cobb salads. I also went shopping for conservative suites.

One night Adam took me out for a congratulatory dinner. As we dined the conversation turned to my new career.

"You know, my dad's really excited that you took Bernie up on the offer," Adam said.

"Really? I find that hard to believe." I always felt a little like Lenny gave me charity, whether I wanted it or not.

"He thinks this will be great for you, and so do I." Adam was still trying to cement the deal.

"We could become a super strong selling team, you know. Me with the plots and you with the funerals." My voice filled with excitement.

"True that!" Adam said, and we clinked wine glasses.

I managed to squeeze in a trip to the salon to get my hair done and a fresh manicure. All too soon, it was April ninth, my first day reporting to work at Rosemonte.

Chapter 3

On my first day at Rosemonte I wore a gray and pale blue suit. Fantastic Stewart Weitzman shoes the exact shade of blue as the suit. My hair was down, pulled back, with a head band. I didn't know why I was nervous, but I was. Nauseous and scared. I felt like the new kid at school.

As I walked in, Bernie called my name from the little office. "Come on in," he growled. I walked in and sat down.

"Good morning," I said.

"I didn't realize how much hair you had," he said with surprise.

"Yeah, it's really long."

Not like Crystal Gayle's, but it was down to the middle of my back. I panicked. Was the entire training just going to be Bernie and me?

Bernie yelled for someone named Brian. A guy came in and sat next to me. We shook hands as Bernie introduced us. Brian looked like a driver's ed teacher dressed up for a school board meeting. Skinny, with strawberry blond hair, thick glasses, and black Levi jeans. I couldn't help but look at the waist number on the back. Twenty seven inches. That was almost starving child in a third world country skinny. His purplish shirt was pilled, accented with a silk Grateful Dead tie. On his wrist was a digital watch.

He asked, "Do ya play billiards, shoot a little pool?" He made a foul gesture that looked like he was jerking off.

"Not really," I said.

Brian started to ramble about his pool league. They practiced every week. His group even made the finals in Los Angeles. Then he said he lived with his mom. Really? I was surprised. Brian was like forty-five years old. The watch should've been a clue.

Bernie said, "We're waiting for one more."

Please be someone normal, I prayed. A woman walked in. No, not normal. No wonder Bernie thought I'd be the superstar of this group.

"Sherry's my name and cemetery sellin's my game," she said. Holy moley. Sherry had barely any hair on her head. I didn't know what was going on there but it looked brutal. Late thirties and almost totally bald? She wore a simple brown dress and black old lady shoes. It looked like she'd never shaved her legs in her life. Maybe she was trying to make up for the hair loss upstairs. She had glasses but couldn't decide if she wanted them on her face or around her neck. The glasses hung on a chain, accentuating the old lady look.

Bernie started our first day of training with a speech about the cemetery world, work ethic, and sales. After a while of him blabbing I lost interest and zoned out. He got my attention back when he said that his training sessions were intense and not all of us were going to make it to the end. The way he was ranting, we were like soldiers going off to war. He announced we would have a short break, and then join the Family Service staff for the morning meeting.

Another meeting, yay. I was glad to have a few minutes, I needed some caffeine. Badly. I got a cup of coffee and made my way to the upstairs conference room where the morning meeting would be held.

I was going to have to get used to having meetings every day. Liz was a pharmaceutical rep; she told me at her office they had three sales meetings a day. Any sales job had a bunch of meetings, rah rah sessions. This sounded boring and redundant to me. However, if I was going make it work, I had to suck it up. Liz could give me some pointers.

Brian and Sherry were sitting next to each other in the conference room. I didn't want to sit next to them. No one else was there yet, so I looked out the window and waited. Spring had not yet sprung, everything outside was grey and dead. How apropos that death was looming outside and here I was in a cemetery. The temperature was in the fifties with minimal sunshine. I checked out at the parking lot and assessed the cars. In my head I was making the match ups. Bernie had the Mercedes; Matt, Alexis, and Ronnie the Subaru, Buick, and Toyota. I saw my Honda and smiled. I pegged Manny for the classy old Cadillac like my grandfather drove thirty years ago. There was a very old Hyundai with no hubcaps. That had to be Sherry's. I knew Brian drove the Kia because of the dorky pool bumper sticker. It looked like a piece of caution tape and said "Caution, I break for pool halls." I couldn't help but roll my eyes.

I turned when I heard a lot of groaning and feet shuffling. People raced into the room, moving fast to beat Bernie, who was trudging up the stairs. Apparently, this journey upstairs was a huge deal for him. He was a very ill man. He had the issues with his knees. Diabetes also plagued him and gave him complications with his feet. This was why he rarely moved from his chair in the little office downstairs.

When I looked around for a seat, Ronnie tilted his head at me. I took that as an invitation to sit next to him. Bernie sat at the head of the table and ordered Matt to get him coffee and water. Matt popped up like an obedient dog. What was with those two? Did Bernie have some secret on Matt? Or did they have a sick relationship boarding on work S&M? I'd seen a documentary on that. I'd have to ask Adam about them.

Bernie talked about the new hires, and how we'd each be paired up with a Family Service salesperson or "counselor." He explained that we'd be rotating so we could see how everyone worked. This would give us newbies the opportunity to see many styles of selling.

"I don't care how you sell, just as long as you make a sale. Got it? Bottom line equals your paycheck." Bernie gave us each a stare down.

Bernie told Ronnie he'd be in charge of giving us supplies. Alexis would show us to our desks. Matt would work on the sales presentation with us. Ronnie announced that our kits were on our desks and everything was ready for us. Bernie said everyone needed to sell more. The first week of the month had passed; the group was in good shape so far, except for Manny.

On the wall behind Bernie was a white board with numbers. This showed the sales goals for the month and what each person had sold. Manny's name sat at the bottom with no sales at all and a goal of $10,000. Judging from the other numbers, it didn't look that hard to hit ten G's in one month. Especially since the other five had done so in one week of work.

Bernie went into detail about the monthly sales. When he got to Manny, he started to yell. Manny and Bernie both became red in the face, Bernie from yelling and Manny from being embarrassed. Bernie did not let up. As I watched him berate Manny, I began to get a little hot myself.

"You need to sell to earn money," Bernie yelled. "How do you feed your family? I realize you don't have a lot of bills. But you must have some. How do you take care of them? Do you need to put your wife out on the corner?"

Ouch. That was harsh. I wouldn't want to be in Manny's spot. Was it even legal, the way he yelled at Manny? It was definitely cruel. Lesson learned. In order to not get yelled at, don't be the last one on the white board list.

Finally, Manny spoke up in a squeaky voice. He said, "You have made your point." He held up his manicured hands for emphasis. "I'll try to do better this week. Please stop yelling."

Bernie stared at him in disgust then said, "Meeting is over. New people, Alexis will show you to your desks. After lunch you'll meet with Matt in the conference room to go over the presentation."

We followed Alexis down the hall as she gave us a tour of the second floor. Alexis looked like a stewardess with her graceful hand gestures as she pointed to each room. Everyone had to share a room except for Matt. His room was teeny tiny, and smelled faintly of mold. There was no window, just one overhead fluorescent light that emitted a low humming noise. Why did he get his own room? Everyone else had to share. This added more mystery to Matt and his accomplice Bernie.

"The kitchen," Alexis said as she pointed to a closet with a coffee maker and a small college-sized refrigerator. The door didn't even close all the way because of the appliance cords. I wondered about fire hazards.

Alexis split us up into the remaining rooms. Sherry and Brian went with her into one, and Alexis sent me into the other with Ronnie. We checked out our new desks. This was the first time I'd had a desk in an office. All of my jobs up to this point had been food related, in restaurants or bakeries. I was excited to look in the drawers and put away my things. I strove to be organized and neat, so setup was always fun for me. Such a dork.

I looked at the massive desk calendar blotter and thought about how I could fill it with sales calls. Ronnie jumped up and closed the door. He looked at me and held his finger to his lips, just as I was about to say, "What's up?"

"I'm so thrilled I won you in the coin toss!" Ronnie exclaimed.

"I don't understand, coin toss?" Won me? Was I a stuffed animal at a carnival?

He smiled at me. "That's how we decided who went in which room."

"I'm happy to be in here with you," I said, looking around. "I like the windows."

Ronnie told me about the meeting from last week. Family Service took a bet to see who was going to quit first. Everyone had picked Brian.

"I don't think Sherry will last long either," Ronnie said. "Julia, you'll be here for the long haul."

"How long are we talking about?" I asked.

Ronnie shrugged his shoulders. "Whatever you need from me to succeed, I'm your guy."

"Thanks."

"This conversation is private between us."

"Okay, got it." Ronnie went to the door and opened it again.

For lunch that day I drove to a Wawa for a turkey hoagie and a Diet Coke. The store was pretty packed. I called Liz. Voicemail, she was probably in a sales meeting. Adam was up next on speed dial.

"Hey, how's your first day going?" he asked.

"Good, just kinda weird. You know, because I've never done anything like this before."

"You'll be fine, honey," Adam soothed.

"I know," I said. "Are you coming by today?" If I still had the business, the magic word would've been snickerdoodle. They were his favorite. Especially hot from the oven.

"No, not today. But I'm scheduled for a funeral over there tomorrow. So I'll see you then."

"Okay, sounds good," I said. Feeling abandoned, I returned to my car.

Adam basically didn't do much at his father's funeral home. He claimed he had responsibilities, but I didn't know what they were. Mainly his job was to drive a hearse. Adam liked to say he was a PhD. Professional Hearse Driver.

After I finished my hoagie in the car, I drove back to Rosemonte. I didn't want to eat alone at work or run the risk of having to eat with Brian and Sherry. As I walked into the lobby, there they were. They'd eaten lunch together at Chili's.

"We were looking for you to go to lunch," they said in unison.

"Oh, maybe next time." I'd really dodged a bullet there.

We walked up the stairs and gathered in the conference room.

Matt strode in holding a can of caffeine-free Diet Pepsi. His can of soda had a bendy straw twirling around in it. Matt had taken off his suit jacket. He was wearing a short sleeve button up shirt with a tie, the Dilbert cartoon look.

"Today we're going over the presentation. I'll do it first for all of you," he said. "When I started here the presentation was awful, and boring. I re-wrote it and got it approved by Bernie. Now you new folks will be learning the presentation direct from the creator, *moi*."

What an ego! Besides, who cared?

The presentation included a binder full of pictures, charts, etc. Matt handed out a CD copy.

"By the end of the week, each of you will be tested and graded on giving this presentation. This is a major part of your training. I cannot stress enough that it is very important," Matt said in a flat voice.

Sherry raised her hand. Matt looked annoyed.

"I don't have a CD player. Can you make me a cassette tape?"

Matt looked stunned. "I'll see what I can do. I don't think that will be too difficult."

The presentation was long; he spoke for forty-five minutes. There was little interaction with us. I thought about doing the presentation for potential buyers. If I was this uninterested, I was sure they would be too. The pictures that went along with the presentation were old and not good quality.

I wanted to figure out what would make people want to buy from Rosemonte. That was the million dollar question. So far I hadn't a clue. From the little bit I'd seen, the place was a mess. I was scared of what I was going to see on the upcoming tour.

When Matt finally finished the presentation, he said. "We're all going in my car as I conduct a driving tour of Rosemonte."

We followed Matt downstairs and out to the parking lot.

"Mr. Matt?" Brian asked.

"Ahhh, just Matt. Yes, Brian?"

"I get motion sickness. I need to ride in the front seat or else it gets ugly. Is that okay with you ladies?" Brian already looked pale.

"Sure, no problem," I said.

Sherry looked upset; she screeched, "I want to sit in the front!"

I said, "You shoulda called shotgun."

Sherry gave me a nasty look. This frightened me. She sure was scary looking with her barely there hair and glaring eyes.

Matt clicked the alarm button on his key to the Subaru. We piled inside, Matt and Brian up front, me and Sherry in the back.

Matt handed us a map of the cemetery. Every section had been broken up and given a letter; some sections had a letter and a number. The map looked like it was drawn by a drunken person with shaky hands. Matt started his car, and we were off.

Rosemonte was one of the oldest cemeteries in the Philadelphia metro area. Built before cars were invented, the roads were very narrow, and in desperate need of repair. As we drove around and around I saw lots of grave stones that had fallen over or were sinking into the ground. How could I convince anyone to buy here? The place looked terrible.

I asked Matt about the unkempt conditions and he explained the grounds guys were in the process of fixing it up. Looking at the poor conditions I guessed it was a never ending task.

As we drove through all the sections, Matt told us a factoid about each one. Some were interesting to me; I had affection for meaningless trivia. One huge section was reserved for poor Jews who couldn't afford a burial. Some families had bought portions of land to keep their brood together and carry on their name. One had started during the Depression and was managed like a credit union. For other sections, anybody could buy in without restrictions.

My grandfather was buried in the front. When we passed his section, I was relieved to see that his grave stone looked pretty good. This was probably because it was in the front near the office and the street. He had good real estate: location location location.

Rosemonte featured a community mausoleum, an above ground structure like a tomb. It had a funky smell, a strong combination of mothballs and bug spray. Puddles surrounded the perimeter, which I thought was odd because it hadn't rained in a few days.

Individual mausoleums cost big bucks. Only a few were sprinkled throughout the grounds. Matt pointed out one Ronnie had sold. What a nice commission that must've been.

At the bottom of the hill sat a huge rustic barn. A hunter green structure with paint peeling off in all the right spots, it looked a back drop for a J. Crew advertisement. This was where the lawnmowers and other grounds keeping items were stored. The barn doubled as a hangout for the grounds guys.

Matt parked the car and we all got out in silence, and walked towards the barn's open door. The grounds guys wore a blue uniform with their name embroidered above the pocket. Matt introduced us to Cemetery Ed. A mammoth man, big and jolly with rosy cheeks like Santa's he grinned and welcomed us.

Cemetery Ed told us, "Any time youse need anything fixed, just call me or one of my guys." His guys included his assistant T.R., Mikey, Spike, Tommy, Julio, and Jose. These were the graves diggers. They also mowed the grass and fixed the stones. A macho group of men, strong with tanned faces and an overdose of testosterone. These guys were not afraid of getting dirty. I smiled at each one, hoping to win them over. It was too soon to tell. Maybe some cookies would soften them up? They all stared quietly as we exited the barn.

Back in the car and up the hill, we returned to the main office. Matt told us, "Go inside to the conference room for another meeting with Ronnie."

Thankfully, Bernie wouldn't be joining us for this meeting. Ronnie was waiting for us as we climbed the stairs and plopped down in chairs around the table. He started to explain some of the everyday ins and outs of working at Rosemonte, policies and procedures. He covered everything from where to find pens, to who was assigned the walk-ins. Finally, he told us we were done for the day, and he'd see us tomorrow morning.

My first day of work at my new job, wasn't what I had expected. I thought it went well, though. I gathered my things and walked out to my car. I took in the scenery for a moment. Tall trees, acres and acres of ground to be sold. I *had* to make this job work. I enjoyed a challenge, and this was a considerable one. I took off my heels and placed them on the floor in the passenger seat, and headed home.

Chapter 4

I called Liz on the way home to see if she wanted to meet me for a slice and some sales pointers. Luckily, she agreed. We met at our usual pizza place in between her house in Queen Village and mine in South Philly. Liz waved at me excitedly as I walked in the door.

We hugged hello, and I dropped into a chair. "What a day. Seriously, how do you sit through so much babble at your job? I'm exhausted."

Liz laughed. "Some of it, no, most of it is boring and meaningless. However, you need to get to know your boss and his form of lecture. Then you'll be able to pick out the two or three important sentences from the blah blah blah."

"I was hoping for some words of wisdom. I feel like we're back in Western Civ class with Mr. Fischer." I tilted my head to the side and pretended to fall asleep.

"Oh God, tenth grade. That was the worst year ever. Remember I grew out my bangs? Pure torture!" Liz shook her mane of auburn hair.

Our slices arrived along with an order of pizza fries. Yum! Chubby like me, Liz didn't count calories either. We'd been friends since high school. Liz and her family always had a seat for me at the dinner table whenever my mother was missing in action. I valued our friendship and secretly envied her relationship with her parents.

Liz told me that in her office there was a slimy yes-man too. She stressed never to be on the bottom of the sales list. That person was always in danger of losing their job.

❧◉❧

The next morning Rosemonte seemed a little different. The sun was shining, and some of the trees on the property had little buds of green. When I got out of my car and started to walk up the hill to the office, I saw a family of bluebirds. Mother Nature was saying hello. The signs of life made me smile. I opened the heavy door, all ready for day two.

Adam was scheduled for a funeral, but I wasn't sure what time. The chalkboard downstairs was full of burials, four in one day. Everyone was buzzing around, much busier than the day before. One by one we all gathered in the little office for the morning meeting.

Bernie was already seated. Ronnie was preparing breakfast for him: two bagel sandwiches with cream cheese and grape jelly. He poured a large orange juice, and a steaming cup of coffee. Without thanking Ronnie, or giving him any kind of acknowledgment, Bernie dove in. Some diabetic diet!

Bernie talked to us about the day ahead. He spoke with his mouth full of chewed-up bagel, a mess swirled with white and purple. He explained that whoever's turn it was to lead in each of the funerals would bring a trainee with them.

"Who's up?" Bernie bellowed.

Manny raised his hand and said in a small voice, "It's my turn."

Bernie gave him a scornful glance and said, "Crap. Take the new people out together to do the prep work."

Bernie asked about the sales from the previous night. Matt had sold, but the rest had struck out. Bernie grumbled about how everybody needed to sell more, and said that Matt was the only one who sold on a constant basis.

Matt just sat there with a smirk on his face. What made him so special?

Bernie asked him where he got his lead.

Matt answered, "One of my synagogue friends." He bragged about his past tenure as president of Shalom Torah, a local temple. Then he lectured Family Service on how easy it was to get leads from being active in the community. Such a suck up. Matt listed the various groups he was involved with in order to get leads. The Jewish Community Center Adult Basketball League. American Friends of Magen David Adom (Israeli Red Cross). The Jewish National Fund. Barf.

At this point I realized Matt was a puppet. Bernie's puppet. Bernie pulled the strings, Matt performed. The nickname Matt the Puppet was born.

The meeting was wrapping up; Manny was going to take us out to perform prep work for the funerals. I smiled extra big at Manny and asked if he could he fix it so I could be on Adam's funeral.

Manny answered, "It doesn't work that way. But I'll try my best."

That was good enough for me.

We went outside to learn about checking the graves. Basically this meant making sure the correct grave was dug. Next we did a quality check, making sure there were a tent, chairs, hand shovels, and bottled water on hot days.

I felt myself sinking into the dirt. I looked down at my black Steve Madden peep toe heels. They were very comfortable considering the five inches in height they gave me. I'd have to invest in a cheap pair of flats to keep at my desk for times like this.

Manny let me pick the funeral I wanted to be on. I picked the first one and hoped it would be Adam's. Next we had to get a map ready. Manny photocopied a map from the main map book and highlighted a route from the open gate to the grave. He explained that we would be leading the hearse into the cemetery. He also told us we should always take our cell phone and a walkie-talkie. He handed me a walkie and told me to give it a test.

"Test one, test one, this is Julia. Who can hear me?" I asked.

Cemetery Ed said, "I'm glad to hear a lady's voice on here."

One of the girls in the office responded, "We hear you loud and clear."

"Looks like we are almost ready," Manny said. "Let's go get my car and we'll drive to the gate and wait."

At the gate, Manny backed in his Caddy to wait for the hearse. He turned on the oldies station and started to sing along. His voice was actually pretty good. I was surprised. He knew all the words to every song, who sang it, what year it was recorded, and on which label.

"I'm guessing you have a passion for music," I said.

Manny explained that his back-ground was in music and he used to live in Atlanta.

"How'd you end up here?" I asked him. "Clearly you would rather be in the music business."

Manny let out a long sigh. He was trapped in a bad marriage with kids. He'd gotten badly burned in the ATL by his old business partner. He and his wife had lost everything and, with nowhere to go, they moved back home and settled in with his in-laws. Rosemonte was the only job Manny could get, and he was barely getting by. An ugly story. I felt bad for Manny. Silence crept over us.

I was relieved when Manny looked in the rearview mirror and said, "Here comes the hearse and it looks like Adam's driving."

Adam followed us as we went winding through the confining roads. Manny's huge Caddy handled the turns without any issues, but I was scared he was going to ding the side mirrors. The roads were paved in some parts and cobblestone in others. There were lots of small pebbles on the sides of the road.

When we got to the section, everyone started to spill out of their cars. The grounds guys met Adam at the back of the hearse. He opened the back door and the guys pulled the casket onto a dolly, then pushed it over to the gravesite. The Rabbi solemnly chanted in Hebrew, following the dolly. The grounds guys moved the casket onto a metal contraption that held it in place above the open grave.

Adam handed out pamphlets to the group of mourners. He also gave me one.

As I watched all of this happen, flawlessly, I couldn't help but think about who was in the casket. Who were the mourners? How did everyone know what to do? There was no dress rehearsal. Would I be able to pull off the same smooth show?

Manny and I returned to his car and headed back to the office. As we were walking in Manny congratulated me on my first funeral. "You handled it like a pro."

Click. The walkie-talkie stood in the charger. Tatyana was filling out a commission form. She lifted her head as I walked by. "How's everything, Julia?"

I smiled. "Good so far."

"Good. Let me ask you, you are Russian? Da."

"I have a grandmother from Russia. She died when I was a child." Was that enough Russian for her? Was this a test?

"Come, we go outside for minute." Tatyana rose from her chair and led me to a side door. It was marked "EXIT". I hoped it wouldn't trip an alarm. "Let me tell you some advice."

"Sure. I'll take anything you want to share with me."

"Be careful around some persons you work with. I cannot tell you who, just be watchful." Tatyana nodded her head and closed one eye. What did this mean? "Such a pretty girl." She pinched my cheek and turned to go back inside.

Watch out for who? Perverts? Con men? Criminals? Thieves? If I had to guess, my money would be on Matt. Maybe Adam could shed some light.

I headed upstairs to my desk. Ronnie was seated at his.

"Do you have any advice for me, like people to stay away from or to get close to?" I asked.

He looked uncomfortable. He shifted in his chair, opened his mouth, and then closed it.

"That's a topic for another time. Have you studied the presentation?"

Nice segue, Ronnie.

I said I had even thought I hadn't. Then Ronnie called my bluff and asked me to do it for him right then and there. What the fuck. "Really, you have a free forty-five minutes?" I asked. Ronnie replied that Bernie asked him to see if I was ready and to work on it with me. "Okay, let's go," I said coolly.

I set up my binder and went over the information. I had a few stumbles but overall I survived. Ronnie was impressed with my practice, or lack thereof. When I was finished, he clapped and said we were going out on sales calls together that night.

"Can't wait," I replied.

Ronnie said, "Meet me at the parking lot at six p.m. sharp, and I'll drive."

After lunch I wasted a few hours pretending to study my presentation. I was never good at studying. I still had some time to kill before I met up with Ronnie. I decided to absorb some cemetery life. Downstairs I went, and saw Bernie sitting in the little office. I think he'd been there all day. He called my name so I went to the doorway; I didn't want to sit down because I was trying to avoid getting stuck there with him.

"Julia, come on in take a load, off. Let's get to know each other," he said.

Yikes, I'd been captured.

Bernie told me tales of when he was a Family Service counselor during the '70s. Stories about a young Bernie with striking looks and no health problems. He told me he'd sold at other cemeteries in Pennsylvania, New Jersey, New York, Florida, California, and Arizona. If this was supposed to impress me, it didn't.

At some point, bored and tired of listening to his dribble, I realized I had to go meet Ronnie. What a great excuse! Bernie told me to have a good night and call him. Not if I need him call him, just call him. Like he was my friend. How strange. I walked out the front door and headed to the parking lot. I looked at my watch: 5:57 p.m. Perfect timing.

Ronnie pulled up in a silver Buick. He rolled down the window and said, "Hey lady, going my way?" I laughed and opened the passenger door. "I'm glad you like my humor, some think it's inappropriate. Some like Sherry."

"Don't worry, I'm chill," I said.

"Do you want a Diet Pepsi?"

"No thanks, I'm more of a Diet Coke girl."

"Can you hand me one?" he asked.

"Sure." I looked around but didn't see any. None in the cup holder. I glanced to the floor, on the backseat. Strikeout again. Frustrated, I shrugged my shoulders and asked, "Where?"

"They're in the glove box," he said. Wow, this was going to be a fun night.

We drove to the Northeast part of the city for our first appointment. The Northeast had changed a lot over the years. When my parents grew up there, it was the place to be. But most people had moved away over the years. Few wanted to admit that was where they were from. I guess they didn't want to be associated with big hair, bamboo earrings, and rough sports fans. As we turned down the street, I saw a familiar sight: block after block of row houses.

The neighborhood was still mostly Jewish, and the family we were going to see had relatives at Rosemonte. We walked up the front steps, and Ronnie rang the bell. An old woman opened the door a crack, the safety chain still on.

She yelled "Go away! I don't want any of your stuff. Get the hell off my stoop!"

Ronnie said in a calm voice, "We need to see you to update

our records. This is very important. There's no obligation to buy anything."

"I don't care," yelled the woman. "If you don't leave I'm going to call your boss tomorrow. You'll be gettin' in big trouble."

"Oh, please. Please call my boss. His name is Bernie Sapowitz. Thank you for your time," Ronnie said. He was as nice as possible. As we left her steps, he called out cheerily, "Don't forget to call."

"Ronnie," I said in a shocked voice. "Are you-"

Cutting me off, he ordered, "Silence."

Inside his car, he explained. "This old bag clearly didn't want us coming in. That makes us look like we didn't try hard enough. But if she calls Bernie and complains, that's great for us. Bernie gets elated when people call to complain about how horrible and annoying we are. I hope she calls. Keep your fingers crossed." Ronnie made some notes about the woman on his legal pad. Then we were off to the next stop. We drove a few blocks, this time headed to see a married couple. They owned ground but nothing else. Hopefully, we'd fill the rest of their need.

"Afterwards, do you want to grab some dinner?" Ronnie asked.

"Sure, I'm starved."

We pulled up to the next place, an older house. The neighborhood was up one economic bracket because it had single homes. Ronnie parked the car and we hopped out. I rang the bell and put on a happy face.

An old man opened the door. "Come on in. We've been waiting all day."

Walking into the house was like traveling back in time. The vibrant emerald green shag carpet met with a less vibrant green velour couch. A TV in a faux wood cabinet, with lots of knickknacks jammed on top in between dozens of framed photographs.

An old woman appeared holding a tray with glasses of water. The couple greeted Ronnie and me and told us to have a seat.

Ronnie chitchatted with the couple about how they met, what

the man's business was, and how many children and grandchildren they had. They seemed nice. Everything was going as planned. The couple nodded along with Ronnie as he went through the book. When we were almost done it looked like Ronnie had it in the bag.

Then he told them what they would need, how much it would cost and how they would get zero percent financing through Rosemonte. The couple looked at each other, horrified. Did they think we were here just for a social call? They asked to have a moment alone to discuss. Could we wait in the kitchen? Ronnie looked slightly alarmed but agreed, and we stepped into the avocado and harvest gold kitchen.

I glanced at Ronnie. "I feel like I'm on the set of *The Wonder Years*." Ronnie held his finger up to silence me.

He was trying to eavesdrop on the old couple's discussion.

The old man came in and told us to follow him. He led us to the den and spoke in a hushed tone. He handed Ronnie a check for two hundred dollars. "Make the payments for seven years and we have a deal."

"Normally, we would only offer a four year plan, but for you, no problem." Ronnie looked at the check. "Let's fill out the paperwork; it'll only take a few minutes."

Everyone signed and we were out the door, on our way to dinner.

Inside the car Ronnie held his freckled hand up for a high five. I met his hand and said, "Good job Ronnie." He said not all sales were that easy.

But really, how hard could it be?

"How about Country Club Diner for dinner?" Ronnie asked as we drove in the direction of Cottman Avenue.

"Okay, if you're buying? Just kidding."

Ronnie laughed "I'm going to treat you because I feel like you brought me good luck. Plus, this is your first night out."

We slid into a booth and ordered dinner. I decided on matzo ball soup and a spinach kinish. Ronnie got the crab cake platter. My phone rang just as Ronnie's did.

"That's weird, Bernie's calling me," I announced as I looked at the caller ID. Ronnie reported the same.

"Do you usually answer him when he calls you out on an appointment?" I asked.

Ronnie laughed loudly and said, "Only half the time."

We both ignored the calls and enjoyed our dinner. Ronnie revealed a little about his personal life. His wife couldn't have children so they'd adopted a baby girl from China. They lived in the Northeast. Ronnie complained about how his wife and daughter lacked respect for him. "They suck the life out of me, everything I got, and then some," he said.

"That's a shame," I said. He looked so sad.

Ronnie shook his head. "It's my own fault. I spoiled the two most important women in my life. I made them feel like princesses. Now I've lost all control. That's why I love coming to work," he explained. "People there, well, most people there, respect me. I bring value to the company."

I really didn't know what to say so I told Ronnie thanks for sharing his feelings with me. All I could really think was ouch; his life was as shitty as mine. Just due to different circumstances.

After a few moments of silence, Ronnie said, "How do you think Brian and Sherry are doing?"

"I'm not really sure. It'll be interesting to see how things go with them tonight on their sales calls."

When the check came, Ronnie took care of it. I thanked him for dinner, and we were off.

Back in the car, I asked Ronnie, "Do we have more appointments scheduled?"

"No, we have to knock on doors."

"What do you mean?"

Ronnie explained when a Family Service counselor doesn't have an appointment they are supposed to knock on doors. "You never know when you can reel in a sale, or at least that's what Bernie thinks."

"It sounds very awkward," I said, annoyed.

"It is, Julia. It is."

We drove a few blocks, and then parked the car. We got out and went up to the door of a house on a street filled with row homes.

"No one's home, or at least no one's answering." I said.

"Most people don't when there's a knock at the door and it's out of the blue," Ronnie said.

"Then why are we here?" I asked, trying not to sound too whiney.

"Basically, we need to kill some time before we call it a night." He marked his notepad with the date and time. We went to another house around the corner and found the same situation. Ronnie again took notes. He looked at his watch and said, "I think we're done for tonight."

"Sounds good to me." It was quarter to ten. Long day.

Ronnie drove me back to my car. We exchanged goodbyes and I thanked him again for dinner. Ronnie waited for me to start my car before he tooted his horn and drove off.

I fished my phone out of my old blue Coach bag. The leather was soft and wrinkled with age. When I was nervous, I would play with the bronze ball chain that held the Coach tag on the strap. I was a little nervous now calling Adam. Da Brat was such a fuddy-duddy. She didn't like him talking on the phone after nine p.m., especially on a week night.

At last he picked up. Hurray!

"So, how's it going kid?" Adam asked.

"Good so far, why? What have you heard?" I sounded worried.

"I know that your boy Brian's getting fired tomorrow," he said.

"What are you talking about? It's only our second day. What

the hell?"

"Bernie said something about him failing the background check."

"Wow, that's kind of a shocker." I was surprised. Brian, a druggie?

Adam told me the details. Brian had had a minor incident with some pot and the fuzz. Apparently, it's still under investigation.

"Why would Bernie tell you this?" I asked.

"Because Bernie's a gossipy yenta and can't keep a secret. The story is all over my office." Adam sounded like, "Duh, you should've known this by now." He just didn't say that.

"Great. So what are people saying about *me* at your office?"

"Nothing yet, kid," he chuckled.

"Stop calling me kid!"

"Okay, I guess I can only get away with one or two kids per conversation," he said.

"Thanks," I mumbled.

I heard a voice kvetching in the background; Adam grumbled, "I gotta go."

"Okay, check ya later." We hung up and I turned on some tunes for the rest of my drive.

By the time I got home, changed and hit the sheets, it was eleven-thirty. I was tired, not physically but mentally. I drifted off to sleep thinking about making my first sale and how good it would feel. I was only asleep for what felt like a few minutes before the alarm went off and I had to get up for day three of training.

Chapter 5

After wearing a uniform for so many years, dressing up for work at the cemetery was fun. I decided to wear a pink and cream houndstooth checked suit, brown croco embossed Ralph Lauren heels, and a Longchamp bag. I thought it was a funny coincidence that both my shoes and bag were equestrian themed. I pulled my hair half up, and pinned it in place with a tortoise shell barrette. I was ready to go.

When I got to work everyone was, surprise…having a meeting. We crowded into the little office.

"You may realize someone's missing," Bernie boomed. "Brian's gone. He failed his background check he has some inner demons he needs to deal with."

Inner demons? That was a little strong. It was only weed.

"So the thorn between two roses is gone, ladies," Bernie said. By the smirk on his round face you could tell he dreamt up that line and couldn't wait to use it.

The day passed quickly. There was only one funeral scheduled. I wasn't assigned to it. Bernie made Sherry and I do the presentation for him and Matt the Puppet. Bernie told me to go first. I was glad that I'd done a run-through the day before, because I'd failed to practice when I got home. There didn't seem to be any time. My whole day and evening had been consumed by Rosemonte. I hoped my schedule would get better once training was over.

I ran through the presentation, pretending to try to sell to Bernie. I was nervous in the beginning, but I soon calmed down. The important bullet points got covered. As I pointed to the various photos, I tried to use my best Vanna White hand expressions. When I pretended to question Bernie about his marital status, he grossed me out by saying, "I'm as single as the number one." I grinned because, honestly, I didn't know what else to do. I must've done something right because Bernie bought a single package from me. Even though I made the sale, Bernie still had some criticism for me.

"You need to relax, and not speak so fast. Remember, people buy from salespeople they like. Don't rush! Before you pushed sugar, now you're pushing dirt."

I nodded my head and tried to look serious and professional. Bernie pointed out that I was a good listener when it came time to do the Q and A section.

"You got a good heart, and youth on your side. Sincerity is not a problem for you," Bernie said.

My pretend commission would have been $900! That was what my mortgage cost each month. This made me excited about the job.

Now it was Sherry's turn. She had a small advantage in going second because she could see the mistakes I had made. But I still felt bad for her. She was a scary mess. People probably stared at her on the street and got frightened.

Sherry started her presentation in the wrong section of the book. When she spoke, her words didn't match up to the pictures being shown. She made a few more fumbles. Bernie didn't buy from her.

"You're all off! Did you study? Clearly not! Matt went and got you a special cassette tape, and for what?" Bernie was almost as loud as when he yelled at Manny.

Sherry stroked her head. I guessed this was her way of nervously twirling her hair. "I'm sorry, I'll study it again."

"You need to do more than study. Feel the intensity of the presentation. If you can't sell to one of us, you'll never be able to sell in the field." Bernie's face had changed from blush to a deep red.

"Okay." Sherry was rubbing at her temples.

"You must study! And you'll do the presentation for Ronnie before going out on appointments tonight. If you can't get this down, you won't be able to hold a job here."

Sherry slumped in her seat, frowned, and then gave me a dirty look.

The afternoon passed slowly. I had a cup of tea at my desk and did some research for leads of my own. I looked in the Rosemonte database on the computer, and made my own list.

Alexis came into the office and sat down on the empty desk next to mine. "We're going out together tonight," she said.

"Oh, cool."

She told me about the lead. "He's this guy I met who wants to take care of things for his mother. I met him at some Jew event. He has the hots for me, but I need to sell him, then cut bait." She fluffed out her hair. "You know what I mean?"

I had no clue what she meant by cut bait, but I didn't want to look like an idiot. I nodded.

"Let's leave around five thirty. We have dinner reservations at six sharp."

"Okay," I said.

"Is that what you're wearing tonight?" Alexis scowled at my outfit.

"What's wrong with this suit? I think it looks really nice," I said defensively.

"It's too professional. You need to loosen it up a little bit," she said. "Maybe unbutton another button on your shirt." She bent towards me and unbuttoned one.

Another button undone? This seemed too revealing for work.

"Much better," she said cheerily and got up. "See you at five thirty. I'll drive."

This was like something out of a movie. Did sex still sell? Did it sell ground in a cemetery?

My stomach was almost on empty. I'd missed lunch because I was busy with my research. Then I was bothered by Alexis. Soon I'd have to go and meet up with her. I went to the bathroom and touched up my makeup. I decided to take my hair down and let it fall naturally around my face. Something told me Alexis would be pulling out all the stops for this guy. I'd need to follow her lead.

Alexis waved to me from her car. She'd changed her clothes and was dressed in something a high class call girl would wear. A super short, tight black skirt and a sweater that fit her like a second skin. It had a cutout keyhole to show some cleavage, and sparkly trim around the cuffs and neckline. On her feet she wore very strappy python-skin heels.

"Nice outfit. I feel like a nun," I said.

She laughed. "Don't worry; you'll probably do this once or twice yourself."

"Great, I can't wait." There was no way I could picture Liz dressing like that to sell meds to doctors' offices. Her approach was to feed them until they said yes.

Alexis didn't notice my sarcasm. She chattered on about her love for foreign horror movies, the gorier the better. She talked about her four legged child, a poodle named Ginger. Then she gave me a nutshell version of her dating history, ending with the usual excuse: she'd never found "the one."

"Now I'm just looking for a good catch. A guy that'll take care of me," she said.

When she asked about my dating life, I gave her a vague no one special answer. I thought it was interesting how the people who worked, at Rosemonte were so open about their private, personal lives.

Alexis asked me, "Do you watch the show *Queer As Folk*?"

"No. Is it still on?"

"No," she answered. "I have them on tape. The show follows the lives of five gay guys who live in Pittsburgh."

"Is it like a makeover show? I'm always looking for new tricks."

"No." Alexis gave a flirty laugh. "It's a fictional show about the intimate lives and relationships of these fabulous men."

"Oh. Is it fun to watch?" I asked.

"Oh, it's fun to watch." Alexis said. "Really fun." She enthused. "I love to watch guy on guy."

"Guy on guy what?"

"Guy on guy porn!" she said in a sultry voice.

"What?" My voice slightly squeaked. I was totally not expecting her to say that. I couldn't help but giggle. I was always squeamish when talking about sex, especially with someone I didn't know well. How inappropriate was this conversation going to get? My cheeks grew hot from embarrassment as Alexis went into detail about pornographic scenes from the show.

"Watching two men is so steamy," she said. "There's something about seeing one man toss another one down and start giving him oral that makes me so hot. I'm attracted to a guy with a take-charge attitude. You know, barbaric-like in the bedroom."

Alexis acted like I knew exactly what she was talking about.

"The men on the show are all perfect looking with great bodies, smooth skin, and muscles. But not too built up because that's overkill. And they're all dressed so well. Really, it's a fantasy show with super hot men enjoying each other. It's *my* kind of entertainment."

Alexis and was getting heated, her thighs squeezed together firmly. She bit her bottom lip, then released a long deep breath. How was she going to be able to focus on work after this?

"This one scene takes place in a nightclub. Most of the men are shirtless and a few are pantless. Everyone's dancing, grooving to the music and having a great time. Everybody's kissing each other and grinding up on one another."

Just when I thought she's going to cream her pants, Alexis turned into the parking lot of the restaurant and announced, "We're here."

"Oh, good. Italian," I said.

"This restaurant has gorgeous waiters, that's why I picked it." She turned to me. "How do I look?"

"A little slutty for work, but good, I guess."

"That's the look I'm going for," she said. "Are you okay?" she asked. She must have noticed my hot pink cheeks.

"I'm good, gay porn," I replied.

"Pardon?"

"Nothing," I said. To myself I said, "Nothing, Gay Porn Alexis."

We walked in the restaurant. She was right; the waiters were easy on the eyes. Alexis waved to a man at the bar sporting a really bad rug on his head. He raised his glass to her as we walked over.

She turned her head slightly, and said, "Forget whatever you've learned so far, and follow my lead."

I swallowed the lump in my throat. "Okay."

"Hi, doll," the portly man said to Alexis. "Who's your gal pal?"

"Big Sam, this is Julia. She's new and training with me tonight. I hope it's okay that I brought her." Alexis spoke in a soft babyish voice.

"Would I say no to you?" he asked. "Especially when you've come with another creature as beautiful as yourself?"

Oh God, how cheesy. I felt like I might barf.

"Do youse want to sit down at a table, eat some clams?" he asked us.

"Sure," Alexis replied.

Big Sam wore a brown polyester suit; his black shoes were the dress-up old man kind, with Velcro. His ensemble would not have been complete without a thick gold rope chain encompassed by a gigantic Jewish star.

He yelled for a hostess, and held three stubby fingers in the air. After we were seated and handed menus, the hostess told us to order whatever our hearts desired even if it was not on the menu.

Alexis and Big Sam ordered wine, I asked for water. I needed to stay clear-headed. Bread appeared, followed by a fancy looking bottle of olive oil. Then a handsome waiter came to our table. Big Sam ordered a feast; Alexis got a soup and a salad. I decided on pasta with broccoli, garlic and oil.

Alexis and Big Sam talked about the Shore and how much they were looking forward to summertime. I wondered if Alexis was running scenes from *Queer As Folk* in her mind. After our first course arrived, Alexis and Big Sam chitchatted about the clams. The plates were cleared, and Alexis took a folder out of her oversized purse.

"Let's get this out of the way so we can enjoy the rest of our dinner," she said sweetly, looking directly into Big Sam's eyes.

She opened the folder and produced a contract. It had already been filled out. There was no presentation book, no long speech; just a contract and a pen. Big Sam patted his chest pockets, feeling for his glasses. He placed the frames on the tip of his nose, looked the papers over, and took a large gulp of wine.

Alexis assured him, "This's the right thing to do for your mother, bless her heart. I've picked a wonderful section at Rosemonte near the road, so it's very accessible. You'll also see a mock-up of the stone; I picked the coral granite because I know coral's your mother's favorite color."

It's also very expensive, I thought as I watched Alexis work her magic on Big Sam.

"The inscription's included, along with the extra floral detail you wanted," Alexis continued, not missing a beat. Then she put her hand on top of his and said, "I know this must be hard for you, but it's better to do it now than later when prices have gone up."

Big Sam nodded his head. "I know." He signed the contract, then he reached in his other chest pocket and took out his checkbook. "How much you want down, honey?"

"As much as you want. Whatever you don't give me tonight we can put into an interest- free payment plan."Alexis smiled, reassuring him.

He gave us a toothy grin and said, "I do feel better taking care of this for my ma." Then he handed Alexis a check and the signed contract.

Wow! I was impressed. Alexis neatly tapped the papers back into the folder, and away they went into her purse. "Now, let's enjoy the rest of our dinner," she said, and gave me a sneaky smile.

As our entrees were served, the waiter also topped off the wine glasses.

"A toast to the two loveliest ladies in the place," Big Sam boomed.

"How nice," Alexis said, with extra sugar in her voice.

During dinner, we kept the conversation on neutral topics. Our waiter cleared the dishes and asked if we wanted dessert. Alexis and I declined, but Big Sam ordered tiramisu, and an after-dinner Lemon Cello for each of us.

"Most people drink Lemon Cello after-dinner on a hot summer night, I like it year round," he told us.

I was a lightweight when it came to drinking, but I downed it because I wanted to get out of there. Alexis must have felt the same way because she drank hers quickly. The bill came and Big Sam insisted on paying. We thanked him for dinner and he shrugged it off. "I enjoyed our time together," he said with a smile.

Alexis thanked him for the business; she gave him a hug, and whispered in his ear, "You did the right thing."

We left him in the restaurant and neither one of us looked back.

I couldn't believe how easy she made it look. Alexis met this man at an event, talked to him on the phone about arrangements for his mother, set up a dinner date, and made the deal!

After a few minutes of total silence in the car, I asked Alexis if she made this type of sale frequently. Were the bulk of her sales to lonely old men? Her answer was cryptic.

"Basically, I do what I need to do to get my sales done. We, as women, have an advantage over men; if we don't use that advantage, then the only person to blame is ourselves."

She dropped me off at my car and we exchanged goodbyes. I thought about Tatyana's advice. Was Alexis the one to watch out for? No way, it had to be Matt. Sure, Alexis used her sex appeal to make sales, but she didn't hide that from anyone.

As I drove home, late again like the night before, I thought about the rest of my training period at Rosemonte. What would tomorrow bring? In only a few hours, I would find out.

Getting ready for bed, I wondered if I could pull an Alexis. Definitely not the gay porn part. But maybe I could use my own sex appeal to make a sale? Who was I kidding? I doubted that would work. I would need to be myself.

Chapter 6

I awoke well rested and ready for work. I decided on a black and white print dress, with a black cardigan. Picking the shoes was always the hardest part. I was torn between red Via Spiga leather sling-backs with an open toe or black Joan & David woven leather heels. I decided to go for the red; I was in a fiery mood. I needed money and hoped to make or a sale soon. Shoes and purses always gave me confidence. I chose my favorite black Prada bag, the one I wore on my interview. I was ready to roll.

I left my house five minutes early. The ride was going smoothly until I got to I-95. A major car accident had turned the four lane highway into a parking lot. "Shit!" I yelled, like someone could hear me. The cars were pretty badly smashed up but the drivers and passengers were out and about, talking to the police. I assumed tow trucks had been called to clean up the mess. A few minutes went by, and a few more minutes. Still no tow trucks. I needed to call Bernie and tell him I'd be late. I didn't even hear the phone ring. He answered straight away.

"Hi, Julia," he roared into the phone. He was so loud. I had to hold it away from my ear.

"Hi, Bernie. There's a car crash on I-95 so I'm running late. I'm sorry. I'll be there as soon as I can."

"No problem, these things happen. You'll get here when you get here," he said.

"Thanks, see you soon." I was relieved he took the news so well.

A few moments later I saw the yellow blinking lights of the tow truck. They started to move the cars out of the way. When I looked around, almost everyone around me was on the phone. I guessed they too were calling their bosses, saying they were going to be late. The traffic started to move and I was on my way.

I arrived about forty minutes late, which meant everyone was in the little office having the morning meeting. As I hurried up the hill, I could hear shouting but couldn't make out who was getting yelled at. I knew Bernie doing the yelling. I hoped it wasn't at Manny. He was nice but I didn't think he was cut out to work for Bernie.

I pulled the heavy front doors open and walked to the little office. The door was ajar, the end seat left vacant for me. Next to Matt the Puppet. I slipped inside and sat down. Bernie was so crimson in the face, he looked like a tomato. Tatyana's words to him were in Russian; and he was screaming at her, "Speak fucking English!" Sherry was in tears. What the hell had I missed?

I gave Matt a what's up look. He shrugged his rounded shoulders and shook his head. What a prick. The bellowing continued.

Bernie shouted, "I don't give a shit. You shouldn't have asked her, you dumb moron!" Tatyana's eyes were glued to her feet, and she was still mumbling in Russian. I looked at Ronnie. He nodded his head, which I translated to mean he'd tell me everything when we were alone in our office. Meanwhile, Sherry was a snot ball mess. I felt sorry for her. I reached inside my Prada and located a purse-sized pack of tissues, handed it over to Sherry, a warm smile on my face. She swatted it out of my hand; the tissues fell to the floor.

"Don't give me this because you feel bad for me," Sherry hollered in my face. "All of you look at me like I'm a circus freak."

She stood up. Tatyana stopped speaking and Bernie quit yelling.

"Why don't you sit down and relax," Bernie said in a gentle voice.

"I've had enough of this bullshit," Sherry screamed at the top of her lungs. She picked up the blue plastic case that held her presentation book and tossed it on the table. Then she took off her coordinating blue plastic name tag, and hurled it at Bernie's face. She moved towards the door, and then turned around sharply. "I have one thing to say to every one of you. Everyone except, Julia," she said.

Suddenly I panicked. This woman was nuts! Why was I being singled out? Oy, what did I do?

"Fuck you, fuck all of you, except for Julia. She's the only one who had enough smarts not to ask me about my hair loss. Everyone else here has no class." Sherry pointed her bony finger at the faces around the table. "You can all go to hell!" She stormed out of the office, slamming the door shut behind her.

All I could think of was the children's nursery rhyme And the Cheese Stands Alone. I was the cheese.

For a moment everything was still. No one spoke, no one moved. Even outside was quiet. None of the grounds guys' were driving by. No birds were chirping. It was like time had frozen.

Finally, Bernie broke the silence. "Sherry probably wouldn't have lasted much longer anyway. Now, let's start our meeting."

෨෧◉෮෨

The next few days of training flew by. Probably because I was the only trainee left. I didn't learn anything new, just reinforcement of the same information. The days formed a pattern. A morning meeting would go on for hours. Then Family Service would do research to find people to sell. This involved pulling names from the Rosemonte database, making phone calls, or sending out letters to people who already owned ground but needed other items. I took my research seriously and soon had enough people on my list to go out on my own appointments.

The night before my first solo appointment, I made plans to go out with Adam for dinner. I was glad he wasn't bringing his girlfriend. I asked Liz if she wanted to join us, but she had a cocktail reception for the debut of a new drug. Bummer. While making our plans for that evening, Adam told me he'd called Bernie to see how I was doing at work. Adam laughed and said, "Don't worry, Bernie gave you a good report." I got the feeling Adam wasn't going to share the details with me. They were most likely discussing how I filled out my sweater, rather than anything to do with my actual work.

Adam would pick me up at the corner of my street like always. He didn't drive down my narrow South Philly street because he didn't want to run the risk of scratching his hubcaps. Adam thought I lived in the ghetto. He lived in Center City, and rented a swanky townhouse apartment that cost twice as much as my mortgage.

I waited for him to pick me up on the corner like a hooker waiting for her pimp. I saw his Jaguar coming down the avenue and quickly ran my hands over my hair to make sure everything was in place. He slowed to a stop and, just as I placed my hand on the door handle, he sped up a little. The car door handle jerked from my hand. "Really grown up, Adam," I said.

He pulled this stunt three more times before I gave him the finger and turned to walk back up my street. He put the window down and called out my name. I pretended I didn't hear him, so he called my cell. When I answered, he said, "Come on, I was just kidding around. Don't be a party pooper. We're going to celebrate. Come on, kid, get in the car. Please, Julia, I won't be an asshole any more tonight, I promise."

"Fine," I said. The car door was open and waiting for me. The luxurious leather seats felt comforting against my body.

"Where do you want to go?" Adam asked.

"I don't care, I can go for anything."

"Okay." We took off, speeding through the tiny streets of South Philly. We ended up at Pesce, a super cute, quaint Italian restaurant. The menu was written on a chalkboard and it changed daily, depending on what the chef bought that day at the Italian

Market. A family place run by a husband and wife, he controlled the kitchen and she handled the front of the house. The place was a B.Y.O.B.; Adam was prepared with a bottle of something expensive. The wine tasted strong and bitter. I ordered salmon with risotto and Adam had a seafood creation with lobster, clams, mussels, and I'm not sure what all else. We picked at the bread, and I waited for him to start the conversation.

"Now that your training's over, are you ready to sell?"

"Yes, I think so. Don't worry; I'm not going to embarrass you."

Adam laughed. "You could never embarrass me."

Our entrees came out of the microscopic kitchen and made their way over to our table. They smelled delicious! The wife asked if we cared for fresh cracked pepper. I shook my head, but Adam said, "Sure thing, hon." She cracked the pepper until Adam held up his nail bitten hand.

She smiled at us and told us, "Bon Appetito."

We feasted. It was so good. The fish was very tender and the risotto extremely creamy. It melted in my mouth. The wife re-appeared at our table to offer us coffee and dessert.

"I would like a cappuccino, please," I said.

"I'll have coffee. And a canolli for each of us."

"I don't want a canolli. Thanks anyway," I told her.

Adam said, "Don't listen to her. Bring it."

"Oy vey," I said, smiling because I thought it was cute how Adam tried to be in charge but really wasn't.

After our canollis, we headed back to my neighborhood. I knew the drill. Adam would drop me off at the corner and wait for me to head to my house.

But tonight he surprised me. As he drove away he yelled out like a cheerleader, "Go get 'em tiger!" How embarrassing! I hoped none of my neighbors heard him.

The phone rang as I climbed into bed. I knew it was Liz and caller ID confirmed it. We often had chats right before we both went to sleep.

"Hey, sista!" Liz cheered into the phone.

"Hey. How was your cocktail thingy?"

"Good, boring, you know, the same shit over again. This new fill in the blank pill is the new miracle pill for fill in the blank disease," she said in a robotic voice. We laughed. Liz asked how dinner went with Adam. "Was Adam the boyfriend type or the big dork tonight?"

I sighed. "He has moved beyond big dork into nerdville. I don't understand him at all. Sometimes I want him to be with me and other times he makes me physically ill. Advice?"

Laughter, then quiet. "I'm sorry, Jul, I don't know what to tell you. Except that you've been dancing to this song forever. If you don't figure it out, eventually something will happen and Adam might make a different choice."

"I know. It's just..." My voice trailed off.

"Listen to me, okay?" Liz said. She was going to give me the cheer-up speech. I'd heard them all. My real problem wasn't Adam. It was not making a decision. I was tired and wanted sleep.

When Liz paused to switch ears, I took the opening and said, "Thanks, I know." We wrapped up our call and I conked out.

Chapter 7

The next morning was my first real day of work. No more training. I felt well prepared walking into the office. I wore my most responsible looking suit; black with white pinstripes. On my feet, black heels with white piping trim. I'd found the shoes at Marshalls in the clearance section for $7.00. It was a no brainer. For a touch of elegance, my Cynthia Rowley purse, white with a smart looking brass chain. I felt put together, and was determined to make a sale on my first night of appointments.

At the morning meeting, Bernie started with a pleasant statement about how we should have a good week. He congratulated me for finishing training. He also added that he'd known the other two were not going to last.

"Who wants to go out to lunch?" Bernie asked.

Of course Matt the Puppet raised his hand. No one else did.

"Okay, Matt and Julia for lunch. Let's go to Vincent's, at 12:30." Bernie ordered.

"What?" I said, startled. "I, um… I'm good."

"No, you're coming to lunch. Matt and I are treating you."

Shit. This was going to suck.

After the meeting, we dispersed to our desks. "How come I got stuck going to lunch?" I asked Ronnie. "I don't want to go. What do I do?" I was hoping he would be able to give me guidance, or come up with an excuse so I wouldn't have to go.

Ronnie shook his head and said, "You have to go. If I can give you some advice, it's this: don't get into any type of conversation whatsoever about who has the best pizza. Trust me, that conversation will not end well." He said this with both hands on my shoulders. "Now, let's get to work." He had a tight grin on his face. It looked like he knew something, but couldn't tell me.

After many phone calls, I secured my first appointment. Hurray! I was going to see Mr. and Mrs. Wasserman that evening 7 p.m. The Wassermans owned land in a family section at Rosemonte. I was going to sell them whatever else they needed and, hopefully, more land for other family members. When I told this exciting news to Ronnie, he said, "That's a big enchilada! Don't get upset if they don't buy, just be happy that you got an appointment on your first day." He gave me a warm smile and a pat on the back. The clock on my desk read twelve on the dot, almost time for lunch.

I met Bernie and Matt the Puppet at Vincent's Pizzeria. They'd come together in Bernie's Mercedes. I chose to drive my own car. When I walked into the pizza joint they were sitting at a table set for six. Bernie sat on one side of the table and pushed the other chairs away so he had extra room. This meant I had to sit on the same side as Matt. I pulled out the middle chair and placed my purse on it. I sat in the end seat away from Matt.

A haggard woman with a nametag that read Stella came over to take our drink orders. She addressed Bernie and Matt by name.

"Is this your little girl?" she asked.

Ew, gross, what the hell? What's wrong with your eyes, lady?

"No," I said before Bernie could muster up a smartass answer. "He's my boss."

I ordered a raspberry Snapple. Matt and Bernie both got root beer. At Bernie's command, Matt jumped up and came back quickly with a bag of B.B.Q. potato chips from the display rack. Matt struggled to open the bag and I laughed.

Bernie growled, "Come on, I'm hungry." He whacked at the bag, but Matt's paws still had a good grip. The bag split open and chips flew everywhere.

"Now look what you did!" Bernie barked.

"Sorry," Matt mumbled and hung his head low, like a little boy who had to take a time out and sit in the corner.

Stella came back with our drinks. "What are you fellas doing, breaking up the place?" She handed us extra napkins, then assumed the position, ready to take our request. Bernie placed an order for the three of us. A large pizza with extra cheese, pepperoni, and mushrooms.

"It's a good thing I like all that stuff," I said.

Matt looked surprised that I dared to speak up.

Bernie cracked a crooked smile. "I know what you like."

I sat up straighter in my chair. The way Bernie had said it made my insides skive.

While Bernie and Matt talked about people who worked in the office, I just sat there and listened. Listening was a great skill to have. Luckily, I was good at it. Most of the gossip they exchanged wasn't relevant. It was boring. I couldn't have cared less who was stealing pencils from the supply closet.

"Your pie will be out in a minute," Stella announced setting down paper plates and a silver stand for the pizza.

Matt grabbed a bunch of napkins from the stack, and motioned to Stella with a weird hand jive. He looked like he was having some kind of seizure.

Stella said in a saucy voice, "One of these days you'll learn how to eat pizza like a big boy." She placed a plastic fork and knife in front of Matt.

I laughed again.

When she turned away, Matt asked Bernie, "Do you notice anything different about Stella?"

Bernie looked deep in thought and said, "I think I do."

Bernie and Matt began to snicker. I didn't get the joke. They exchanged glances and secret eye signals.

"What are you laughing about?" I asked.

Bernie cleared his throat. "Matt likes to play the real or fake game. Our lovely waitress, Stella, has just come back from a leave of absence to get her boobs back where they belong. I think she also traded in her old ones."

I looked at Matt, then at Bernie. "Seriously, how old are you guys that you like to play the real or fake game? Thirteen?"

They smirked. Real mature.

The pizza was arrived piping hot and greasy.

"How's your recovery coming along?" Matt the Puppet asked Stella in a phony voice.

He's such a jerk.

She smiled. "I'm still a little swollen, but getting better every day. I should be bathing suit ready by Memorial Day. Thanks for asking, Matt. Do youse need anything else?"

Bernie said, "No, thanks, hon, we're good." He served slices to me and Matt.

Matt looked like a goober fiddling with his plastic utensils. If the guys from my old pizza shop saw him, forget it. They would've made a mockery out of him and his pizza antics.

After my first bite, Matt the Puppet asked, "Well, what do you think?"

"It's good," I said, remembering the warning Ronnie had given me. I steered the conversation back to work and away from pizza. We discussed our appointments for later that night. Bernie told me it was not important right now if I made a sale, but it was important to get in and see people. I thanked him for the advice and words of encouragement.

Stella delivered the check to Bernie. I reached into my wallet and produced a twenty dollar bill.

Bernie engulfed my hand and boomed, "Put it away, Matt and I are treating you. Anyone want ice cream next door?"

"I have to get back to work," I said. "But thanks anyway." I waved to them as I walked off to my car. I could only imagine what they were saying about me over their ice cream cones.

༄ৎ◎৴৹

The rest of the afternoon was spent preparing myself for my appointment with the Wassermans. While I finished my afternoon cup of coffee, I made sure I had everything I thought I would need.

As I drove over to the condo, I felt ready to sell. They lived in Plymouth Meeting, a suburb, in a gated community. The place was large with many beige buildings, each about ten stories high. Driving through the gates I looked for their building, then parked in a visitor spot. I smoothed down my suit and gathered my things.

I entered the lobby of the building, I needed to sign in at the desk and show my I.D. An old woman pointed out the elevator. I went over and pushed the UP button. I watched as the digital display came down from ten to L. I got in and pushed eight. The trip up was fast. When the doors opened, an old man was standing there.

"Julia?" he asked me.

"Yes. Hi," I said. "You must be Mr. Wasserman."

"I am indeed. Come on, follow me," he said. "The missus has some refreshments for us."

"Oh, what a lovely surprise, you didn't have to go to any trouble."

We got to the door of his condo, and Mr. Wasserman opened it. A faint smell of mothballs mixed with baby powder reached my nose immediately. I walked inside and he introduced me to Mrs. Wasserman, who was wearing a lacy apron over a muumuu. I kept smiling. "What a darling home." I said while Mr. Wasserman gave me a tour, and Mrs. Wasserman frequently interrupted, asking me questions about my life.

When the tour was over, we sat down at the dining room table. The wooden chairs were upholstered in a tan and brown zigzag pattern.

On top of the fabric was a plastic see-through seat cover. "You never know what could happen," Mrs. Wasserman said with an arched eyebrow. My smile got bigger and my cheeks were beginning to get tired. Mrs. Wasserman poured some room-temperature chocolate cherry soda. I took a sip that was a mistake. It was nasty, and probably past the expiration date. Well, too late now. What were a few more sips? No harm done.

As we drank the vile soda, I opened my presentation book. I started with the pictures and proceeded on; things were going well. They both looked interested in what I was saying. Mr. Wasserman informed me they owned land next to his parents in a family section.

"I know," I said. "You two are very smart to plan for the future."

Mr. Wasserman asked, "What are you here to sell?" He looked a little skeptical, peering at me over glasses that were perched halfway down his nose.

I took a big sip of soda. "There's no obligation to buy anything. I'm just here to inform you of the many other services we offer," I said in a cool voice, and went back to the presentation book.

When I arrived at the point of the presentation when I would have to go over what they needed and how much it was going to cost, I took a deep breath. Then I told them the prices, trying to remember to breathe.

Mr. Wasserman said, "We're not getting any younger and we've talked about this many times. When the missus got your call last week, we thought, now's the time. And here you are."

Mrs. Wasserman piped up, "We don't want to leave this for our daughter, she's an only child. Not married."

They looked at each other and linked their hands. The Wassermans fingers were all tangled and covered with age spots. How cute were they? The Wassermans had been married for fifty-three years, and they still seemed majorly in love. Their old-fashioned marriage had a certain sweet factor about it.

"We want to take care of this, we don't want to put it off

anymore," said Mr. Wasserman. "I mean, we don't want anything fancy or over the top as far as the stone goes."

I reached inside the file folder and pulled out the picture I had taken of Mr. Wasserman's parents' stone.

"How's this?" I said, showing them the picture. "It can be exactly like this."

They smiled and I smiled back.

"I know this can be a really uncomfortable subject but I agree that you are doing the right thing. You are doing a mitzvah by not leaving this for your daughter to deal with," I said with confidence in my voice. I prepared the contract. My sale totaled $4,200.

"We can handle that," he said, turning to look at his wife. He winked at her like a young man in love. Mr. Wasserman wrote out a check for $200.

"This brings the balance to $4,000. It'll be divided into monthly payments over the next four years of $83.00. That's not so bad," I said, finishing my awful soda. The math problem appeared in my head. I'd get half of their deposit in my next paycheck. Then a few bucks every month until my commission was met.

"Thank you both for the hospitality. It's very hard to find cherry chocolate soda at the Acme."

Mrs. Wasserman walked me to the door and we waved goodbye. As I left their condo and walked into the hall, I was proud of myself for making my first appointment, and my first sale. Some might have said it was beginner's luck. I would've had to agree.

As I lay in bed trying to go to sleep, I thought about the next day. Tomorrow I'd be able to add my name to the white board and write my sale on it. The first of many, or at least I hoped so. As I drifted off, I wondered if any of the other counselors had been successful that night.

Ronnie called me as I was driving into work. He was at Dunkin' Dounuts. Bernie had given him his order of two bagels with cream cheese, coffee, and six chocolate Munchkins. "Would you like anything while I'm here?" he asked.

"That's thoughtful," I said. "I'll just have coffee from the office."

"As you wish," Ronnie said. "Do you like flying saucers?" he asked.

"Like a U.F.O.?" I asked. What a strange question.

"No," Ronnie laughed. "It's a kind of donut."

Now I was laughing because I'd never heard of that donut, and I'd worked in the bakery business for ten years.

Ronnie said, "Oh you have to try one. They're the best. I'll pick you up one."

"Okay, see ya soon," I said.

I arrived at the cemetery a few minutes later. Bernie was in the little office as usual having breakfast. I smiled and waved; he was too busy eating to speak, but he bobbed his head at me. I walked upstairs and down the hall to our office, excited for the meeting to start. As I entered my office, I spied a huge Dunkin' Donuts bag on top of my desk.

Ronnie was sitting at his desk and swiveled his chair around to greet me. "Hello darling. That," he said pointing to the bag, "is a flying saucer."

"Thanks, Ronnie." I opened the bag and looked inside. "This is gigantic! Do you want to share?"

"No, I've already had two."

"Two! Really?"

"Yes." He hung his head. "I had a bad night last night. I got lost, made no sales, it was downright shitty."

"Bummer," I said, as I sampled the flying saucer. It was twelve inches in diameter and covered with a sugary honey glaze. While I chewed I speculated, about how Ronnie had managed to eat two.

I came out of my sugar coma when Bernie called everyone on

speakerphone to come down to the little office for the morning meeting. He started with Matt, then Alexis's office, and called ours last. I assumed Bernie couldn't find Tatyana because he was calling each extension at every desk downstairs and upstairs; it didn't matter if it was occupied or not. She probably wasn't coming in today. Lucky her. Tatyana sometimes worked from home and got to miss Bernie's endless meetings. Ronnie and I gathered our notebooks and headed downstairs.

Bernie had a smudge of cream cheese on his chin. No one told him it was there. Not even Matt the Puppet. Which was unexpected, because he was such a suck up.

"How did everyone do last night?" Bernie asked in a bland voice. I didn't want to be the first to announce my sale, but I couldn't help smile a little. That must've been a dead giveaway, because Bernie asked, "How did you do on your first night out alone?"

I was quiet and handed over my contract and check from Mr. Wasserman. Bernie looked at it, then looked at me.

"Not bad, but you didn't get any referrals from the Wassermans." I immediately sputtered, "Sorry, I forgot."

"It's okay, you can always call them," Bernie said.

What? Was he for real? What about saying "good job"? I realized at that moment my special treatment had already ended. I was no longer the new kid, my time as the rookie was finished. I was a counselor like the rest of them.

"I will, this afternoon," I said to Bernie.

"Anyone else?" he asked, looking around the table. Alexis handed her paperwork over to Bernie. He looked at it and threw it back. "What is this shit?"

Alexis let out a long sigh. "The couple I saw were arguing from the minute I got there. They clearly did not see eye to eye on anything--"

Bernie interrupted her. "Get to the point! Why did you sell them half of what they needed? I know this couple, they have a shit ton of money."

Alexis said, "The people didn't want to take care of everything in one shot. It was a miracle I sold anything. I did the best I could."

"I don't believe you," Bernie fired back. "This should have been done, fully taken care of, no excuses." He roared, face blazing.

All I could think about was Alexis watching gay porn. I wished she'd never told me that tidbit of her life. Alexis was silent and Bernie waved his hands at her. "No more out of you today," he said.

Manny was next in the line of fire. He actually had a contract in his hands. This could be good for him. He said, "It's not much, but it's something," as he glided the papers across the table to Bernie. Manny placed his hands on his bouncing leg to stop it from nervously moving.

"What the fuck is this?" Bernie yelled. "You sold a stone removal? You don't make any commission on that! What goes on in that pea-sized brain of yours? Every day you come into this office looking like you have everything, and yet you have NOTHING! No money, no sales, you live at a relative's house in their unfinished basement, you have nothing! Explain to me, to everyone here in this room, where your money comes from. Because it's not from Rosemonte. We don't pay you. How much money do you have in your wallet today? Right now? Take out your wallet and empty it. I want to see how much money you have."

His face pale, Manny, silently took out his wallet and looked inside. In a very small voice he announced, "I have $11.00." I watched as Manny swallowed hard. Like a lump had formed in his throat.

"Eleven bucks," Bernie said, laughing. "Where'd you get that from? Who gives you an allowance?"

Manny said, "Okay, Bernie, I see your point. I need to try harder."

Bernie moved on to Matt, who had made two sales. One big and one medium-sized, together they totaled $22,750. Bernie began to pray thanking Jesus for giving him Matt. "If it wasn't for you I would have no one who makes sales," he said, winking at Matt. What was that? Some sort of secret sign? It looked kinda kinky, maybe they were involved in a covert relationship. Matt looked like he'd be the one to take it in the tush.

Matt just sat there as Bernie continued to stroke his ego. The expression on Matt's face was pure enjoyment. The rest of us stared with annoyed looks on our faces.

"New topic," Bernie said. "Mother's Day is in two weeks. Who wants to tell Julia what we do on Mother's Day?"

No one volunteered, so Bernie told Alexis to tell me the scoop. Alexis groaned, and took an extra long sip of her coffee. She cleared her throat and said, "Mother's Day is one of the busiest days at Rosemonte. Tents are set up at both gates and we hand out flowers, and surveys to the cars that come in. Family Service helps people find their loved ones. After we get the surveys back, we use them as tools to try to sell people."

"Why flowers?" I asked. "Isn't that a goyish thing to do, flowers in a Jewish cemetery?" I refrained from rolling my eyes at the thought of flowers. Rocks would be more appropriate.

Alexis answered, "Yes, it is, but a lot of people appreciate it. We need to go over who's doing what for Mother's Day. Ronnie's in charge of supplies: flowers, paper towels, and buckets of water for the flowers, map books and copies of section maps for both gates." She gave orders, "Matt, you're responsible for the survey forms front and back, getting them to and from the printer. Also I need you to have lots of pens for people to use then and there if they choose to fill it out on the spot. T.R. and Cemetery Ed know to have the tents up by the gates, and by the bathrooms with coolers of bottled water."

When Alexis finished giving out the tasks, she looked exasperated. After another long sip of her coffee, she said, "A lot of people don't like the fact that we do the survey thing. In past years people didn't take them or they didn't fill them out. Last year someone tried to run over Ronnie's foot." She was holding back a grin.

Ronnie said, "I am very proud of my cat-like reflexes." The laughter eased the tension in the room.

"Also, you don't want to wish them a Happy Mother's Day. You get the idea right?" Alexis said to me.

I nodded my head. This was a ton of information to process.

Bernie informed us he would be driving the grounds all day, offering people rides and giving directions. "This is a great opportunity to find people who have relatives here but don't own here," he said. "If there's an open lot next to or near their loved one, take advantage and sell sell sell. Got it? Mother's Day can be very lucrative. I had a meeting with Cemetery Ed and he and his team have been working hard fixing stones, planting flowers and making things look nice for the big day."

Bernie continued to babble for a while telling stories of Mother's Days in the past. Finally he asked, "Who wants to go to lunch with me and Matt?" No one volunteered. I hoped he wouldn't pick me again.

After a minute of silence, he looked at Matt and said, "It's just you and me, pal. Should I call Adam?" As he dialed Adam, he ordered Alexis around, "Update the white board. Everyone needs to sell tonight!"

As I exited the little office, I heard Bernie complaining that Adam wasn't answering his phone. "It's still just us, I got voicemail." he said. Matt stared blankly out the window.

Chapter 8

The next few days ran together. I'd made another sale and was working very hard on getting more. The cemetery really was starting to shape up. The grounds guys were putting in over time fixing fallen stones and making things look pretty. Now that daylight savings time was in effect, we had extra hours of daylight.

I remembered Liz's advice. The end of the month was close by and I didn't want to come in dead last on the white board. All the counselors were driving hard sales. Whenever I saw Alexis going out looking like a whore, that meant she already had the sale. Matt the Puppet was in first place on the board. He had sold almost $50,000 in one month! Ronnie was next at $39,000. Alexis was close behind him at $34,500. I needed only a few thousand to beat Manny. I had no appointments scheduled. It was time to call Adam and get some leads.

I took a deep breath and dialed his direct office number from my desk phone. He answered in a mature work voice. "Adam Cooperman."

"Hey, it's me."

"Oh, what's up, babe?"

"Not too much," I said in a slow voice. "Remember when you said you could give me some leads?" I peeked into the hall to see who was around.

"Yeah, I remember," he answered. Then he said nothing.

"Do you have any for me?" I asked in a sugary voice.

"Let me look and see what I have, I think my dad may have something for you. I'll call you back in five."

"Okay, I'll stay close."

After what seemed like forever, but was actually only seven minutes later, my desk phone rang. Since I'd hung up with Adam I had sat there and stared at it, thinking good thoughts. I cleared my throat and answered.

"Hello, this is Julia."

"Hey, sweet cheeks."

"Why do you call me all sorts of fakakte names?" Now was not the time to get snippy with Adam, I told myself. He's just trying to push my buttons and it's working. "Sorry. I'm trying to have a good month, and the end is near."

"It's cool, honey bunny. I got a name for you," he said. "Actually, it's from my dad."

"Great," I said, excited. "What do I owe him?"

"A blowjob," Adam said, laughing.

"You're such an ass, I hope your dad doesn't hear you." But I wanted Lenny to hear Adam and tell him he needed to be more professional at work.

He stopped laughing and gave me the information. "He's expecting your call. Good luck, Young Grasshopper."

"Please tell your dad I said thanks."

"I will."

We hung up and I went to the Rosemonte database to see what I could find out about my lead.

The lead Lenny gave me was fair. The Levines were a mother-son duo. Mrs. Levine lived in a nursing home, and her son, lived down the Shore. He was in charge of her estate and arrangements. I decided to strike while the iron was hot and forced an appointment for that night.

Traffic wasn't too bad on the A.C. Expressway. I knew the way to the Shore but plugged in my GPS once I was in Atlantic City.

Tonight's lead could make or break the month for me. My head was in the game, all systems go.

Mr. Levine actually lived in Margate, a suburb of Atlantic City. Only fifteen minutes from the casinos. Margate's a somewhat wealthy area, mostly inhabited by the Jews who live there for the summer.

His house was a cute bungalow. An off-white clapboard with a brown roof and matching brown shutters. The driveway off to the side of the house had a car sleeping underneath a draped cloth. Located three blocks from the beach, this was pretty good real estate.

I got out of my car and took a deep breath. The salty ocean air smelled familiar and reminded me of my childhood. The sun was almost down and the sky was a pinky peach, filled with lots of fluffy clouds.

I walked up the stone path to the front door, rang the bell, and waited. A moment later I rang the bell again. I shifted in my shoes. I was wearing a drop dead gorgeous pair of stiletto heels. They had a crazy design in burgundy, black and cream with a very pointy toe. So pointy that I almost hated wearing them, but they were too fantastic to sit at home in a box. The things I do to my poor feet, I thought as I waited at the door. Another moment went by and I pushed the bell for the third time. If this guy stood me up I was going to be so pissed off!

I looked around the porch. The swingy chair with overstuffed pillows on it looked so inviting and comfy. I sat down and got my phone out of my purse. I called Mr. Levine. Maybe he was hard of hearing and didn't hear the bell, or maybe he forgot.

He answered his phone. "Hello?"

"Hi, Mr. Levine, it's Julia from Rosemonte. I'm outside your house. Where are you?" I asked him in a nice way. I wanted to say are you home or not, jerk off?

"Oh, Julia, I forwarded my calls from my house to the cell. I'll be home in a few. I had some time before you got here so I ran down to the casino."

"Okay, see you soon." I rocked back and forth. At least I could enjoy the view.

Twenty minutes later a horn beeped down the street. A car parked behind mine and a very tall man got out.

"You must be Julia," he said.

"I am," I said, standing up to shake his hand.

"Sorry I'm late," he said. "I found a fifty in the couch cushions and wanted to try my luck with the roulette wheel."

"No worries." What I really wanted to say was, you can waste all my time; clearly, I don't matter to you.

He opened the door and I followed him inside. Mr. Levine looked like he was a lifer at the casino. He wore glasses that had a smoky tint and lots and lots of jewelry. Mr. T and Mr. Levine shopped at the same jewelry store. He had on a bunch of gold rope chains that were twisted together, many of them with charms: Jewish star, Chai, Italian horn, dog tags with pictures of people on them, and a football. His hands were hairy and he wore too many rings. I was surprised to see he only wore one lonely bracelet. The bracelet said MARV in gold nuggets with diamond chips on all the letters. So tacky.

I forced myself to stop thinking about how bad his jewelry was and refocus. "Where can we sit, Mr. Levine? We have business to discuss," I said in a serious tone. I needed this sale and he'd made me wait for him. I wasn't leaving without a signed contract and a check.

Mr. Levine told me to follow him. He led me toward a table in the breakfast nook off the kitchen. The house décor was shabby chic. We sat down at a whitewashed table and chairs. I took out my presentation book.

Mr. Levine moaned. "This is going to take forever," he said in a whiny voice.

Shit, this was going badly and I hadn't even started yet. "Don't worry," I said. "Most of this you know and I can skip."

As soon I started the presentation, I felt like I was losing him. Mr. Levine was looking all around the room. He wasn't making any eye contact with me. So I changed gears. "Do you prefer table games or slots at the casino?" I asked him.

He grinned and answered, "Both. I like them all. Poker, blackjack, roulette, and slots. Whatever strikes my mood."

"Okay," I said. "I get it. You're a gambling man."

"What does this have to do with my mother?"

"Look, Mr. Levine, I drove eighty-two miles to come talk to you about the arrangements for your mother. This is serious. Plus, I have to drive eighty-two miles back home, and it's getting late. I don't want to waste your time. I'm going to give you the bottom line on what loose ends your mother needs taken care of at Rosemonte. This will have to be done, now or later. So, let's flip a coin. Heads you take care of this tonight, tails I'm out of your hair and you take care of it when you want to or when you need to, depending on your mother."

Mr. Levine smiled. "Lenny was right about you, he said you were feisty." He held up his hands to make cat claws. I stared back at him and felt around until I found a quarter in the bottom of my purse.

"Okay, on three," I said. "One, two, three." I flipped the quarter and before my eyes I saw that I'd fucked up. The quarter landed tails side up. I'd gambled and lost.

I looked at Mr. Levine and said, "You won. I'm just going to pack up and I'll be out of your hair."

He picked up the quarter and handed it to me. There was a sheepish grin on his face.

"Thanks," I said in a small voice. I felt like such a fool. How could I have done this? I turned around to get my purse, which was hanging on the back of my chair. My stupid blue plastic nametag fell off the lapel of my blazer, landing with a clink. Could I be any clumsier? I just wanted to get out of there. I felt so stupid! Get it together, I told myself.

Mr. Levine picked my nametag off the tile floor. "Thanks," I said, but he was holding it in the palm of his hand and studying it, looking closely at my name. Then he looked me directly in the eyes.

"Do you know a Jim Daniels?" he asked in a quizzical voice.

"Yeah," I said.

"I went to Northeast High with him. Is he related to you?"

"That's my dad."

"What a small world," Mr. Levine said, a smile breaking out on his face. "I remember him from high school. He's a smart guy, your dad. Wasn't he president of the Audio-Visual Club? What's he up to now? I would love to shoot the shit with him."

"He..." I cleared my throat, "He's dead. He died when I was a kid."

"Oh honey, I'm so sorry. I feel like such an asshole. Here I am going on and on. I'm sorry, I didn't know."

"No, I know, it's okay," I said. I was almost done gathering up my stuff.

"No really, here I am, so lucky to still have my mother, and you lost your father when you were a tiny tot. Stay right here. I'll be back in a minute," he said as he left the room.

I was packed up and ready to go. What did I need to wait for? Was he going to get a yearbook or something? I wasn't in the mood for that. I looked at my watch, it was really late. I needed to get going.

Mr. Levine came back holding a small brown paper bag. The kind a little kid would take their lunch to school in.

"Let me tell you a story," he said. "Way back senior year, the first nice day of spring, flowers blooming, sunshine, you know, real nice day, I decide to take my father's 1964 Studebaker out for a drive. My father loved that car more than life itself. He didn't know I took it out for a spin. I was trying to impress Josie Johnson; she was a real looker, a cheerleader. Anyway, I digress. I'm out in the car, the top's down, and I'm cruising through town."

What did this have to do with anything? I wondered how I could get out of playing remember when with Mr. Levine. I needed an exit plan.

"Suddenly, a dog breaks away from its leash. I swerve to miss the dog and hit a pothole instead! I blew the tire right out, and dented the hubcap pretty badly. It was an awful scene. I knew my father was going to go ape when he found out what I'd done. All of the sudden, I see your dad walking out of a luncheonette. He comes over to me and looks at the car."

Daddy? Suddenly, he had my attention.

'I had a booth by the window, and saw what happened. Are you okay?' your dad asked me. He looked at the car and said, 'these your wheels?' I told him how I 'borrowed' the car, Josie Johnson, the whole megillah. Your father tells me to 'pop the trunk'. He changed the tire. I didn't know how. Your dad said, 'I have a friend who has a garage and can fix the hubcap to look brand new.'"

"I'm amazed," I said, interrupting Mr. Levine. "I've never heard this story before. This is incredible!"

Mr. Levine nodded his head and continued with the story. "So we go over to the garage. His buddy fixes it up, just like your dad said. The tire and hub cap looked good as new. I told your dad I owed him one. The only bummer in the story was I never got to go for a ride with Josie. Come on, you gotta see this."

I followed him outside to the driveway. He turned on a light and removed the drape from the car. "This," he said with his arms open, "is the Studebaker. When my father died he left it to me because he said I never got to drive it. He never knew, thanks to your dad. I never got to pay back your dad for the favor. So now I can. Come on back in the house, let's take care of my mom's needs at Rosemonte."

"Really?" I said, my mind racing in many different directions at once.

"Yeah, now I can even my debt."

We sat down at the table. I reached for the folder I had made for his mother. "Everything all together comes to $5,095."

Mr. Levine opened up the brown paper bag and took out neat stacks of bills, all hundreds.

Holy shit! Who keeps that much cash in the house? I was shell-shocked. I told Mr. Levine, "But I lost the coin toss."

He just laughed. "Don't worry, I won't tell anyone you lost." We both grinned. "Now start counting."

A few minutes later I had all the money in another brown paper bag. I also had a signed contract. I was still in a bit of a daze. At the front door, I said, "Thank you so much. For the sale, but more importantly, for that story about my father. We don't have much to do with his family and my mother, she's... I don't know. I'm at a loss for words."

Mr. Levine held out his arms for a hug. I gave him one knowing I would smell like his nasty cologne. I didn't care.

"Thanks again," I said.

Mr. Levine said, "No. Thank *you*." He stayed on the porch as I walked to my car.

I waved to him and started the engine. I opened the sunroof and looked up at the stars twinkling in the night sky. I said out loud, "Thanks Daddy. I miss you too."

❦

In the morning I woke up ready for work with a smile on my face. I felt like my new career was a good fit for me. April was almost over; I'd had a nice first month, really a partial month due to training. The smile stayed on my face as I drove from the city into suburbia.

For some reason, I couldn't sit still. I was tapping my steering wheel to the beat of the radio. I kept checking to make sure my earring backs were secure. I hadn't even had any coffee yet. Why was I so jittery? Maybe the brown bag stuffed with cash was making me a tad crazed. I couldn't wait for the morning meeting to start so I could hand in the sack of dead presidents.

Bernie called everyone on speaker phone, then sat watching us skeptically as we all entered the little office. The meeting started with Bernie asking, "Who sold anything last night?" Everyone was silent.

"I did." I raised my hand.

Bernie said," Let's see," and motioned for me to hand him my contract. I gave him the contract and the brown paper bag. "I didn't ask for your lunch," Bernie said. He appeared amused.

"That's the payment. In full." I told him.

Bernie read the contract and opened the bag. His eyes grew large. "Nice, Julia, you even got the references. You learned from your mistake. In the future, when you get a payment in cash, a large payment, don't take it home with you. Call me."

"Why?" I asked.

Bernie said, "Let's face it, you don't live in a safe neighborhood."

"What are you saying exactly? You've never been to my neighborhood." I was offended.

"Look, South Philly's a little rough, somewhat ghetto. And you're walking around with thousands of dollars in cash? It's for your safety," he said in a condescending voice. "Call me and drop it off at my house."

This ticked me off. "Look," I said. "No neighborhood is completely safe all the time, there's crime everywhere. Don't pick on me or where I live. I'm the only person who sold last night. Why are you picking on me?"

Bernie looked at me, the room quiet. Then he nodded and said, "Julia's right. What happened last night? What's wrong with the rest of you?" Bernie launched into another one of his tirades.

Manny hung his head and mumbled, "I struck out at every place I went to last night."

"Of course you did," Bernie shouted. "Well, I'm waiting,"

Alexis and Ronnie were having some sort of telepathic conversation. Probably trying to figure out who was going to go next.

Matt the Puppet volunteered, "The decision maker was not present last night, there was some sort of emergency with another family member. I needed to reschedule the appointment."

"God damn it, Matt! You know how I feel about be-backs. Be-backs are not green backs!" Bernie was foaming at the mouth.

I hadn't seen him upset with Matt before. It was shocking. I felt so good for sticking up for myself, I could ignore Bernie's ranting. Soon the meeting was over. We dispersed to our desks and started work for the day.

Bernie called everyone again on speakerphone and told us all to go to the conference room. Once we had assembled, Matt called down to Bernie. They spoke for a moment, then Matt replaced the receiver and pressed the speakerphone button. I raised my perfectly maintained eyebrows at Ronnie across the table from me, as if to say, what's up with this? Ronnie pointed to the white board behind him. The end of the month had come and it was time to tally the sales.

I don't know why I had butterflies in my stomach, but I did. I had a feeling my partial month was enough to push me ahead of Manny. I was not a huge fan of competition, so I was going to have to get used to this part of the job. Especially because we had a sales tally at the end of every month.

Matt the Puppet took first place. Ronnie came next, Alexis was a close third. Then me, and in last place, Manny.

I have not seen many grown men cry. Manny had tears brimming in his eyes when he saw the new kid had beaten him. He fumbled with a shiny cuff link as he congratulated me. I felt sorry for him. He just was not cut out for this cutthroat job.

We all stared at the board while Bernie shouted, "Sell, sell, sell," from the speakerphone. I was content with my sales for the month.

All I needed to do was sell more than I had and I would be in the clear. That didn't seem so difficult. How hard could it be?

Chapter 9

The month of May started out very wet. Every day it poured buckets. In spite of the bad weather going out at night to sell was starting to become rhythmic for me. I was in the groove. The first week went well for me. I had a few sales under my belt and more appointments for rest of the month.

To reward myself for my earnings, I went shopping with Liz. I wanted a few more suits. Liz got her makeup done at the MAC counter. The money was coming in but I still didn't divert from the sale rack when I went to Macy's. I also had a coupon for marked-down finds.

After shopping we grabbed a Starbucks and chitchatted. Liz had been causally seeing a stock market guy named Scott. They were going away for the weekend. I had no man on the horizon, so I listened to Liz swoon. I was happy for her, but sad for me.

Might being with Adam make me happy? Maybe, but he would never go for me; I didn't have a trust fund. Even if I made a small fortune at Rosemonte, I wouldn't be good enough. Liz said, "You'll find someone when you're not looking." Yeah, that's what I'd been told for years.

The second Monday of May, I wore one of my new suits, a tweed fabric of pinks, yellow and coral, a pale pink blouse, and lots of big chunky necklaces. I loved it! I felt very Chanel in that outfit, even thought I could never afford a real Chanel suit. Or fit into one. But just saying Chanel made me smile. It stood for class, refinement, and reminded me of my grandmother. As I was pulling onto I-95, my phone rang. I reached for my Longchamp purse. Adam was calling.

"Hi," I answered excitedly. "How are you? I haven't talked to you in forever."

"Hey, baby," he replied. "Why you working so hard? I never see you anymore, let alone talk to you. What's up?" His voice made me grin. It sure sounded like he missed me.

"Just working. I don't want to let you down and make you look like a shithead to Bernie."

"Thanks," he said laughing.

We chatted for the rest of my ride into work. Then I asked if he knew about the events scheduled for Mother's Day at Rosemonte.

Adam let out a sigh that turned into a snide chuckle. "You'll see," he said. "It's a circus. A ton of people will be there, all complaining about the place lookin' like shit. Be prepared, it's supposed to be really hot."

"Great," I said as I pulled into the parking lot. We talked for a few more minutes, and then hung up after promising to make dinner plans soon.

Our meeting that morning was all about Mother's Day, which was the following Sunday and fast approaching. We had to vote on flowers and colors. My suggestion of daisies in multi- colors got shot down by Bernie. The winner was carnations in red, pink, and white. Bernie also told us he was considering having a hotdog cart.

The Family Service team all looked at Bernie like he was nuts. "Why feed people at all?" I asked. That was a mistake.

Bernie gave me a lecture about Jews and food. "All Jews love to eat!" he said. "What's better than a juicy hot dog on a nice spring day? Maybe we could get challah hot dog rolls."

"I agree, Jews are all about food. But this is a cemetery. Where does a hot dog cart fit it?" I said.

"Hot dogs have been around forever!" Bernie said. They

are delicious and nutritious, full of vitamins. My great-great-grandfather, Yossel Steinhass, helped perfect the hot dog design back in the old country. He was a butcher, and very good with his hands."

I looked around the table; everyone was staring at Bernie like he was an alien from another planet. Alexis was shaking her head.

Bernie continued his tall tale and added some more fibs about how the Jews had invented the wheel. "You know why onion rings are round?"

"Duh, because onions are round." I knew that one from my culinary background.

"No, smart ass. The Jews created the onion. What's wrong with you people that you don't know these things?"

Seriously? I waited for his nose to grow.

"Bottom line, Julia, you need to go back and study Jewish history."

Alexis slipped me a note to stop leading him on or we would be there all day. Her eyes were squeezed into little slits and the look on her face frightened me.

"So, Julia, do you have a better idea?" Bernie asked.

"No. I retract my statement. I think a hot dog cart is a unique idea. Sorry to have disagreed with you," I said, hoping to smooth things over.

"Then it's settled. Hot dog cart!" Bernie sounded victorious. "Now do we offer Hebrew National or Nathan's?" We all voted for Hebrew National. "Ronnie, in addition to the other supplies, we will also need napkins, mustard, ketchup, and an assortment of relishes. Don't forget a trash can. I don't want to see a bunch of garbage everywhere. Rubbish blowing in the wind looks tacky."

Ronnie scribbled away in his notebook.

I couldn't believe it. What a joke Mother's Day was going to be. Adam was right, it was going to be a circus, and Bernie was the ringleader.

Sunday morning the sky was a pale blue, not too many clouds. The Weather Channel called for rain late in the day and a high of eighty five degrees. It was going to be a hectic day. Besides the obvious, I was leading in my first funeral all by myself. I didn't feel confident to do the lead in, but then again, how hard could it be? I knew how to drive.

I picked out a comfortable khaki dress that had a military feel to it. Brown woven flats were a smart decision because I would be out on the grounds all day. I pulled my hair up into a ponytail, and put on a headband to keep flyaway strands of hair tame. My outfit felt boring, so I looked for something to snazzy it up. I found an armful of copper enamel bangle bracelets that had recently become popular. I had received a bunch of them years ago when my grandmother was traveling through Russia. Now high-end fashion designers like Hermes, and Van Cleef & Arpels were making them a must-have accessory. The pop of color and jingle of sound would remind me of my grandmother all day. I would hear her voice in my head, smoothing my annoyances away.

Everyone needed to be at work extra early to finish all of the last minute details. Bernie told us to park at his house, which was a few minutes from the cemetery. He and Cemetery Ed were going to run a shuttle service. I squished in the middle with Ronnie in Cemetery Ed's truck.

"Sorry," Ronnie said.

"For what?"

"I have been drowning my problems with Reese's Peanut Butter Cups," he said, embarrassed. Ronnie had been stressed out. "Same old problems," he said. "Nothing seems to ever get resolved in my household."

I'd noticed he had put on some poundage but I certainly wouldn't have brought it up. I was far from being svelte myself and had no right to talk. However, my weight didn't fluctuate like his. "You know, I'm here to lend an ear any time you need." I said, and gave him a kind smile.

"I know, thanks. You are wise beyond your years."

Not knowing what to say, I was relieved to see we were making the turn into the gate of the cemetery.

"Wow," I said to Cemetery Ed. "Everything looks so nice! You guys have been putting in a lot of work, and it shows."

"Thanks, Julia," Cemetery Ed said in a gravelly voice. A man of few words. He dropped us off at the office ready to start what would be a very long day.

Bernie yelled my name when I was halfway up the stairs to my office. I wanted to put my things down at my desk but knew I should go back down and see him first. So I turned around in the narrow staircase and marched into the little office. Bernie sat there looking like a slob kabob.

"Today we are going to be very busy," he announced.

Duh, I knew that already.

"Have you mapped out where you need to go to lead in your first solo funeral?" he asked.

I nodded my head.

"Good. Do you know how to get there?"

"Yes, I do. When do I leave to get my car for the funeral?"

Bernie looked at me, a bit puzzled. There was only one funeral today, and it was all me.

"What time Bernie?" I prompted him.

"Well, why don't you take my car for the lead in?"

"I don't want to take your car," I said. I didn't want to take his Mercedes Benz for a two very good reasons, the first being it cost as much as my house! The second was I wasn't used to driving it, let alone in the cemetery. Today was not going to be my test run. "I really would feel more comfortable in my own car."

"No, you'll be fine." He tried to convince me. "Listen, there will be hundreds of people here today. Just take my car, that way we don't have to worry about shuttling you back and forth."

"Please, Bernie, I would prefer to use my own car," I said in my nicest, most ladylike voice. Just the thought of hundreds of people was bad enough. Driving a very expensive car past all of them made me even more nervous.

"You will take my car and that is final!" Bernie boomed. "When you lead in the funeral, I'll take a break and have my lunch."

I nodded and left the little office, trying not to worry too much.

At nine o'clock we went outside to the tents to greet visitors. It wasn't too hot, not yet. The hot dog cart was scheduled to arrive at eleven and stay until two. Ronnie, two girls from the office, and I were armed with flowers, surveys, pens, and maps. Manny, Matt, and Alexis were stationed at the other tent.

I asked Ronnie, "How come Tatyana doesn't have to partake in this mess?" Actually she didn't have to do a lot of stuff the rest of us were required to do.

Ronnie chuckled. "Tatyana has a special deal with Bernie. When he first started working for Rosemonte, he inherited Tatyana from the man who held the position before him. Tatyana told him she deals strictly with Russians. She doesn't want to have anything to do with Family Service, so that meant no funerals for her."

"She doesn't go to a lot of meetings either. Hardly any," I complained.

"Tatyana does her own thing. She made a deal with Bernie, and it works. She sells and Bernie doesn't get involved in her business."

"I need a deal like that!" I exclaimed.

Ronnie agreed. "We all need a deal like that." We laughed.

The first car was slowing down to turn into the gate. I approached and greeted the people inside. "Just give me the flowers, hon," the man ordered from behind the wheel. "You can keep that paper. I'm not interested in any of that crap."

I handed him the flowers. I gave him the survey just in case he changed his mind. As I turned to go to the shelter of the tent, something hit me in the back. I spun around in time to see the man in the car stick out his tongue. He shouted, "I told you I didn't want that shit." He floored it and zoomed up the hill.

I picked up the survey and unfolded it. "Can you believe he threw this at me?" I asked Ronnie.

Ronnie patted my shoulder and sighed. "Yes, I do believe it."

The next car drove in. They were going way too fast. Ronnie was at the post to hand the driver the flowers, but the car didn't stop. It passed him and kept going.

More cars were coming through the gates; most of the people took the flowers. But they were not too thrilled about the surveys. No one was terribly rude, after the one guy who chucked the survey at me. But they weren't friendly either. Bernie was riding around in his car with the windows down, checking to see if we were doing our job. He shouted at people, "Hey, why don't you have any flowers?"

They would respond, "We don't want any."

Everyone looked annoyed. But that answer wasn't good enough for Bernie. He would reach down into the bucket of flowers in the passenger side of his car, pull out a bunch, and throw them at the visitors. As if he was a middle aged newspaper delivery boy. It didn't matter if the people wanted them or not. Most of the flowers just stayed wherever they landed. What a waste.

I looked at my watch. 11:15. The hot dog cart had arrived but I couldn't see it from the tent. The pungent smell of rolling beef was in the air. It wafted all the way over from where the cart had been set up.

"I'm going to head back to the office, I need to tinkle, then do my funeral; I'll be back in a little bit," I said.

Ronnie took a slow gaze around the grounds and told me, "Be careful. There's a bunch of people and cars all over the place."

"Thanks," I said. Ronnie was not trying to make me more nervous than I already was. Still, the crowds were scaring me.

I went to the bathroom, touched up my makeup. I grabbed my phone, a walkie-talkie, and paperwork for the funeral, then called

Bernie to see where he was. "Lunchtime for you," I chanted into the phone, "and funeral time for me."

He said, "I'll be at the front office in a few minutes."

While I waited for him on the front steps, I went over my map again.

Bernie pulled up in his giant car. His Mercedes looked like it had grown another foot since the morning. It took him forever to heave his legs out and grab onto the door to help himself up. Once he was steady on his feet, he started moving towards the steps. He took them one at a time. How does he not have a handicap license plate, I wondered. He'd left the keys in the ignition and the engine running. "Be careful!" he shouted at me from the top step.

"Okay," I whispered back.

When I settled in the driver's seat, my feet were nowhere near the pedals. I looked to find the buttons to adjust the seat. It would've been nice if Bernie had shown me where they were. Why did he have to be such a jerk all the time? I finally figured it out, then adjusted the mirrors. Okay, ready to roll. I put the car in drive and arrived at the bottom of the hill safely. Now I had to turn around. There were way too many people for me to make a U-turn, so I drove out of the cemetery and made a turn in the street. I was in position and waited for the hearse.

In the rearview mirror I saw the gleaming black hearse coming down Oak Hill Road followed by, not one, but two limousines and a bunch of cars. I called over the walkie-talkie to the office to see if the girls knew how many cars were in the processional. A minute later, Cathy radioed back that there were at least twenty-five cars, maybe more.

Lucky me, I thought. Just take your time, I told myself. I put my foot on the brake and moved the car from park to drive. The hearse was behind me so I started the journey to the grave.

The main street of the cemetery was filled with people walking to and from graves. Many of them looked sad and some were crying.

The stench of death was everywhere. A car was parked in the middle of the road ahead of me. There wasn't enough space to pass on either side of it. I looked at my map to see where I could make the next turn to circle back, then turned left onto a narrower road.

Shit. I hadn't realized the road didn't go all the way through. I was in trouble! I couldn't believe I'd fucked up, my first funeral!

I grabbed the walkie-talkie and called for help. No one answered. I was headed toward a dead end, with a bunch of cars behind me. I bellowed for help on the walkie. "Anybody, please, I need help! This is Julia, I screwed up!" The hearse stopped behind me. Both limousines and the long line of cars halted. Yikes!

Cemetery Ed crackled, "Where are ya?"

"I'm not sure," I said. "I took a wrong turn, and now I'm at a dead end."

Cemetery Ed's pickup truck ran on diesel and had very large tires. He was extra high up and had a better view of the grounds. "I see ya," he said. "Stay there, we're comin' to help."

T.R. gave instructions in Spanish to the rest of the grounds guys. I could see from what seemed like miles away the fleet of pickup trucks coming to my rescue.

I was sweating. This was terrible. What else could go wrong? The threat of losing my job ran through my mind.

A man appeared at the passenger side of Bernie's Mercedes. He looked to be in his late eighties, very thin and scrawny. "Do you work here?" he yelled.

"Yes," I answered in a small voice.

He shouted about his wife's gravestone, how it looked like garbage, the whole place looked like a dump. A big bulging vein on his neck looked like it was going to burst any second. Oh God, I thought, please don't let this man die here now, in front of me.

"What can I do to help?" I asked. Some of the cars in the processional were blaring their horns. "Help!" I cried again into the walkie as I scanned the grounds for the trucks. They were getting closer. "I need back up, please. Anybody, come out here. Ronnie, Alexis, Manny, Matt? Anybody?"

The old man threw his arms up in the air and flailed about, angry. That's when I saw he had a shiny silver hook for a hand. He put the hook on the ledge of the car window. I was fearful of this real life pirate, and worried he would damage Bernie's car.

T.R. jumped out of his pickup truck and hurried over to the hearse. He looked like an angel coming to save me. His muscles poked out from the sleeves of his cut-off shirt. His skin was tanned from the sun to a lovely shade of café au lait, and it glistened with just the right amount of sweat in the spring sun. He was pointing to the grounds guys and giving orders, fixing the mess I'd created.

The grounds guys moved the casket from the hearse to a rolling dolly; they pulled it up the road toward the gravesite. Cemetery Ed used a bullhorn to give directions to the funeral-goers. He announced that we'd had them park because it was such a busy day; and would be easier to get around on foot. Everyone spilled out of their cars and followed the casket. All of this teamwork had a touching effect. I exhaled a deep breath of relief.

I told the old man with the scary hook, "Please calm down."

He wouldn't. He was getting more and more upset. "Listen, dear, I'm not moving until my wife's grave is fixed!"

"We're very busy today. I promise I can have things fixed for you as soon as possible," I said. Although I was not sure what the problem was. But Captain Hook wouldn't leave. I started to freak out. I didn't know what else to say.

A man a few years older than me jogged up. "Grandpa," he called, and the old man turned his head. "It's fine, come on, we need to get you back home. Mom made her famous chocolate cake." The two men walked off. After he handed off Grandpa to another member of the family, the guy came back. He bent down to the open window of the car. This guy was a hero, at least in my eyes. "I'm sorry for how Grandpa acted."

"Oh, it's fine," I said. "I understand why he's upset. What's the name on your grandmother's stone? I'll have it fixed, I promise."

"That's just it," he said, "There's nothing wrong with it, he's just starting to lose it." The young man tapped the side of his head with two fingers.

"Oh," I sighed. "I'm sorry. That must be difficult." I looked down at my wrist full of bracelets and smiled, thinking of my own grandmother.

"He likes to freak people out with his hook hand and scratch stuff up, but your car looks unharmed," he said.

"That's a relief; this is my boss's car."

"I'm Sam, Sam Sendars," the guy said. "Here's my card. Would you like to go out for a drink sometime? It looks like you could use one after the way my grandfather yelled at you."

Sam had a twinkle in his eyes. He looked like a mensch. I took his card and put it in my pocket. "Thanks, Sam. I have to get back to work now, but maybe... that would be nice."

Sam said, "Yeah, I have to get back to the family too." He waved and jogged off.

I called Bernie and he answered on the first ring. He yelled a loud, "Hello," in between chews of food.

I started to explain what happened, but Bernie cut me off. "You're so smart! What a great idea! Brilliant, actually. We should do it more often."

"Uh, okay," I said. Maybe Bernie had taken some drugs with his lunch. "So, should I leave your car?" I asked him.

"No, stay there. Cemetery Ed will be there soon to open up the fence."

"Huh, I don't understand. I'm not by the gate," I said.

"Yes, you are. Each ten foot piece of iron fence is moveable so we can open the fence at any spot."

"Okay," I said. I was super confused.

"I don't know why we never thought of it before. Having the cars park down a one way street and then moving the fence. That way no one gets lost going out. They just drive straight out. You'll get a little something extra in your paycheck this week."

"Really?" I asked.

"No. I'm being a kibitzer. On your way back to give me my keys, you gotta stop and have a hot dog. They're so tasty. I'm glad we went with Hebrew National." Click.

While I waited for Cemetery Ed, I pulled down the visor to look at myself in the vanity mirror. I looked like hell! I was a sweaty mess; my hair had dozens of flyaway frizzes. The headband was no help. I couldn't believe Sam Sendars had given me his digits. Things like that rarely happened to girls like me. But Sam was right, I did need a drink.

Cemetery Ed arrived and Spike hopped down, to move the fence. I bowed to both of them, started up the car, and drove carefully. I stopped when I passed to say, "I owe you guys' big time!"

"No, you don't," said Cemetery Ed. "We're just doing our jobs. But it's nice to know youse appreciate us."

"You guys got me out of a very sticky situation. I will always be grateful," I said, smiling. Then I drove through of the opening in the fence.

As I parked Bernie's car in front of the building, I took comfort in the fact that I would never drive it again. Too much pressure. I passed the tacky hot dog cart and walked up the steps to find Bernie waiting in the doorway for his keys. "Get a hot dog." he ordered.

"I don't want one, thanks anyway."

"Eat one, they're wonderful. You will insult the man if you don't have one," he said.

"Maybe later."

"Julia, he's only here until two."

"Okay, when I'm done with my paperwork I'll have one," I lied, just so he would leave me alone.

"Good girl," Bernie said. Like I was his trained pet.

Bernie limped down the stairs. He grunted each time he lifted a foot. The railing looked like it might crumble from the years of abuse it had taken from him.

The rest of the day was a whirlwind of cars speeding by the tent. Most people honked their angry horns if we approached them. I received a few middle fingers, one from a woman who looked as old as Grandma Moses. Few people actually said thank you for the flowers.

At four o'clock Ronnie told our tent team to pack it up. I was relieved. My feet ached from running around all day, even though I'd worn flats. Bernie had given me a headache; he had bugged me for hours to get a hot dog from the cart. He kept calling me on the walkie-talkie and my cell to tell me the countdown, how many minutes I had left. He'd acted like an annoying child.

By five o'clock everything was broken down and cleaned. The cemetery was quiet, still, and peaceful. I asked Ronnie, "What are your Mother's Day plans?"

"I'm going to take my wife out to dinner. I bought her a bracelet."

"That's nice."

"I'm giving her the gift receipt because she's notorious for returning gifts. She doesn't care for my taste," Ronnie said in a mocking tone, touching his chest.

"I'm sure it's a lovely bracelet." His wife sounded like a piece of work.

On my way home I called Adam and told him about my horrendous day.

"You sound beat," he sympathized.

"I am. I feel like I've been run ragged."

"What are you doing later on?"

"Taking a nice bath, then relaxing with some Malibu Coconut Rum and a Diet Coke."

He laughed. "That's a ghetto drink."

"I don't care, I like it."

"Can I come over and join you in the tub?"

Was he serious? "Yeah, but I don't think your girlfriend would be happy."

Adam laughed again. "Probably not."

"Oh, I almost forgot to tell you about this dude who gave me his digits today," I said.

When I filled him in on the details Adam got quiet. Then he said, "That happens to me all the time. It's no biggie."

"Okay, one upper. Don't be a hater."

Adam seemed a little jealous. Yet he had a girlfriend and I was alone.

When I got home I kicked off my shoes, slipped out of my dress and headed for the bathroom. I loved my bathtub, an original claw foot tub from the 1920s. I got the water going and put on a terrycloth robe. Next stop was the kitchen to make a cocktail for myself.

With the glass in one hand and a bottle of rum and soda in each pocket, I headed back upstairs. The water in the tub was full, nice and toasty. A stack of magazines next to the tub doubled as a table for the bottles. My robe dropped to make a pink puddle on the floor. The tub was gently calling my name.

I eased in, leaned back and sipped my delicious beverage. Finally, peace and serenity. My phone was ringing in the distance, but I ignored it. Whoever it was could leave me a message, I simply did not care.

A few hours later I woke up in the tub. I was wrinkled like a raisin and, judging from the almost empty rum bottle, I'd had too much to drink. I couldn't remember the last time I'd passed out from drinking. It was 8:30. What a nap. I felt much better. I grabbed my robe and got out of the tub.

After cleaning up the party in the bathroom, I went to look at my appointment book for work. The rest of May was looking light. I had to get more appointments. But how? The next few weeks at work I would really have to hustle.

Chapter 10

The rest of May was on the quiet side. Mother's Day was over and we still had a few weeks before round two, Father's Day. I hadn't made a sale in ten days. It wasn't just me, Ronnie and Alexis were also in a drought. Something had gone awry.

One afternoon, Alexis and Matt were in his office with the door closed. Alexis was in one of her selling outfits. They argued loudly.

Tatyana was eavesdropping from the kitchen. She gave me the stink eye when I walked past. I gave her a hopelessly confused look. She threw her hands up in the air, and pulled me in close. I saw she was overdue for her moustache waxing. Eeek.

"Well?" I asked.

"Julia, in that office is the one you need to watch for. Don't make the mistake everyone else has."

Why wouldn't she just straight out tell who? "Matt? I already know he's slimy."

"Yes. This is the truth, but don't let him get to you," Tatyana warned.

"I can handle my own. Thanks, Tatyana."

"Do you know old saying keep friends close and enemies closer?" she asked.

I nodded my head.

"That is what I have done, and it made me very rich lady," Tatyana said in a low voice. "Now, I have to go on appointment.

Good luck, Julia."

I sat at my desk and waited until the screaming match was over. Alexis made her way back to her empty office. Manny, had taken a few days off, claiming it was for his mental health. Matt was making sales, but fewer than usual. What did he have that I didn't? Sure, he was much older than me and had more experience. But he also had a secret to sales, and I wanted to know what it was. Remembering Tatyana's warning, I decided to have a chat with Matt the Puppet.

I knocked on the door to the dark closet that was Matt's office. He answered, "Come in," without looking up.

"Hi," I said brightly as I sat down. The chair had been upholstered in orange wool. It scratched my bare legs. "Could I pick your brain for a few moments?"

Matt sat back in his squeaky leather-like chair and pushed his glasses farther up his pug nose. "Sure."

"I know you are heavily involved in many organizations, but how does that translate into getting appointments?"

He laughed. "Do you think I would tell you?"

Ew, that was rude. "I thought you might want to share by taking a young salesperson under your wing," I said. Yuck, that was difficult to get out.

Matt asked me, "Where do you go to solicit?"

What am I, a streetwalker? "Nowhere, I just go where I have appointments."

"You should try to solicit," he said. "There are many old age homes in the Philadelphia metro area that are filled with Jews. Go and talk to them, be their friend, and then …try to sell them." He put his head back down in his paperwork and asked, "Anything else?"

"No," I answered, "Thanks, Matt."

Sell to old people in nursing homes? This was going to be a lot harder than I'd expected.

I went back to my desk and sat, staring at the wall in front of me. I moved to the computer table and Googled old age homes.

In a nanosecond, many pages popped up containing long lists of places to go. I started at the top with Cedar Ridge. I looked at their website; it appeared to be a fancy place. There were many buildings that housed lots of people; surely I could find one of them to sell to. The cemetery had a cool computer program. It pulled the street address of Cedar Ridge and matched it with Jewish sounding last names. I hit the print button and immediately had a manifest of over two hundred names. What a treasure trove! Now, off to the phone to score appointments.

I was successful. Soon I had set appointments with Mrs. Gold and the Cohens. On my way to Cedar Ridge I reflected on my short conversation with Matt. He'd actually given me good advice. I was surprised.

Cedar Ridge was far away in a newish suburb. From Rosemonte the drive took an hour. I was almost there when the sky turned dark. The clouds were moving super fast and lighting was striking everywhere. The roar of thunder was loud. I wanted to get inside before the rain started. I didn't want to present looking like a soaked shlub.

I had on one of my favorite pairs of shoes. My fantastic leopard print heels were a fab find at the Miu Miu sample sale. They were on crazy markdown because one of the heels was missing the bottom part. That wasn't a big deal for me. I scooped them up for a third the normal price. My shoe guy, Salvatore, fixed them up in two minutes flat. So the shoes getting wet was non-negotiable.

When I arrived at the gate to Cedar Ridge, the husky man at the guardhouse waved me right by. He didn't even look up from his glossy magazine. I didn't have to stop to show my I.D. or anything. Some security. Ahead of me was a circle. In the middle was a gigantic fountain sprinkling water to music. I drove around and took the first exit, then found a visitor parking spot. It was actually the second one from the door; the first was reserved for an ambulance. Naturally, the grounds were lush and green. It had to be pricey to live there.

I got out of my car and gathered my things. Just as I was walking through the automatic doors, the sky opened up. Rain pelted the sidewalk. I was safe inside with dry Miu Miu's and armed to sell.

The lobby looked like it belonged in a five star hotel. The vibe was an Asian theme. Under my feet was a massive Oriental rug, at either side of the door were large painted urns. A bamboo desk sat near the elevators. It was vacant. I looked for someone to point me in the right direction, but nobody was around. So I went to the elevator and pushed the UP button. I checked out my reflection in the mirrored doors. I looked professional, grown up, like I meant business.

Inside, I pushed the button for seven. Lucky number seven, I thought. The doors opened and I walked out with a confident attitude. I looked at the arrows of the addresses painted on the wall and turned left. When I got to the door of apartment 703, I knocked and pasted on a smile.

"Hi, I'm here to see Mrs. Gold." I said when a wrinkly old man in an undershirt and slacks opened the door. He kept the chain on.

"Who are you?" he snapped.

"I'm Julia, from Rosemonte. I spoke with her on the phone a few hours ago. She made an appointment with me."

An old woman appeared behind him. She looked kind and sweet. Her white hair was in a loose bun. Elderly hands rested on top of her blue flowered housecoat. She tapped his shoulder and whispered something to him.

"Why would you do that?" he screamed at her. "She's just here to steal from you!"

Man, was this guy taking lessons from Bernie? "That's not true," I said in a loud voice. "I'm here to help you, Mrs. Gold. We have important business to discuss."

"What are you doing, sneaking behind my back on the telephone?" he yelled.

Oy, this guy was going to be difficult. He kept her on a very short leash. Mrs. Gold said in a tiny voice, "I need to talk to her."

"AHHHH," he yelled and walked away, throwing one hand in the air.

Mrs. Gold stood at the door. "I'm so sorry."

"That's okay," I said brightly. "Can I come in?"

"I thought he was going out to a card game but because of the storm he didn't want to leave."

"I can still come in and go over your needs," I said.

"No, you don't understand, Julia. I have a plot at Rosemonte with my first husband, may he rest in peace. But he," and she motioned, meaning Mr. Grumpy, "wants me to be buried with *him*. I can't do it," Mrs. Gold said, looking somewhat scared.

Shit. From our conversation on the phone, I knew Mrs. Gold had a plot with her late husband. However I didn't know she'd remarried. Note to self: ask about current marital situation.

"I understand, Mrs. Gold, but you need to do what's right for you. I can help you do that," I said with the kindest look in my eyes, "Please let me help you so your wishes can be carried out the way you want them to be."

"But I … I'm in a difficult situation," Mrs. Gold said gingerly.

Just as I was about to lecture Mrs. Gold on her rights, I felt a tap on my arm. To my surprise, two security guards were standing in the hallway. Clearly a good cop bad cop duo. Porky looked like he'd had way too many doughnuts. The belt that held up his pants looked like it might scream from the pain of riding around his girth. Young Buck was by the book, his uniform pressed perfect.

"That's her! That's the woman who's trying to steal from us! Take her away, and throw away the key! This woman is a criminal!" Mr. Grumpy screamed from inside the apartment.

What the hell was going on! Me, a criminal? This couldn't be happening.

Young Buck kept his hand on my shoulder. He said, "Miss, you need to come with me."

"I have an appointment with Mrs. Gold. Please, Mrs. Gold, say something." My eyes locked on her frail body.

She looked down at her worn slippers and said, "This was a mistake. I shouldn't have made the appointment, I just wanted some company. I thought my husband was going out tonight."

My mouth dropped open. I said, "I came here tonight to help you."

"I'm sorry, Julia," Mrs. Gold said, still looking at her slippers.

"Come on, miss," Young Buck repeated. Mrs. Gold closed the door and the screaming began. I cringed, glad to be leaving Mr. Grumpy's yelling behind.

I pleaded with the security guards. "This isn't what it looks like."

"We know," they said in unison.

Porky said, "We get a lot of calls from him. He's an old man and thinks everyone's trying to steal from him. The pizza guy, his cleaning girl, even his neighbors. It's sad. He has Alzheimer's."

"Bummer." I looked at my watch. I was going to be extremely early for my next appointment. We all walked to the elevator together. "The rain's pretty bad, huh?" I complained to the guards.

"Yeah," they said nodding in unison. "Do you have a long drive home?" Young Buck inquired.

"Yes, to South Philly. But I have another appointment here, so the rain should let up by then." I pressed the UP arrow and Porky pressed the DOWN arrow.

"No," Porky ordered. He looked at me with squinty eyes.

"No, what? I'm confused."

"Because of section code QTZ 341:9, you'll have to vacate the premises," Young Buck said. He looked impressed with himself.

"But I have another appointment." I said firmly. "It's imperative I see the Cohens."

"I'm sorry," Porky said, "You've been banned from Cedar Ridge."

The elevator doors opened and we stepped in. Porky hit the L button. "But I don't get it," I stammered.

"No one checked you in, so it looks like you snuck in, and that's against the rules here."

"No one was here to check me in at the lobby, and the guy at the gate just waved me right by. He was too busy reading a magazine to care." I had a fierce attitude. My nice girl manners were gone.

"Look, I'm sorry you're banned from here, but do yourself a favor and don't come back," Porky said, matching my tone.

The elevator doors opened. As we exited, the two guards made a Julia sandwich. "Sorry to have caused you trouble tonight, that wasn't my intent," I said to them.

"We know," Young Buck said.

They walked me to the double glass doors, which opened automatically. It was still nasty outside. I looked down at my Miu Miu's and sighed. I put down my presentation case and started to take off my shoes.

"Freeze! What are you doing?" Young Buck yelled.

"I'm taking off my shoes. They were very expensive and I don't want them to get wet. Chill out!" I said. I placed my shoes in my presentation case. "Good night," I said with a head nod.

The guards came out and stood under the overhang to watch me get into my car. I took a moment to settle myself in. I was drenched from top to bottom. I retrieved a napkin out of the glove box and wiped my face dry. I started up the engine. The guards were still standing outside. They weren't going to leave until I did.

I shook my head in pure disgust. Tonight had been a complete bust.

Over the next few weeks, I made some sales. None that were huge. I came into work early, sat through the morning meeting, and then went back to my desk to find leads. In the evening I'd go out and try to sell. I only saw Adam when he came to the cemetery for a funeral. Liz too was becoming a stranger.

I started having a sensitive stomach. I wasn't sure if it was from the work or the stress of being yelled at by Bernie. When I did eventually make it home I'd have a pint glass of Malibu Rum and Diet Coke. That probably wasn't helping my situation.

All in all I enjoyed my new job, and was I fond of the money I was making. I felt like I was working harder than I ever had. My social life, which wasn't that social before, was even more pitiful now. It had been ages since I'd been out for some fun.

Summer came early at the end of May and it was very humid. Alexis beat Matt for the month by $300. Ronnie came next, then me, and finally Manny. Manny had no sales, nothing, a goose egg for the month. We had our end of the month wrap-up meeting upstairs. The white board held the monthly results. I had switched my morning routine from coffee to Diet Coke because it was so hot.

Bernie was extra cranky because we hadn't had a good month. Also he was in severe pain. He didn't like the heat. Bernie was a shvitser, he sweated more than most normal humans. His perspiration output would only grow worse as the summer progressed. Alexis suggested he try Botox in his armpits. Bernie wanted nothing to do with that. Bernie's dry cleaner was probably happy that he'd passed on that brilliant idea.

He suffered more and more from symptoms of diabetes. He claimed his doctor couldn't get the medication right. Bernie had become quite the pill popper. One of the side effects from his meds, was he went to the bathroom, a lot. Normally not a big deal for the average person, when your legs don't work that well it can be a problem.

We sat in silence as he yelled at us for all the usual stuff. Then he pulled out a red folder and looked at it for a moment in silence. In a loud voice, he said, "I have two words for you, Manny. Do you know what they are?"

Manny shook his head slowly from side to side. He looked

especially dapper in a navy pinstriped suit with a pale blue shirt that had a white collar and cuffs. His tie had a G-clef on it, probably from his days back in the music business.

"Really, no clue?" Bernie asked sarcastically. "The two words for you are, YOU'RE FIRED!" Bernie's voice was so thunderous and ferocious I was surprised fire didn't dance off his tongue.

Bernie fired Manny in front all of Family Service. Yikes!

Ronnie and I exchanged glances. Alexis was staring out into space. She was probably thinking about a steamy sex scene involving two hunks. If Manny was dunzo, then I would be the bottom rung salesperson. That wasn't good news for me. My stomach started to knot as I took a swig of my soda.

"Okay then," Manny said in a casual tone. He stood up offered his hand for Bernie to shake. Bernie snarled like a dog and gave Matt the Puppet a signal.

Matt stood up and said to Manny, "I'll escort you to your desk to collect your personal effects, and then to your vehicle where you will promptly leave." As the two men walked out of the office, we all gawked at Bernie.

He had the floor and gave a mini speech. "Now that Manny, that piece of shit, no good, lazy ass, is out of here, the rest of you need to get some work done. No more excuses, people. May's over, June starts tomorrow. We have Father's Day coming up. Who knows what happens when it gets hot out?"

I knew that whatever I thought the answer was would be wrong, so I just sat there. Alexis and Ronnie traded looks. Apparently they had been through the conversation before. Yet neither of them offered any answers.

Bernie said in a jovial voice, "People drop dead. It gets hot and people plotz. We capitalize on the funerals coming in, and sell to the remaining loved ones." He rambled on about the summer of 1975. When he was selling at a new cemetery in Miami, Florida. He regaled us with how great it was. The sales, the Cuban coffee, and babes in bikinis at the beach. What a snooze fest.

From my seat I had a clear view of Manny's office. I watched Matt lead him to his desk. On top of it sat a small brown cardboard box. Matt made a gesture toward the box.

Manny plopped down in his chair for what would be the last time, emptying his personal belongings into the box. He picked up a framed picture of his family and placed it carefully inside. Next he tossed in a handful of cough drops, some tea bags, Band-Aids. When Manny started to sort through a pile of business cards Matt knocked them out of his hands.

"You can't take these with you. They're Rosemonte property."

Oh, please. Give the guy a break. Poor Manny looked defeated and hung his head low as he wrapped the cord around his cell phone charger. He must have said something because Matt shouted loud enough so we could all hear him.

"One more thing, I need to collect your name tag." He outstretched his bony hand and held it flat, until Manny placed the blue plastic name tag in his palm. Then Matt curled his fingers around it as if the name tag would grow legs and escape. "Now, I will escort you to your vehicle."

Manny followed Matt into the hall, down the stairs, and outside to his car.

Nobody in Family Service got to say goodbye to Manny. He vanished as quickly as a pair of Louboutins on the sale rack.

ю⊙ю

The next day was Friday and I couldn't wait until it was over. We didn't make appointments on Friday or Saturday night due to Shabbat, the Jewish Sabbath. I was really looking forward to doing absolutely nothing on Saturday. I needed to relax. I'd been working a lot lately and was extremely stressed out. As I sat at my desk, staring at my calendar and sizing up the rest of the month, the phone rang.

"Hello."

"Hey, doll."

"Hey, Adam, what's up?"

"What're you doing tomorrow?"

"A whole lot of nuffin."

"Settle down there, gangsta. I got an email invite to this new place that opened up recently. It's a nail salon where you get your digits done and have a cocktail at the same time. Joy wants no parts of it. Wanna go?"

"Sounds good to me," I said. "We haven't hung out in forever." I looked down at my feet. I could use a pedicure. And it seemed like I was always up for a cocktail these days.

"Great," Adam said. "I'll book us an appointment so we can have our pedicure chairs next to each other. Do you want to go out for a bite after?"

"Okay." Bernie was calling Family Service on the speakerphone. "I gotta go, I'll see you tomorrow," I said.

As I prepared for another boring meeting, in my head the countdown clock had started ticking. Only eight hours left until I could leave for the day. Yay.

Chapter 11

I hailed a cab and drank my morning cup of coffee on the ride over to the salon. Adam was leaning against a newspaper box. He paid the cabbie for me and we walked inside. The salon had a Zen-like feel to it. Everything was in neutral tones, yet the decor wasn't boring.

We sat down on a cream colored couch with dark brown velvet pillows. In front of us was a bamboo table with drink menus. I picked one up and started to peruse it. Adam put his arm around me and looked over my shoulder at the menu. I turned to give him a nasty look and got him his own menu from the table.

"Here you go," I said.

He frowned at me and looked at the menu. "What color are you going to get?" I asked him.

"Haha," Adam said. "I'm going to get a no polish pedicure."

"That's very manly."

He punched me hard.

"Ouch," I said as I rubbed my shoulder. "You know I bruise very easily." I gave him another dirty look. I thought about Liz and her question about which Adam I was hanging out with. Too soon to tell. My mood was kinda into him, but playing hard to get. I scolded myself: he had Da Brat, I couldn't forget about her.

"So," I said putting my menu down. "How's Da Brat? I mean Joy?"

Adam shrugged his broad shoulders. "She's okay. We're having some problems."

Really? What a shocker. "Duh. Maybe because you're only dating her because of her bank account. Of course there are going to be problems."

Adam looked at me with his sad green eyes. I felt a little bad, but it was true. Sometimes the truth hurts.

A girl appeared before us wearing a zebra print uniform. "Adam, party of two." She looked at us. "Follow me."

We did, down a quiet hallway to a room lit with candles that smelled like vanilla beans. A display of nail polishes was mounted on the wall near two spa chairs with the whirlpool tubs attached.

"Please pick your color and select your drink order. I'll be back in a moment to take them," she said in a calm, mellow voice.

I looked at Adam. "This is heaven. Thanks for inviting me, man."

"Thanks for coming."

Adam sat down in a chair. I walked over to the display to pick my color. I heard the water splash when he placed his size twelve's inside the tub. I looked at the rainbow of colors and tried to make a decision. They all looked so pretty and shiny in their petite bottles. I decided on a purplish pink with iridescent sparkles. I turned around. Adam looked relaxed.

I took the chair next to him and slipped my feet into the hot water.

"Ahhh," I said out loud, "that feels really nice." Someone had put rose petals in our water. I wasn't sure what they were for, but it felt fancy.

The zebra girl appeared again to take our drink orders. She smiled at us. "What's your poison?"

Adam said, "I'll have a SoCo and 7 Up."

I returned her smile and said, "I'll have the same."

Adam looked at me. "I'm surprised."

"Why?"

"I thought for sure you would have your ghetto hood rat drink, Malibu and Diet Coke." He smirked.

"Very funny." The Adam I didn't like was here.

Two girls came into our room, one wearing cheetah and the other giraffe. They announced they were here to do our toes. "Yay," I said and softly clapped my hands. Both girls were silent as they started to work on our feet. I looked at Adam. "What are your problems with Joy? Is this the end of your relationship?"

"No," he said, looking a little shocked. "It's just, you know, she's no fun. She is the complete opposite of her name. She never wants to do anything or go anywhere."

A man came in dressed in eighties-styled Skidz pants in a reptile pattern. The girls definitely had the cuter uniforms. He served us our cocktails. Mine came with a fun polka dot umbrella.

Adam continued to bitch about his issues with Joy and I sat there and lent an ear, knowing that nothing was going to change. Adam always complained about her, but he never did anything to modify the relationship. It was the same cycle over and over. While he was talking, I played around with the remote that controlled the massage chair. Between the massage and the booze, I was really starting to unwind.

The girl doing my toes put my flip-flops back on, careful not to smear the wet polish. I thanked her and gave her a tip. She winked, and gave me her card, told me to ask for her next time.

Adam asked, "How long do you want to sit for?"

"Until I'm dry," I commanded.

"Okay, I'm going to go pay up front. That should kill some time." I took out my wallet and held up some money.

With a wave of his hand he told me, "Put that away."

"Thanks, Adam," I said "I appreciate it."

"Get outta here. Like I would ever let you pay." He hooted.

We exchange a smile and it reminded me of when we were kids. When Adam would buy me a slice from Frank's, our neighborhood pizza parlor, he would always tell me to put my money away. Some things never changed.

By the time he came back, I was semi-dry. "Where do you want to go for lunch?" I asked him.

"I don't care."

"How about Little Pete's?" I suggested.

"Done deal, I could go for some eggs."

"Did you drive over or take a cab?"

"I drove," Adam said, waving his valet slip in front of my face.

"We can walk from here, can't we?"

"Yeah, if you want to." Which sounded like Adam didn't want to. "Let's drive."

"Okay."

Adam wasted a ton of money parking his car in garages all over the city. It was ridiculous.

Outside, Adam and I walked the few steps to the neighboring garage. He sent the valet guy for his Jaguar. The valet didn't have to go far; it was in the first spot. After Adam tipped him, we got inside the immaculate automobile and drove a few blocks to Little Pete's. Adam pulled into a lot next to the restaurant. He threw his keys to the attendant and told him, "We'll be back in about an hour, keep her close."

I rolled my eyes. Sometimes he sounded like such a douche.

We grabbed a booth by the window. The waitress greeted us and handed out menus. At the same time we both said, "I know what I want."

She laughed and smiled. "Ladies first."

"I would like coffee and an egg white omelet with American cheese, and rye toast, please."

She asked, "Do you want potatoes?"

"Not today, thanks."

Adam ordered coffee, a western omelet without peppers and onions, a salt bagel and hash browns. "Is it possible to have the potatoes that she doesn't want?" He pointed at me.

The waitress was all giggles, "Sure." She vanished and was back almost instantly with two steaming mugs of hot coffee.

Little Pete's wasn't too busy. We people-watched while we waited for our food. It came out quickly. We enjoyed shooting the shit and reminiscing about the old days. I was just glad not to be talking about work. Saturday was half over. It felt nice to relax and be lazy.

The check came and Adam paid it. "Do you want a lift home?" he asked.

"Only if you don't mind going to the ghetto."

"Not for you." An inside joke that never got old.

We freed his car from the lot and Adam drove towards South Philly. As we were coming up to the corner of Moyamensing Avenue and Sigel Street, Adam pulled over and put on his hazards. I turned to thank him for a lovely day. He engulfed me in a huge hug and kissed my cheek. I hopped out and walked up Sigel to my house, the third one from the corner. Before I went up the front steps, I looked back. I knew he'd be waiting to make sure I got in safely.

We waved.

∾⊙〜

I had to work on Sunday. When I was growing up, Sunday's were all about bagels and lox. I didn't care much for lox, but I did enjoy a freshly toasted bagel smothered in cream cheese. Sunday at the cemetery started out the same way. The task of getting the delicacies rotated among, all the Family Service counselors. It was Ronnie's turn to buy.

I popped in and grabbed a cinnamon raisin bagel, then headed up to my desk. Bernie didn't say boo, he was too busy eating from what looked like a Shiva-sized tray of food. He was in hog heaven between the lox, whitefish salad, and crudités. Off to his left was a white cardboard box of cookies, rugelach, and mandelbread. To the right sat a carton of Tropicana and a thermos. It was almost 95 degrees outside, way too hot to eat that much. My stomach started to feel cramped at the sight of Bernie feeding his face.

When I got to my desk, I popped two chewable Pepto-Bismols before I took a bite of my bagel. I made some phone calls to people I'd met on the grounds and made appointments for the week. So far so good.

Bernie called for me on the speakerphone. His voice sounded hard to understand, probably from his throat being coated with cream cheese and fish fragments. I picked up the receiver. "I'm getting a lot of static can you please repeat what you said?"

"No, just come down here."

Damn. I grabbed a notebook and pen and hurried down to the little office.

Bernie was gulping a translucent cup of orange juice when I appeared in the doorway. "Sit down," he barked. I took a seat and tried to look like my stomach wasn't doing cartwheels. "Father's Day is coming up soon," he said.

I nodded. "I know. I thought we were having a meeting about it this week."

"We are. I want to make sure you'll be okay." He said this in a gentle voice.

"Yeah, why wouldn't I be?" I asked.

"Because your father's dead."

Thanks for the kind reminder, Bernie. "I'll be fine; really, it's not an issue. Is there anything else?"

Bernie poked around in the white box, sampling the different kinds of cookies. "Take a look at my pen."

I picked up his Montblanc pen and said, "Oh, this is nice." I knew diddly about fancy pens.

"No!" Bernie shouted. "Jesus! Put that down! The other pen."

"Oh," I said as I picked up the other pen. "This one's nice too."

"Pull the lever on the side, but be careful," he instructed with a mouth chock-full of cookies. I pulled the lever out carefully, and a scroll of paper unraveled from the barrel of the pen. Written on the paper was SORRY FOR YOUR LOSS. "That's what we're giving away at Father's Day this year. They're very expensive."

"Wow. These are the nicest pens I've even seen. I don't want to know how much they set you back." Bernie was so focused on his feedbag; I don't think he realized how sarcastic I was being. "I gotta get back to my desk; I'm working on getting set up for the week."

"Good, good. Go." Bernie said. He fixed another bagel and hollered for Ronnie on the speakerphone.

Those pens had to be a joke, they were so bad. Who was going to want one? What was Bernie thinking when he ordered them? What a waste of money.

The next morning at our meeting we discussed Father's Day. It was going to be similar to Mother's Day with the tents at both gates, and surveys, but instead of flowers we were going to hand out the pens. Bernie changed his mind mid-lecture and requested a few buckets of flowers for people who might want them. He ordered blue and white carnations. How lovely.

Bernie showed us pictures of a classic Buick Riviera and vintage Ford Model T. "I met the owner of these two cars over the weekend. His parents are buried here, in section L." We all nodded but I didn't know where he was going with this. "Beautiful cars, wouldn't you agree?" Again everyone bobbed their heads. I looked at Alexis, who raised both her eyebrows at me. "I made a deal with him," Bernie crooned. "He's going to park his Model T near the hot dog cart and let us take photos with it."

What photos? This made no sense. But I had learned my lesson from the Mother's Day meeting, so I wasn't going to ask any questions.

Alexis asked, "Who's going to take the photos?"

How daring of her.

Bernie answered, "I didn't figure that part out yet. Does anyone know a cheap photographer?"

"Can people sit in the Model T?" I asked. Did both sides of my brain not agree? Why had I asked a question?

"Yes, of course," Bernie replied in an excited voice. "That's the draw of this beautiful car; you can sit, get your picture taken, have a hot dog and visit your loved ones."

"Don't forget about leaving with your limited edition pen," Matt added.

I couldn't tell if he was being cynical or serious. Father's Day was going to be even worse than Mother's Day.

That evening I headed to my only appointment. It was in Center City. Hopefully it would go smoothly and I could make it an early night. I drove into town and parked my car at a garage Adam frequently used. The building I was going to was not far from the one he lived in.

It was a hot sticky night. My feet ached. I had on strappy black sandals. On the back of each heel was an embroidered dragonfly. I loved these shoes, but they killed my feet. When I was riding up in the elevator I looked down, I couldn't help but smile. I had on hot shoes and a fresh pedicure. From the ankles down, I was a total babe!

The elevator stopped on the nineteenth floor. I'd never met Dr. and Mrs. Fine, but I had sold plots to their relatives and got them as a referral. I arrived at their door and rang the bell. The welcome mat, was black with an assortment of colorful footprints. How fun. I tried to see if one matched up with my foot.

The door opened and both Dr. and Mrs. Fine stood in the doorway. "Hello!" they chanted in unison. "Come on in!" Oddly, they seemed excited to see me. I introduced myself and we all shook hands.

A cute older couple, they both had the same short hairdo with curly salt and pepper hair. Mrs. Fine had cat eye glasses on a neck chain with chunky, exotic looking beads. She wore a caftan circa

1969, tie-dyed and very cool looking. Her fingers and toes showcased a different colored polish on every nail. Dr. Fine was dressed like a preppy grandpa. Khaki pants, a cotton plaid shirt, and brown leather boat shoes. The Fines had a delightful back and forth between them.

They welcomed me into their home, and Mrs. Fine asked, "Would you like something to drink, sweetie?"

"That's very kind of you; I'm parched. Could I have some water?"

"I'll go get it." She darted off to the kitchen, her caftan swirling around. "Go and get settled in the den."

I followed Dr. Fine. The den was paneled with faux wood on the walls and a lime green carpet. The walls housed shelves from the floor to the ceiling. On the shelves were tons and tons of knickknacks, all of them feet. Big feet, little feet, white, black, multi-colored, silver, bronze, and papier-mâché. I felt like I was in a foot museum.

When Mrs. Fine came into the den with three bottles of Fiji water, she shrieked with delight. "Look at your shoes! They're fantastic!"

"Thanks," I said with a smile. "As fabulous as they look, they're murder on my feet."

Dr. Fine got up to take a gander at my shoes. I felt like Dorothy in *The Wizard Of Oz*, when all the Munchkins were checking out her Ruby Slippers. Oooohing and aaaahing.

"That dragonfly is absolutely marvelous," Mrs. Fine exclaimed. "Do you know what a dragonfly represents?"

I shook my head. I thought a dragonfly was cousin to the butterfly.

"A dragonfly," she cleared her throat, "is symbolic for power and poise. The elegance and grace of a dragonfly is often compared to that of a ballerina. You, my dear," Mrs. Fine said as she cupped my chin, "have all of these qualities; I can tell. I can see it in your magnificent ebony eyes."

What the fuck! Did they smoke a joint before I got here or what? I had none of the qualities she'd listed. However, I wanted the sale so I went along with her foolishness. "Thank you for your insight."

Now she was circling around me. "I want to drink you all in."

I was getting dizzy from watching her twirl about in her sea of color and motion. My face must have turned a little green, because Dr. Fine clapped his hands and Mrs. Fine stopped. "Let's all have a seat," he said.

I was grateful and smiled at him.

We sat down at a black lacquered table with matching chairs. A paisley foot statue stood in the middle of the table. Dr. Fine told me, "I know why you're here." He was aware that I had sold a double package to his relatives. "They're more," he paused and said, "*traditional* than me, and my beloved." He reached for Mrs. Fine's hand and gave it a squeeze. "Look, Julia, just give us the info. We'll think about it and let you know."

This wasn't what I wanted to hear. I needed to make a sale. Tonight. Mrs. Fine also didn't want to hear this because she ripped her hand away from her husband's and snapped, "That's not what WE talked about. I want to do this now. Tonight."

I needed to take charge of the table. "Look, if I were in your shoes," I said, "I would take the time to discuss it right now. We can handle all of this tonight. That's my job. That's why I came out to your home, to put your mind at ease, and give you all the important information. I don't want anyone to have ill feelings about anything having to do with Rosemonte. So everybody just relax, take a deep breath in and exhale out slowly."

"Sorry," Dr. Fine said after I'd finished my mini lecture. "I just get a little funny about this stuff."

"That's okay; you don't need to be sorry."

"See, what did I tell you?" Mrs. Fine said in a smooth voice full of power and poise. Maybe she was the dragonfly.

I took out the folder I had prepared for the Fines. "Your family's in this section." I highlighted it on the map and showed it to them.

Mrs. Fine fired back, "We want to be cremated. Well, actually, I want to be cremated he wants to be buried in the ground. My darling hubby gave in after many years of me fulfilling his foot fetish."

She seemed to be getting a little hot and bothered talking about the topic. She moved the neckline of her caftan back and forth to create air flow.

I smiled. "That would explain all the feet." I let out a nervous giggle.

"That's only one part of it," Mrs. Fine said. "My husband had a very successful podiatry practice. He would come home from work, and tell me in great detail about the feet he'd looked at. I thought this was normal. One day we were making love and he started giving me a foot rub and kissed my feet." Mrs. Fine closed her eyes. "Eventually, he was sucking my toes. All the time." She winked at her husband. "And that was just the beginning! He loved eating off of my feet, painting my toenails, licking the bottom of my feet like he was a mischievous kitten, and smelling between my toes. Of course, he wanted me to urinate on his feet. At first I said no way, but look at that face. How could I say no? We discussed it like adults and bought rubber sheets. The golden shower wasn't that bad after all. Eventually I became fond of it myself. Very freeing, you know? I drew the line when he wanted me to insert my big toe into his anus." Mrs. Fine shook her head, "exit only."

Oh God, I think I just threw up in my mouth. This had to be a dream. No, a nightmare. Did she really say "golden shower" and "anus"? Mrs. Fine was seventy-something years old. I felt ill. Where was my Pepto?

"Back then we didn't know what it was called; we just kept it a secret," she said. "These days everyone talks freely about sex and the word fetish is used all the time. We just joined a social group called Fetish Fun For Seniors." Mrs. Fine smiled and blew a kiss to her husband.

I needed to stop this fetish forum. It was downright creepy. I was gonna need at least two drinks tonight after work.

"Okay, let's switch gears," I said to the frisky couple. My cheeks were hot from embarrassment. I didn't know why, but I felt like both

Dr. and Mrs. Fine were thinking about my feet. Thank God I'd gotten a fresh pedicure. I had a feeling that might win me the sale.

"Here we go," I said, turning to the picture in my presentation book. The glossy photo was taken in spring, all the colors were popping. "A compromise for both of you. This is a columbarium. It works out well for you two because you're buried in the ground and memorialized with a plaque." I looked at Dr. Fine. "You can still be cremated." I glanced at Mrs. Fine. "It's a wonderful marriage of both your wishes. Isn't that what life is all about? You'll be with each other forever."

At this point I could feel the sweat running down the back of my neck. Mrs. Fine looked over at her husband. Their eyes were speaking to each other in their secret language. I almost drank my entire bottle of water during their silent conversation.

Finally, Mrs. Fine ordered, "Go, get your checkbook."

Dr. Fine obeyed and returned with a check and a pen. I wrote out the contract, got both signatures, referrals, and the payment.

I was thrilled the appointment was over. "It's been a pleasure meeting such unique people," I told them as I gathered my things.

Mrs. Fine placed her hand on my head and closed her eyes. I'm not sure what she was doing, but it felt icky. I looked over at Dr. Fine. He was licking his lips, staring down at my feet. Ugh.

They escorted me to the door and watched as I walked down the hall to the elevator. I felt the need for a shower to cleanse myself of their kinky foot filth. I couldn't wait to get to my car and take off my shoes.

When I got home I tucked the dragonfly strappy heels back in their box. I closed the lid and placed them in the closet, thinking how every time I wore the shoes I would think of the Fines.

Chapter 12

My house phone was ringing. Who would call me at 6:30 in the morning? I saw the 310 area code flash.

"Hello, Mother." Why was I number one on her drunk dial list? Seriously, it was 3:30 a.m. in California, she should have been sleeping, not calling me drunk.

"Julia? Is that you? You sound like you put on a few pounds. Are you all right?" She slurred her words.

"Yes, Mother, it's me. Why are you calling so early? I'm about to leave for work."

"Father fathersss day is soon. Are you still upset about Dad?"

Déjà vu. Had she talked to Bernie? I heard her fumbling with a lighter. Smoking was such a disgusting habit. "I'm fine. Are you okay?"

"Yup. My new boyfriend just walked in so I gotta boogie. I'll talk to you before your birthday. Tootles."

She hung up before I got a chance to think up a smart retort. My birthday wasn't for six months. How depressing that my drunk mother had a boyfriend and I didn't.

At work, Ronnie and I prepared for Father's Day. He stickered up the pen boxes and I stacked them inside two larger crates.

"You know, we get a break until the High Holy Days," Ronnie said.

"A break? What do you mean?"

"None of this extra bullshit work," Ronnie said. "The stupid giveaway chozzerai, pens for Father's Day, the car photos. That has to be the dumbest idea Bernie's ever come up with."

"Oy vey," I groaned in agreement.

When Ronnie and I finished the pens, we moved on to the cheesy oak tag frames. The idea was to fold along the perforated lines. Ronnie complained he could barely see them. I had an issue with paper cuts.

Upon completion my hands were a mess. I looked like a cutter. This was very unattractive. I searched the supply closet, hoping to find a solution. I could picture my father wearing these rubber finger covers during tax season. He'd been a CPA. As a little girl I'd steal them from him and make them into finger puppets. He would break into a tight grin, then scold me for messing around with his things.

The next day, Ronnie and I finished up the boring prep work just before noon. We took our lunch break and returned along with the mailman. Ronnie held the door for both of us. "Funny," I said to Ronnie. "This is the first time I've seen a mailman here at the cemetery."

He introduced himself to me. Max was a hearty looking man who'd made the postal service his life-long career. "I don't think I have any contracts today, but I do have some postcards for you," he said as he placed the mail on the counter. I felt my face blush as he tipped his hat in my direction. Max was very 1950s. "See you tomorrow," he announced. Then turned on his heel and headed for the exit.

Over the speakerphone we heard Bernie ranting, "Bring me the mail. Now!" Ronnie took the pile into the little office to give it to Bernie for sorting.

When Ronnie returned I asked him about the postcards. He held up one finger as if to say hold on, walked behind the counter and grabbed a map. He gave it to me and said, "Look at the bottom."

"I don't know why I never saw this before," I said. At the bottom of the map was a tear- off portion where you could fill out the blanks and mail it back to the cemetery postage-paid.

"For some reason," he said, "the postcards all seem to arrive in a bunch, then we won't get any for a while. This is a great tool for people who are tracing their roots, or doing family tree projects. Especially because the cemetery has records that go back one hundred and fifty years. Of course, Bernie thinks this is a great way to try to sell to people."

"I think Bernie thinks any way to sell people that's tricky is a good way," I said and we both laughed.

In the morning meeting the next day, Bernie distributed the postcards. Ronnie, Alexis, and Matt each got two and I got one. Bernie went on to bore us by lecturing on how we could sell so much to these types of people because clearly they had family here and wanted to be here too. I looked at my postcard it was from a woman who lived in Juneau, Alaska. How'd she get the map? I didn't think there were any Jews who lived in Alaska. What was the time difference there? Why was I always getting stuck with all the weirdos?

The meeting was over and Bernie commanded us all to, "go call our people from the cards. Right now!" he yelled.

Matt the Puppet added, "We need to strike while the iron's hot." Alexis gave him a dirty look as we all shuffled out of the little office.

Upstairs at my desk, I reread my card. Veronica Stern from Juneau was looking for her relatives. She listed Sylvia Braunberg and Ruth Stein. I plugged both names into the computer database and waited. The postage mark indicated it took almost two weeks to get here. Ruth Stein was a popular name so I printed out the page with all the locations. Sylvia Braunberg was a little more complex.

Many early immigrants had arrived in the United States without knowing any English. The people who worked at Ellis Island asked for names and simply wrote down what they heard. In a lot of cases, mistakes were made. For this reason, many people do not know the original spelling of their family name.

I printed out Sylvia's page and tried to match the two to see if they were related. No luck.

I spun around in my chair and asked Ronnie for his advice. He said, "Why don't you call her? Maybe she can give you some insight."

"Good idea," I said. This wasn't a good idea at all. "I think it's an eight hour time difference, so what should I do? Seriously, what time is it in Alaska? I can't do the math."

"Call her."

"Okay." As I started to dial Alaska, I said, "I'm pretty sure this is the first time I'm calling anyone in that state."

The phone rang three times before a deep hoarse voice answered. "What?"

"Hi, can I please speak with Veronica?"

"This her."

The voice sounded masculine, which made me pause. But I started my spiel about the postcard and Veronica gave me a "yessum." I went on to explain that I needed more information to narrow down the search. Veronica didn't like that at all.

"What do you mean you need more information?" she yelled. "I followed the directions on this here map, now you're supposed to do the work for me." She continued to yammer. "I've been working on my family tree for a long time. Soon I'll be dead, and no one will take over this job. So I have to finish it!"

I imagined Veronica wearing a checkered wool cap, the kind with ear flaps, long john's and furry snow boots. A shotgun lay across her lap and she was ready to shoot at any moment. What a combination. I had to be serious, so I sat up straighter in my chair and let Veronica finish yelling. I waited for the slightest pause.

"Listen, Veronica, I'm more than happy to assist you. I just need you to cooperate with me." Veronica didn't like that one bit.

"Cooperate? No, you listen to me, missy. You send me everything you got. I want information, maps, photogs, bills, whatever. Anything relatin' to me, you send it my way. You understand what I say?"

This woman was totally insane. Clearly, she didn't know what I was dealing with. Photogs? Did she mean pictures? I couldn't believe I was conversing with such a hillbilly.

"Have you ever been here before?" I asked. "Do you realize how long that's going to take me? That's a very big job."

"No," she answered in a nasty sounding tone. "I've never been to Rosemonte or Pennsylvania. I've never left Alaska. I don't care to. You do it or else I'll have your head hung on my wall here in front of my TV set." She hung up.

I looked at the clock. It wasn't eleven yet and I already needed a cocktail.

"This is bullshit!" I announced to Ronnie. I pushed my chair back and marched downstairs to see Bernie.

I stormed into the little office. Bernie and Matt were gossiping and eating danish. "Sorry to interrupt the girl talk, but I'm having some issues with this postcard." I slammed it onto the middle of the table.

Bernie read it and asked, "What's the problem?"

I explained about Veronica. "She's mentally unstable, and she wants me to send her photos of all the possible stones that could be related to her relatives."

Matt said, "So?"

I rolled my eyes at him, and continued to speak to Bernie. "She's never been to Rosemonte, so I doubt she wants to buy here."

Matt interrupted again. "Oh, where does she want to buy? Or didn't you bother to ask her?"

"Ew!" I said to Matt's gnarly face. "I didn't ask her because she told me she's never been to Pennsylvania, she's never left Alaska!"

I shoved the card to Matt the Puppet. "You sell her. When you do, you have my permission to rub my nose in it. Good luck with that." I turned to exit the little office.

Outside the office, I paused to listen. Matt said, "Fuck this. I'm not going to call her, she sounds like a waste of my time." I heard the paper shredder whine as it devoured the card. Goodbye, Veronica.

Bernie said, "Man, Julia's a spitfire! We need to see more of that side of her. If I wasn't married and an old man, oooh, the things I would do to her." The two men erupted into laughter.

Ew! Gross!

That night, as I poured myself a cocktail in the tranquil serenity of my house. This was becoming a nightly ritual of mine, coming home and having a drink or two, followed by a gulp of Pepto-Bismol. Not a good habit.

I called Liz. I wanted to see how she dealt with work stress. Voice mail. She was probably busy with Scott.

Father's Day was coming up, I had joked with Ronnie, saying the circus was coming back into town. But I was stressed. I put on my robe, stuffed the pockets with a bottle of rum and a can of Diet Coke. I grabbed a box of Cheerios out of the pantry as I made my way upstairs to run a bath.

The Saturday before Father's Day was humid. The streets of South Philly filled with the smell of barbeque while the hum of window air conditioners ran on high. I lay in bed thinking about how much of a loser I was. No boyfriend, no family of my own, no prospects. I couldn't remember the last time I went out on a date.

It didn't help that I'd had to talk to my mother on the phone. She always made me feel like I was her biggest mistake. Sometimes just hearing her voice speak my name was enough to ruin my day. I rolled over and squeezed my eyes closed, as if that would make her go away. When I opened them, I decided to get up and do something. Staying in bed all day would do nothing for me.

After a shower, I walked a few blocks to Carmine's. A neighborhood gem, Carmine's sold the best water ice in town. As soon as I walked in the door, everyone greeted me. "Ciao bella, Julia, so good to see you." I waved and ordered my usual medium cup of cherry. I always got a medium because I felt that was a good spot to be in. If I got a large I would feel like an oinker, if I got a small my tummy always wanted more.

On the front stoop I found a spot to enjoy my water ice and people-watch. Some of the neighborhood folks were chatting about the Phillies. One man spun Frank Sinatra tracks on an old record player. I waved goodbye and walked home, thinking about the rest of my day.

Unfortunately, the rest of the day my mind was mostly focused on work problems. Father's Day would be crazy and I wasn't exactly looking forward to it. My days at the cemetery were long and filled with too much nonsense. Bernie yelling all the time didn't help. He caused me to have headaches, stress, and stomach issues. Not to mention my new love affair with rum. I racked my brain about how to change my troubles at work. Before I knew it, it was time for dinner, then bed.

A loud crash of thunder woke me up in a panic a little before four a.m. The rain was coming down hard. I got out of bed and looked out the window. Everything was soaked and slippery. How would this affect the events we had scheduled? I closed my eyes and tried to go back to sleep. It was useless, I was up. But the rain beading against my window screen had a calming effect. It came down in a pattern. I listened until my alarm clock went off at six. I felt very relaxed while getting ready for work.

Seven on the dot, I was out the door. The rain had not let up. My driving skills were extra keen because of the wet conditions. I phoned Bernie right before making the turn into the cemetery because I didn't know where to park. He yelled, "Because of the goddamn rain, just park in the far lot. No one's showin' up today." He hung up without saying goodbye.

The tents at the gates were a soppy mess. Some of them needed to be poked to push the large puddles off the top. I parked my car and trudged up the hill.

The little office door was partially closed, so sneaking in past Bernie was easy. Ronnie was in our office, feeding his face from a sixty-count box of Munchkins.

"Oy, Ronnie, it can't be that bad."

"Oh, it is," he whined, powdered sugar all over his face. "Ever since Manny got fired I've been Bernie's punching bag, and frankly, I'm sick of it."

"I know, but you need to stand up to him. He's a big bully." Ronnie smiled at me and got up to get a cup of coffee.

I opened my desk drawer to place my Fendi purse inside when I realized the light on my desk phone was glowing red. This couldn't be good. The red light blazed as I stared at it. It seemed to get more vivid the longer I stared. Who would call on a Saturday? Could it be a past customer of mine with a problem with something I sold them? I always thought the worst. Oh shit, what if it was the Fines?

Scared but curious, I picked up the receiver to play the message. I couldn't believe my ears. Sam Sendars had called me. I had forgotten all about him, his card, and his grandfather with the hook hand. Adam had made it seem like no big deal, but apparently Sam Sendars wanted a little more of me. I replayed the message and wrote down the number he'd left.

Ronnie came in and placed a cold Diet Coke on my desk.

"Check this out," I said. Ronnie must have gone to the bathroom because his face was powder free. "Remember Mother's Day, the horrible mess I made?"

"Oh yes. But it wasn't as bad as you think."

"Well, the hook hand guy's, grandson called me and left a message asking me out on a date," I said, my voice perky. "Here, I'll play it on speaker."

"Hey, Julia, it's Sam. Sam Sendars. Ahhh. I was thinking, would you like to have dinner with me this weekend? I was intrigued by our conversation a few weeks ago. Call me. I'd like to take you out. Bye."

"Well? What should I do?" I bit my lower lip.

"Go. You are young, gorgeous, and need to have some fun. Go."

"I don't agree with you about the gorgeous part," I said, "but I do think I'll go. I was just thinking how I needed more fun in my life."

"Ask and you shall receive," Ronnie said, quoting gospel.

The rain outside wasn't letting up. Today would suck. We finished our morning beverages and headed out to our posts. The cemetery looked like a painting where the colors had all run down the canvas. We were sitting in the folding chairs at the tents, armed and ready with surveys and the new pens.

Bernie was ranting over the walkie-talkies about the car guy. "He doesn't want to bring his car out in the pouring rain," Bernie yelled. "He's afraid something bad will happen to it. I thought this guy was a cool dude, but he turned out to be a little bitch. What a waste."

We laughed at Bernie acting like such a brat. Finally, a car turned in and stopped at our tent. I went over to the car and offered them a survey and a pen.

"What kind of gimmick is this?" the middle aged man in the driver's seat asked.

"It's no gimmick, sir. It's a free pen with a pull-out section. You can take it if you like," I said, trying not to laugh. These pens were so dumb and cheap looking.

"It looks like something you'd see in a Kung Fu movie," he said.

"Instead of a piece of paper, I would expect to see a switch blade or something."

I had no words for the guy. I just smiled and asked if he needed help finding his loved one. He grabbed the pen and threw it in the passenger seat, and drove up the hill.

Around lunchtime Ronnie told me to go on break, the hot dog cart had arrived. I was on my way to get a hot dog for lunch when Bernie intercepted me. "Can I give you a ride?" he asked from the rolled down window of his car. Normally I would have said no, but with the rain, I caved.

"Thanks," I replied, and walked around to the passenger side. "I'm going to see the hot dog guy for lunch."

He took the scenic route. "I wanted to invite you to my house for dinner tonight."

The invitation came completely from left field. Shit. I did not want to go! "Um," I sputtered trying to stall and buy time.

Bernie said, "Tonight, come for dinner."

"No, thank you. I can't; I have plans."

"Julia, please, I'm your boss. I'm ordering you to come for dinner. I know you don't really have plans. You shouldn't be alone today."

"What? How do you know I don't have plans?" My voice was hostile. "I do have plans, and I'm not going to break them." I attempted to stay calm. What did he mean, I shouldn't be alone? Big fucking deal, it's Father's Day and I don't have a father anymore. I'm over it. I didn't like this conversation.

Bernie kept rambling on about how I should be in good company tonight, be in high spirits. The offer still stood if I changed my mind. I was so relieved to see the hot dog cart, I nearly wept.

Bernie pulled up to the curb and locked the doors. He placed his massive hairy paw on my knee and said, "Think about it. We're having a wonderful meal cooked by my wife. Matt and his wife are coming over, too. I think you need to get to know him better, outside the office."

I shuddered at the thought of being the oddball at that dinner table. Gross. I didn't want to ever think about it again. I wanted nothing to do with Matt the Puppet outside work. I manually unlocked the door and hopped out. Bernie's window rolled down. What now?

"Hey, get me two dogs, both with the works. And extra napkins. I got leather seats in here," he shouted. Naturally, I had to get his order before my own.

❧⊙❧

Father's Day was pretty much a washout. The few pens we gave out barely made a dent in the full crate. The recipients seemed less than thrilled. As we were packing up and leaving for the day, Bernie called my cell.

"Remember my offer," he barked into the phone. "Just show up if you want. You don't need to call, just come."

I managed a meek, "Thanks, but no thanks," and hung up. I didn't want to be a liar. I needed to find something better to do. But what?

I swiveled in my chair and got to my feet. My plan for the evening was to give Sam Sendars a call.

After my evening cocktail, I looked at the scrap of paper with Sam's number on it. I took a deep breath and dialed his digits. The worst thing that could happen would be nothing at all. The phone rang three times. By the fourth ring, I was ready to hang up. Then Sam picked up. We chatted for fifteen minutes before he asked me out to dinner.

"So, I was wondering if you would, ah…like to eat dinner with me? On Friday night? I mean, you know, like a date?" Sam spit out. He sounded nervous. I thought it was cute.

"Sure, I'd love to go." How nice that he asked me out in advance.

Most guys call and ask the day before. So not classy. We made plans to meet at Lamberti's Cucina, an Italian restaurant in Old City.

I called Adam and told him the update. "Don't go," Adam advised.

"Why? Sam seems nice."

"He sounds like a douche to me. Lamberti's? Come on, that place is SO LAME!"

"I disagree. Besides, I just want to have some fun. What's the big deal? Why are you being such a dick?"

"I just… I know how this will turn out. He's not good enough for you," Adam said, lowering his voice. Da Brat was probably in the next room.

"Really? Relax. I gotta go. I'll talk to you later."

Talking to Adam was becoming more difficult. I had enough stress, I didn't need more from him.

Chapter 13

Mazel Tov! I'd made a whopper of a sale that pushed me ahead of Ronnie and Alexis. In the morning meeting, Bernie remarked, "The kid's hot, she's on fire. Watch out!" June was turning out to be my best month.

Alexis asked if I wanted to get a manicure with her at lunchtime. I accepted. We went to Smarty Nails, a few blocks from the cemetery. Alexis went every Friday, she had a standing appointment. I felt slightly honored that she'd want me to go with her. I wasn't sure what we were going to talk about, but the timing couldn't have been better since my date with Sam was later that night.

We both decided on French manicures. We agreed it was a clean and elegant look. We sat side by side, so we could have some girl talk.

Alexis chuckled. "You know, Bernie tried to set me up on a blind date once. I'll never forget it. Noah Kirshbaum, he drove an ancient yellow Yugo. This guy had really bad psoriasis all over his body." She pointed her finger in her mouth and gagged.

"Ew," I answered, "he sounds horrid."

"This poor guy was just that," she said. "He was destitute and Bernie should have known better. He knows I need money. I don't want to have to work forever." She blew on her nails. "You know what, Jul. If I knew then what I know now, oh my God, my life would be totally different."

She surprised me. On the outside she appeared almost normal. Inside, she was a gold digger obsessed with watching dudes getting busy.

The conversation was giving me a headache, so I changed topics. "How's your dog?"

"Good," she answered. "That's so sweet of you to remember," she said in a sugary voice. "You'd think I would be able to pick up a man with my dog." She elbowed me in the ribs. "But nope, that's not happenin'. I got her a Coach collar and matching leash to try to look fancier but that's not working either. I think it has the reverse effect and makes me look high maintenance."

"I don't think so. It's just Coach. I mean that's the cheapest in the luxury department, right?" I said, hoping I wouldn't insult her.

"I just don't know anymore."

"I wish I had an idea for you," I said. "But I'm not doing so well in the dating department either. Although I do have a date tonight!"

"You do?" she shouted. "Dish. Details, now!"

I laughed and told her about Sam Sendars. "I'm not even into him at all. I just want to have some fun. How bad am I?"

"Not bad at all. Trust me, I have used men for a lot worse reasons. No, for a ton worse reasons than that."

She gave me a devilish grin because she knew I knew that was the truth.

ℛ◎ℜ

Deciding what to wear on a date always took me forever. I was a horrible decision maker. After many outfit changes, I ended up in a pale pink sleeveless sweater with some beading on it, a denim pencil skirt, and a pair of sand-colored espadrilles. My outfit was cute, summery, and girl next door. I took a cab over to Old City and met up with Sam.

He was standing outside the restaurant. I almost didn't recognize him, he looked totally different than that day in the cemetery. He was wearing khaki pants pulled up almost to his armpits with a braided leather belt, the kind that was popular in 1993. His striped Polo shirt was tucked in, not only into his pants; but into his underwear. The waistband of his Fruit of the Loom was showing. As if his appearance couldn't get any worse, he had on sneakers with bright red socks. He waved to me when I got out of the cab. At least I thought so, he might have been shooing away a mosquito. The expression on his face was odd, like he had smelled something bad.

"Hi," I said, as he tipped his head in my direction. When he did that I got a good look at the botched hair plugs under his thinning hair. What a handsome Casanova.

The restaurant was a huge space with two floors of dining area. Sam had made a reservation for upstairs. After we followed the hostess, a tall Italian beauty, to our table, she wished us Buon Appetito.

The menu at Lambertis was filled with traditional Italian fare. Everything looked yummy. Just like getting dressed, it took me forever to decide what to eat. I was trying to not be so indecisive, but that was harder than it sounded.

The waiter came over and filled our glasses with water. "Would you like anything from the bar?" he asked.

He turned to me first so I answered, "Yes, thank you. I would like a Southern Comfort and 7 Up."

The waiter said, "Of course," and looked at Sam.

Sam said, "No. I only drink water from the tap."

Suddenly I felt like a boozehound. Was I turning into my mother? *I only drink water*? What about iced tea or soda? Only water, how boring. I looked at him after the waiter left. He was squinting at me.

"Do you drink a lot?" he asked.

Yikes. "Just for fun." I suddenly felt like I had a drinking problem. "What looks good to you?" My eyes quickly glanced at his calculator watch.

"I'm going to get the mesclun salad, dressing on the side."

I waited for him to say something else but realized that was his dinner. A small dinner salad, with water. Oh shit, this date wasn't going to be any fun. At all.

"How about you, what looks good to you?" he asked.

"I think I'll go for a Caesar salad, I love Caesar salad."

"What about the dressing?" He frowned at my dinner choice.

"What about it?" I asked, totally farshadet.

"Do you want it dressed, or on the side?" He voice sounded annoyed.

"It's fine however it comes." After all, Caesar salad, duh, comes tossed. What was his problem?

The waiter came back with my drink, which I was glad to see and consume. He told us about the specials of the evening. The waiter was very passionate about the food he was describing. He used his hands to help illustrate. When he was finished, he paused and waited for us to order.

"Just the salads, then?" The waiter looked disappointed.

"Yes, that will be all. Don't bring us any bread, we don't need it." Sam eyed me up and down.

Ouch. How come I wasn't consulted on this decision? Didn't my vote count?

"So, how's your grandfather doing these days?" I asked.

"He's fine."

"What do you like to do for fun?"

"I like to pop into the background of live television broadcasts," he said.

For real? Is that even a hobby? Do other people do this, too? Oy vey. Was this the same guy who seemed normal, nice, and friendly at the cemetery and on the phone? No way. Maybe he had a twin brother.

The waiter must have felt sorry for me because our salads came out lighting fast. "Would you like any fresh ground black pepper?"

Sam said "No, it only makes me sneeze." Of course it did.

After a few bites, I said, "My salad's good. How's yours?"

"It's fair." He sneered. Snobby about salads?

The waiter came back. "Would you like another drink?"

Sam answered for me. "No."

I would've liked another one, or ten. But I wasn't going to order anymore because of how Sam acted when I ordered the first. We munched on our salads in silence. I made sure I chewed every bite slowly. I didn't want to finish before him, even though I wanted to get out of there. With a few bites left, I excused myself to the ladies room. I didn't have to go; I just needed a break from the putz.

After I reapplied lip gloss, I returned to the table. Our salad plates had been cleared, as well as our glasses. I guess I was done eating. "Did you get the check?" I asked.

"It's on its way," he answered. I could see the waiter marching across the room with the leather folder in his hand. I sent him a telepathic message to go faster, but the opposite happened. A busboy bumped into him. They collided and the busboy dropped an overflowing bus pan of dirty dishes. Crash! We were never going to get out of there. Broken china was all over the place. Our waiter got up off the floor, his white apron stained with marinara. He looked pissed and bellowed something in Italian, but the bus boy didn't seem to understand.

The bus boy yelled, "Man, you always in my way, yo!"

A manager came over to mediate. We sat in silence for a few minutes until things were cleaned up and back to normal.

The check arrived and Sam opened it. "Okay, let's see here," he said, as his lifeless eyes danced over the bill. The tab couldn't have been more than twenty-five bucks. What was there to see?

I opened my purse and took out a twenty. "This should cover mine." I laid the green on the table.

Sam looked at me like I was a monster. He cleared his throat and announced, "I'm a gentleman, and will be treating you to dinner."

I bit my tongue. This was no treat. He slipped some cash into the folder and stood up. "I'll walk you out," he said.

"Great."

Down the iron steps we went to the first floor. "I'll walk you home," he said.

"I'm gonna catch a cab."

"Allow me." He raised a pale skinny arm and hailed a cab. He opened the door and told the driver, "Take her wherever she wants to go."

I rolled my eyes. What a dork! I thanked Sam for the measly dinner. He held his arms out for a hug. I didn't know how to not hug someone when they had open arms like that, so I gave him what Adam called a bro hug. A one armed hug sorta slap on the back deal. Then out of nowhere, he tried to kiss me. EWWW! I saw him licking his dry lips, trying to make them seem more appealing. I turned my cheek before he could land them on my lips. That was close. A set of way too wet open lips left an imprint on my face. I dashed inside the cab and waved a polite goodbye.

I told the cabbie, "Step on it, please." He sped out of there like his hair was on fire. I kept wiping my cheek where Sam's kiss had landed until I removed all of the cooties left behind. I still felt disgusting.

As soon as I walked in the door, I ditched my date clothes for schlumpies and settled in front of the TV with a bag of Doritos and a pitcher of water. There was nothing good on. I watched until I received a text from Liz. She invited me out drinking with some of her friends. I ignored the text. I felt like such a dud.

I couldn't believe I'd put so much effort into the stupid date. What's worse, I had told Ronnie and Alexis about it, and now I felt foolish. Adam was right. I shouldn't have accepted Sam's offer. I didn't know which would prove more humiliating, having a bad date or hearing Adam taunt, "I told you so," with that condescending look in his eyes.

Chapter 14

Monday was the hottest day of the summer. The weatherman predicted triple digits and high humidity. Yay. Our morning meeting was extremely uncomfortable. The back of my legs stuck to the cracked vinyl of the chairs. Bernie was berating us with hot his coffee breath. I drew a doodle of him in my notebook. He looked like the lovechild of Jabba the Hutt and a dragon.

"We only have a few more days left in June, people," he screamed. "We need more sales! Am I speaking to myself? Are any of you listening to me?"After an hour of his usual rants he dismissed us and we dispersed quickly to the calmness of our desks.

Ronnie pulled his chair over and asked how Friday night had gone. As I looked into his eyes I could see how much Ronnie wanted to be young again. To be free from his horrible wife, mess of a daughter, and deep money woes. He wanted to live vicariously through me, at least for a few minutes.

So I exhaled and said, "Oh my gosh, Ronnie, it was so bad." I told him all the details, from my outfit to Sam and his attempt to kiss me at the cab. "Ugh, I am so glad it is O.V.E.R. I don't know what happened," I said, still puzzled about the evening.

Ronnie uttered, "This guy's a real piece of shit."

I was surprised to hear him curse.

"He must be unbalanced," Ronnie said. "Let me tell you something, if we were the same age and didn't work together ... Ah, forget about it."

I smiled and thanked him for cheering me up. I knew Sam was a big goober and all I wanted to do was erase him from my mind. Hopefully, he'd sense my wishes and vanish.

All day the heat index kept rising. I had one appointment for the afternoon and none in the evening. In a perfect world, I'd make a sale so I could go home and cool off all night. My appointment was with Joe Steinberg, a bachelor around age sixty. His brother and parents were buried at Rosemonte. He didn't own anywhere. Surely by the end of the appointment he'd own at Rosemonte.

I was sweating as I left my desk. Walking to my car made it worse. Sweat ran down my face and the back of my neck. Putting my hair in a high ponytail didn't help. I wore a cotton wrap dress a la Diane von Furstenberg. It was expensive, even with the outlet price tag and a coupon. The dress was so lightweight it felt like I had nothing on, perfect for a day when it was Africa hot. My car was an oven. Why did I have leather seats? I put the key in the ignition and ran the AC for a few minutes before I shut the door and started on my way.

Joe Steinberg lived in a townhouse community not too far from the cemetery. I pulled through the security gate without any issues after the guard gave me directions to Joe's unit. A nice complex with a small manmade pond and a birdbath in the middle, lots of trees offered a nice amount of shade for parking. I picked a spot close to Joe's place. Now that I was cool and dry, it was time to get sweaty again.

Out of the car, I schlepped my stuff to his door. There was a lot of humming in the air; it seemed everyone had their air conditioning units on full blast.

I looked at my watch. Punctual as always, I thought as I rang the doorbell. Joe had an end unit. The pale blue townhouse stood tall, with dark blue shutters. A man's voice bellowed, "I'm coming."

The door opened. Joe Steinberg wore an open, threadbare

bathrobe. My eyes widened. I didn't know what to do.

He opened the screen door and called out, "Julia, come on in."

He was old and naked. A mammoth man, at least six feet tall and easily three hundred pounds. His wrinkled body was covered with age spots and white hair. I stood my ground.

He scolded, "I'm losing all my AC. Get in here."

"Can you put on some pants?" I asked, feeling foolish.

"Do you know how hot it is outside?"

"Yes, I do, but I'm not coming in unless you put on something," I said, getting control again.

"No can do, sweetheart," Joe said as he took a pack of smokes from his bathrobe pocket and began tapping the pack against his hand.

Oh, God. I swallowed a lump in my throat. "Then we'll have to reschedule."

"How about when it's a little cooler? I only wear bottoms when it's less than 88 degrees," he said as he lit a cigarette.

"Okay," I said. "I'll call you towards the end of the summer."

"Righto." He grinned at me and blew a few smoke rings.

As I turned away, I suddenly could not believe that this was my life. People with foot fetishes. A long forgotten friend of my father, and now this, a naked giant. What kind of life was I leading?

I went back to the office and tried to salvage the rest of the evening. I hit the phones to make an appointment for the next night. Being freaked out like that totally made me more motivated. It also made me think about Joe and his situation. His immediate family was gone, he was obese and all alone. He didn't see anything wrong with answering the door naked. I didn't want to end up like him, that was for sure. Crazy, unkempt, and, worst of all, alone.

I made an appointment with a woman named Dottie. She knew my family from back in the day and, with that on my side, I was confidant I'd make a sale. At least I had faith that she would be dressed.

When I left the office later that evening; the sky was a pretty pink. The drive home was peaceful and cool. From my car to the front steps I saw a few of my neighbors and waved. They waved back. All I could think about was Joe Steinberg all alone in the world, and here I was, alone as well. I needed to get out more. My life was all work, no fun. Pathetic. The only thing that distinguished me from Joe was a DVF dress and a shmatte.

✌◎〜

Driving to work the next morning, I answered my cell. Bernie yelled, "What the hell is your problem?" He was so loud I was afraid my eardrums would burst.

"Excuse me?"

"Are you afraid of a little skin?" he asked.

How did he know what had happened? Had Joe Steinberg actually complained to Bernie? Why would he do that? My stomach started to turn and twist.

"Well, I'm waiting," Bernie ranted.

"Look, I'm about to get on I-95. We can talk about this when I get to the office," I said. I hung up before he could say anything else. My phone wailed. Bernie again. Oy vey. I didn't answer. After a few more tries he gave up.

I sweated the entire drive to work. I hated when Bernie screamed at me. What a way to start the day.

The minute I opened the front door, Bernie shouted, "Get in here!"

Why did I suddenly feel five years old again, and in 'Big Trouble'? The only thing missing was Bernie calling me by my full name.

"Yes," I said with a major 'tude as I walked in the little office.

Bernie and Matt the Puppet were both eating giant sticky buns loaded with nuts and raisins. The buns looked delicious.

"I got a phone call. You didn't follow through on your

appointment," Bernie said.

"The man was naked, and three times my size. I was not going in there," I said in a calm voice.

"What did you think he was going to do? Jump you and thrust himself on you?" Bernie asked. He finished his sticky bun and waved his fingers at Matt for a piece of his.

"Joe Steinberg knew I was coming over. I didn't feel comfortable going into his home and trying to sell him because he was naked and refused to put on clothing. He didn't even want to close his robe. Why is this so hard to understand?"

"Was it hard?" Matt the Puppet asked a smirk on his face. Then he and Bernie both burst into giggles and high-fived each other.

I shook my head. "You two are so ridiculous. Thanks for worrying about my safety." I walked out and went upstairs to work. What jerks!

At the morning meeting, Bernie played us the message from Joe Steinberg. The guy said I had declined his invitation to come in because of his nudity, and when it was cooler we'd reschedule. I wasn't sure who was sicker in the head, Joe Steinberg for calling and leaving the message or Bernie for making fun of me and playing it back for everyone to hear. My coworkers burst into laughter.

"All right, enough. Leave it alone!" I made a tight fist with one hand. I would've loved to punch Bernie right in the face. A good solid shot.

"Oh, did I hit a nerve?" Bernie asked. "Are you upset because you like Joe Steinberg? Or are you mad because I'm pulling your chain? Hmmm, is that it?"

I raised my voice. "Stop acting like a fuckface."

The room immediately fell silent. The tension was thick in the little office. I wasn't going to speak first. If I did that, I would look weak. I stared at Bernie's cold eyes and he stared back.

After a few long moments, Bernie cleared his throat and said, "Joke's over."

The score was Julia one, and Fuckface zero. The meeting continued and I sat there feeling smug. Alexis and Ronnie gave me nods of approval while Matt the Puppet had a look of disgust. I looked at him like, you want some of this? He quickly averted his eyes and glued them to Bernie's face. Two shmucks.

At the end of the meeting, Bernie read the totals for the month. The shit-eating grin on my face stayed there because I knew I was in second place. Matt was in first, followed by me a close second, then Alexis, and finally Ronnie. Bernie was shocked that my sales numbers were so close to Matt's.

"Very impressive, kid. If you keep selling like this, you can call me whatever you want," Bernie said and winked.

Gross. Don't try and kiss my ass now, I thought. I'm no dummy. I can see through your games, Bernie. Matt too. Something was up with the two of them.

"Fine by me. You guys are my witnesses," I announced to the rest of the group.

"Now," Bernie said. "July is here. You know what that means: summer vacations, the fourth. It gets hot, hot, hot, so people will drop dead from the heat, hence, more funerals." Bernie paused to gulp his coffee. "The month of July's usually a good month, so let's continue on the high from June and make July even more profitable."

This was a rare nice pep talk from Bernie. The key was to get out now before he turned ugly and mean. "All of you can go except for Ronnie," Bernie said.

Oh no. I knew Ronnie was going to get a talking to, maybe verbally beaten with a wide leather belt, and it wasn't going to be pretty.

I went back to my desk. I had a client coming in for a look at the grounds after lunch. I was hoping to give such a good tour she'd want to buy on the spot. I could dream, couldn't I? Tours were not my specialty, probably because I rarely did them. I had to prepare and make this afternoon's tour extra smashing.

I grabbed a salad from the corner deli and ran an errand on my lunch break. I arrived back in time to greet Mrs. Solomon. She walked into the office with children clinging to her sides. This was a surprise; she was supposed to come alone.

She smiled at me and said, "This is Jacqueline, she's four, and this is Sloane, she's five. My precious grandchildren."

I bent down to eye level with the girls and said, "Hi."

"I'm so sorry to bring them here. My daughter needed me to babysit last minute and I didn't have the card you sent me with your number on it to reschedule," she explained.

"That's okay, I understand," I said as I pulled two Tootsie Rolls from my purse and gave one to each little girl. They both smiled and appeared pleased with their candy. "How about we reschedule and make a date for next week?"

Little Jacqueline pulled on Mrs. Solomon's pinky finger. "Bubbe, I have to go now!"

"Okay, sweetie," said Mrs. Solomon, looking down at her granddaughter. "Is there a restroom nearby?" she asked, scanning the office.

"Yes," I replied, "follow me." I led the way through the kitchen to the bathroom, "Right in here."

"Be a dear, and stay with Sloane for a minute?" Mrs. Solomon asked me.

"Sure, no problem," I said. "We'll wait for you in the seating area."

As we walked out of the kitchen, Bernie emerged from the little office. I was startled. I rarely saw Bernie moving around. He was almost always stagnant.

"Are you coming from the bathroom?" he growled.

"No, someone's in there," I said.

"What? Who…. Who's in the Goddamn bathroom? I need to go. What the hell? This place…" Bernie shouted.

So nasty in front of a child! I clasped Sloane's shoulders and said, "The woman I was giving the tour to, she's in there with her granddaughter." I tried to steer Sloane away from Bernie.

"But I … Fuck," Bernie yelled. "Forget it!"

He limped back into the little office and slammed the door. That was the fastest I'd ever seen him move. I was embarrassed he'd cursed in front of Sloane. I hoped she wouldn't say anything to Mrs. Solomon. He had such anger issues. What could've made him so upset? So embarrassing.

I guided Sloane to an empty desk and gave her a pen and a piece of paper. She seemed like a happy child. A moment later, Mrs. Solomon came out of the bathroom with Jacqueline. She thanked me. "That was a close call. This one," she pointed to Jacqueline, "had too much juice at lunchtime."

I smiled and gave a little laugh I hoped wouldn't sound too phony. We made another appointment and I walked them out. On my way back, I passed by the little office door. I knocked and asked, "Can I come in?"

Bernie hollered, "No. Go back to work." He acted like such a baby sometimes. What was his problem?

I went upstairs to my desk to finish some paperwork before going out on my evening appointment. Upstairs was on mute. I liked it that way.

Ronnie and Matt were out on an appointment together. They came back with a sale, and I heard Ronnie and Matt knock on the door of the little office to tell Bernie the news. Bernie wouldn't let them in. He was acting very peculiar.

Ronnie and Matt marched upstairs to fill out the commission forms. They were squabbling in Matt's office but I couldn't make out what they were saying. Ronnie looked angry when he entered our room. He muttered under his breath about sales, commission, and unfairness.

As soon as Ronnie sat down at his desk, his cell phone buzzed.

He spoke in a low inaudible voice, turning around to face the corner of the room. From his shirt pocket he retrieved a small notepad and wrote in it. After he hung up, he gathered a few supplies. Ronnie's eyes danced on the paper. He crossed them off in red ink. I watched him for a moment. He looked like he was preparing for a secret mission. Under his arm was a roll of paper towels, in his hand a plastic trash bag and scissors. He was searching for something else, I could tell by the look on his face. His glasses slid down and his mouth hung open.

I gave him another minute to scramble about before I asked, "Can I be of any help?"

"No, no," Ronnie said in a loud voice, "you just stay up here, and keep working." Then he followed the statement with a stern nod.

He backed out of our office and stopped in front of the supply closet, where he took out a can of Lysol. He placed that under his other arm. I peeked into the hall and watched him make his way downstairs. His cell phone rang again as he was midway in the stairwell. Ronnie answered it, a little out of breath. "I'm coming, I'll be there in twenty seconds."

When he arrived at the door of the little office, he knocked. Bernie shrieked, "Use your fucking key." Ronnie hunted for the key to the little office door. His belt housed a massive keychain, the kind a night watchman would wear. He had a key for every door in the cemetery, keys to the other office at the bottom of the hill and the barn. Why he had all of these keys, I wasn't sure. Ronnie let himself inside the little office.

Curious to find out what was going on, I stayed close on Ronnie's tail. I made my way downstairs to the main office and hid behind the counter. I needed something to do while I spied. The maps were always a disaster, so I decided to organize them.

Inside the little office was a lot of commotion. Bernie yelled at Ronnie, "You need to blot the stain, don't rub it in a circle. That's making it worse! You're no help, you fucktard. Where's the seltzer?

I told you to bring it. Look at all the pieces of lint you're leaving behind. This stuff smells like kitty litter, what it is? You are no fucking help at all! My suit is ruined!"

Clearly there was a mess of sorts, but I needed more information. How much time could I kill with the maps, before I needed to go on my appointment? As I looked at my watch the front door opened and a man entered.

"Hi." I greeted him in a peppy voice.

He looked awkward. "I'm here to see a guy named…uh… Bernie," the man said, looking at a crumpled napkin.

"Okay. What's your name?"

"Vic. I'm here to discuss computer programs with him."

"Have a seat, I'll be right back." I marched over to the little office. Excellent timing, this was my in.

The door was still closed. I tried to open it before I knocked, but it was still locked. Bernie yelled, "What do you want?"

"Vic is here to see you," I said.

Ronnie opened the door. Bernie was sitting in his usual chair. His tan suit pants were stained on the inside of both legs. Just as I registered what the stain must have been, the smell hit me. Urine! Bernie had peed his pants! Holy shit!

Ronnie was fumbling with a room deodorizer. The small trash can was overflowing with balled up paper towels.

"Send him in," ordered Bernie.

"Are you sure?" I asked, pretending I didn't see an adult male in pee-soaked pants.

"Yes," he boomed.

"Okay, I'll be right back with him."

Ronnie asked Bernie, "Why didn't you go home to change? I mean, after all, you do live less than a four minute drive from here."

"I just had my car detailed. I don't want to ruin the leather seats in my Mercedes. If you had a nice car, Ronnie, you'd understand that."

I asked Vic to follow me and led him back to the little office. After introductions, Bernie stated that he was sorry to make Vic wait. He said, "I'm on medication, but don't worry. Nothing's contagious."

Yeah, he was sick all right. Sick in the head. Who would sit around in pee-soaked pants, taking business meetings and pretending everything was normal? Bernie had sunk to a new low. I couldn't wait to call Adam to tell him all about this latest chaos. Unfortunately, when I dialed I got voicemail. "Call me back. You are NOT going to believe the story I have for you," I said in a giggly voice.

I left for my appointment and drove into the Northeast, to the neighborhood of Bell's Corner. At one time a nice section, now the neighborhood was kind of rough. At least it was light out. The house looked like it might be the worst one on the block. Great, I thought, this lady's going to have no money. She's not gonna buy. This was going to be a huge waste of my time.

The grass was brown and bare in some sections. Both the front path and the sidewalk were full of cracks. The house hadn't been painted in a very long time. I checked my hair and makeup in the mirror before I got out of the car. Maybe I could at least get a referral from her.

When I rang the doorbell, I wasn't sure if it worked or not, because I didn't hear a chime. The storm door had no screen and was dented in numerous spots. I looked down at my feet and saw many busy anthills. Yuck. I waited with a smile painted on my face. There was a scuffle from behind the door.

"Just a minute," a petite voice called out.

"Okay," I said.

The door opened to unveil a hoarder's dream. Stuff was everywhere! Boxes of cereal and crackers were stacked to the ceiling. Yellowed newspapers in piles taller than I was. Even in my heels. A dense coat of dust covered everything. It was dark inside the house; the shades all drawn. Plastic shopping bags from the supermarket filled with God only knew what sat along the walls.

I didn't want to go inside this house. I was afraid of what I would see and even more afraid of what I wouldn't.

The frail anorexic woman who answered the door held her hand out for me to shake. "Hello," she said. "I'm Jessica Goldblum Johnson."

"Wow, Jessica, I love your glasses. Not everyone can pull off red frames," I said.

She blushed and said, "Come inside."

I followed her through the maze of junk. Everything from board games to empty orange juice containers. Jessica led me to a room with a bed in the center of it. Circling the bed were scads of pillows, all different shapes and sizes. I couldn't see the flooring under my feet. On the bed was a woman, Jessica's mother, Sonja. We exchange hellos and Jessica moved some clothes off a chair for me to sit on. Behind the chair was an open closet. It overflowed with stuffed animals.

Sonja thanked me for taking time out of my busy day to visit her. She sounded strangely normal considering the environment we were in.

"It's part of my job to visit people in the Jewish community," I said and gave her my scripted story. How was I going to sell this person? No way!

A teenage boy of sixteen or so walked into the room holding a basketball. He was very tall and very black. "This is my son," Jessica said. "Say hi to Miss Julia, Jon," she instructed him.

"Hi Jon," I said as he turned around, trying to bounce his ball on the crap-covered floor. He left the room, completely ignoring me. On his way out, he kicked some of the pillows.

"I'm so embarrassed," Jessica blurted out. "Teenagers these days." She raised her hands to tszuj her hair.

"I understand," I said. She babbled about her relationship with Jon Sr., her ex-husband.

I really couldn't focus. I was too busy checking out the room. Along one wall were cans of food, stacked according to size. Some were pet food but I didn't see any animals. How old was the food in those cans? I couldn't get over all the stuff!

"That's why I called you," Jessica said. I snapped back to attention. "We own at Rosemonte," she said motioning to herself and her mother, "but what about my son, what happens if…"

"Stop. There's no need to get upset." I said in a caring voice. This could be it. I pulled out the map of the cemetery as well as the section Jessica's father was in. I showed it to them. "Here's your father. The space next to it is reserved for Sonja. Your father was smart. He purchased this space for you. There's a space available next to yours, Jessica, if you want to save it for Jon. That would be a smart decision, just like the decision your father made for you." I paused for symbolic effect.

Jessica broke the silence by asking, "How much?"

"Before I tell you the price, I want to tell you that we work with all budgets."

"How much?" she repeated.

I looked at my price sheet and felt the heat of their pupils on me. "The space is $4450."

Their eyes bugged out like cartoon characters. "We can't afford that," Jessica said in a meager voice.

I held up my hand and said, "Let me be a little creative with the numbers, just a minute." I reworked the math and cut a few dollars off. "Okay, this is as low as I can go: $4100."

Sonja started to tear up. Jessica remarked, "That's still a lot."

"I understand, but I want you to realize you can pay it out over six years with zero interest. Look at the map," I said. "Every other spot in this section is gone, sold, goodbye."

The women looked solemnly at one another.

"Julia." Jessica cast her eyes on her mismatched socks. "We don't have any money. We're both on government assistance. I have a medical condition."

Duh, it's called you're a hoarder. You live in filth. But I needed a sale. I dug deep down into my soul, which was becoming shallower by the minute. Then I took a shot in the dark. "Do you have cable TV?"

They nodded in unison.

"The only suggestion I have for you is to cut your cable. The cost of basic cable is the same as the plot for Jon. If you cut your cable you'll have the money to pay for your son's plot. God forbid anything happens. You know what else? If something happens you need to pay all the money up front. There's no payment plan, no exceptions. Ahead of time you can pay it out, six years with no interest. I'll fill out the contract, and you call the cable company."

Jessica pleaded with her mother. "We need to do this, Mom."

"I know," replied Sonja. "I know."

They both looked at me, scared and helpless. I reassured them they were doing the best thing for Jon and their family.

"One more question?" Jessica asked.

"Yes," I said and looked up from the paperwork.

"Do you accept money orders?"

I nodded, still in shock that I had actually told them to cut the cable. "I just need a signature from you and a down payment of one hundred dollars."

Jessica signed by the X. Sonja reached into her shirt and removed a mix of tens and twenties from her bra. I felt queasy.

I took the cash. "Thank you," I managed to meek out.

Jessica walked me through the maze of garbage to the front door. She shook my hand and told me it was a big relief. I smiled and said, "I'm glad you feel better."

"We tried to do this before, but no one wanted to come to our house."

"I don't know why." I shrugged my shoulders. "I'm glad I got to come here and meet you and your family."

Jessica opened the door for me. I walked outside and was never happier to see the sun and breathe the fresh, clean air.

A day to remember. As I drove home I realized my life could be way worse. Like Bernie's with his medical problems or Jessica, living as a hoarder with no money. At least I had a future. Why was I so hard on myself?

Then I thought about how I had convinced them to give up cable TV to buy a plot for a healthy teenager. Was this what I had become? How much lower was I willing to sink for a sale?

Chapter 15

At the next morning meeting, Bernie was mum about the pee pants. We all knew he had done it. The little office reeked of stale urine. Partly because there wasn't ventilation, but mostly because of the overflowing toxic trash can. No one had bothered to crack a window. Everyone pretended the stench of day-old pee wasn't there.

I was very proud of my sale, and told all the other counselors about it.

"I made an appointment with them last year. I went in, but I didn't make it past the first tower of cereal boxes," Alexis said. "I cannot believe you stayed long enough to sell! That place gave me the creeps. I still have nightmares about it."

I forced a smile, even though I felt ashamed. I handed my paperwork to Bernie.

The phone rang. Bernie looked very angry as he listened to the person on the other end. He slammed down the receiver and announced, "That was Rhoda from the accounting office."

I tried to place Rhoda, but I couldn't remember which old lady she was; they all looked alike down there. White hair, long fake nails, and stretchy outfits in pastel colors.

"Rhoda claims we are way over our budget for items from the wholesale club. Ronnie, what's the official count?" Bernie barked.

Ronnie pulled a folder from his notepad and robotically read aloud. "We get coffee, creamers, pretzel nuggets, hot chocolate mix, paper towels, and cups. Each month, Cemetery Ed shops for us and spends anywhere from three to four hundred dollars on these items."

"Something's got to give," Bernie shouted. "Rhoda ripped me a new asshole. She says we are spending excessively." He paused to stare at us. "How many cups are you using a day?"

Matt the Puppet answered. "I only use one a day, like my vitamins." He was the only one laughing at his stupid joke.

"Well, what about you Alexis?" Bernie asked.

They were staring at each other with heated eyes. I waited to see who was going to blow up first.

"Some days I use more than others, it all depends on what I'm drinking." she said in a coy voice.

Bernie started to lose it. "And you?" he asked, as his head spun in my direction. A ripple in his neck danced back and forth.

"I usually don't use any," I said.

"What? How can this be?" Bernie asked. "I want answers, not riddles." He slammed his hand on the table.

This investigation was such a waste of time. "Well, in the morning, I have a soda in a can, so no cup. Then, if I have a cup of coffee or hot chocolate, I use a mug that I brought from home. Save a tree, you know."

"Well, what about you, Ronnie?" Bernie asked.

Ronnie looked hard at the paper in front of him. "I'd have to say, I use two a day, one for cold beverages, the other for hot."

"Add it up," he ordered to Ronnie as he shoved a calculator over to him.

"That will be hard to do since Alexis did not give an exact number," Ronnie said.

"Well, whatever the total number is, we need to cut it," Bernie shouted. "Cemetery Ed is spending too much money at the wholesale club and we need this fixed yesterday." He looked at Alexis.

I couldn't believe we'd just had a meeting about cups. What

would be next, how many squares of toilet paper we were using when we went to the bathroom? I couldn't help but laugh. Bernie was saving money, using his pants as toilet paper.

"Why are you laughing?" Bernie shouted.

"I'm sorry. I thought of something funny, I'm so sorry." I said. Bernie must have bought my apology because he left me alone after that.

"Get to work," he yelled at us as we vacated the room.

Once we were upstairs, Ronnie went into the coffee room to count how many cups were left in the dispenser. Oy vey! Was he going to check the number of cups each morning? He marched back to his desk and made a chart to keep count of cups used daily. He added it to the report he already kept about the wholesale club. Just what Ronnie needed, more bullshit work for Bernie.

The rest of the day slipped by. I didn't have any appointments for that evening, so it ended up being a hot, lazy summer night. Around dinnertime I left the office. I was the last of the counselors to leave, so I turned off all the lights upstairs and made my way down the staircase. Bernie was sitting in the little office with the door wide open. There would be no way I could sneak out without him seeing me. But I tried to anyway.

"Julia, come in here." Bernie beckoned to me.

Damn it! Foiled again. "Yes?" I peeked my head in.

"Come in, sit down for a minute," he said.

Shit. I slumped into a chair and waited for the lecture to begin.

Bernie was looking at a large calendar in front of him. "Every summer we have a picnic. This year I want you to make all the desserts for it. We, I mean the cemetery, will of course reimburse you for the expenses."

"When is this picnic?" It sounded like a real good time. Not.

"In two weeks. It'll be outside and it's for all the employees. Between both offices, the grounds guys, about fortyish people."

"What do you want me to make?" God only knows what

meshuge list he'd give me. Bernie didn't have a sweet tooth, he had all sweet teeth.

"Whatever you want to make. I know the results will be delicious."

"This is the first time I'm hearing about a picnic," I said, surprised that no one had mentioned it.

"It's a lot of fun. There's music, and the grounds guys play dominoes. Cemetery Ed does the barbecuing, and now you'll make dessert. Which will be a tasty addition," Bernie said winking.

He must have remembered the cookies from my interview. "Okay."

"Save your receipts," Bernie squawked.

I nodded. "Can I go now?"

"If you wish."

I wished, all right!

As I drove home, my mind raced with ideas of what to make for the picnic. For the first time since working at Rosemonte, I felt alive again. It would be wonderful to get busy in the kitchen. The hum of my KitchenAid was music to my ears. Butter, flour, sugar, yay!

The next day, I gave Bernie a menu of desserts I had planned for the picnic.

He held up his hands like I was trying to give him a squirming animal. "No, I want your treats to be a surprise. I know whatever you make will be great." He gave me a toothy grin. Behind Bernie's smile was a chunky little boy, an emotional eater, especially with sweets.

July was going by slowly. It seemed to get hotter every day. I hadn't sold anything since I'd told Jessica Goldblum Johnson to cut her cable. Was this karma telling me it was cutting my sales for the week? I had to push the negative thoughts out of my mind and concentrate on the positive. As I rummaged through my notes from meeting people on the grounds, one name stood out. Our information in the computer indicated the woman owned a plot but needed other things. So I called her and, to my delight, she made an appointment with me for that evening.

Ronnie came into our office holding a small flowery gift bag. He was humming a tune and seemed really happy.

"What gives?" I asked.

"Today is my anniversary." He beamed.

"Mazel Tov!" I cheered as I walked over to Ronnie's desk to peek at the gift he had bought. He unveiled a blue velvet box. Inside was a necklace, a silver chain with a medium size heart dangling from it. Not my taste, but lovely. Ronnie divulged his plans for the evening. Dinner at a romantic Italian restaurant, a stroll in the park near their house, and hopefully he'd get lucky. I blushed at the last part and told Ronnie congrats and good luck.

I had some time to grab an early dinner before my appointment. It was downtown so I headed in that direction. I called Adam on the way to see if he wanted to meet for a last minute bite. Big surprise, I got his voicemail, again. Adam was never around anymore. He was always busy, with what I wasn't sure. Suddenly I had a horrible thought. What if he married Da Brat? Was she powerful enough to take away my friend? No. He wouldn't dare. Money wasn't everything, even when it came to Adam.

I called Liz.

"Hey you."

"I know it's last minute but do you want to grab dinner? I have a late appointment." I had my fingers crossed.

"Boo. I wish I could. I'm meeting up with Scott at his office, I'm bringing Chinese."

"That's okay. You guys have fun. It sounds like things are getting serious between you," I said.

"He's so great, Julia. I'm really falling for him," Liz said, her voice totally in love.

"Good. I'm happy for you. I gotta get hoppin'."

We hung up. Dinner on my own? That's okay, I was a big girl. I was independent.

I remembered a cute place on Spruce Street that offered huge yummy salads. A great location because I'd only need to walk a few blocks to my appointment and I wasn't wearing walking shoes.

On this hot sticky day, I had on red leather sling-back pumps. Red shoes always made me feel powerful. I didn't know why, they just did. They looked extra fabulous with the suit I had on, a blue and white seersucker jacket and capri-length pants. My outfit was very look at me and slightly patriotic.

After I parked, I went into the café and ordered a Diet Coke and a Caesar salad. The girl who took my order handed me a number and said, "Your food will be out in a moment."

"Thanks." I took a window seat and sipped my refreshing cold beverage. As I pulled out the paperwork for my appointment and gave it a once-over, I thought I heard my name being called. I swiveled my head around and there he was.

Oh no, Sam Sendars! He had just walked into the café. He made a beeline in my direction. What to do? I was trapped.

"Hi," I said as he showed up at my table. Ugh.

"Hey. What are you doing here?"

"I'm just grabbing a quick bite before I have to go back to work."

"Can I sit with you?" He looked lonely and sad, like a lost puppy.

"No, I really have a lot of work to do," I said, pointing to the stack of papers. Most of them were blank, but Sam didn't know that.

"Oh, okay," he said, sounding desperate. "Well, what about another date? We could go out this weekend?"

No way. I would've rather nailed my feet to the floor. "I don't think so, I'm really busy," I said.

"You don't like me, do you?" he asked in a no-nonsense way.

"It's not that I don't like you, I just feel that we don't have anything in common," I said, feeling bad.

Sam looked worse than the night we'd gone out. His nails were gnarled, his cuticles torn and bloody. Yuck. Why was he wearing corduroys in July? And with Teva sandals of all things. Ew.

The girl brought my salad to the table. She opened her mouth, probably to ask if I'd like anything else, when Sam turned on the rage. He leaned in and yelled, inches from my face. "Well, I don't like you either. I think you're fat and ugly."

He turned around so quickly he knocked into the girl with the salad. The waitress was a pure professional because my food made it to the table. After she set it down she rubbed her shoulder. Sam stormed out of the café.

"I'm so sorry," I said to her. She looked miffed.

"S'okay."

"I'm sorry," I said again. "We went out once and it didn't work out. This is so awkward, sorry."

The girl walked away. I ate my salad in silence. The words Sam yelled at me were on replay in my mind. I knew I wasn't ugly. Curvy, yes, but not fat. Clearly, he was unbalanced. I looked again at the papers and got ready for my appointment. I left an extra generous tip for the trouble I caused and off I went.

I walked the few blocks to a high-rise building. I double-checked the address to make sure I was at the correct one. A doorman was stationed behind a podium in between the curb and the front door. He rushed around the podium to open the door for me. I smiled and thanked him as he winked at me. He looked like a solider going off to a gala wearing his fancy dress blues. His suit had gold buttons and lots of brocade on the shoulders of his jacket. He wore a matching hat and shiny patent leather shoes. Poor guy, he had to be roasting in the heat.

As I crossed the lobby of the building, my high heels clacked across the marble tile. The elevators seemed to be hidden. I couldn't find them anywhere. I spotted a man sitting at a desk in a corner of the room. As I approached him, he looked up and smiled, showing all his teeth. "Hi," I said. "I have an appointment with Miss Rozen. Where are the elevators?"

The man extended his massive hand to me. "I'm Linus Williams," he said. "It's my pleasure to meet a lovely lady like yourself. Are you here for business or pleasure?"

Linus sported a custom-made suit. I could tell from the details. Adam always pointed out things like that to me. If Linus could afford these threads, then why was he a desk jockey for the building?

By the way Linus pronounced pleasure was barfy. Why was this creepy forty-something man all up in my business? "Elevators, please." I said.

"Through the doors and around the corner, sugar. But you need to sign in first." I scribbled on his clipboard and started towards the doors.

Linus got up from his desk. "Let me escort you to Miss Rozen's apartment."

Too tired to fight, I let him follow me into the elevator and push the button for her floor. He fumbled with his shirt cuff, exposing an expensive looking watch.

"What do you do, besides look smashing?" Linus asked, licking his lips.

Oy vey. "I work for a cemetery in the 'burbs."

"Which one?" He licked again.

"Rosemonte," I replied.

"That's a Jewish one, right?"

"Mhm," I said, nodding my head, acting bored.

"There are lots of elderly Jews who live in this building."

"Really?" Suddenly I was intrigued. I changed my attitude to a much nicer one. A lightbulb was flashing in my brain. If I could somehow pull an Alexis move and get some inside information from this chump, that might prove lucrative for me.

The elevator stopped at Miss Rozen's floor and I got off. I turned around and said, "Thanks for the ride." I gave him a big smile.

Linus smiled back at me and ordered, "Stop by my desk on your way out." He gave me a flirty finger wave goodbye.

"Oh, don't worry, I will." I wasn't sure what I was going to do or say, but somehow I was going to get something from him.

Miss Rozen was waiting for me in the hallway. She had the door
to her apartment wide open. "Do you want to come in or do our
business in the hallway?" she asked. Oh boy, was there a full moon
out?

"Can I come in? Is that okay?" I asked. She shrugged her rounded
shoulders and I followed her inside. Her apartment was one tiny
room, a studio unit.

"Do you want to sit on my bed?" she asked.

I cleared my throat. "No thanks. Is there somewhere where we
both can sit, like a table and chairs?" This was going to be a difficult
sale.

She opened up a folding chair and a TV tray. "This's the best I
can do," she said. She chose to sit on her bed.

I pulled out my presentation book and started to go through the
information, but she wasn't paying attention. I had a flashback to
all the times I'd daydreamed in school until the teacher called out
my name. Now I was the teacher and Miss Rozen was the student.
The room was cramped and hot. She didn't have the air on, and the
place was cluttered with a bunch of dime store crap.

Miss Rozen interrupted my selling speech. "Why are you here?"

I replied, "To assist you with plans at Rosemonte." I picked up
her paperwork and showed it to her. She frowned and looked upset.

The woman had to be in her eighties. She had on oversized
glasses that made her face look like an owl. Her hair was pure white,
so were her overgrown eyebrows. I wondered what color her hair
had been when she was younger.

"Are you married?" she asked.

"Not yet," I answered.

"Me either," she replied. "Do you have any children?"

"No," I answered in a short tone.

Again she replied, "Me either."

I could see where this was going, but how could I save it?

Miss Rozen said, "I have no family. I'm the only one left." Her words saddened me. "The only one left," she repeated slowly. "My parents are dead. My siblings are dead, and they never had any children. I have no cousins left, no relatives, and no blood," she said, tight lipped. "Julia," she continued, her voice sounding weaker. "I want to give my body to science when I die. My space will be left alone just as it is now. Dirt, grass, and earth." She made this statement so soundly there was nothing I felt I could do to change her mind.

I was annoyed. If she knew she didn't want to buy, why had she accepted my offer to make an appointment? Why would she have me come out there and waste my time? I didn't get it. So I asked her.

"Because I'm a lonely old woman," she said. "No one visits me anymore. All my friends are already in the grave or have one foot in it. I'm eighty-four years old, and even though I look like shit my mind is as sharp as ever."

I was done. I had surrendered my sale to Miss Rozen. I thanked her for her time, packed up and left. I didn't want to be old, alone, never married. It was too sad to see Miss Rozen. I didn't want to end up like her. Even though I had lost the sale. I'd realized something. I would have to change my life. Miss Rozen had taught me a valuable lesson. I would have to *make* the change I wanted, not just sit around complaining about it. Or else it would never happen. Tomorrow was a new day and I was going to make the most of it, I thought as I waited for the elevator to arrive.

The elevator ride down was prep time. I used it to apply fresh lipstick. When I arrived at the lobby and the doors opened, I strutted out like a peacock. I sauntered over to Linus's desk and said, "Did you miss me?"

He drooled over me, like I was a lamb chop on a silver platter and he hadn't eaten in days. But I was there to work whatever assets I had. I channeled my inner Alexis, smiling, flirty, full of sex appeal.

"Here's a list of all the residents in the building." Linus held up an envelope with 'Sweetheart" written on it. Yuck. "Have drinks with me and this is yours." He placed the envelope in his inside jacket pocket.

What would Alexis have done? I said, "Drinks? Lovely. When do you want to meet?" I could handle a drink with this middle-aged black guy. No problem. Tops, all it would take was an hour of my time.

"There's no time like the present," he said. "How about Thursday night?"

I took out my planner and met his eyes. "I can fit you in around eight."

"Perfect. Do you know the Swan Lounge at the Four Seasons Hotel?"

The Swan Lounge? Really? Linus was pulling out all the stops. I was entering territory I knew nothing about.

"Of course. See you then," I said in a sultry voice. I turned around a little too quickly and made myself dizzy for a moment. I sashayed off, knowing that Linus was watching me walk away. When I reached the front door, the doorman was at the ready to open it for me. I looked at Linus over my shoulder. He waved and I swallowed the little bit of throw-up in my mouth.

❧

The next day I arrived at work before anyone else. I needed to do some research without being interrupted. Focus was very important. I knew as soon as Ronnie came in he would tell me all about his anniversary night with his wife. It wouldn't be long before he would be in to make the morning coffee run.

At exactly nine a.m. sharp the speakerphone crackled. "Ronnie!" Bernie's voice made me groan out loud. I looked at Ronnie's empty desk. The speakerphone again crooned his name. I'd only have a minute before Bernie would go through all the numbers and call to my extension.

Today was going to go well, I told myself. I tried to remain calm as I smoothed down my perfectly straight hair and took in a deep breath. Bernie was acting more and more like a monster. My stomach was always upset and I'm sure my habit of an evening cocktail was not a good one. It seemed like I had Pepto-Bismol everywhere. In my desk at work, in the car, on my kitchen counter and on the nightstand near my bed. I even had a box of the chewable tablets that I moved from purse to purse.

As I listened for him to yell my name, I felt a surge of nausea. When I reached over for the relief of Pepto, I heard, "Julia!" So loud it hurt like I'd been struck by a bolt of lightning. What the fuck?

"Good morning, Bernie," I said as I picked up the receiver.

"Coffee. Now!" Bernie barked, then disconnected.

I walked down the hall to the coffee room and started a fresh pot. There was coffee left over from the day before. I was tempted to spit in it and reheat in the microwave, then serve a cup to Bernie. But I chickened out.

As soon as the pot finished brewing, I poured a cup for him. Ronnie had showed me the way Bernie liked his coffee with an excessive amount of sugar and lots of creamer. This was Bernie's first cup of the day. Too bad Ronnie wasn't around to mark the cup chart.

I made my way downstairs to give Bernie his cup of joe. "Sit down and stay for a while," he said.

"Okay." The flare of nausea fought with the Pepto-Bismol. I smoothed my skirt and sat down, crossing my ankles and clasping my hands in my lap. I had on a summery white dress with pink trim. I wore with it sassy pink shoes. I looked at Bernie's face, red from the sun and covered with beads of sweat. Ick.

Bernie took a colossal gulp of coffee. "This is perfect. I see Ronnie has trained you well."

I said nothing. If I was silent, maybe he'd let me go work. "So, who are you dating now?" Bernie asked, like we were two girlfriends having a tea party.

"No one. Why?"

"I'm just curious," Bernie said. "We never talk. How come?"

I stayed mute. Eventually, I broke the silence by saying, "I have work to do. Can I go back to my desk now?"

"Atta girl," Bernie cheered. What was wrong with this man? One minute he was yelling like a banshee, and the next he wanted to know what was going on in my social life. One thing was clear, the man was disturbed.

When I returned to my desk, Ronnie was sitting at his. "How did you get here?" I asked.

"In my car," he said with a chuckle.

"No, I mean how did you get past Fuckface?"

"Is that what we're calling him now?" Ronnie asked.

"Yes." I said in a matter of fact voice.

"I snuck past you while you were being grilled."

"Oh, sneaky. I see how you operate." I asked "How was your anniversary?"

"It was sooo good."

I turned my chair around and said, "Dish. I want all the deets."

"Well, let's see. We went down to South Philly for a romantic Italian dinner. It cost close to my last commission check, but it was worth it to see my wife happy. For once I didn't look at the price of what I was ordering, I just ordered."

"What a nice idea for you two to celebrate. Forget about everyday life for a night. I like it."

"So true." Ronnie described the restaurant. "The staff was so hospitable. We both had two glasses of wine. That's a big deal because both the missus and I aren't big drinkers. The wine sat in wicker carrier thing. It was so cool. And when we wanted more, the waiter would pour it for us."

That's what waiters do. That's their job. "Where was the

restaurant at?"

"I don't remember," he said. "But Julia, you have to go there. You would appreciate all the fancy food details because of your culinary background. This place was top shelf fancy. The décor was like being in Italy; it was fine dining at its best. Stars across the board."

"Tell me more. What did you eat?"

"The bread was out of this world," he exclaimed. "We got so many baskets, they just kept bringing more out. It had just enough salt and oil. Our dinners came with a huge salad bowl. We could pick out what we wanted on it. My wife can be a big pain in the ass when it comes to ordering food, but the waiter made it exactly how she wanted it."

I nodded my head.

"Then our entrees came out I got some sort of seafood ravioli. They were in the shape of little moons," he said with a sparkle in his eye. "We weren't going to get dessert but the restaurant asked us if we were there for a special occasion. My wife said it was our anniversary and all of a sudden we hear clapping and a bunch of waiters are marching over to our table singing. With a cake! On top was a sparkler. It was awesome. We kissed and everyone cheered." He looked truly happy. "All in all, it was the best anniversary we've had in about twenty years."

"I'm so glad you guys had a great time," I said. "You'll have to find out the name of the restaurant for me. It sounds so fabulous."

"I will," Ronnie said as I turned my chair around and started to organize my research from earlier. "Oh wait," he yelped. "It was the Olive something. Garden. I think. Yes. The Olive Garden. For sure. You must check it out, Julia."

I tried not to laugh. "I will."

Luckily, my back was turned or he would have seen the silly grin on my face. Who *were* these people I worked with?

Chapter 16

The rest of the day was filled with foolishness. We had our morning meeting and Bernie yelled at us. I had lunch with Alexis. I wanted to tell her about my plans with Linus, but Alexis monopolized the conversation by talking about the difference between cubs and bears. At first I didn't know what she was talking about, then she explained it to me.

"A bear is a sexy hairy manly man who's gay. A lot of the time they don't seem gay. Picture the Brawny Man." She closed her eyes. She twirled about in her seat, looking dreamy.

"The guy on the paper towels is gay?" I asked.

"No, well, I don't know. But that look, like a lumberjack. A man's man, and hot," she said. She leaned in way too close to my face. "A cub is a mini version of a bear." Alexis blotted her neck with a napkin.

I started to laugh.

"Why are you laughing?"

"All I can think of is Yogi and Boo Boo bear, Jellystone Park," I said. Suddenly I felt like a dummy.

Alexis ignored my statement and gabbed about a series she was watching on Showtime with a bear who had caught her eye. She described the bear of her dreams. "If only he were bi," she said, and groaned while squeezing my hand. "Then my life would be perfect. I would have it all," she shouted a little too loudly.

Whenever I was out with Alexis I felt uncomfortable. I decided not to say anything else for the rest of lunch. Alexis continued to ramble on about a fantasy life in which she lived with two gay men; one bear, one cub. And her dog.

Did that make her Goldilocks? No, she'd need another bear. Unless her dog dressed up. I'm pretty sure Alexis has played with that scenario.

When we got back to the cemetery, she said she had to run home for something she'd forgotten. I wanted to believe her. But something about the way Alexis moved made me think she was going home to take care of business. Private business.

The rest of the afternoon I was at my desk. Right as I was packing up to leave, someone knocked on the door. I looked up. Adam.

"Hey stranger. How's my favorite Rosemonte employee?"

"Good. It's so great to see you," I said, standing to give him a hug. "Where the hell have you been?"

"Very busy." He hung his head.

"That's no excuse." I pinched his arm. "Do you have time to chill?"

"Always for my Julia, but only for a bit. I have to talk to you about Joy."

My Julia? This was going to be interesting.

"Sup?" I raised both my eyebrows and tried to look interested.

"We've been going through a rough patch." Adam brushed his hand through his hair. "She doesn't get me."

"Obviously. I know that. I've always said that to you."

"Well, after lots of fighting and yelling, she wants to be with me." Adam said, looking away from my face.

"I'm confused. She *is* with you."

"No, she wants to be MARRIED to me," Adam said, head even lower.

I turned Adam's face with my hands and looked into his eyes. He was still rambling about Joy wanting this and that.

Oh no, it's happening. I let go of his face and flung my hands up. "Do you want to be with her?" I asked him. "Money aside. Just her, do you want to be with her?"

Adam had no answer. Then he slowly mouthed the words, "I. Don't. Know." He paused, and said, "I do know if I end up with her, I want her to be more like you."

WTF? "This is major bullshit. You don't call me for weeks, you don't return my calls. Now you show up at my office and release this load on me when I have an appointment to go to," I said, my voice rising. "You are going to need to go shopping for new pants, Adam, because suddenly your balls have grown." I gathered my things and pushed him out of the way. I quickly left my office and headed down the hallway.

Adam shouted for me to slow down, but I ignored him. I made it downstairs and headed straight for the front door. I didn't stop to say good bye to anyone.

I clamored in my heels to my car, tossed my belongings on the passenger seat, and jumped in. I wasn't sure what had just happened, but I hadn't liked the conversation. If Adam wanted Joy to be like me, then he should've wanted me, Julia. The only reason he wanted Joy was because of her money.

After I started my car, I looked up and saw Adam at the top of the hill by the office. He'd given me a good head start but I needed to get out of there pronto.

I floored it as I drove down the driveway, past the gate and onto Oak Hill Road. Adam hopped in his car. He caught up to me. He was calling my cell, but I didn't answer.

Luckily, I knew lots of short cuts, most of them through not the best neighborhoods. I knew where Adam wouldn't want to drive his Jaguar. I turned onto 2nd Street and lost him in an array of Chinese food carts and other street vendors.

I needed time to cool off. Adam knew I didn't agree with him dating for a trust fund. Plus, I couldn't come up with one person who actually liked Joy. He was making a huge mistake.

I cut down a side street. Why couldn't we both have the right feelings for each other at the same time? If he was even considering marriage to Joy, honestly, he was not good enough to be my man. Liz was right. All her lectures rang true.

I slowed to the speed limit. My gas tank was almost empty. I pulled into a Sunoco station and filled up, then I walked into the minimart. I needed something to chill my nerves. I bought a Snickers and a Diet Coke. As I snacked, I took a deep breath, held it, and let it out, pulling myself together. Back in my car, I touched up my face and practiced making sultry eyes. After all, I had a bigger fish to fry and his name was Linus.

I headed over to the Four Seasons Hotel. If I decided to valet, would Linus pick up the tab? I didn't feel like searching for a spot on the street.

The valet helped me out of the car and escorted me to the front steps. I smiled at him and did a test run with the vixen eyes, hoping he would think I was just flirting and not a prostitute.

In the Swan Lounge the vibe was swanky. A baby grand piano was being played by a jazz pianist. He looked too cool for school with his Kangol hat on backwards and retro framed Ray-Bans. I took a seat at the bar and drank in the scenery of the room. Big comfy couches, tall vases with orchids perfectly in bloom placed on swirly marble-topped tables. A fireplace gave off a French feeling. The few other people there were all doing business deals of some kind.

I looked over the drink menu. Linus sauntered in. He was taller than I remembered, at least six feet, maybe more. He had in one hand a long-stem red rose, and smelled it before giving it to me. "A beautiful flower deserves to be held by an even more beautiful woman."

I smiled as I took the rose. "Thank you," I said, gagging slightly.

Linus asked, "Do you want to stay at the bar or move to a settee?"

"I would like to stay here." I was thinking about my safety. Here, the bartender would be kinda close.

"Very well, then," he said, and sat down on the bar stool next to mine.

We ordered drinks. I asked Linus about himself, trying to keep the focus on him rather than me. It was a good thing because Linus loved to talk about himself. He told me about his daughters, his pets. It turned out that he wasn't a desk jockey. Linus owned the building, he said, and worked as the concierge in order to stay in touch with his employees. He enjoyed traveling and was looking for a new travel companion. Wink wink, nudge nudge. No thank you. Linus was fond of the arts; he held a yearly membership for the Pennsylvania Ballet.

Eventually Linus ran out of things to say. As he asked me an array of questions, I felt like I was on a job interview with Bernie. I gave short non descript answers. "Mostly, I work. I work all the time. I'm focused on my career and not really looking for anyone at the moment."

Linus frowned. "What do you do for fun, excitement, thrills?"

I didn't want to sound like a total nerd, so I lied. I filled the conversation with fiction. It seemed to work. Our glasses went empty. The bill came and Linus paid for it. I offered and he shooed my hand away. "This was my sweet treat."

Ew. I could tell Linus was trying to be suave, but it came off purvey.

He asked, "May I take you home? Or did you drive here?"

"I drove," I said in a smooth voice.

We walked over to the valet stand. When he tried to hold my hand, I wouldn't let him. The date was creepy enough, I didn't need actual physical contact. That could send me over the edge. I wondered how Alexis would have handled the situation.

I handed the valet the stub for my car. He left in a hurry to retrieve it. I turned to Linus and looked into his dark brown eyes.

"Thank you so much for a lovely evening. If I ever have a free night, I'll call you," I said, knowing I never would.

Linus smiled at me and reached inside his jacket to the chest pocket. He handed me the envelope marked "Sweetheart. You, my dear, are exquisite." He held up one of my arms and twirled me in a circle. As he spun me around, I saw my car coming up the alley.

"These are my wheels," I said. The valet hopped out with a miniature clipboard with a form on it.

He handed it to me. "Please sign."

I read it over quickly, and signed my name at the bottom by the X. I opened my Cynthia Rowley purse to find my wallet.

"Allow me, please." Linus said as he paid the valet.

"Thanks again for everything."

Linus bent down to kiss my hand. Suddenly I felt like we were in another decade. Who was this ass clown? His manners made me feel icky. Granted, on the outside he was a nice guy. But way too old. That's where the raunchiness set in.

He held the door for me to get inside, then closed it softly. The window was rolled down and Linus stuck his head in. "Please, if you ever have any time, call me," he practically begged. "Girl, you put me under a spell!"

I smiled but I was a little freaked out. I put the car in drive and zoomed away. Linus stood abandoned on the curb of the Four Seasons Hotel.

When I got home, I opened the envelope. Inside were six neatly typed pages. On top of the first page Linus had attached a Post-It note saying he did the research himself to find out who was Jewish and who was not. And if I ever needed anything, not to hesitate to call him. He enclosed his card with all his info on it. I'd scored big time. I placed the envelope inside my work bag.

I went into the kitchen to find something to eat. I couldn't recall the last time I'd gone to the grocery store. A jar of peanut butter looked like my best option. At least it had protein. As I reached for the silverware drawer, I looked at the calendar on the wall.

There it was, staring me in the face: the picnic. I had almost forgotten. It was coming up in less than a week. I needed to get myself in gear. I had a bunch of desserts to make. How could I have let this slip my mind?

With the jar of peanut butter and a spoon in hand, I sat down at the dining room table and started to make a plan.

Chapter 17

The next day at work, I went through the list from Linus. I was worried because I hadn't sold much in July. Then again, neither had anyone else. I knew the week would be a waste considering any free time was going to be devoted to prep work for the picnic.

Alexis asked me if I wanted to go to lunch. I declined. When I explained I had to work through lunch, she looked slightly miffed. But really, I couldn't take anymore of her gay porn antics. She was so inappropriate. Actually, everyone who worked at Rosemonte was inappropriate.

I made phone calls during lunch and tried to set up some appointments for the next week. I scored a few from Linus's list. Wouldn't it be super funny if he had other concierge friends who could get me lists too? Ugh. What if I had to have drinks with all the concierge guys? Gross. I'd be acting like a whore, but without the sex. Just for some leads. Oy!

At 5:15, Ronnie and I looked at each other. We decided to leave together. Safety in numbers. We gathered our things and started to slink down the hallway. Ronnie's cell phone rang. "Oh no," he moaned. "It's Bernie."

"Don't answer, we're almost outta here," I said. I could see the front door, only a few steps away.

Ronnie didn't listen. He answered the phone. "Yes, Bernie." He hung up and said, "I can't leave, but you go. I'll see you tomorrow."

I looked in Ronnie's sad eyes. I didn't want to leave him, but I also had a bunch of baking to do. I didn't have a choice. "See ya in the morning," I said, patting Ronnie on the back. I slipped around him and headed for the door. I had escaped unscathed.

I headed towards home. My first stop was the market. I had my list and I was ready to shop. I pulled into the parking lot. All the close spots were taken, just my luck. I found a spot, grabbed my reusable grocery bags and got a cart from the corral. As I entered the store, I realized my double platform Giuseppe Zanotti heels were not a smart supermarket option.

I navigated through the aisles, picking up all the supplies I would need. My stomach started to feel uneasy, so I popped a Pepto. All the registers were backed up. My feet were aching. The checker rang up my order. She was chewing gum super fast, but doing everything else extra slow. I paid with my debit card and placed the receipt in my wallet. I needed to hand it in for reimbursement. I could already hear Bernie yelling at me. "What do you mean, you don't have your damn receipt? I told you to save it. What the hell is wrong with you? Do you ever listen to me?"

When I got home, the first thing I did was change into schlumpies. I washed my face and pulled my hair into a ponytail. Now I was ready to get to work. The menu I picked out for the picnic consisted of individual fruit tarts, dark chocolate fudgy brownies, snickerdoodle cookies, and coconut caramel dreams. I'd bake something that appealed to everyone's taste.

First I made the tart dough. I put it in the fridge to chill. Next I made all the cookie doughs. They also went into the fridge to chill. My plan was to prep one day and bake the next.

As I cleaned up my tiny kitchen, I felt a sense of pride that had evaporated once I closed my business. It felt good to work with my hands again. Time had flown by. I couldn't believe it had been almost three hours. It felt like so much less. Probably because I was enjoying myself, listening to some tunes and doing what I did best.

I was only a few minutes late getting up the next morning. By the time I got out of the house and on the road, the few minutes had turned into ten. When I arrived at Rosemonte, I was a full twenty minutes late.

When I opened the heavy front doors I could hear Bernie yelling. Shit. I was late for the morning meeting. I placed my belongings outside the door to the little office and went in with a pen and notebook. Bernie's face was bright red. A full-on stream of sweat ran down the side of his fat face.

"Why are you late?" he yelled.

"What is your reason for being tardy?" asked Matt the Puppet at the same time.

"I'm just late, sorry," I said.

"That is no excuse," yelled Bernie. His head looked like it was going to burst.

"I know, I'm sorry," I said.

Matt shook his head from side to side and scribbled something in his notebook, then showed it to Bernie. Bernie held up his hand to Matt the Puppet. "Later," he said.

The meeting dragged on. Bernie ranted about us not selling. He took on each of us and went over our numbers for the month. "Everyone sucks," he screamed. "What the hell do I need to do to motivate you people?"

No one said a word. Bernie banged his massive banana hand on the table for emphasis. "You have barely made enough money to support the picnic," he boomed. Matt the Puppet leaned over and whispered something in Bernie's ear. "I would never do that," he said to Matt.

I couldn't believe Matt had whispered in Bernie's ear. First off, because it's rude. Second, because Bernie's ear was so fugly. A clump of hair sprouted out of it. His ear canal resembled a bee hive. Lord only knows when the last time he took a Q-Tip to it. And the smattering of skin tags on his neck had started to spread to his ears. Just seeing Matt get that close to Bernie made me ill.

I must've had a strange look on my face because Bernie asked, "What's your problem?"

"Me? I think it's rude to whisper," I said. Alexis and Ronnie looked at me with shocked expressions on their faces.

"You do, do you?" asked Bernie.

I nodded my head and stared straight into Matt's beady eyes.

Bernie yelled, "All of you get out." When Matt stayed behind, Bernie bellowed. "Did you hear me? I said out!"

"What was the meeting about, other than the fact that we all need to sell more" I asked Ronnie.

"That was the gist of it," he said.

We trudged upstairs single file to our desks. Ronnie closed the door to our room and explained that Bernie had been under pressure from the owners of Rosemonte about the counselors not selling enough and that it could affect his bonus. That made sense. No wonder he was acting like a shmegegge.

"I hope he changes his attitude before the picnic tomorrow," I said. Ronnie just gave me a blank stare.

The day went by quietly. We had a few funerals, but Matt assisted. Cemetery Ed and T.R. were busy getting ready the festivities for the picnic. It looked like it might actually be fun. A double tent was set up with lots of tables and chairs. There were games like dominoes, horseshoes, and bean bag toss. A large barbeque grill sat under a smaller tent. Without Bernie, the picnic could be enjoyable.

By the end of the day, I'd made a phone sale. Yippee. I sold a grave stone to a lady who lived in Virginia. She gave me her credit card info over the phone. It was a piece of cake. When I walked by Bernie on the way out, he couldn't give me too much flack.

As I passed the little office, he called me in. I had the contract in my hand, ready to give to him. I didn't take a seat. I was trying to avoid wasting time chatting with him. He looked over the contract and said, "Okay. Where are you going now?"

"Home to bake for tomorrow," I said in a chipper voice.

Bernie nodded his bulbous head. "Be good," he said.

I drove home with a smile on my face. I thought I was going to get yelled at for something but didn't. No need for an upset tummy today. As I unlocked the front door, my land line was ringing. The caller I.D. had Adam's number. I picked up the phone.

"Hey," he said.

"Hey, man."

"Are we cool?" he asked.

"Yeah, but I think you're making a big mistake with her."

"I know," Adam said, sounding down. "What are you up to tonight?"

"I'm baking for the stupid picnic at work tomorrow. You're welcome to come over and hang, but I can't go out."

"Okay, honey. I'll see you in a little bit. I'll bring dinner," Adam said.

"Awesome, see ya soon."

I went upstairs to change my clothes. As I was dressing, I thought how the night would be like old times. Adam would want to hang, but I'd put him to work. He'd scoop cookies like a machine. I'd work the oven and he'd eat too many of the cookies. We'd laugh a lot.

Minutes later the doorbell chimed. Adam had stopped at Mr. Chicken on the way, and he held the bag in front of his head when I answered the door. I laughed when Adam spoke in a dumb voice and it sounded like it came from the chicken on the bag. The chicken was fried and crispy with a bunch of sides. As he unpacked the bag, I got us beers from the fridge.

We sat down at my dining room table, a wobbly glass-top piece from Ikea that seated six. I had cheap plastic chairs to go with it. They so didn't match and Adam always ribbed me about it. As we ate dinner we caught up on work stuff. I told him about all the loons I'd sold.

He laughed and said, "Yeah, you meet all kinds of people in this industry."

He caught me up on the gossip in his office. Then I told him how Bernie had peed his pants and acted like it was no big deal.

"Holy shit," Adam sputtered. "Wait until tomorrow when I tell everyone at the office."

I looked at him, and rolled my eyes.

"Okay, cookie time," I said when we were done eating. I cleaned up the take-out containers and pulled out the doughs from the fridge. I turned on the radio and gave Adam a scoop, pointing to the sheet trays I had lined with parchment paper. I started on the pastry cream for the tarts. As I mixed the ingredients, we were both quiet.

After the tart shells cooled I stood at the island, carefully filling to the top of each tart. The yellow color resembled the sun. When they were all filled, I wiped my hands on a towel and threw it over my shoulder. I began to place fruit in different patterns. Berries, kiwi, star fruit, and peaches. Then glazed with apricot jam that I'd melted down and pushed through a mesh strainer. Adam was watching me. His eyes had been glued to me the entire time.

"What?" I asked.

He smiled. "I forgot how passionate you are when you're baking."

"Shut up and get back to scooping," I ordered.

He grinned again and I felt tingly on the inside. If only he were like this all the time.

Hours passed. When we were finally done, dozens of fruit tarts and a few hundred cookies sat on my counter. I'd lost count of how many cookies Adam had eaten. I didn't care, honestly. I was happy he'd hung out with me, and even happier he'd actually helped.

Adam plopped on a stool at the island and while I washed dishes. "Do you think you'll ever go back to baking?"

"I don't know. I feel like it will always be a part of me, but I can't support myself with it."

Adam sat there and finished the beer that was in front of him. "It's late, I gotta jet."

"Okay. Thank you sooo much for your help," I said. I walked him to the front door.

"Don't let this much time go before we hang out again. You hear me?" Adam said in a serious voice.

"Sure, I mean, yes." I wondered if he meant the question and if I was sincere with my answer. We hugged and Adam left. I locked the door and hiked upstairs to bed. I was exhausted.

❦

The morning of the picnic was hot, but not a scorcher. I pulled my car around to the front of my house to pack it up. After a few trips back and forth, I was ready to leave for work. Suddenly I had a flashback to when I had my business and would make the deliveries myself. The delicious smell would linger in my car for a few days.

When I got to the cemetery I pulled up to the tents first to drop off my baked goods. Cemetery Ed was wearing an apron over his uniform. "There's the girl of the hour," he said in a lively voice.

"Why am I the girl of the hour?" I asked.

He smiled from ear to ear. "Fuckface has been talking all week long about your cookies."

Suddenly my cheeks got red. "You call him that too?"

Cemetery Ed roared with laughter. "We all adopted your nickname, it fits him so perfectly."

I gave him the boxes of goodies. "See you at lunch time," I said. He waved and winked goodbye as I drove to the parking lot.

Bernie didn't hold a meeting. He told us to work until noon, so we could enjoy the afternoon off. I went to my desk to start my work. Bernie called me on the speakerphone.

"Can I have a cookie?" he begged.

"I gave them to Cemetery Ed. You'll have to ask him."

"Go get me some," Bernie ordered.

"No." I said. "I'm trying to work."

"Please? Pretty please with a cherry on top?" he said, trying to sound like a little kid.

I picked up the receiver and told Bernie, "You are asking the wrong person. You need to call Cemetery Ed."

"Forget it." He sounded irritated and hung up on me.

"What's his issue?" I asked Ronnie.

Ronnie said. "He can't be by himself."

"He is so annoying." Ick. What a baby.

The morning ticked by. At noon I realized I didn't want to attend the picnic. Baking for it was fun. But I didn't want to go outside and be forced to socialize with my coworkers.

The music playing was loud and in Spanish. Thick smoke from the barbeque filled the air. Slowly, all the counselors slumped out of their offices. We made our way downstairs, and outside. It looked so strange to see a peppy party with a cemetery as backdrop.

Bernie drove down the hill in his car. When he hoisted himself out, T.R. came over and offered his arm to assist him to his seat under the tent. Bernie pushed T.R. away and used a cane whittled from a cylindrical piece of wood with intricate carvings all over it.

Bernie had ditched his usual blazer and tie for a colorful Tommy Bahama shirt, but he'd kept on his pinstriped suit pants. When he settled into a sturdy folding chair, his pants rose up and showed off argyle socks held up with garters. His wingtip shoes looked silly with the rest the ensemble. He started tapping his cane, but not in rhythm with the beat of the music. What a tool.

He was yelling for Ronnie. Everyone could hear him as we walked down the hill. Ronnie didn't answer back. "Three two one," Ronnie said. His cell phone started to ring.

I erupted with laughter. Ronnie answered his phone. "Yes,

Bernie. I'm almost there. I'm only a few feet away."

When we arrived at the picnic area, Ronnie hurried over to Bernie. Bernie gave him his order and Ronnie, tail between his legs, went to make the boss a plate. He delivered it with a smile.

I got a hot dog and a few chips. Everyone seemed to be in their own cliques. As much as I wanted to sit with the office girls, I couldn't because I was a counselor. The grounds guys formed a Spanish-speaking circle in the grass. Bernie sat with the old ladies from the accounting office. He was eating like a pig and kept ordering Ronnie to get him more. It was like high school all over again. The counselors were at a card table not too far from Bernie. I sat down next to Alexis and Tatyana, across from Matt the Puppet.

"Tatyana," I said. "I haven't seen you in forever. How's life?"

"Life is good. I have health and my family and good fortune," Tatyana said.

"Can I ask you a question?"

"Question? Yes, you can, Julia."

"Ronnie told me about your set-up with Bernie. I want to know how it works. How it *really* works."

She cackled, throwing her head back and shaking it from side to side. Her large gold earrings made chiming noises as she laughed. "Basically," she said, "I sell lots only to Russian peoples and Bernie, or should I say Fuckface, he leave me alone. In sales, if you sell lots you can do vhatever you vant."

I stiffened. "Does everyone know I called Bernie that name?"

Alexis, Matt, and Tatyana all said "yes." In unison.

Oy vey!

"Julia, it took me long time to get along with Bernie," Tatyana said. "Underneath all that fat is good man, but you need to be patient and be willing to dig deep."

I smiled at Tatyana. Gross, I thought. No digging for me.

"I work hard in Russia. Here in America I work hard, but not as intense," she said. "Bernie's a big baby boy, he cries if you take his candy away. You understand, Julia?"

I did, or at least I tried to understand. Tatyana had many years invested with Bernie and Rosemonte, a lot of experience. And her results had been economically rewarding.

I was not as confident in myself. I doubted I could last as long as Tatyana had. She was a tough lady from Russia; she'd experienced the Cold War, waiting in line for toilet paper. She'd started over in America where she knew no one. I, on the other hand, grew up in the suburbs. No comparison.

The music came to a halt. "Testing one two. Testing one two," said a voice. I didn't need to turn around to know who that voice belonged to. What I wanted to know was, who the hell gave Bernie a microphone? "Can everyone turn around now and look at me?" he asked.

After chairs had been turned and Bernie had everyone's attention, he said, "Thank you to Cemetery Ed for working hard on the barbeque." Everyone clapped. "There's plenty more food, so come back up if you're still hungry."

I looked at Ronnie and whispered, "Do you need to make Bernie another plate?"

Ronnie muttered back, "I hope not."

Bernie yapped about team work, about how we were all working well together but of course needed to work harder. Finally he wrapped it up by saying, "Dessert is served courtesy of Julia." Another round of applause, one of the grounds guys took the microphone away from Bernie. The music came back on and the picnic resumed.

Ronnie got up to gather Bernie a sampling of the desserts. Other people formed a line after him. I liked to watch people's expressions when they ate my food. It was interesting to see smiles appear or an expressive eye movement. Body language always intrigued me. I must have been in a trance because when Matt sat down next to me I didn't even notice. He had a plate full of desserts in front of him.

"I only eat a small portion of each one. That way I get to sample them all, but I don't over indulge myself," he said.

Such a dork. I was about to get up but he kept talking.

"These are wonderful treats."

"Thanks," I managed to meek out.

"Would you mind giving my wife some of your recipes?"

"Yes, I would mind," I said with attitude. "I worked very hard perfecting each item you're eating. I don't just give out my recipes to anyone who asks for them."

Matt the Puppet glared at me. "Fine. Next time you need help, don't ask *me*."

"No problem. I won't," I said.

Matt walked away with his plate of barely eaten desserts. What nerve! When did he grow a pair? Now I disliked him even more. Tatyana looked at me and shook her head, tilting it in Matt's direction. What was it about him that she wouldn't divulge?

After a few hours the picnic wound down and the grounds guys packed up the chairs and tables. Soon the tents would come down and they'd be done for the day. The counselors still had sales calls to go out on. I didn't have any appointments, though, so I headed back to my desk to work.

Chapter 18

Back at my desk, my phone was lit up. I had a bunch of messages. I picked up the receiver and listened. Adam's dad had called me with a lead. Hurray! I called him right away to get the info.

Lenny was just back from a funeral when he took my call. "You know what happens when I work a funeral, don't ya?" I pictured him chewing his Dentine. Lenny had given up smoking when Adam and I were twelve. He immediately started chewing gum. He always had his jaws moving.

"No, what?" I answered, knowing he was going to tell me something dumb.

"I put the fun back in funeral," he said, laughing. We chatted for a minute or two, then he gave me the details. "The name's Brownstein. I just arranged the funeral for the mother. She's old and going to croak any day now. If I was you, I'd get over there sooner than later."

"I'll call her soon," I said. "Thanks, Lenny, you're the best." We hung up. I gathered more information on Mother Brownstein before I called.

A woman answered the phone with an old-fashioned greeting, "Afternoon, Brownstein residence."

I told her who I was and that Lenny had given me her number. She seemed interested and wanted to make an appointment. I told her I'd be in her neighborhood that very night. Would that work for her?

"Splendid," she answered. "My husband and I will both be home."

"Perfect. I'll see you this evening," I said. Score.

The Brownsteins lived in New Jersey, in the suburban town of Cherry Hill, about forty-five minutes from the cemetery. As I was printing out the directions, Ronnie came into our office. "What's on tap for tonight?"

"I'm headed to Jersey."

Ronnie exclaimed, "Me, too!"

"Hey, do you want to meet up afterwards for some dinner?"

"I would love to. Dinner's one of my top three favorite meals of the day," he said with a chuckle.

A few hours later I arrived at the Brownsteins. Their house was on the large side with a three car garage. They had a straight driveway as well as a half-circle one in front of the house. Parked on the straight driveway was a massive trailer with an airboat attached to it. The airboat looked like it had seen better days. There were tons of crusty dried-up critters on the boat. Eek! Lots of dead grass was tangled in the wheels of the trailer. Mud and grime stained the bottom of the boat.

I rang the doorbell and waited on the front porch. The outdoor furniture was older than me, and in worse condition. The metal frames were covered in rust. Bird poop made the seat cushions look like a Jackson Pollack painting. The light above my head flickered on and off.

The Brownsteins greeted me and shuffled me into the kitchen. We sat around their massive octagon-shaped table. Mrs. Brownstein was around four and a half feet tall. She had extremely long acrylic nails, the kind you pay extra for when you get a refill. Her full face of makeup was approximately three inches deep. She was dressed up in a silk kimono with matching slippers. Mr. Brownstein towered over her at, five feet eight inches. He didn't dress like a geisha, but wore plain shorts, a fishing-themed Big Johnson t-shirt, and a Gilligan style hat. What a pair.

"Tell me about that airboat," I said to them to break the ice.

Mounted on every wall was a fish that had been lacquered and stuffed. A few fishing rods were also hung as prized trophies. Their living room couches were covered in a camouflage fabric. The dining room was dominated by a glass-topped table with tall backed chairs and burgundy seats. A large mixed metal piece of artwork hung on the wall. A wall unit housed many porcelain clown dolls in ornate costumes. Outfits similar to what Mrs. Brownstein was wearing.

Somewhere in the background was a fountain. I couldn't see it, but I could hear water trickling. The sound was supposed to be Zen-like and promote relaxation. Running water always made me have to go to the bathroom. I tried not to think about it.

Mr. Brownstein gave me a lesson in air boats. I nodded my head as he talked about the fun times they'd had out on the boat. Mrs. Brownstein just stared into space like she'd heard the story a hundred times already. When he finally finished talking, I said, "I can tell you enjoy fishing." That sparked another batch of stories. While Mr. Brownstein talked, I tried to figure out what he and Mrs. Brownstein had in common. They didn't look at each other at all. I knew about the law of attraction, and opposites do attract; but this was bizarre. They looked like two strangers sitting together in someone else's kitchen.

When Mr. Brownstein ran out of tales to tell, I brought up his mother. I reviewed what they had done with Lenny. Then I started my presentation. I went over the material, showed them the pictures and went through the motions. I told them Mr. Brownstein's mother needed a few more items.

When I told them the price they stared, motionless. He said, "Okay. Can we pay you today?"

"Absolutely," I said. "I'll fill out the paperwork and be out of your hair in no time." This presentation had been practically painless except for the scary fish eyes that seemed to follow me around the room. "May I use your powder room?" I had to give in, the fountain won and I needed to pee.

"Right this way," Mrs. Brownstein said, and I followed her down a hall to the powder room. I turned on the light and shielded my eyes. The entire room was mirrored: walls, ceiling, even the floor. I felt like I was inside the fun house from the Purim carnival. Only the sink and toilet were white. The soap dispenser and tissue box were both mirrored. The Brownsteins sure carried out their decorating themes to the max.

When I got over my initial shock, I pulled down my pants. Oh my God, watching oneself urinate was so not normal! I closed my eyes.

This had to be the powder room of Alexis's dreams. It wouldn't have surprised me if she had a pee fetish. Did she give people a golden shower? Or worse, receive one? Ew. I had to get the image out of my head. I was so thankful I didn't have to go number two.

When I returned to the kitchen, Mr. Brownstein had his check book out. I filled out the contract and asked them to sign. He handed me a check. Paid in full. Nice, I'd get the entire commission of $375 in one chunk. I offered them each a leftover pen from Father's Day. They said thank you in unison, but didn't touch them after I placed them on the table.

As Mrs. Brownstein walked me to the front door, she started to tear up. "Thank you again," I said, while she shed the first tear. A big black blob ran from one eye down her cheek. Then a tear from the other eye did the same thing. The flood gates opened and Mrs. Brownstein began crying hysterically.

"I'm sorry." She sniffed. "It's just you're never ready. Know what I mean?"

"I do," I said, feeling sorry for Mrs. Brownstein. Her mother-in-law was almost one hundred years old, but that didn't matter.

Mrs. Brownstein placed her claw-like hand on my arm. "You've been a great help to us. Thank you."

I didn't feel like I'd done anything special. I was just myself. I smiled at her. "You have my card if you need anything; feel free to call me at the cemetery."

She opened the door for me, and I walked out quickly. The Brownsteins were nice people but their house gave me the willies. I was happy I got a sale. Now I was off to meet up with Ronnie for some grub.

When I got to my car I called Ronnie. He answered on the first ring. "Helloooo, Julia."

"I'm done with my appointment. I guess you are too?"

"Mine never showed up. Assholes. Let's meet at Ponzio's Diner on Route 70."

"Sounds good to me. I'm on my way."

I arrived at Ponzio's before Ronnie did, so I grabbed us a booth and looked at the menu. Ronnie strode in a few minutes later. Our waitress came over and plunked down water glasses, then took our order. I got a grilled cheese sandwich with French fries. Ronnie ordered the crab cake dinner platter.

"Do you want to share a milkshake?" he asked.

"No, I'm okay. I'm not a huge fan of milkshakes. But I'll share a dessert, if that interests you."

Ronnie spun the dessert menu carousel. He was weighing some options. "So tonight was a bomb," he blurted.

"I did all right," I said.

"I'm so tired of no show appointments."

I understood where he was coming from. I too had had my share of no shows. It sucked.

"Tell me about your appointment tonight," Ronnie said. "You always have an intriguing anecdote to share."

I told him all about the Brownsteins, the strange décor, the ornate costume, the mirrored bathroom. "Now you tell me a story," I said.

"A story…" Ronnie repeated. His voice trailed off.

I scanned the diner. An old man sat at the counter by himself drinking coffee. His appearance was stuck in the 1970s, probably his prime. This guy looked like he was straight out of the movie *Saturday Night Fever*. His shirt was halfway unbuttoned and he had a collection of gold chains around his neck. His white hair was perfectly feathered. A porn-style moustache matched his outfit. I wondered if he had been stood up by a date.

He finished his coffee stood up and walked towards the door, passing our table on the way. I smirked when I saw him carrying a man purse. It totally matched him; I wasn't sure how I'd missed it before.

Ronnie asked, "What are you giggling about?"

I pointed discreetly to the man purse. Ronnie turned to see the man just before he slipped out the door.

"What?" Ronnie asked. "I wore one of those in the seventies."

I burst into laughter. I couldn't stop. It was the kind of laughing that hurts your bellybutton. When I pictured a seventies version of Ronnie in my head with a man purse, it was too cruel. "What did you carry in there?" I asked when I finally caught my breath.

"Well, obviously my wallet, keys. SEPTA tokens. ChapStick, gum or Tic Tacs, Condoms. And medication."

I made a strange face. "Medications? Were you sick?" I asked.

"No." He said and looked around and, in a lower voice, said, "Weed."

"Oh, I follow you," I said, still giggling.

The waitress brought our dinner and we ate like two people starved after fasting on Yom Kippur. Ronnie decided to share a piece of chocolate cake with me. Yum. After the cake and a round of coffee, we got the check. "Thanks for having dinner with me," I said.

Ronnie smiled and said, "No, thank *you*."

In the parking lot we chatted for a few more minutes before we got in our cars.

July was drawing to a close in a few days. At home I pulled out a legal pad of paper and calculated my sales thus far for the month. I was in second place, Ronnie in third, Alexis last. Matt the Puppet was in first place. He was in first place every month. How did he stay there? He was like a *Nancy Drew* mystery.

I didn't know if it was thinking about work or the greasy diner food, but something was not agreeing with my stomach. The Pepto next to my bed was within reach. I grabbed the bottle and took a swig. Tasty.

It was time for bed, but I wasn't tired. I turned on the TV and watched reruns of *Sex And The City*. Eventually I drifted off.

Chapter 19

The next morning the counselors showed up like clockwork. We all sat squished in the little office. Bernie was on the phone. He was silent and turning redder by the second. I really thought his head was going to explode.

He finally broke the silence by softly saying "okay," then he hung up. He let out a deep breath, then yelled at the top of his lungs, "Everybody out!" I'd never seen Ronnie move that fast. He looked like he was running a footrace. The rest of us didn't move as quickly, but we all fled.

We stood out in the lobby looking at each other. Matt the Puppet suggested we have our morning meeting upstairs. Everybody shrugged and mumbled. We followed him up the stairs to the conference room, where Matt the Puppet took Bernie's tall leather back chair. I didn't think that was a wise move. Even though Bernie hardly came upstairs, it clearly was his seat, his territory. Matt started the meeting. Alexis pulled out her phone to keep her occupied. Ronnie paid attention. I zoned out.

Matt announced the totals for the month, and said there were only two days left and one of them was Saturday. Saturday was the Sabbath, the day of rest, so we really had just one day left to sell. Matt announced the totals and Alexis changed them on the white board. Then Matt the Puppet gave a lecture about closing the deal.

Matt was like a bad substitute teacher. He lacked our respect, and he dressed like a tool. None of us were paying attention, not even Ronnie, who was making his supermarket shopping list. Alexis was still involved with her phone and I was fading fast. Matt finally finished up his speech. He held out his puppet hand, trying to get us to do the same. He wanted us to do the teamwork thing; like everybody puts their hands in and then we shout "Go Rosemonte!" That would so never happen.

Alexis glared at Matt. "You've got to be fucking kidding me."

He scolded her, "Language, Alexis."

Ronnie didn't realize the meeting was over and the hand thing was the cue. I laughed because Matt the Puppet looked like such a dork. I was prepared to tell him that if he asked for my input. Which he didn't. Bummer.

When I got back to my desk, I started to work on the next month. I tore the July page off my desk calendar and looked at August. I had a few things lined up. Summer would be over soon, then the High Holy days would be here. I looked at my commission sheet for July. I wanted to exceed what I had accomplished. I wrote down the dollar figure I wanted to sell and taped it to the wall in front of me as a motivational technique.

I needed a Diet Coke so I went to the coffee room. We were out. Crap. I asked Ronnie if he wanted anything from the corner store. He said, "Can you get me a Tastykake?"

"Sure." I grabbed my purse. "I'll be back in a few."

I went behind the big counter in the lobby and told the office girls I was going out for a quick errand. As I turned around to leave, I heard my name being called. A woman was waving at me. When I got closer I realized it was my favorite English teacher from high school, Mrs. Fishman.

"Hi," I said in a super excited voice. Tall and confident, Mrs. Fishman wore a floppy brimmed hat, white pants, and a white shirt with a cream stripe running through it. She looked fresh from the beach with her summer tan and metallic sandals. She was with a much younger woman, a blonde in her late thirties.

"Hello, Julia." Mrs. Fishman said again as she engulfed me in a big hug. "How are you?"

"Good. I mean I'm doing well, I should say." I giggled. Mrs. Fishman smiled back at me. "Hi," I said to the other woman.

"This is my daughter," Mrs. Fishman said. "Her name is Jill. Say hi, Jill."

Mrs. Fishman had never mentioned Jill back in school. I'd thought she was childless. Surprise.

Jill raised her head. I could see it in her face. She had Down syndrome.

"Hi," I said brightly.

Jill returned my greeting with a shy, "Hello."

"Jill, sweetie, have a seat for a minute. Okay?" Mrs. Fishman said.

"Yes, mama," Jill replied.

Mrs. Fishman waited until Jill was seated. "What do you do here, Julia?"

I explained my position, then said. "Is there any way I can be of service to you and your family?"

"Actually, yes. My husband and I are not getting any younger, and you know, with Jill…" Mrs. Fishman paused for a moment. "I want to take care of our arrangements now."

I nodded my head. "That's very wise. I can help you, if you like."

"That would be a grand idea." She pulled out a planner from her giant Burberry tote bag. "How about the day after tomorrow?"

"Perfect," I said.

"Do you know downtown well?"

"Yes, I live in South Philly now."

"South Philly, such a marvelous neighborhood, we love to dine there." Mrs. Fishman wrote down her address in her perfect cursive. "We live in a building on Rittenhouse Square. If you go to this garage, you can park in our visitor spot."

"Great. Thanks for the parking tip. I'm looking forward to seeing you and Mr. Fishman."

Mrs. Fishman pinched my cheek and said, "Look at that shayna punum. Come on, Jill, we're off."

Jackpot! This could be my biggest sale ever, I thought to myself on the way to my car. August was going to be a very good month.

I hopped in my car and went to the store. I decided to be funny and buy Ronnie a family-size box of Tastykakes. I grabbed a six-pack of Diet Coke and headed towards check out.

Back at my office, I placed the box of Tastykakes on Ronnie's desk. I'd started to research information for the Fishmans when Ronnie walked in. He laughed when he saw the big box of Krimpets.

"These'll be gone by the end of the day. You do know that," he said.

"Whatever," I said with a wave of my hand. I too could house an entire box of Tastykakes, but I wouldn't do it at work. Ronnie didn't care who saw him eating out of control. Which was impressive.

The rest of the day was filled with annoyances. Bernie was still acting strange. He was bored and wanted people to sit with him and keep him company. Ronnie got suckered in to babysitting. But when it was my turn, I simply said no in a stern voice. Just like when I got a Shih Tzu for my fourteenth birthday and had to train him.

My mother had been hopped up on pills and told me she felt sorry for me, not having a father anymore. Then she had a car service pick her up and take her somewhere. The next day, she tried to make amends by giving me a puppy. The dog was inbred and didn't understand most commands. She'd bought him at a black market puppy mill. He was always having accidents. Eventually, he registered my stern voice. I still knew how to use it. In more ways than one, Bernie reminded me of my dog, Pepper.

After I pulled up the information for the Fishmans, I looked up Down syndrome on the web. I didn't know much about it. I remembered a TV show from when I was younger about a boy named Corky. In the middle school I attended, there was a class of slower kids who got nicknamed "Corkies" by some bullies. I didn't want to appear ignorant in front of the Fishmans, so I wanted to get a few facts under my belt so I didn't look like an ass.

I called Adam to see if he wanted to go shopping on Saturday. Adam always wanted to go to the mall. He answered the phone, "Wassup, slut."

"Ew!" I yelled.

"I'm just joking. What's up, honey?"

"Not much. Do you want to go to King Of Prussia tomorrow?"

"The mall? You don't need to ask me twice," he said.

"Awesome. Do you want me to drive?"

"No way. I'll pick you up. What time, doll?"

"Eleven. We'll do lunch and hit some stores. I have coupons for Macy's and Bloomingdales."

"Of course you do," Adam said, mocking me. We went back and forth a little more, then hung up.

I was excited to go shopping with Adam. He was a good shopping partner. He always told me the truth about how clothes looked. In the past I had wondered if he was gay, but he was just really into superficial things like looks, money, and stuff on the outside. Either way, I was happy to hang with him.

That evening I chilled at home and ordered dinner in. It was too hot to cook, and also a little depressing to cook for one. Lou the pizza man was getting to know me better and better. He was a frequent visitor to my house. He'd come to my door, ring the bell, and sing in Italian until I answered. I think he sang to get better tips, which worked on me. I felt special whenever he serenaded me as he handed over my grub.

"Whaz a nice Italian girl like you doin' home on a Friday night? I could introduce youse to a lot of nice fellas," he'd say, trying to tempt me.

I thanked Lou for the compliments. "See you next time, Lou."

The aroma of the pizza filled my tiny house with the delicious smell of sweet sauce and Italian spices like oregano and basil. I liked a little salt on my pizza. As I opened the box, a perfect looking pie smiled back at me. The cheese had melted and the crust was a golden brown. I sat down at the table and gave the pie a quick shake of salt, Parmesan cheese, and red pepper flakes. Now I was ready to eat. The first slice flopped over just the right amount when I picked it up and moved it towards my mouth. I closed my eyes and enjoyed the moment of silence. As I chewed, all my stress from work went away. I didn't think about the pressure from Bernie to sell sell sell. The cast of characters I had sold to didn't parade through my mind. I didn't care that Matt the Puppet was a shady mofo. I just sat and enjoyed what I considered to be the best pizza in the city.

❧❦❧

Adam picked me up the next morning and off to King Of Prussia Mall we went. I was surprised to see that Adam had come alone, without the company of his girlfriend.

"Where's Joy?" I asked, trying not to sound too excited that she wasn't there.

"She decided to go down the Shore and spend the weekend with her family at their place."

"Oh nice," I remarked, doing a cheer in my mind.

Adam took a shortcut out of the city and onto the highway that would take us to the mall. I looked out the window and watched the landscape change from South Philly to expensive high- rise buildings to the ghetto and finally to I-76. Soon we were at our exit for the mall. Adam had sung along with the radio the entire time. He had a good singing voice when he wasn't playing around or smoking too many cigarettes.

He asked, "Where do you want to go first?"

"Wherever's fine. Do you want to park at Sears or K-Mart?" I laughed when I saw the face Adam made at me, his nose crinkled up.

"I would rather die," he said in a snotty voice. He pulled around to Neiman Marcus and parked there. We got out of the car and Adam beeped the alarm on. As we walked towards the store entrance, he said, "Let me guess, shoes?"

"As if you had to ask."

Inside, I led the way to the shoe department. They were having a big sale so things were a little chaotic. I looked around and held up various shoes to see Adam's expression. After I had a few pairs to try on, I joined him in the chairs. Then I modeled the shoes for Adam, turning in a circle and asking, "What do you think?"

Each time Adam gave his opinion, asking which outfit I would wear the shoes with. I'd answer, then look at the price. My grandmother had taught me it was free to try on anything. Clothes, shoes, especially diamonds. Sometimes that wasn't the smartest move. Then again, how bad could it be? Everything I had picked out was off the sale rack.

I narrowed my choices down to three pairs and tried them on again. I asked Adam to pick the ones he liked best. He chose a fantastic pair of nude-colored patent leather heels. The price was not too steep. I smiled and went up to the counter to buy them.

When I returned, I asked, "Next?"

His answer was simple. "Lunch," he said as he pointed to his big belly.

We made our way through the mall to the food court. I wanted a salad and Adam was going for mall Cajun. The salad place was next to the Cajun place, so we ordered our food and met at a table. Adam grabbed my receipt off my tray and placed the money I'd laid out for lunch in my purse. I rolled my eyes and mumbled "thanks" at the same time.

Over lunch we caught up and discussed our families. I was almost done with my salad when Adam asked, "Do you think you'll work for Rosemonte forever?"

"No way," I said in a strong voice. "How about you? Will you work for the funeral home forever?"

"That's a loaded question," he said, "and you know that." Adam stared right into my eyes. He told me how depressing it was to work there. I understood that completely. But he had never worked anywhere else. He had to be used to the work. Plus, being a funeral director was in his blood. From time to time, Adam had bitched about working in his Dad's shadow. This time he seemed to be really annoyed.

"So, back to you," Adam said. "Why did you say no way?"

I let out a long breath and scratched at the side of my face. "This job is good for me for now. But this is not a forever career. Honestly, I seem to be able to sell only to freak shows. And Bernie puts so much stress on me, I feel like I'm getting an ulcer or something. Someday, I want to go back to being my own boss."

"Don't let Bernie get to you," Adam instructed. "He's all show and no go."

"That's a lot easier said than done."

Adam took our trays over to the trash can. He asked me, "Where to now?"

"I have coupons for the private sale at Bloomies, let's head over there."

Adam nodded. We walked in silence, pausing here and there at a store window. "Do you mind if we go by cosmetics?" I asked "I want to get some free samples."

"Of course you do, Miss Frugal. No, I don't mind."

When we arrived at Bloomingdales, we walked the black and white checkered floor of the cosmetics department. I graciously accepted samples of lotions and potions that promised to make me prettier, less wrinkled, and lovely smelling. It was like trick-or-treating for adults. Adam also got a few samples from the Bumble and Bumble counter.

After the cosmetics department, Adam asked, "What's the plan?"

"I don't really have one," I said. "Do you want to wander around, do a lap?"

"Sure," he said. "I need some new shirts for work. You can't let me forget."

"Got it." I replied.

We walked around the sales floor at Bloomingdales. I looked at a few dresses but didn't want to try them on after my dinner date with the pizza. Adam got a few shirts for work and a tie. When we left Bloomies Adam asked, "Do you want to go for ice cream? Please?" I looked into his big blue eyes, and he gave me a wide grin.

"How can I say no to that?"

I got medium cookie dough in a cup and Adam got a large cone, triple chocolate with rainbow jimmies. Then we made our way back to Adam's car. I was happy with my purchase and all my freebies. "Today was nice," I said as we drove home.

"I agree. You working tomorrow?"

"Yes. It's my turn to bring the bagels and babysit Bernie." I moaned with disgust.

"That blows."

"I know, but I have a good appointment after that, so I hope my day will turn around."

The ride home seemed to go much quicker than the trek to the mall. Soon we were back in the city. Adam pulled up to the corner and dropped me off. We went through the motions of a hug goodbye. As always he waited until I got to my front door, then he beeped the horn as he drove away.

I was mentally prepared for the next day at work. Ronnie had gone over the bagel order, as well as the topics to stay away from while babysitting for Bernie. I also had my appointment with the Fishmans, which I was hoping would be fruitful for me. I poured myself a glass of Malibu Rum and Diet Coke, and watched some TV until I was sleepy enough to turn in.

Chapter 20

On Sunday morning I got up extra early and made good time getting ready. The night before I had picked out what I wanted to wear. I needed a power outfit, something that made me feel sophisticated and in control. I chose a white linen pantsuit and paired it with a honey colored t-shirt. My new shoes looked great with it. I needed something else, so I tied a scarf loosely around my neck. The different shades of brown swirled and swished in a fluid motion. I parted my hair on the side and scooped it up in a tight bun. My Fendi barrel bag in khaki and dark brown pulled everything together. A glance in the mirror for approval, and I was ready to go.

The main reason why there was a rotation for picking up the food on Sundays was the bagel place. It was a mad house. I took a number from the red deli machine and waited. Eventually my number was called. Hurray. I made my way up to the high counter to place the order. The man behind the counter saw my blue plastic name tag and said, "Oh Rosemonte. I got a spot over there for me and my old lady."

I gave him a weak smile and read the order off my notepad. "Three dozen bagels assorted and sliced. The works platter, please." This consisted of crudités, cream cheese, and fish.

"You got it." He shoved a slip of paper at me and said, "You pay over there."

"Thank you." I looked at my notes. I still needed to get the sweets. Bernie would lose his shit if he didn't have cookies. I went over to the dessert counter and ordered a tray of cookies large enough for twenty people. Bernie would eat most of it.

I paid, darted out the door and headed to work. I checked my watch. Still on time. At the front door I dropped off the stuff, then went to park. I popped a Pepto-Bismol because I had the feeling I'd be stuck with Bernie all day. My stomach was already off.

Bernie sat in the little office, waiting with his coffee and orange juice. A napkin was spread on his lap, another one tucked into his shirt collar.

"Good morning," I said brightly.

He just sat there. He reminded me of a dog waiting for the master to put the food out. But once I handed over the food, he told me to sit. Role reversal, now I was the dog.

Trapped, I sat down and tried not to watch him eat. Watching Bernie eat was so disgusting. I didn't want to make conversation because I knew he'd talk with his mouth full of food, some chewed, some not. Midway through his first bagel sandwich, I prepared his second sandwich. I sipped some orange juice and checked the email on my phone.

Bernie broke the silence by asking, "Do you want to split a bagel with me?"

I answered, "Sure." I did so to be cooperative. I wasn't hungry.

We waited for the rest of the Family Service counselors to arrive. Once everyone was present, the cookie tray would come out.

I tried to escape but Bernie wanted to talk. He told me stories about when he was a young boy. How his mother would show him love by serving baked goods. He would come home from school to fresh baked cookies, and wake up to apple cake still warm from the oven.

"That's nice," I said. Where was he going with this? Did I really need to hear about his childhood obsession with sweets?

He praised the ruggelah his mother would roll by hand. The mandle bread that won first place in the B'nai B'rith bake-off. Oy vey. I didn't care. His eyes were getting wider as he spoke about different baked goods.

"You know, my wife, she doesn't bake," he said.

"I didn't know that. How interesting, because you have such a sweet tooth."

"Well," he said, "she's goyim."

"Oh, that explains it." I said sarcastically. "Baking is not for everyone."

After a bit of silence, Bernie asked, "Do you like dogs?"

"Not big dogs." I wondered what was up with this line of questioning. What could possibly be the motive behind this kind of interrogation?

"You know," Bernie said, "my wife and I are going on vacation at the end of the month."

"Where're you going?" I was interested in any and all details about an upcoming break from Bernie.

"We're going out west," he said. "Part business and part pleasure. A cemetery industry convention in New Mexico. We're going for that and then for some fun. See the Alamo and all that stuff."

"Wow, that sounds great," I said, trying not to sound excited that Bernie would be out of the office. "How long are you going for?"

"Ten days," he said.

Hallelujah! Ten Bernie-free days! "Nice. Enjoy your trip." I said. I held down my legs so I didn't jump for joy.

Bernie took out his wallet and fumbled for a minute. "Ah, here it is." He showed me a tattered picture of his dog, a little white fluffball. "Her name is Sugar. She's a mix of Poodle and Bichon."

I laughed because all I could think of was the Conan skit with Triumph the Insult Comic Dog and his lust for the Bichon. When I mentioned it to Bernie, he looked at me like I was nuts. He had never seen the show or the skit.

"So, moving on," Bernie said, looking me in the eye. "I wanted to know if you'd be interested in staying at my house while we're on vacation. You can take care of Sugar and bake some cookies. You know, stock up my freezer. You could also drop us off and pick us up from the airport. We're flying out of Philly International. We'd reimburse you for gas as well. Of course, we'd take care of you for your time and your talent."

What the fuck? "Let me understand," I said slowly. "You want me to babysit your dog and your house, and bake for you while you're on vacation?"

Bernie said, "That's right."

There were too many creepy thoughts running through my head. I didn't want to step one foot inside Bernie's house, let alone sleep there for ten fucking nights. I imagined his bathroom with pee all over the toilet seat and floor. Every place had its own distinctive smell. Bernie's house would smell like a combination of bad potpourri, Drakkar Noir, and urine. Whatever gave him the impression I was his bitch?

"I have central air conditioning, cable TV, and you can use the pool," Bernie said, trying to sweeten the deal.

"I don't think this is appropriate. You're my boss."

"It's fine; we're one big family here at Rosemonte. I thought you knew that." He winked at me.

"I wouldn't feel comfortable doing that. Sorry. Bernie, the answer's no." I kept my voice soft.

Flames lit up Bernie's eyes. "Fine. Then Ronnie will dog sit for me. I'll have the neighborhood girl pick up my mail. As for the airport, I suppose my father can schlep us there and back. He's only eighty-nine." His voice was pissy.

"I'm sorry, I just don't feel comfortable," I said again.

"That's fine," Bernie said. His voice was loud. I felt the rubble racing around in my tummy. I popped another Pepto.

Bernie pulled the phone towards him and called the counselors down to the little office. Time for the morning meeting. I was grateful for the company. Bernie was extremely angry. He looked like I had personally offended him. He didn't care when I called him a fuckface. I think he may have even liked it. But now he looked like I'd kicked him in the nuts. He was a tiny wimp who hid in a body of a monster.

Our meeting was brief. Bernie didn't discuss any business relating the cemetery. Instead he rehashed the conversation we'd just had about house sitting.

Bernie said to me, in front of everyone, "Why don't you want to stay at my place?"

"Is this really necessary?" I asked.

"I'm insulted," he said.

Alexis tried to come to my rescue. "Bernie, leave her alone. She doesn't want to stay at your house. Get over it."

Bernie's nostril's flared. "The meeting is over," he yelled. "Everyone out but Matt."

I was overjoyed to get out of there. The tension was growing by the second. "Thanks," I said to Alexis on our way up the stairs.

"He's such a bully, but if things don't go his way he turns into the biggest baby. Come on, let's scoot," she said. I followed Alexis into her office and sat down at Manny's old desk.

"Do you think Bernie will hire anyone else?" I asked.

"Probably towards the end of the month. I'm not looking forward to whoever ends up in my room. I've gotten used to being in here by myself." Alexis stretched her arms out.

I went to my desk to prepare for my appointment with the Fishmans. It was quiet in my office. Ronnie was out somewhere. So I got a little startled when my desk phone rang. "Hello," I answered.

"Julia, this is Estelle."

"Hi Estelle," I said. I had no clue who she was. Then it hit me. Duh, Estelle was Mrs. Fishman.

"I wanted to invite you to have dinner with us before our appointment. It will be great fun to catch up," she said.

"That would be lovely. What can I bring?" I asked, thinking, how I had no time to go home and bake.

"Nothing, my dear, just yourself. See you tonight," she said, and hung up before I had a chance to say anything else.

On my way to the Fishmans I stopped at a state store to get a bottle of wine. When it came to wine, I knew nothing. I asked the store sommelier what would be a good bottle to bring to a dinner for around twenty bucks. He pointed me to a few bottles of red and white. I picked the one that had the prettiest looking label.

I pulled into the garage and parked in their guest spot. A quick check of hair and makeup. Rittenhouse Square was a fancy area. Big money lived there. A beautiful tree-filled park, the Square was also home to many popular restaurants and high rise luxury buildings. Tonight the place was packed with people having fun and enjoying the summer evening.

The Fishmans lived in the Barclay. I'd never been inside before but had always wanted to explore it. Built in the late 1920s the building was absolutely gorgeous. A doorman at the helm of the building looked like Superman, larger than life in his impeccable uniform. "I'm here to see the Fishmans," I said, trying to sound elegant and grown up.

"Right this way, miss." He walked me to the elevator. The lobby looked like a movie set. The floors glistened. All the furnishings looked regal and expensive. I rode in the dark wood paneled elevator up to the top floor.

At the Fishmans door, I knocked. A young ethnic woman answered the door. I was surprised to see she was wearing an old-fashioned uniform, a throwback to the 1960s and the TV show *Hazel*. "Hi," I said. "I'm here to see the Fishmans."

"Follow me. The Fishmans are in the parlor." I followed the maid into the apartment. Wow, I had no idea Mrs. Fishman was so loaded. Her home was fantastic. The herringbone wood floors looked original. The kitchen boasted a Viking French door double oven, granite countertops, and a small wine refrigerator. The parlor featured ten foot tall windows. Mr. and Mrs. Fishman were seated on a silk couch overflowing with plump pillows. The maid announced my arrival.

The Fishmans greeted me warmly. Mrs. Fishman said, "Thank you Cecilia," and the maid left. As I handed the wine to Mrs. Fishman I said, "I love your home." I was hoping I didn't sound like a suck up.

"Thank you," she said. "Would you fancy a tour?"

"Very much so." I nodded. Cool!

"All right. But first thing's first. I'm not your teacher anymore, so please call me Estelle."

I swallowed the lump in my throat and said, "I'll try, but it'll be a little difficult." We both smiled.

She led me on a tour of the bedrooms, each with its own working fireplace. The dining room had an antique hutch purchased from a quaint shop while summering at Martha's Vineyard. Intricate woven rugs from India lined the hallways. I was way out of my league.

"Come, let's break bread," she said enthusiastically. She called out for Jill and Mr. Fishman to join us at the dinner table. Cecilia served us a spring mixed salad with pecans, and blue cheese, then poured a light vinaigrette.

Estelle and I did most of the talking. Jill just sat there and ate. Mr. Fishman made a comment every now and again. I talked about going to culinary school and the internship I'd had at the William Penn Inn. Over beef bourguignon with steamed vegetables, I told them about my baking business. Estelle said it was wonderful that I had become an entrepreneur.

"That was then. Now I work at Rosemonte," I said. "But one day I'd like to be an entrepreneur again. It's so exhilarating being your own boss. I loved working with my hands. The best was when I'd watch people eat something I'd baked and see their faces light up with smiles."

Mr. Fishman seemed to like that, and gave me a kind wink. "Tell us more about the bakery. We're always looking for a smart investment," he said.

Whoa. Invest in *me*? Smart. Really? Shit.

Be calm. You can't blow this, I told myself. The bakery again? My emotions twirled with excitement.

"Right now, I'm sort of in a holding pattern, trying to save money and prepare for my next venture." That sounded good. Like I was open to partnering up.

Mr. Fishman raised his glass of wine and tipped his head in my direction.

Dinner plates were cleared and petit espresso cups with a piece of lemon rind were brought out. Estelle talked about how wonderful I had been as a student. It was nice she thought I was so wonderful because I'd been a C student. However, I did try hard. Dessert was a light mango sorbet with a slice of star fruit and an almond-flavored crescent cookie.

When we were finished, I thanked the Fishmans for a delicious dinner and joked, "I haven't eaten that well in a long while."

Estelle led us back into the parlor. Jill retired to her bedroom. Estelle called on the intercom for after dinner drinks. "Now let's begin," she said, looking at me.

"Okay," I said.

"We don't need to go over all the official procedures." Estelle made a motion with her hands, waving them away as she spoke. I'd seen her do that a million times in class. "Both of our families are at Rosemonte, and one day we'll be there too. You already have the sale. Let's just pick locations. Naturally, we will need three of everything. Because of Jill."

I was flabbergasted. I looked down at my presentation book, then skipped ahead to the end. According to my research, the Fishman family was spread out around the cemetery, so I asked them a few questions to help select the best section for the three of them.

Mr. Fishman sipped his cocktail and asked, "Would you ladies like a chocolate?" He opened a fancy looking box of truffles. He popped one in his mouth and closed his eyes. "One of my clients sent us a box of confections from France. Pure Heaven."

I showed her a map in a nice section up front near the office. "This is near your parents," I said, and she nodded her head in approval.

"I think we should buy an extra space on each side. Don't you, darling?" she said to her husband.

"Whatever you like," he said as he ate another truffle.

"So, you want to buy five spaces? I just want to be clear," I said.

"Yes, we do," she said in a matter of fact tone.

My mind was going bananas. I was going to make a humongous commission!

"Also, I think a triple stone would look best. With Jill in the middle, of course," Estelle stated. "A group of single stones does not suit me. I will not have it."

"It sounds like you and Mr. Fishman have really thought this through," I said.

"Julia, you are so much easier to deal with than that pushy Matthew." Estelle frowned.

What? Matthew? I just smiled and thanked her for the lovely comment. "I take my job very seriously, so that means a lot to me."

My mind churned. She must have meant Matt. But how did Matt the Puppet know my old teacher? It was hard to figure out because he was active in so many groups. Still, I wondered. For the moment, I pushed him out of my mind and got back to finishing the sale.

I punched the numbers into my calculator to give them the grand total. "Here's the bottom line. For the spaces and the triple stone, $34,500." I held my breath.

Mr. Fishman asked, "If I pay in full, what can you do for me?"

"I can take off five hundred. That would bring the total to an even $34,000," I said.

"This is your call, Estelle," he said to his wife.

"Let's do it and be done. I would much rather have Julia, my former student, get the credit than that annoying Matthew. He's constantly calling me. All because he met me at a walk-a-thon for Down syndrome," she said, getting a little steamed. If we were back in school I know Matt would be sent to take the rest of English class from the hallway.

Mr. Fishman told me "Write the contract and I'll write out a check."

My commission would come to $2,300 bucks. My heart was pounding. At that moment, I felt like I could do anything.

A few minutes later, Estelle walked me to the door. I thanked her again for her business and for dinner. She gave me a hug and thanked me for helping her. "Now I can go to bed and know things will be taken care of and Jill has nothing to worry about. To me, that's priceless." As she opened the door for me she said, "If you're ever if the neighborhood, stop by. I would love to have tea sometime."

"I'll keep that in mind," I said.

I couldn't believe it. My biggest sale ever! Matt was going to be so pissed! But it wasn't my fault the Fishmans didn't like him. My previous relationship with Mrs. Fishman was worth way more than his walk-a-thon meet and greet. This was a victory for me, but I knew it would launch a war between me and Matt.

That night I slept like a baby. I couldn't wait to go to work the next day.

The morning meeting the next day, began normally. Bernie

called us all down to the little office. He was in an extra cranky mood. Ronnie told me that Bernie had gotten some test results back from the doctor and was not happy about them.

I was the last to arrive and took the only open seat in between Alexis and Bernie. Matt sat directly across from me. I had a full view of his beady eyes and mouse-like face. No one knew about the whopper of a sale I had made. Bernie opened his mouth and roared, "Who has a contract?" Everybody's eyes switched from one to another.

Ronnie was the first to break the silence. "I do, but it's not that big." He pushed the paper across the table to Bernie.

Bernie looked at the amount of the sale and shook his head in a disappointed manner. "This is pitiful," he said without missing a beat. "Well, what about you?" He stared at Alexis.

She stared back and said, "I presented, but I didn't make the sale."

"Why the fuck not?" Bernie screamed. His face turned beet red, and his eyes were squinty. "You are going to have to wear shorter skirts and no underwear if you want to sell." Alexis looked like she was going to say something back but decided to hold her tongue instead.

Matt the Puppet gave Bernie two contracts. Oh no, could he have outsold me last night? Did I just shoot myself in the foot? "One is small; however, the other is quite considerable," Matt said. "The total's just shy of $27,000."

He looked at me, Ronnie, and Alexis like we were a bunch of chumps. I maintained a straight face, but in my head I was laughing. Matt was about to be knocked off his pedestal, and the new kid was going to push him.

I was quiet as I handed Bernie my contract. He looked at the total, then grinned. "How did you do this?"

"She was my English teacher in high school," I said.

Bernie dropped my contract in the middle of the table for

everyone to see. I watched as Matt's eyes moved from the contract up to my own eyes. He was angry.

"I have been working on the Fishmans for almost ten months," he screeched. "This is an outrage."

"Yes, Mrs. Fishman told me how you met her at a walk-a-thon," I said in an extra snarky voice.

"This is unfair!" Matt exclaimed.

"How?" I asked calmly.

"The Fishmans were mine," Matt whined.

"You know what, Matt? Mrs. Fishman didn't even mention your name until the end of our meeting when she walked me to the door. Life's unfair. Get used to it," I said in a cool voice. My eyes did not leave Matt's. He squirmed in his seat and eventually looked away.

Bernie's mood had done a one-eighty. He'd gone from cranky to joyful. He loved to watch drama unfold in front of his eyes. "Sorry, Matty," he said. "Looks like the kid beat you to the punch."

"But the Fishmans are a big money client," Matt whined. They deserve my level of service and experience. Did you get references?" he asked, trying to stump me.

"Yes, I did."

"So what you are going to sell to the Philadelphia elite now?" Matt asked, thinking this was funny.

"I will sell whatever to whoever wants to buy from me," I said. "I got news for you Matt. Sales 101: customers buy from the people they like. Obviously, the Fishmans liked me, not you."

"I don't understand why," Matt murmured. "How could this have happened?"

I let out a long sigh and said in a very ghetto voice, "Cuz they don't like you." I rolled my head from side to side to add a little extra punch. I glared at Matt because he was staring at me.

Bernie broke the tension, "The kid wins again. Meeting adjourned."

The rest of the day went by in a blur. I was in stellar mood while

Matt was miserable. Alexis came into my office and sat down next to my desk. She wanted to know what had happened word for word during the trash talking of Matt by the Fishmans. She seemed slightly bummed when I told her it wasn't much. "Mrs. Fishman is much too classy to do that in front of me."

Alexis stood up and patted me on the head. "You did well. Now the hard part will be keeping Matt dethroned. He's sneaky. You'll need to be careful."

She turned and left my office. Now Alexis was giving me a hint about Matt being unethical. Why was everyone so scared of him? He was such a wimpy nobody.

I made lots of phone calls to try to stay on my hot streak. I was able to set up a bunch of appointments. My goal was to keep Matt down and out. I was a force to be reckoned with.

That evening I went back to the building where Linus worked. I had an appointment there which turned out to be a no show. I knocked on a few doors but got nowhere. Linus was off that night so I didn't have to worry.

On my way home, Adam called. "Hey," I answered, surprised to hear from him.

"Hey," he said. Something was awry. He sounded very down.

"What's wrong?" I asked.

"I think it's over."

"Really?" I doubted it.

"Where are you? Can you come over?" he asked.

"I'm a few blocks away. See you in a minute," I said.

I drove over to Adam's building and hunted for a parking spot. After I parallel parked, I checked my face in the rear view mirror. I wasn't sure how I felt about the situation. I didn't care for Joy, but I didn't like seeing Adam depressed either.

When the elevator doors opened, I walked down the hall. Adam was standing in his doorway, slumped up against the jamb. He held a squat glass with two ice cubes and golden-colored liquor. Oh boy,

I thought. This was going to be interesting.

I strode inside and sat down on his black leather bachelor pad couch, put my feet up on the coffee table. "Well? What happened?" Adam came over and sat down on the coffee table. I heard a ruckus coming from the bathroom. "Is she here?" I asked Adam in a hushed voice. "You know I don't like coming over when she's here." Now I was annoyed.

Joy exited the bathroom. Her eyes were puffy. She'd been crying. "Of course, you're here. You're the first phone call. I'm so sick of you! I wish you would go away and never return."

Her eyes were like laser guns melting holes in my head. She was pulling a wheelie suitcase, her initials monogrammed on it in large, cobalt blue letters. She wore sweatpants and her hair was in a messy ponytail. The tank top she had on sported a bleach stain. As she walked across the room, her cheap flip flops squeaked.

I couldn't believe this girl who was worth tons of dough looked like such a shambles. "I'll be at my parents' estate if you need me," she said, to Adam. "What is so special about you?" she asked me. "You're nothing but a half-orphan with a drunk as a mother."

"Come on. Get out of here." Adam shoved her into the hallway. He locked the door and put the chain on.

Yikes. That was a lot of unnecessary words. What a bitch. She wasn't telling me anything I already didn't know.

"Do you want to start talking now?" I pleaded.

Adam sunk into a reclining black leather chair. He looked exhausted. "You know I love money," he said. I nodded. "But I don't love her, and that's a major problem."

It got quiet and I felt uncomfortable. "You need to do what's right for you," I said, trying not to sound like a know-it-all.

"That's the problem. I don't know what's right for me."

He sipped his drink, staring into space. Granted, Joy and I were not fans of one another. But I didn't want to totally rip her apart. Even though she'd torn me limb from limb. Adam loosened his tie and unbuttoned the top button of his shirt. He took off his Tourneau watch and smoothed the face. He stared at the watch. Did he think his prized procession would tell him what to do?

Adam drank the rest of his drink and got up for a refill. I just sat and watched him. "So, what can I do for you?" I asked, trying to sound sensitive. I felt like I was wasting my time sitting there.

"I need time to think about what just happened," Adam answered.

"Right." I said. "So what did happen?"

"That's the problem, I'm not sure. I feel like we're going in circles. She wants to get married and have kids. I don't want that, at least not with her." Adam filled his glass.

"I understand how you feel," I said. "If this is not a good match for you, then get out now while you can." I stood up and moved closer to him. "Trust me, there are plenty of honeys out in the world with big bank accounts, she's only one of them. You'll land one who's hotter and has more cash." I smoothed his hair and gave him a wink.

I felt like such a cheese ball for saying such crap to him. Joy's words still rang in my head. *Special.* If I was so special, why wouldn't Adam have made a move by now? He knew me well enough to know I'd never make the first move. If he wanted me, now was the time. Kiss me, I thought.

Instead he nursed his drink. The moment was gone. Over.

His problem was his obsession with only dating girls with money. He looked for bank accounts, not for love. Could that really be what was holding me back? Cash? My bank account had gotten fatter since working at Rosemonte, but I was a lowly peasant compared to Joy and her trust fund.

I started to feel sick. I didn't believe any of what I'd told Adam. I felt the same feelings in my stomach as I did when Bernie yelled.

Suddenly, I jumped up. "I gotta go," I announced and pushed past Adam. I ran to the bathroom, closed the door behind me, and puked. Luckily for me and Adam, I made it into the toilet bowl. Yup, there was my lunch, looking back at me.

I flushed the toilet and went to the sink to splash cool water on my face. Adam was banging on the door. "Are you okay?"

I opened the door and said, "Sorry, my stress levels are getting out of control from work."

Adam looked concerned. "I'm worried about you. Do you want me to call Bernie and tell him not to ride you so hard?"

"No." I shook my head. "It's fine, I got it."

I needed to get out of his apartment. Looking at my watch, I yelped, "I gotta get home."

Adam walked me to the door. "Are you straight to drive home?" he asked.

"I'm good. What about you? Are you going to be all right?"

"As soon as I figure out what's happening, I'll let you know. Right now, I think Joy and I need some chill out time." He stood in the doorway as I walked down the hall to the elevator.

How could he still want to be with her, when she'd verbally assaulted me? My God, everyone had their price, but Adam's was so high.

The night air was sweet. The moon was full and slightly yellow. Autumn was coming and I couldn't wait for summer to be over. As I walked to my car I felt another wave of nausea. I was also a little dizzy. I got in my car and drove home slowly.

I went right to bed. I tried to relax but the room was spinning, I had a headache, and worst of all, I had made no sales that day. I didn't want to think about the monster Bernie had become, and I couldn't deal with knowing I had to face him in the morning. I prayed that Matt had no sales either. Then fell into a deep sleep.

Chapter 21

During our meeting the next morning, I still felt like shit. The only good thing was no one else had made a sale. Bernie held a staring contest with each of us. Then the yelling began.

"What the hell do I need to do to motivate you people? This is piss poor selling," he ranted. "What the hell is happening to my sales team?" Bernie looked like his face was going to explode. His skin was tanned from the summer sun, but his cheeks were garnet-colored. This aged him, and showed off his deep-set wrinkles. It was not a pretty sight.

I was sitting next to Ronnie, who was humming. A short, sweet little tune. I couldn't recall the words but I knew I had heard the song before. Ronnie often hummed this tune. He had hummed it so frequently that it had become back-ground noise. It was going to drive me crazy if I didn't figure it out. I wrote a note to myself to ask Ronnie what the song was.

Bernie continued to scold. He slammed his hand on the table. We'd seen all his moves before. He desperately needed some new ones.

"The High Holy days are coming, people! We need to be on our A game to sell to the future land owners here," he squawked, pointing out the window towards the grounds of the cemetery.

After twenty more minutes of the same one-sided conversation, Bernie dismissed us. We retreated to our offices to start work.

"What song are you humming? A showtune? A slogan for some product?" I asked Ronnie.

"What song?" His face was clueless.

"You know." I did an imitation.

"That's not a song," Ronnie said, and erupted into hoots of laughter.

I was surprised at Ronnie's response. Usually he was so well composed. Suddenly I felt really dumb, like this song or tune should be obvious to me. And it wasn't.

"Where do you think it's from?" he asked.

"I don't know," I wailed. "Tell me."

Ronnie held up a finger. "Let me stop laughing first." He began breathing in and out, trying to calm himself.

"The four questions from Passover Sedar," he finally said. "Ma nishtanah ha-laylah ha-zeh mi kol ha-leylot." He chanted in Hebrew. "In English, 'What makes this night different than all others?' Whenever Bernie starts, it's always the same thing over and over, it's never any different. Bernie's constantly yelling about the same damn thing."

I laughed until my eyes watered.

"In all the years I've worked here, Bernie has never caught on. I'm always humming that. He's such an idiot!" Ronnie shook his head.

I finished up some paper work and made phone calls to set up appointments. One of the calls I made was to Joe Steinberg. He was surprised to hear from me. He said he'd thought he scared me away. I set up another meeting with him for later in the week. I hoped for my sake he'd be wearing shorts. The weather outside had cooled slightly, so I figured Joe would've started to clothe himself again.

More hours of the day ticked by. I was curious about how Adam was doing. I sent him a text but he didn't respond. Then I heard the crackle of the speakerphone being fired up. Great, another meeting. Bernie made the calls. Everyone was needed down at the little office again.

When I arrived I was surprised to see Tatyana. She looked upset. She had a snotty tissue balled up and shoved in her sleeve. She sat next to Bernie.

"Why are you crying?" I asked her.

She held up a hand. "It's okay Julia. I fine." She wrote in her notebook, something in Russian. The letters looked fierce and aggressive in red ink. "I not done with you, Bernie," she said.

With a push of his paw, Bernie dismissed Tatyana. "Get outta here. I don't want to see your fat ass anymore today."

Tatyana gathered what was left of her dignity and exited the little office. I wanted to speak with her. What had brought her to tears? The secret meetings between Matt and Bernie, something with sales, or the person she had so mysteriously warned me about? I looked out the window and saw her driving off. Damn.

"I called you all down because I am pissed off. The word on the street is that no one is happy working here. Is this true?" Bernie searched our faces. I put on a poker face, no emotion. "Well, I just got reamed a new one from the owners. So slap on a smile even if it's a fake one. Okay? We need to boost morale around here, at least that's what I'm being told. Now, everyone out. Go sell something."

I went back to my desk. Without a lot of work to do, I sat thinking about what Bernie had said. Was I happy working here? Life was precious. I was wasting my time, my youth, in this unhappy, stressful place. I was too young to be stressed out all the time. I didn't want to end up being a lifer like Alexis or Ronnie. Yes, the money was good. But money wasn't everything. Hadn't I just said that to Adam? I was deep in thought when my phone rang.

On the other end of the line someone clucked at me. An old lady who had been referred by someone I'd sold in July. She rambled on about how she lived in Florida but would be buried in Rosemonte with her late husband. I pulled up her name from the computer database while she was talking about her dogs, CoCo and Chloe. The records showed she didn't need anything. The woman was paid in full. I couldn't sell her anything, even if I wanted to. Something wasn't adding up.

I informed her I was getting an emergency call and I'd call her back in a few. She said, "Splendid," and we hung up. I went to find Ronnie. He was in the coffee room making a fresh pot and shoving doughnut holes in his mouth.

"Sorry," he mumbled. "You know I'm an emotional eater."

I nodded my head and changed the subject. "Question for you," I said holding back a laugh at Ronnie's powdered sugar moustache.

"What can I do for you?"

As I explained the odd phone call, Ronnie interrupted. "Let me guess," he said. "Goldie Wasserberg?"

"How did you know?"

"She calls every now and again. Sweet lady, but she's starting to lose it, poor thing," he said.

"That would make sense," I said. Alzheimer's is an ugly disease, and it seemed more and more people were affected by it.

I returned to my desk and dialed Goldie back. "Hello?" I could hear the dogs yapping in the background.

"Hi Goldie," I said. She started to chitchat. Eventually, Goldie told me no one ever called her back from Rosemonte. I was the very first one. Hmmmm, I thought. This could work in my favor, but how?

After another fifteen minutes of hearing Goldie talk about her garden, I asked her about her family. She said her parents were buried at Rosemonte, and her sister and her sister's husband would be there also. Bingo.

When I asked for the sister's name, Goldie gave it to me. Then she kept talking while I looked her up in Rosemonte records. Just as I'd suspected, she owned ground, nothing else. That was my appointment. I let Goldie yammer on for a few more minutes. Then I asked her if she thought it would be all right if I called her sister.

"Oh, yes, mamaleh. She'd enjoy that very much. Especially

because you're such a good listener."

I thanked her and we hung up.

I called Goldie's sister, Mrs. Lillian Cohen. "Hello, Mrs. Cohen?" I said.

"Hello, mamaleh." Her voice sounded identical to Goldie's. Lillian was younger by five years, and she didn't sound as far gone. We chatted for a bit. Lillian used a lot of Yiddish, most of which I understood. I made an appointment to see her later in the week. Score!

❧❦❧

A few days later, I went to meet Lillian Cohen. She lived in a fancy condo building in Jenkintown, only a few minutes from the cemetery. I don't know why but I had a good feeling about this appointment. Maybe my good feeling was coming from my Prada purse. Almost every time I wore it, I made a sale. It was my good luck charm.

I parked in a visitor spot and gathered my things from the trunk of my car. The sun was starting to set. The early evening sky was painted coral and the sun a bright orange.

When I walked into the lobby of The Plaza, it was wall to wall with blue hairs, all waiting for the complementary shuttle bus to schlep them to the shopping center. No doubt this was one of the busiest runs of the day. After all, it was 5:00 and the sunset specials for Morty's Deli clearly states you must be seated by 5:30 p.m. Through the crowd a woman emerged waving a cane. I waved back.

Lillian had on dozens of gold necklaces: she looked like a native African tribeswoman from the pages of *National Geographic*. I was surprised she could hold her head up. I had made plans to meet her at her apartment, but it seemed she preferred to meet in the lobby.

"Hello, Mrs. Cohen," I said bright and cheery.

"Hello, mamlea," she said. "Please call me Lillian."

"Okay, Lillian. Shall we go upstairs?"

"No, let's sit here for a moment," she said, walking the living room area of the lobby. I followed her over. The bus had arrived and the lobby was starting to empty out. A moment later, it was just us. Lillian talked about how long she had lived there and how much she enjoyed it.

"That's nice," I responded.

Twenty minutes later, I asked Lillian, "Do you want to go up and start the meeting with your husband?"

"He's taking a nap and I don't want to disturb him," she said.

"I understand. We can keep having girl talk until he gets up."

"Oh goodie," Lillian said, clapping her hands.

"How did you and Mr. Cohen meet?" I asked. I figured that would kill some time and then he'd wake up and I could begin the presentation.

"The matchmaker set us up on a blind date." Lillian said, settling in for a long story. "We hit it off immediately. I was kasha and he was the bowtie."

"That's so sweet, and cute!" I said, afraid I sounded corny.

"We decided to get married the next day. It was a huge upset to our families, but eventually both sides got over it. After all, it was war time and he was going to be shipped out four days later. I was a nervous wreck while he was stationed on the shores of France. Killing Nazis and freeing Jews in camps. Three and a half years he was there. Every day I prayed to the big man upstairs. He answered my prayers, you know. My Heschy came back safe and sound. Not a scratch on him."

OMG, this story was touching my empty heart. It made me believe in love. I blinked away what I hoped wasn't a tear.

"When he came back home, we got stationed in Hawaii. Let me tell you, Honolulu was an experience! The people, the culture, and so many beautiful flowers. We lived on the base. The Px is just a tad shy of Neiman Marcus, if you know what I mean." Lillian winked.

"We went to the beach almost every day! When Heschy's time was up over there, we came back to Philadelphia and started our family. And here we are."

I peeked at my watch. Almost seven o'clock. When Lillian paused to catch her breath, I asked her again if she thought Heschy was up yet.

She said, "No, he's a sound sleeper and takes very long naps."

I was hell-bent on getting a sale. I needed more time so I asked Lillian about her children. She again looked delighted. On cue, she reached into her pocketbook and pulled out a brag book. She described each one as we looked at the photos. "I have three children and five grandchildren," she boasted, her eyes gleaming with pride.

When the bus came back from Morty's Deli, a parade of alter kockers marched through the lobby, most of them carrying their leftovers in crisp white paper bags. They made a large ruckus with their walkers and canes as they shuffled by. It was eight p.m. Now I was annoyed. Again I asked Lillian about waking Heschy for our meeting.

"Lillian," I said sternly, "I have to discuss some very important information with you and your husband. Both of you need to be present so you both understand what I'm going over with you. Please, this is for your own benefit, and Heschy's." I tried to make my eyes look fierce and important.

Lillian was silent. Miss Chatterbox had run out of things to say? Impossible!

"You don't understand," she said. "Heschy can't come downstairs."

"Then let's go upstairs."

"No, you don't understand about my Heschy."

I placed my hands on top of hers and said, "Make me understand. I'm here to help you."

Lillian looked extremely sad all of a sudden. Her bright eyes turned dull. She looked down at her left hand and played with her wedding ring. She let out a sigh and looked up at me as she blurted, "Heschy's dead. I had him cremated after he died years ago. But I couldn't let him go. I didn't want to be one of those widows who went to the cemetery every day. He was and will always be the love of my life."

Fuck me.

"Okay," I said. "I understand, thank you for sharing that with me." I wondered if being a little nutty ran in the family. "Let me ask you a question. Do you wish to be cremated too?"

"No! My parents wouldn't be happy with that decision. They'd roll over in their graves! I want a traditional Jewish burial. I'll wear a white shmatte, be buried in a pine box, the whole deal."

"I understand," I said. "Give me a moment." I pulled out my notebook and the photocopy of the map I'd made of their section in Rosemonte. "You have two spots," I said showing her the map. "When the time comes, you can bury Heschy with you, or next to you in his own grave. Whatever you want to do. And you can still have a traditional Jewish burial."

Lillian looked confused. "When he died, someone at Rosemonte said I couldn't do that. Did the rules change?"

"No. I'm sorry, but you were misinformed. You *can* do that."

The color in Lillian's face returned. "But I don't have to give him up now, right?" she asked.

"Absolutely not, you can do it whenever you want." I felt empowered to deliver such happy news.

"Now let's talk brass tacks," she said.

"You still want to stay down here?" I asked.

"Why not? I'm comfortable."

I got out my calculator and gave her the prices both ways, with Heschy in his own grave or in a single plot with her. "The price difference isn't that much," I said. "What's nice is, because you own the ground, you can do whatever you want with it. Give it to another relative or keep it empty, it's up to you."

Lillian looked over the proposals I had written out for her. She twisted her wedding ring around her antique finger. "I think I'll pick this one." she said. She wanted Heschy to be buried in her grave. An extra tall single gravestone would finish their love story.

"Very nice choice," I said. "Now you two will always be together. Forever." She got a little teary eyed. "I didn't mean to upset you."

"No, these are tears of joy." Lillian sniffed. She opened her pocketbook and stuffed in her brag book of photos, took out her wallet. She handed me her AMEX. "I get airline miles if I use this one. I want to go and see my sister Goldie in Florida; with this purchase, my ticket will be free."

"That's a lovely idea," I said as I filled out the contract. "Your signature is all I need and you'll be set."

Lillian signed and put her credit card away. "I feel like a weight has been lifted off my heart," she said. "Thank you, Julia, for helping me with this."

"I'm just doing my job," I said. I felt my cheeks grow warm.

"You have manners, grace, and the patience of a saint," Lillian said. "One day you will find your Heschy, your own true love, and you will understand how I'm feeling right now."

I smiled back at her, not knowing what to say. We rose to our feet and said our goodbyes.

As I drove home, I realized I actually felt good about the sale. I thought about what Lillian had said, how she was so in love with Heschy, even after he died. Their bond was powerful. Would that kind of love ever happen to me? Would I experience a love so deep it could withstand death?

I smiled just thinking about it, and before I knew it I was home.

Chapter 22

The next few days at work were extremely busy. The High Holy days were just around the corner. Naturally, we had a meeting about the plan of action. Everyone packed into the little office.

Bernie was looking heavier by the day. He'd put on some major pounds over the summer. If I had to guess, I'd say a solid thirty. He would start to sweat from just sitting in a chair! How repugnant. He never wore shoes with laces anymore, because tying them was too difficult. He was too fat to reach his own feet.

When the phone rang, he'd always answer on speaker because it was too much effort to pick up the receiver. He'd uncap his pen in the morning and leave it that way all day, so no extra energy would be lost taking it on and off. How much lazier could he get?

So there we all were in the little office. Bernie looked like he had just run a marathon, drenched in his own perspiration. The rest of us were giving each other dirty looks because we'd had to race to get there. Whoever got there second to last and last had to sit next to Bernie and run the risk of getting sweated on or picking up his rank B.O. But on the other hand, if you beat your way to get there early, you had to have alone time with Bernie. That could only lead to problems or an argument. Or both. Any way you looked at it, it was a terrible situation.

I was the last to arrive, as usual. I'd decided I would rather run the risk of sweat or stink from Bernie than have to have alone time with him. Matt sat across from Bernie. Alexis and Ronnie had played rock, paper, scissors in the lobby to see who'd have to sit next to Bernie. Ronnie had won. Alexis and I bookended Bernie.

"A rose between two thorns," Bernie said, with a stupid grin on his oversized face. Didn't he use that line before? Lame.

"Don't you mean…." Alexis started, then said, "Forget it."

In the middle of the round table sat a jar of honey and a calendar. The calendar was for the Jewish New Year, and the honey was to represent a sweet New Year. Bernie pointed to these items and said, "Listen up. The calendars will be here in a few days. The rule is one per family." He emphasized one by holding up his Twinkie-sized finger. "The honey jars are here, they need to be stickered. We have new stickers this year. Make sure they are all put on straight and proper," Bernie said to us like we were a bunch of idiots.

"Should we use a ruler or a level?" Matt asked.

Bernie mouthed the word no.

"Do not mail any calendars," Bernie screamed "The postage is outrageous! I'm still paying for the postage Ronnie ran up last year." He gave Ronnie a dirty look. "I thought you were going to take over the payments," he said to Ronnie.

"It was under ten bucks. Really, enough is enough," Ronnie said.

Oh no. I could feel an eruption brewing.

"Ten dollars and change!" Bernie screamed at full volume. "What about the lecture I had to take from the owners? What about that, Ronnie? What is the price for *that*?"

Ronnie was silent. Bernie was just warming up. "Are your wife and daughter still sucking you dry? Because if they are, you should definitely not mail any calendars. Here we are, a whole year, later and nothing has changed. They are still taking you for everything you got, and then some. When are you going to start sucking? I hear you are pretty good? You need to make money somehow because you're not making any here."

Bernie threw both arms in the air, revealing yellow armpit stains.

Ugh. I flinched.

Then he moved his fist towards his left cheek moving it in a back and forth motion, while sticking his tongue out in his right cheek. Holy crap. How totally inappropriate was he? How was he able to get away with speaking to Ronnie like that? His behavior had to qualify as some sort of illegal workplace harassment.

Ronnie held his tongue and wrote in his notebook. Bernie was a hot air balloon, giant and round. The sweat ran off his chin and landed in his coffee. Would he taste that in his drink? "Cat got your tongue?" he asked in a lower tone. I couldn't believe he would treat Ronnie this way when he was going to be taking care of Bernie's dog soon. Didn't he care about Sugar?

Matt decided to sway the beast and asked Bernie, "Is there any other news to discuss?"

"Yes. When I get back from vacation we are going on a field trip. The company that we buy gravestones from is taking us out to lunch." Bernie flashed a big grin.

"Where are we going?" I asked, afraid of the answer.

"The company is treating us to lunch at the Palm restaurant downtown." Bernie seemed very pleased with this news. I surveyed the looks on my co-workers faces. All of them looked sad except Matt, who was thrilled because it was a free meal. He was such a suck up to Bernie, he always had to be on board as his bitch. "Lunch isn't for a few weeks, so, we don't have to figure out the logistics yet," Bernie said.

Lunch at the Palm was going to be so weak. But I couldn't think about that. I still had to finish the month, try to beat Matt for first place. And put stickers on a bunch of jars of honey. The only light at the end of the tunnel was knowing Bernie was going on vacation and giving us all a much needed break.

The meeting continued with Bernie talking about closing sales and not leaving a person's home until we did. When he went into story mode, I tuned out. I came back to life when the meeting was over and we could return to our desks to start work for the day. I looked at my watch. It was almost lunchtime. Did we really just have a three hour meeting? Oy vey!

At lunch I stayed in and got some work done at my desk. I'd made way with a few calls and caught up on paperwork when I heard giggling in the hallway. I got up to see who it was. T.R. was bent over, fixing an outlet under Alexis's desk. She stood behind him, drooling as she watched his glutes move in his tight jeans. She giggled like a school girl. When she saw me watching she bit her lower lip and rolled her eyes.

A moment later T.R. popped up from her desk and said, "The outlet's all fixed, Alexis." He was wearing a tight, thin, white t-shirt with a v-neck. His nipples popped out at attention. The shirt was tucked into his jeans and a brown leather tool belt accented his trim waist line. He picked up a screwdriver and placed it in the loop while Alexis licked her lips.

"Thank you so much," Alexis said in a husky, come hither voice. "Let me ask you a question." She cooed, "Do you think you could come to my house and help me clean up my sun room? It's gotten a lot of debris from the late summer storms and it's too much for me to do. Of course, I'd pay you for your time."

"Sure, that's no problem," T.R. said. "I could use some extra cash. My daughter starts driving soon and I want to help her out with her car insurance."

"Oh, T.R.," Alexis said, tapping him on his bulging biceps. "It's so hard to believe you have a daughter that's almost sixteen." She made a screechy noise that sounded like a cat in heat.

"Well, I do," he said, looking down at his worn work boots.

"So, I'll see you on Saturday." She handed him a slip of paper with her address written on it.

"Yeah, okay, see you then." He winked at her and left her office. "Can I fix anything for you Julia?" he asked me on his way out.

"No, I'm set, thanks."

T.R. strutted down the hallway like a proud peacock. Alexis watched his every move. "Oh. My. God." she exclaimed. "What're you doing on Saturday?"

"Nothing."

Alexis was fanning her face with a manila file folder. "I need you to come to my house. I cannot be left alone with that man. He is one hundred percent, grade A beef and I don't trust myself. Julia, please come by and keep me company. If not for me, then for T.R.'s sake."

I thought for a minute. I wasn't doing anything. It was pretty clear I had no life. "Okay, but you have to do something for me," I said.

"Sure. You name it," she answered.

"I need you to go with me to the naked guy's house. Joe Steinberg. I'm pretty sure he'll have shorts on because it's getting cooler out, but I'm afraid to go by myself."

Now I was looking at my shoes. I didn't want Alexis to think I was a baby. When I looked up, she was snickering.

"Isn't it obvious I love men? All men. Old, young, fat, thin, gay, circumcised or au natural. If there's a chance of seeing some skin, I'm in," she said with great enthusiasm.

"Okay, deal," I said, and we shook hands.

༄☉༄

That night when I went out on appointments, I didn't have any strong leads but I had a vigorous attitude. My first appointment was a bust. I got nowhere fast. It turned out they owned at another cemetery but took my appointment because they wanted the free crap we give out. The couple kicked me out when they realized it was a little too early for the freebies. How sad. Were people really that lonely for company that they would accept a sales call just for some bogus conversation and a jar of honey? In the end, the joke was on them because I didn't have any gifts.

My next stop turned into a sale. Yippee. I had met this old man, David Greenberg, while walking the grounds of Rosemonte. We'd talked a few times on the phone, but every time I wanted to visit him it was a bad time. Finally, he gave in. A bachelor, David had no family. I seemed to do well with that type of customer. Did that mean something? Was my destiny to end up like them? Old, alone, never married with no family? I shuddered at the thought.

On my way home, I scolded myself and tried to be happy about making a sale. My focus was to throw Matt from his throne so I needed to keep my head in the game. I drove to my house trying to think positive thoughts. I was a young girl in my twenties; I had plenty of time for marriage and a family later on. Now it was go time, and I was going.

⚬⟅◉⟆⚬

The following days were long and filled with lots of Bernie. He held extra meetings with long lectures about closing the sale. He had one of the office girls make up a PowerPoint presentation explaining the proper way to place a sticker on a honey jar. Things felt incredibly tense during discussions of sales.

Rosemonte employees had Bernie's vacation circled in red on their calendars. We all felt each other's pain, no matter what our jobs were. We were united in our difficulties in dealing with this horrendous mound of a poor excuse for a human.

One day just before Bernie left on vacation. I came into the office a few minutes early. He was sitting in his chair, waiting. He was dressed in white, a more casual look for him, with crisp linen pants and a button-down shirt in the same fabric. White loafers adorned his feet, making them look twice the size. If he'd had on a hat, he would have looked like Boss Hogg.

I tried to tiptoe by. "Who's there?" Bernie barked.

I took a deep breath and poked my head in the door. "It's me,"

I said.

"Come in here," he ordered. I walked into the little office and waited for whatever he was going to shoot at me. "Are you wearing men's cufflinks?" he asked.

"Yes, I am," I said confidently. I was dolled up in a black pencil skirt with a cream colored short sleeved blouse. It was very unique because it had French cuffs, and I wore cuff links that had belonged to my father. I felt close to him when I wore them. On my feet, I had a fantastic pair of black and cream leather heels. I felt very fashion forward in my outfit. I wasn't going to let Bernie tear me apart.

"Did you buy them just because they had a J on them?" Bernie asked. Why was he so nosey?

"No, I didn't buy them," I said. "They were my father's."

"They look old," he said in a flat voice.

So did Bernie, but did I point that out? "They are. They're from the late '60s or early '70s. Why are you so interested?"

"Did I strike a nerve?" he asked, a glimmer of evil in his eyes.

"No. I just don't understand your sudden interest in my wardrobe."

"You look lovely, as always," he said.

For some reason, I didn't believe him. "If that's all, I'm going to my desk."

He winked his evil eye at me, so I turned and left to go upstairs.

Ronnie was sitting at his desk. He had moved up from Munchkins to regular doughnuts. The box that had once held a dozen only had three left. I didn't judge Ronnie. I myself had become a frequent drinker from working at Rosemonte. Perhaps I was even becoming a functioning alcoholic.

"I can't wait until he's gone," Ronnie said.

"Forever or just on vacation?" I asked. Ronnie smiled.

"I wish forever, but I'll be happy with vacation," he said. "Do you want one before I finish them off?"

"No thanks. You enjoy."

After Ronnie finished the last of his doughnut breakfast, he told me what Bernie had verbally dumped on him that morning. Bernie had started by asking why he and his wife couldn't have any kids. Was it because of a low sperm count? Maybe it was his wife's issues with her lady parts. No sexual attraction between them, so they just bought a baby? Why did they buy one from "the Orient"? Was it cheaper than buying a white baby? When his daughter started to act like a monster, was that when they decided not to roll the dice and get her a sibling?

Jeez. No wonder Ronnie had inhaled a dozen doughnuts. Poor guy, he was well past his breaking point. I'd gotten off easy with Bernie's low blow about my cufflinks. "That is sooo terrible," I said to Ronnie. "He's the one who's a monster, not your daughter."

"I know," Ronnie said. "But damn, he knows what buttons to push." He shook his head.

At lunchtime I went out to grab a hoagie. As I was walking to my car, I saw Bernie driving around the cemetery. He pulled up to T.R.'s truck and honked his horn. Then he pulled out a bullhorn and yelled instructions. Actually, they were more like orders. About how to fix a gravestone that had fallen over. Bernie didn't have any hands-on experience fixing stones. This was the same man who couldn't reload a stapler by himself, let alone work with cement and power tools. But he was relentless. It didn't matter who it was, no one was safe from his buggering. When I got to my car I could still hear Bernie over the bullhorn. I popped a Pepto- Bismal and tried to sink into the silence of my surroundings.

I put the key in the ignition. The engine wouldn't turn over. Shit. I tried again. Nothing. My battery was dead. I got out and trudged up the hill to where T.R. was getting browbeaten by Bernie.

"Hi," I said to T.R. "Can you or one of the guys give me a jump? My battery's dead."

"Sure," T.R. said. He radioed in Spanish to the grounds guys. Bernie started talking to me over the bullhorn, which was making it more difficult for T.R. to use the walkie-talkie. It was also giving me a headache.

"How do you know your battery's dead?" Bernie asked.

"I know." I held up my hand, like I was some sort of car whisperer.

T.R. announced, "Spike will meet you at your car and give you a jump."

"Thanks."

I turned and walked back toward my car. Bernie went back to tormenting T.R. Spike pulled up when I was halfway down the hill. He had spotted me and drove over to pick me up.

"Muchas gracias," I said as I climbed in the truck. Spike nodded his head in my direction.

We pulled up to my Honda and I popped the hood. Spike got out his jumper cables and clipped them to his truck's battery. He hooked up to mine and snapped his fingers. Voila! My car roared back to life.

Spike stared at my car. He looked concerned. Oh no, what now? He went to the bed of his truck and came back with a contraption I'd never seen before. It was shaped like a large canister with a small hose attached. He knelt down and filled my tires with air.

"You look a little low," he said. Man, was that the truth.

"Thanks, Spike," I said. I didn't know he knew any English.

"You all set," he said. Lunch plans cancelled, I was off to Sears.

In the auto department at Sears, I got a salty snack from the vending machine while I made the best of sitting for an hour in the waiting room. The surroundings were drab and gray. To make the time go by, I called Adam. It had been a few days since we'd spoken. I wanted to check on him, to see how he was doing after the breakup with Joy.

"Hey, baby." He'd answered on the first ring.

"You sound a lot better." I was pleasantly surprised.

"I feel a lot better," he said.

"So, what's going on?" I finished my last Goldfish.

"Nada and it feels soooo good," he sang into the phone. "Joy and I are dunzo. Honestly, it was never going to last. I'd rather move on with my life and find a newer, better looking skirt. And if she has money, that's a bonus."

"I am floored," I said. "What brought this on?"

"I'm just tired of looking for money first. It isn't necessarily the most important asset," he said in a serious voice.

"I'm impressed. When did you grow up?"

"Enough about me," he said. "Whaasup with you?"

"I'm sitting in Sears waiting for my car to be finished."

"What's wrong with your Honda?"

"My battery died, so I'm getting a new one. Nothing major."

"Why didn't you call me? I would've come over to help you." He sounded upset.

"I just got a jump from one of the guys and now I'm getting a new battery," I said. "It's no big deal."

"I feel bad. I should have been there to help you."

"It's cool." As I tried to smooth his upset feelings, a confused thought popped into my head. Why was Adam acting all protective of me just when he'd finalized his breakup with Joy?

Maybe I was reading this the wrong way. I pushed those thoughts out of my mind and changed the topic. We chatted until my car was ready, then wrapped up with loose plans to hang out over the weekend.

I paid for the battery. When I started the car, it hummed to life. I smiled as I revved the engine. The power of the new battery ran through the entire car, like my Honda had received a new lease on life.

As I drove back to the cemetery, my happy feelings dwindled. Maybe I needed a new lease on life too. The only question was, where could I go to get a new battery for *me*?

Chapter 23

When the first day of vacation for Bernie finally arrived, I woke up feeling fresh, happy and alive. Everything seemed to be brighter in color, the air cleaner, people dancing down the street. Okay, no one was dancing, but I certainly felt like cutting the rug.

While I was driving to work, Ronnie called me on my cell to see if I wanted coffee. When I answered the phone, he was singing. "It's getting cooler out, does that mean coffee this morning?" he crooned.

I laughed, "Sounds good to me."

Our morning meeting was going to be run by Matt the Puppet. We gathered upstairs in the conference room instead of the little office. Ronnie had brought coffee for everyone. The meeting was so short I still had a half cup of coffee left. Matt told us to finish the month strong, and start September off stronger. I loathe admitting it, but Matt was a refreshing change in leadership.

When Ronnie and I were back in our office, I asked him, "How's the dog sitting going?"

"My wife's in love with Bernie's dog. That dog is so sweet and loving, the total bipolar opposite of Bernie." Ronnie chuckled. "You'd think Sugar would pick up nasty habits from him, but all she does is give love."

"So Sugar doesn't eat things she shouldn't, resulting in an upset tummy? Does she have accidents?" I was laughing so hard I could barely get out the words.

Alexis came in and pulled up a chair. Soon we were telling stories about Bernie and how horrible he was. We were rosy-cheeked from laughing. Alexis told us how Bernie once set her up on a blind date he had come along with his wife to chaperone.

"Oy vey," I shrieked. "Were you a sixteen year old girl, out for her first time?"

Alexis said they all went to a movie, then to Denny's for dinner. Everyone traveled together in Bernie's car, but Bernie made the guy ride up front with him and stuck Alexis and his wife in the back seat. She scoffed at the meal at Denny's. "Who does he think I am?" she asked, her voice an octave higher. "I don't eat at Denny's! So that was the end of that guy. And of me taking dating advice from Bernie."

Soon our laughter billowed out into the hallway and found its way to Matt's office. He marched down the hall and told us, "Get to work or I'll tell Bernie." His threat was so lame. I looked at him with a get real expression. Finally Matt turned and slithered back to his office.

Alexis looked up at the clock. "I have to dash. I have a lunch meeting with a gentleman of a certain age," she said, reapplying more lipstick. The color was cherry red.

"We might as well get some work done," I said to Ronnie.

With a round of phone calls I was able to make an appointment for later that evening. At lunchtime I popped out for a quick bite. I called Liz. Our friendship had been stretched thin. Nothing bad had happened, but I felt awkward. Her life was progressing with Scott. All I had to show for the summer was my bank account. It had fattened up to a nice figure just north of sixteen thousand dollars.

Big surprise, I got her voicemail. Her message informed me she was on vacation. Probably away with Scott. Relaxing, having fun, and drinking it up. Good for her. Still, I felt alone. A fat bank account wasn't great company.

When I got back to my desk, a large brown envelope was waiting for me with a return address of Tucson, Arizona. Who did I know from Arizona? I opened the envelope and emptied the contents on my desk, then read the handwritten note on top.

Written in shaky cursive, the package was from a Mrs. Leiber. I had totally forgotten about her. I'd tried to sell her over the phone months ago; she'd been one of my first cold calls.

The note said she'd had to wait to discuss with her children and to please dismiss her tardiness. I eyeballed the contract. This was good news. I had a chance at beating Matt again. I called Mrs. Leiber and told her I'd received her contract and thanked her for her business. Then I took care of the paperwork and got that squared away.

I went to Matt's office and knocked on the half-open door. "Come in," he said.

I handed him my contract. He examined it.

"Did you update the white board?" he asked.

"No, not yet. I thought I'd wait until tomorrow since it's the last day of the month." I was trying to stay cool.

"Very well, then," Matt did not look up from the contract. "It's only one month," he said as I left his office.

"Pardon?" I turned around and met his glance.

"Nothing," he said. "Absolutely nothing."

I had him, at least for August. I'd won.

Almost done at the office for the day, I had an appointment later in the evening. The only thing left to do was to go out to the cemetery and check a grave for my appointment. I went downstairs to make a section map. Everyone was in a wonderful mood. I made a copy of the map and grabbed a walkie-talkie.

The evening sky was closing in and a cool breeze was in the air. I took a deep breath in and let it out slowly before I walked down the front steps of the office.

I needed to go to section Q5, which was a bit far. But it was nice outside and I wasn't in a rush, so I decided to walk. Q5 was located behind the Russian section, Tatyana's territory. Almost all the Russian gravestones featured etched pictures of the departed. Very expensive. As I made my way through them I looked at all the faces. Many appeared hardened, probably from years of living under Soviet Russia. Others appeared truly happy, buried in the United States of America. Still, the faces were starting to give me the willies.

At the end of the row I noticed a stone with an extra eerie picture: Jakob Brushkova, a war hero, at least according to his epitaph. He rocked a patch over one eye. The man looked really depressed. I would be too if I had to wear a pirate patch. I tried to do the math to figure out what war Jakob had served in. The war might have been one, fought in Russia. I would never know.

As I approached Q5 I heard a whistle. Who would blow a whistle in a cemetery? I spun around and saw Alexis and her dog, Ginger, leading a pack of people and their canines.

Alexis announced, "Thanks, you guys. We'll meet up next week at our usual location."

The people dispersed to their cars, dogs in toe. I waved to Alexis and she gave me a head nod back. She walked towards me, so I met her halfway.

"Hi," we said in unison. I bent down to pet Ginger on the head, then rubbed behind her ears. She was a gentle breed.

"What are you doing, leading a dog parade?" I asked.

"This is my dog walking group," Alexis said. "Bernie doesn't let us come through, but with him on vacation I figured, fuck it." she laughed. "Don't forget T.R. is coming over to my house this weekend," she reminded me.

"I remember, don't worry."

Ginger started barking furiously.

"What is it, girl?" Alexis asked.

Ginger kept barking, louder and louder. We scanned the

cemetery. Maybe she saw a squirrel or some other furry animal? Across the parking lot, Jose and Spike came out of the barn, looking for the commotion. Ginger pulled away from Alexis. "Stop it, Ginger!"

The dog jerked until Alexis accidentally dropped the leash and Ginger took off. "Oh no, Ginger, stop!" Alexis screamed. She ran after her dog. I walked after them as quickly as I could in the heels I had on.

"Ginger!" Alexis continued to scream.

I heard the sputter of an engine as Jose and Spike hopped in the Gator Quad and drove towards us. They stopped briefly to pick me up. Ginger was up ahead acting crazy and barking up a storm. We passed the Russian section and reached Q5, where Alexis had just caught up to Ginger.

WTF? I felt as if my eyes were playing a trick on me. Jose and Spike were frantically speaking to each other in Spanish. I radioed for help but I didn't know who I should ask for, so I just said, "HELP! 911! Q5!"

Alexis had Ginger's leash back in her hand. She yelled, "What the hell is going on? What are you doing?"

A man was laying face-down on the ground in front of us. He was humping a hole he had dug right in front of a grave. His bare bony ass moved up and down. He gyrated faster and faster, then uttered a low moan as he ejaculated into the dirt hole. After a few seconds, he stood up. I had to look, his member was soft and recoiled.

I couldn't believe it! I wanted to look away but my eyes were frozen. What kind of sick freak was this? Did he know the person who was buried there? Was what he had just done considered rape? Was he breaking any laws? Was he mentally all there? How many times had he done this? I had a zillion questions, but said nothing.

The man looked scared. I was afraid of him. His dirty jeans were down around his ankles and he wore no underwear. His pale legs were covered in cuts and bruises, probably from the dirt and rocks on the ground by the grave he'd just violated.

"I'm not here to hurt nobody," he said in a calm voice, but his hands were shaking.

Jose and Spike moved slowly towards him as Alexis demanded, "What the hell do you think you're doing? This is a private cemetery."

"I was just having some fun until your mutt came over and ruined my hard on," he said. The man buttoned his jeans; he looked ready to take off.

Alexis had Ginger's leash tightly wound around her hand. "You're in trouble, serious trouble. And for your information my dog is not a mutt!" she said, just as Jose and Spike both pounced on him. Ginger started to bark again.

The man yelled, "Get off of me. I didn't do nothing wrong." He was crying and screaming for mercy.

Again I radioed for someone in the office to help. Alexis pulled out her cell phone and called 911, describing the man as a necrophiliac. More grounds guys arrived on the scene. Numerous pickup trucks were racing over. The guys all took turns holding the man prisoner mobster-style until the cops arrived.

Alexis and I huddled together. "Do you think Ginger will be traumatized by this?" I asked her.

"No, but I think we will be." she said.

The spinning blue and red lights arrived and two uniformed officers spilled out of the squad car. One asked us what happened while the other got the man out from under the gang of grounds guys. Alexis took charge and spoke with the officer. She told him exactly what had happened and didn't spare any details. Meanwhile, the other officer led the man over to the squad car. He verified his I.D. and ran it for other offences.

This was not the first bizarre crime on record for this guy. He'd been caught humping the ground elsewhere. If Bernie hadn't been on vacation, Alexis would not have walked her dog group that day and Ginger would never have smelled that something wasn't Kosher in the cemetery. So I would have been alone with that freak. Ginger was my hero.

The officers took down our information and put the guy in handcuffs, seating him in the backseat of the squad car. One officer gave Alexis his card and told her if she needed anything to call him. Alexis gave him a sexy, "Thank you, officer," and tucked the card in her pocket.

Everyone watched as the squad car drove away. Then one by one the grounds guys left. Alexis walked Ginger home. I finished gathering the information I needed from Q5 and got a ride back to the office with Spike. He was nice enough to wait for me. I did not want to be alone in Q5.

"Once again, I'm grateful for your help. Thanks so much," I said and I leaned over and gave him a hug. Spike blushed and kept his eyes on the road. I climbed out of the Gator and waved goodbye.

What a day, I thought as I gathered my things. How lonely was that necrophiliac guy? How desperate? The privacy of his own home wouldn't do? I shook my head as I walked to my car. I couldn't get the memory of his bouncing white butt out of my head. I was sure I'd never go to Q5 by myself again.

I was still slightly skived by the time I got to my appointment, an apartment building in the neighborhood of Fox Chase inside the Northeast section of the city. The surroundings were mostly blue collar. I parked and walked up to the front door where I searched for the name Silverman in the call box registry. I found it and pushed the button. Mrs. Silverman buzzed me up without asking who I was.

The lobby was bare and the elevator smelled like old mothballs and wet newspaper. At the eighth floor I got out, found my way to the apartment, and rang the bell. I had to buzz twice before Mrs. Silverman answered the door. I didn't even get a glance. She opened the door turned away and said gruffly, "Come in."

I entered her small apartment and closed the door behind me. Mrs. Silverman sat down in an easy chair, lit a cheap cigar and started to puff away. Her housecoat hung off her body with no shape. She had on men's brown Velcro shoes with knee-highs. Her bare knees were freckled and creased with age. Her very short white hair looked like it had been cut at the barber shop.

The theme of her apartment didn't reflect her hard exterior. Countless shelves housed knickknacks of dogs and cats. A painting on the wall of a rainbow with a swarm of butterflies looked bright and cheery. Next to Mrs. Silverman's easy chair was an old couch covered with a sheet and a bunch of stuffed animals. On the other side was a mismatched ottoman with a cat sleeping on it.

"Where should I sit?" I asked her.

"Right here." She jerked her thumb towards the ottoman.

"I don't want to wake your cat," I said, trying to sound sensitive. I wasn't a fan of cats.

Mrs. Silverman burst into laughter. She was howling and shaking so hard, I was afraid her cigar might ash on the carpet and possibly cause a fire. She picked up the cat and said, "Sophie's stuffed." Then she dropped Sophie in her lap and started to stroke it.

Did I miss the memo, or was today freak show day?

When Mrs. Silverman calmed down and I felt I had her attention, I showed her photos and charts and gave her the information she needed to be buried at Rosemonte. That's when she dropped the bomb. "I know all this. That fella with the stupid haircut, what's his name...?"

Hmm bad haircut I knew who that was. "Matt?" I offered up.

"Yeah, that's it Matt already came to see me."

So Matt had been here but didn't get the sale? Crap.

"I told him I ain't buying," Mrs. Silverman said.

"Why?"

She explained that she'd had to scrimp since her husband had died many years ago. Her children had disowned her because of family disputes. That would explain her apartment. Mrs. Silverman went on and on about her horrible children, and a nasty brother-in-law.

"What does this have to do with Rosemonte?" I asked. Something wasn't adding up.

"The answer's no," she said looking down at Sophie. That cat had been getting a lot of love. Mrs. Silverman constantly petted it.

After a long pause, I asked, "What was Sophie like when she was alive?"

She brightened. "Sophie was a wonderful cat. My best friend. I loved her very much." Her grip tightened on the feline.

I asked a few follow up questions about her BFF. She was starting to soften. "So, when Sophie unfortunately died, who took care of her?"

"I did! I wouldn't let anyone else go near her."

"I'm sure Sophie would do the same for you, but she's technically not here. So who will take care of you when it's time?" I asked. Never mind the fact that Sophie was a cat. A dead stuffed cat.

Mrs. Silverman stared at me, then at Sophie. She puffed away on her cigar for three more minutes before she communicated again. "All right," she said quickly. "How much?"

I was floored. Did I actually have this sale in the bag? I looked at my paperwork and gave her the total. She made four smoke rings in a row before putting her cigar down in an ashtray. She reached under her housecoat and pulled out a small change purse she had lodged in a garter. The change purse was a vivid green vinyl with a brass closure. She opened it up and started counting out bills.

"Here," she said as she shoved a handful of twenties at me. "Invoice me for the rest." She put the change purse back in its hiding place and picked up the cigar again.

I nodded and prepared the contract. I worked hastily and was soon ready for Mrs. Silverman to sign. She scribbled her name. "I like you a lot better than that Matt fella. He's what my mother would call pixilated."

I nodded, not knowing what pixilated meant. When I finished I offered her a jar of honey. "For a sweet New Year."

"Hell no, I don't want none of that," she snapped.

"Very well then, have a good evening," I said as I stood up.

Mrs. Silverman wasn't going to get up from her chair to let me out so I walked myself to the door and called out goodbye. Once I was out in the hallway, I felt relieved. I had beaten Matt for the month of August, with money to spare.

Tonight I was going to have a double Malibu Rum and Diet Coke. I'd certainly earned it.

Chapter 24

I strutted into work the next morning full of power and confidence. I wore a no name black dress with a smart looking collar. On my feet, a fierce pair of Manolo Blahniks. My only piece of jewelry was an oversized, almost obnoxious looking cocktail ring on my pointer finger. Naturally, my lucky black Prada bag was on my arm. I was ready for the morning meeting. Matt knew I had beaten him for the month, but he didn't know about my sale from the previous night.

We all filed into the little office, Matt sat in front of the phone in Bernie's chair. I made sure I sat across from him.

"This is going to be short and sweet, people," he muttered. He went over a few bullshit announcements before giving the totals for August. "Being that it is September first," he said in a monotone voice, "we will go over the totals." He shuffled through some papers to find Bernie's tally sheet. "Well, it looks like Julia beat me," he said.

I beamed at him. Alexis and Ronnie broke out in a round of applause.

"You don't need to clap for her; she only beat me by one hundred and fifty dollars, that's not a big deal at all," Matt said. He looked annoyed.

"Actually, I have another contract from last night." I pushed the papers across the table.

"You made another sale?" he asked, dumbfounded.

"I did," I replied in a matter of fact voice.

I clasped my hands and sat up a little bit straighter while Matt looked over the contract with Mrs. Silverman's cash attached. His eyes danced over the paperwork, looking for a mistake, an error, missing referrals. He found nothing to cite me on.

"So how much did she sell?" Ronnie asked, while tapping his hands on the table in a drum roll.

"Her sale totaled seven thousand dollars," Matt said in a quiet voice.

"Wow," Ronnie and Alexis chanted in unison.

Ronnie put a finger on my shoulder and said, "Ouch, the kid's on fire!" He pretended to shake his burnt finger. Alexis laughed.

"So I actually beat you with *seven thousand one hundred fifty dollars*," I said sweetly.

Ronnie pulled out a chart from the back of his notebook. He ran his fingers over the colorful lines then, announced "The last person to beat Matt's totals for the month was eleven months ago, Robin Seltzer. She doesn't work here anymore."

"Good job, Julia," Alexis said as she gave me a high five. "You should call Bernie and tell him," she suggested to Matt.

"I will do no such thing," Matt shouted. He was hot under the collar. His glasses slid down his pointy nose. Sweat began to appear all over his face. This was better than I had imagined it would be. "One month," Matt told me. "September is a brand new month. Anything can happen."

"True. I could beat you again. You said it yourself, Matt, anything can happen." I stared into Matt's inner being. He looked even more furious.

Alexis chimed in again. "Let's call Bernie."

"If we call him, he'll only bite your heads off for not selling enough," Matt warned.

Alexis and Ronnie looked at each other. Ronnie said, "We don't care, call him." I couldn't believe they were willing to get thrown under the bus, just to hear Bernie put Matt through the ringer. How touching.

"You asked for it." Matt dialed Bernie's cell on speaker.

"What time is it?" I asked.

Ronnie looked at his watch and answered, "9:19."

"So, it's 7:19 there?"

"Oh, shit!" Matt had forgotten about the time difference. He reached for the flash button, but it was too late.

Bernie answered the phone, with a scream. "What do you want?" I hadn't missed that gut-wrenching sound.

"Uhhh, good morning, Bernie," Matt stammered. "I wanted to give you the results for the month of August."

"This couldn't wait until I was awake?"

"We forgot about the time change," Matt explained. "Sorry."

"Not we. *You* forgot," Alexis bellowed into the speakerphone.

Matt had lost control. The results were amazing to watch. "Well, the totals are: Ronnie, Alexis, Matt and Julia."

"What?" Bernie roared. "You got beat by the kid?"

"She had a last minute sale that put her over the top," Matt explained.

"That's not true." I stood up and moved closer to the speakerphone. "I beat Matt by two sales."

Matt shot me a dirty look. "It was only one month, one lucky month," he whined.

"I can't believe you can't handle things there without me," Bernie squealed.

"I can," Matt said in a small child-like voice.

"And you two," Bernie said. "What the fuck is wrong with you? Both of you need to sell, you have no money. I don't know which one of you is worse, Alexis or Ronnie. Alexis, you should be out there shaking your moneymaker and preying on desperate old men or sex-deprived married ones. Ronnie, we've been over this again and again. You need to knock the dick out of your ass, act like you have a pussy, and start selling."

"I don't even understand what that means," Ronnie said.

"Well, you better figure it the hell out, or else you're not going to have a job for much longer," Bernie roared. "How's Sugar doing? The missus wants to know."

"Sugar's fine. Nothing to worry about," Ronnie said.

Matt glared at Alexis and Ronnie and held up a piece of paper that said, "I told you so". Bernie continued to ramble for a few more minutes, but I wasn't listening. I was thinking about what Bernie had said to Matt about him not handling things. What did that mean? Matt was shady and a suck up, but what did that have to do with his sales?

"What else?" Bernie asked.

"Nothing," Matt said. "Have a good rest." But Bernie had already hung up.

We all sat there staring at Matt. He stared back at us. "I guess the meeting's over," he said. "Let's try to have a blow-out month of September."

Alexis, Ronnie and I walked out of the little office and went to our desks. Matt stayed behind to work from the little office.

Later in the day, Alexis and I met with Joe Steinberg. Thank goodness he opened the door with shorts on. They were very short running shorts: the material overlapped and there was a slit up the side. They weren't appealing, but better than nothing. He appeared excited to be in the company of two women. I was relieved that Alexis had agreed to come.

Joe's house had a bachelor feel to it. Worn plaid couches, no throw pillows, a wooden coffee table with a humidor in the middle of it. In the entryway a talking fish hung as a prized piece of artwork. An enormous TV took up one wall of the living room. The remote control looked like one you'd use to land an airplane.

Joe turned off the TV and announced, "Julia, you have the floor."

I started the presentation, but Joe kept interrupting. He was more interested in asking Alexis questions. He wanted to know all about her social life, where she grew up, if she was single. Oy!

I interrupted Joe. "Hey, go over the numbers with me and then you can have some coffee talk with her," I said. Alexis laughed and twirled a strand of her of golden locks around one finger.

"How much are we talking, here?" Joe grumbled.

"Give me five minutes," I said. I did the math, then showed him the total on my calculator.

Alexis stood up. "I'll make some coffee," she announced.

"Bottom line, this is what you need and how much it will cost," I said. "If you want, we can spread it out over a few years, no interest."

"I like things simple," he said. "You're a nice girl and you put up with my shenanigans. Plus, today you brought me a little candy."

Gross.

Joe stood up and walked across the living room. He opened the drawer of a small table. "I'm not getting any younger." He came back with a checkbook and asked, "Who do I make it out to?"

"Rosemonte. Smart decision, Joe," I said.

Alexis came back in with the coffee pot and three mismatched mugs. We sat and chatted for a while. Alexis played matchmaker and set up a date for Joe with her mom. Soon we wrapped it up and Joe walked us out.

"Thanks for the peace of mind and the possible romance," he said to us.

We both giggled as we left Joe's house. I thanked Alexis for tagging along.

"I hope it works out for your mom," I said. She winked at me and waved as we got into our cars.

When the weekend arrived, I had nothing planned, as usual. Adam was busy doing God knows what. The only thing on my to-do list was to hold up my end of the deal with Alexis. How depressing that my big event, for the weekend would be to babysit my sex crazed co-worker.

My phone rang angrily as I was getting ready. I was having one of those days where I didn't know what to wear and everything I put on looked frumpy. Clothes were strewn all over my neatly made bed. I decided to ignore the phone. However, it kept ringing. I was late and still not dressed. For some reason, I was nervous about going over to Alexis's.

"Hello?"

"Hey, baby girl," Adam cooed. "Why did it take you forever to answer? I lost count after twenty rings."

"I'm running late. Can I call you when I'm in the car and on the road?"

"Fine." He sounded upset. Sometimes he acted like such a diva.

Ten minutes later, dressed but officially tardy. I called Adam back.

"Why are you going to Alexis's?" he inquired.

I explained about Joe the naked man, our deal, and how Alexis needed me to chaperone her with T.R.

Adam roared with laughter. "I always thought Alexis had a thing for *me*."

"She has a thing for anyone with a dick," I said, joining in the laughter.

"What are you doing later?" he asked.

"Nothing."

Adam was starting to come out of his funk. I was glad he was acting like himself again.

"If you want, roll over and hang," he said.

"Okay. I'll see how I feel." We hung up when I reached Alexis's development.

Her house was super cute, a cottage from a fairy tale. The front had darling shutters that framed the windows. Along the flagstone walk were purple flowers. A large crab apple tree sat in the middle of the front yard.

I saw T.R.'s truck coming up the street as I exited my car, so I jogged up to the front door. I wanted to look like I was already there hanging out. Alexis opened up the door before I rang the bell and pulled me inside.

"T.R.'s almost here."

"I know. That was close timing," Alexis said.

The bell rang and Alexis tszujed her hair and licked her lips before she opened the front door. When she leaned forward to push the screen door aside for T.R., her blouse fell open. I was sure Alexis had rehearsed that move.

T.R. greeted us both. "Hey, how you two doin'?"

"Would you like a glass of iced tea? I just made some." Alexis, bit her lower lip ever so slightly.

"In a little bit," T.R. answered. "Where's the work you need done?"

"Follow me," she said in a crisp voice.

She walked in front of us, clopping her high heels on the hardwood floors. She stopped in front of a screened-in patio. It was filled with leaves, grass, dirt and dust. The furniture looked grimy. A faint smell of mildew mixed with potpourri was in the air.

"I need this room cleaned up. Most of the junk can be swept up and out," she said, her hands moving towards the back door of the room. "The furniture will need to be hosed down and dried off."

"That's no problem. Let me get my tools," T.R. said. He brushed past us and went out to his truck.

Alexis clutched at her heart. "That man is so sexy," she whispered.

I didn't get it. T.R. was nice and easy on the eyes. But we worked with him. I didn't look at him that way.

He returned and got right to work. Alexis and I sat in the kitchen and drank iced tea. She asked me. "Do you want your iced tea to be naughty?"

"Um, no thanks." Huh?

"Suit yourself," she said, pouring a generous amount of vodka into her glass and stirring slowly with a long-handled spoon. Alexis talked about how freaked out Ginger had been after tracking down the sexual freak show in Q5. "I took her to the vet. Ginger actually needed a mild antidepressant."

"I can understand that. I had to put that insanity out of my mind also," I said.

We heard heavy footsteps coming and T.R. said, "Now some iced tea would be great." A bandana was hanging from the back pocket of his jeans. He'd removed his t-shirt and his chest muscles were slightly sweaty.

"No problem, coming right up." Alexis said.

Here we go, I thought.

"Would you like your tea a little dirty?" she asked T.R., holding the bottle of vodka in her hands like she was a model on *The Price Is Right*.

T.R. shook his head. He reached for the bandanna and patted at the sweat on his forehead. Alexis looked at me with wide eyes. She handed him the glass, then the three of us were silent, sipping our tea.

T.R. finished off his glass in one long gulp and said, "Well, I gotta get back to work." After he left Alexis put her head on my shoulder and bit my arm.

"Ouch!" I shrieked. I pushed her off and rubbed my shoulder. "Alexis, you broke the skin."

"Oh, relax," she said. "That's nothing compared to some of the love wounds I've gotten in the past."

Ick. Yesterday's dinner swirled around in my stomach. Alexis sat down and stared out back where she could see into the sun porch. She watched T.R. "He's such a hunky man. Why can't I find a man like that?"

Shit. She was actually hot for T.R.

"Julia, watch him bend over and stand up again. Oh. My. God. Look at that perfect ass!" she kvelled.

"No." I said. "Stop looking at him like he's a piece of meat. He's your co-worker. Remember that."

Alexis was ignoring me. "Bend and up, bend and up," she chanted while she watched T.R. working.

"He is not one of your dreamy porno guys. T.R. is your friend and co-worker. Have some respect."

"Oh, I almost forgot," Alexis said. "You have got to see this!" She led me into the living room and popped in a video tape in her VCR.

"You still have a VCR?" I asked, stunned. What a dinosaur!

Alexis ignored me. "Grab a seat and watch this. I made a tape of all my favorite scenes mostly from *Queer As Folk* and some hot, sexy, man on man porn. I love it," she said in a loud voice.

I grabbed a throw pillow and plopped down on her floor. "Alexis, I really don't want to watch this. Porn is not my thing."

"I need something to help me resist T.R.," she claimed.

"Right. Do you really think watching a porno tape is going to help? I mean, isn't that why I'm here? To help you stay... calm, while he's here?" I felt like I was starring in a bad afterschool special.

"You're right. I need a shower, a cold one. I'll be back in a few."

She bolted up the stairs. Something told me she wasn't taking a shower. I turned off the VCR and leafed through an art book on her coffee table. Of course, the art in the book featured men, some gay some not. They were all naked. Oy vey.

I closed the book and sat back. On the wall in front of me was a painting of a naked man looking at himself in a mirror. The artist's name appeared in the right hand corner. Alexis.

T.R. walked in the room. "I think I'm almost done. Where's Alexis?"

"Here I am," she called out and galloped down the stairs. She sure didn't look like she'd showered. "Let's take a look out back." She led the way. "Everything looks so clean."

"I just have to hose down the furniture. But so far you think it's good, right?" T.R. asked.

Alexis nodded. Her eyes wandering up and down his torso.

When T.R. walked off to find the hose, I pulled Alexis back into the living room. "Seriously, Alexis, you need to get a grip. We both know you're thinking about T.R. working that hose." My voice was shrill and sharp.

"You're right, Julia, but hey, I already took care of business upstairs so I should be good until he leaves."

Gross. T.M.I.

"I didn't need to know that, Alexis. Let's just chill out until he's done, okay?"

She sat down on the couch and flipped through a *People* magazine and I turned on the TV. We both zoned until we heard T.R. approach.

"I'm all done, Alexis," he said. "Do you want to check my work?"

We all walked out to the patio. It looked nice. Everything was neat and clean.

"Thank you so much, T.R. You're a lifesaver," Alexis said. "Let me get my purse."

She crossed the living room and opened the coat closet. She stood on her tiptoes to grab her pocketbook, then walked back with a big smile on her face. After she took out her wallet, she handed over a wad of cash to T.R.

"Thanks, Alexis. My daughter will be happy. This will cover some of her car insurance," he said.

"My pleasure." Alexis's voice was too deep. I gave her a look and a mini shake of my head. So inappropriate.

We stood at the doorway and watched T.R.'s truck disappear. I fetched my Kate Spade and announced, "I think I'm going to go also."

Alexis grabbed my arm."Thanks, Julia, I'm sorry I bit you. Sometimes I get a little too intense."

I laughed, "It's cool."

I was relieved our deal was done. I'd held up my end of the bargain, Alexis had held up hers. But I was too emotionally exhausted to hang out with Adam. I just wanted to go home and chill. Bernie was due back the next day and things would be normal again. At least, as normal as things ever got at Rosemonte.

Chapter 25

I awoke feeling sick to my stomach, and I knew why. Bernie was back. His vacation had zoomed by.

At work I could tell everyone else felt his presence also. The smiles had vanished. The happy music that played in the background was gone. Everything was bleak, blah, and routine again. Nobody danced in the streets.

Bernie had a long meeting with Matt in the little office. A private meeting. The door was closed for a few hours. It was quiet: no yelling, no screaming, nothing. Very strange. This was not Bernie's usual protocol. Eventually he got on the speakerphone and called us all down to the little office.

Bernie sat in his chair, his face scorched from the New Mexico sun. He didn't look rested from his vacation. If anything, he looked crankier than usual.

"We have the lunch at the Palm coming up this week," he grumbled. "The company that supplies us with tombstones is taking us out. I'll go over the rules." While Matt handed out memos, Bernie lectured us about our clothing. "Wear only your best threads to lunch." He used quote fingers when he said the word threads. He thought he was cool using the slang. Dork. "We're being treated to lunch and should order what we want, but don't be excessive."

This was funny coming from Bernie, since everything about him was so excessive.

"Familiarize yourself with the menu so you don't take up a lot of time ordering. No one will order anything marked market price." Bernie glared at Ronnie. "The car pool situation is as follows: I, will go in my own car and meet you there. Alexis, Ronnie, Julia and Matt will go in Matt's car."

Great, a car ride with Matt the Puppet. I couldn't wait.

Bernie continued. "Only speak when spoken to. You may order one alcoholic beverage, or as many soft drinks as you like."

I couldn't believe Bernie thought we didn't know how to behave in a nice restaurant. At the bottom of his memo was a signature line. He wanted us to date and sign, agreeing to the rules he'd just gone over. Ronnie was signing. Next to him, Alexis was scribbling her name too. Matt had already given his John Hancock and was staring at me, waiting for me to sign. Unbelievable.

"Now that that's out of the way, what happened to sales last month?" Bernie yelled. "Ronnie, you suck so much I can't believe you still have a job here. How much money's in your sock drawer? Halloween's coming up soon, will you be collecting a grant from UNICEF? Or going door to door with a tzedakah box? Alexis, what happened? You were one of my best and now you are one of my worst! With your looks, you should have no problem closing any sale. You should be acting like the babe in the movie *Basic Instinct* you know, running around in a short dress with no underwear on. You'd get 'em then."

Alexis looked at him in disgust. "You are such an ass. I make sales because I'm a good saleswoman, not because of my looks," she fired back.

That was only partly true. However, now was not the time to split hairs. Bernie was being extremely rude and nasty. I was pretty sure that, legally, he couldn't speak to his employees this way. Although that never stopped him. I reached into the pocket of my suit jacket and found a chewable Pepto. Even though I wasn't being yelled at, my tummy still felt the effects.

"What appointments does everyone have lined up for the week?" Bernie asked.

Matt, of course, volunteered first. "I have four lined up so far."

Alexis boldly announced, "I have nothing so far," and flashed a big smile at Bernie.

Ronnie said, "I have three appointments."

"At this time," I said, "three."

Bernie didn't like any of our answers. He continued to yell at us. "I am trying to motivate you people to sell!" he screeched.

My sole motivation was to beat Matt again. I wasn't sure about anybody else.

Later in the day I was on the phone with Adam and he was giving me some leads. We chatted about how nasty Bernie was. "I almost forgot his name was Bernie, I'm so used to you calling him Fuckface." he said.

He had to go drive a funeral. After we hung up, I started researching his leads.

In the middle of super sleuthing my desk phone rang. A woman said, "Hello, my name is Kristen Holbrook Weinstein." She said she had received my card from a friend, but was very vague about which friend. Then she said, "I'm not Jewish, but my husband is. Many of his relatives are buried at Rosemonte. I'm putting together a family tree." She asked for my help in her quest.

"Sure." I was hoping I could eke out a sale later on. "I can take down the names you'd like me to look up," I offered.

"Oh. Can I just fax you? It'll be easier for me," she said.

"No problem." I gave her the fax number and told her I'd be in touch in a few days. We hung up and I made a few notes about Mrs. Kristen Holbrook Weinstein.

Cathy from the office downstairs buzzed me, "You got a fax."

That was fast. I flew downstairs to retrieve it.

Cathy was stapling a few pages together. "Here," she said. I took the pages and looked them over. Fuck, this was going to be a ton of work.

Over the next few days I slaved over Kristen's requests. Then I called her to make an appointment to show her what I'd found. Kristen invited me to her home in Chestnut Hill. She seemed upbeat and thrilled about the progress I'd made so far. After we hung up, my mind started to drift. I wondered about the Weinsteins. How they'd met, why she was doing his family tree, and how I was going to get a sale out it.

That evening I drove out to Chestnut Hill, one of the most expensive neighborhoods outside Center City. The homes were humongous and old, many registered as historic sites. A handful of big names lived there. Germantown Avenue, the main street, was made of cobblestones. The Avenue, as locals called it, was filled with restaurants and quaint shops and featured an old school trolley that ran up and down.

I pulled up to Kristen's mini mansion. White with columns, and a large porch, it looked like a house from the movie *Gone With The Wind*. A half-circle driveway broke up the front of the yard, with a straight one leading to a three car garage. Yellow rose bushes in full bloom sat on both sides of the pitch black double front doors.

I rang the bell and waited. A woman only a few years older than me opened the door. "Hello, I'm Kristen," she said as she held out a hand adorned with a massive diamond ring. I eyeballed her rock to be at least six carats.

I greeted her and tried to stifle my surprise. She couldn't have been much more than thirty. She had long, wavy, vibrant red hair. Her green eyes were shielded by Dolce & Gabbana glasses. Her crisp white shirt and black slim pants were very plain but probably cost a small fortune.

"Let's go into the study," Kristen announced. I followed her

Gucci loafers and took in the grand entryway as we crossed the two-story foyer with an oversized crystal chandelier. "It's original to the house," Kristen told me, as if I were on a historic tour.

We entered the study. A large side by side desk was flanked by two high backed leather chairs. On the wall was a life-size portrait of Kristen and her husband. He looked more like her father. "Would you care for a drink?" she asked, and gracefully walked over to the bar.

"Water's fine, thanks."

She poured a bottle of Voss water into a crystal goblet and fixed herself a gin martini, three olives. Vintage, and very classy.

"Please, sit. Let's see what you found," she said as she handed me my drink. Excitement sparkled in her eyes.

I pulled out the file I'd been working on. The fruits of my labor included maps, photos, and old bills of sales. Kristen looked amazed.

"You've been putting in a lot of hours," she said, opening a drawer to take out her paperwork on the family tree. Together, we tried to fit in the missing pieces, or in this case the missing persons. An hour or so later, we finished up.

Kristen was elated. "You've helped me tremendously!"

"I'm so glad. Would you like to come to the cemetery and see the graves? I'll give you a guided tour." This could be it. My invitation to close the deal.

"I would love that," she said.

"Do you and your husband own ground anywhere?"

"No. We discussed it once. He's dead set on Rosemonte, no pun intended. But we just haven't done anything about it."

I put on the best laugh of ease and delight I could manage. "I can assist you with that."

"Can I be buried there?" Kristen asked. "You know, because I'm not Jewish."

Really? What a shock, a girl named Kristen not being Jewish! "As long as you're still married to your husband, you can be buried there."

A look of relief crossed Kristen's face. "You have given me very good news," she said.

I pulled out my date book. "Next week is good for me."

Kristen played on her iPhone and we compared schedules. We talked for a few more minutes before I was graciously walked to the front door.

I called Adam on my way home to see if he wanted to grab some dinner. He told me to order some grub and come over. I picked up a pizza and a side of fries, then headed to his apartment. As we sat and enjoyed our take-out, I brought him up to speed about the crazy stuff that had happened at Alexis's house. He filled me in on his office gossip.

"Have you ever eaten at the Palm?" I asked.

"No way. That place has sucky service and tacky décor." He gave me the thumbs down gesture.

"What's tacky about it?"

"The dining room is bumble bee yellow with caricatures on the wall and the chairs are sooo fucking uncomfortable," he said.

"Really?" I was disappointed. I told him about the lunch and how Bernie made us sign off on all these rules.

Adam laughed. "You are going to have the worst time. Bernie's going to try to act like a big shot. He's such a jackass."

After dinner we vegged and watched a movie. Adam sat next to me on the couch, which was kind of strange. He never sat right next to me, especially when there was lots of room. I took off my heels and rubbed the balls of my feet.

"Do your feet hurt?" he asked.

"Just a little. These shoes make my feet ache if I wear them too long."

"Do you want me to give you a foot rub?" he offered.

"No." I scooted away from him. "Why are you acting funny?"

"I'm not. I'm trying to be nice," he said.

"You're freaking me out, man."

The movie continued but I felt out of sorts. I reached for a Pepto from my purse. The weird out of place feeling didn't go away. I decided to leave.

"I'm not feeling well. I'm gonna go."

"You can stay here, if you don't feel up to driving," Adam said.

"Thanks for the offer, but I'm okay to drive. I just want to go home and get some rest." I slipped on my shoes and was out the door in two seconds flat.

As I drove home, I took mental stock of what was happening in my life. I was making decent money at the cemetery, even though I was putting in tons of hours. But my decision to have more fun was not exactly working out the way I wanted it to. Stress was pretty high at work and probably not the best thing for me. This was brought into focus by my Pepto-Bismol habit.

I told myself I needed to look on the bright side. I should be grateful I had a good job, and a cute house. I needed to stop the pity party and focus on getting ahead.

❧

The next morning, Adam swung by with coffee and a flaky pastry.

"What a surprise," I said when he popped his head into my office.

"Hey, I just thought I would bring you a little sweet," he said. He plopped down and began to eat his own pastry. "Are we cool?"

"Sure, why wouldn't we be?" I asked, knowing exactly why we wouldn't.

"You know, last night…" His voice trailed off.

"Ancient history." I waved my hand for effect.

"Okay, good." Adam popped the last bite of sugary goodness into his mouth.

Bernie started his morning go-round on the speakerphone. When he got to my name, Adam held a finger up to his mouth and answered for me. I held back my laughter as Adam said, "What do you want, Fuckface," into the speaker. Bernie yelled and I started to laugh. I couldn't hold it in! Ronnie was chuckling too.

"You little piece of shit. If it wasn't for your father, you would have nothing!" Bernie screamed.

Adam shouted, "Come upstairs and face me like a man."

Bernie hung up, then called back immediately. "Get your asses downstairs! Now!"

I knew a lecture from Bernie was coming but I didn't care. Adam's joke was an unexpected and fun office prank.

Adam announced, "I'm going out the back door to avoid Bernie's rage."

"Smart move," Ronnie said as he patted Adam on the back.

Adam grabbed my hand and whispered, "Call me later."

"I will." Why he was acting extra nice, I wondered. Did he need me to bake something for him?

As soon as everyone was seated, Bernie unloaded. I zoned out right away. Every now and then I'd glance in his direction. His face was red with anger, sweat beaded all over his forehead. At one point, a little string of spit connected his lips. It was a bad magic trick, as his lips opened and closed, the string never broke. Finally, after making a bunch of hand motions, Matt the Puppet whispered to Bernie and Bernie wiped his mouth with the monogrammed cuff of his sleeve.

After an hour of yelling, Bernie looked disgusted enough and ordered everyone to get out and sell big.

That evening I struck out on my appointments. I smiled, I was kind and considerate. I handed out calendars and jars of honey. And I didn't make one sale. I called Ronnie on my way home to see how he'd made out.

He whined, "I haven't made a sale in what seems like forever."

"Don't worry," I said. "Things will turn around."

He moaned. "I'm in deep doodoo!"

We hung up and I parked on my street. I hurried inside and made my evening cocktail, just to take the edge off. The rum tasted smooth and sweet going down my throat. Relaxation was setting in.

My phone rang. Liz! One more day and I would've sent a search party.

"I'm in love! Scotty is a dream come true!" She crooned about her man, their vacation to the Caribbean, and how he totally got her.

I sat and listened. I was happy for my friend, but sad for me. As I topped off my Diet Coke with more rum, I thought about Adam. He could never make me as elated as Liz was about Scott.

"He wants me to meet his parents," she squealed.

"Are you thinking what I'm thinking?" I asked.

"I can't confirm, but this is exciting. We're going up to New York at the end of the month."

We wrapped up our conversation and Liz promised to have a spa day with me before she left. I would have to keep my fingers crossed.

As I prepared for bed, I tried not to think about the upcoming morning meeting. No good could come from it. Instead, I planned my outfit for lunch at the Palm. I ran a few looks through my mind and drifted off to a booze filled dreamland.

Chapter 26

I woke up feeling dizzy, sick, cold and clammy. When I sat up, I felt the familiar nasty swirling in my tummy. Only it was worse this time. Oh no, I groaned, and ran to the bathroom, where I vomited up everything I'd eaten the day before.

Yuck. I splashed cool water on my face. I couldn't take a sick day. Today was the day of the big lunch. I had no choice, I'd had to go to work. I took a hot shower and got myself in gear.

An hour later, I was on my way to work dressed in a brown checked suit, dark brown Ralph Lauren snake skin heels, and a cream colored Tod's purse. A large smokey topaz necklace looked like an expensive collar. When I arrived, Bernie was waiting in the lobby. He was inspecting everyone's outfit, making sure we were up to his standards.

"Looking good, kid." Bernie said as I walked through the door. "Now, do a spin," he ordered.

"What?" Was I on the catwalk at Fashion Week? Give me a break.

"A spin. You know do a turn."

"I'm not doing either one." I still felt dizzy.

"Why are you starting with me?" Bernie asked. "All I'm asking is that you do a runway walk with a twirl," he said in a snarky voice.

"I'm not starting with you. You're acting like an asshole. If I pass your inspection, then I'd like to go to my desk."

"You take all the fun out of being a boss."

I walked up the stairs in silence, satisfied that I'd passed his stupid test. All I wanted was to put my head down on my desk.

Matt was standing in the doorway to my office with his hand out. "Five dollars each," he said to me and Ronnie.

"For what?" I challenged. Ronnie was counting out five singles, then recounting them.

"For gasoline and parking."

"I'm not paying you. You volunteered to drive," I said.

"Actually, I was assigned to drive by Bernie," Matt said.

"Then get the money from him," I growled. Matt eventually left with Ronnie's five bucks.

Alexis didn't pass the dress test. She had to go home and change. Bernie wanted her to wear a skirt, not pants. She argued with him, but eventually gave in. It was just easier to do what he wanted. She was back in time for us to leave.

We rode in Matt's Subaru. His car didn't have a radio. Who doesn't have a radio? Alexis and I sat in back and Ronnie rode shotgun. Matt parked the car in a cheap lot a few blocks from the Palm. He instructed us to turn our phones on vibrate before we went inside. None of us did.

Walking past the foreign vendors selling street meat I started to feel nauseated again. When we walked into the restaurant my nausea grew worse. The smell from the kitchen wafted through the dining room, a mixture of grilled steaks and bacon grease, which combined with the heavy cigar smoke in the air.

"I need to go to the bathroom," I said to Ronnie and Alexis. "Please make sure I do not sit next to Bernie." They nodded their heads.

I walked very quickly to the ladies room. Once inside the stall, I hung my purse on the hook on the door, then vomited. How was I going to eat a steak now? I walked out of the stall and washed my hands. Then I fixed my face.

The bathroom attendant peered at me. "Can I get you anything?" I shook my head and put on more lipstick. "You pregnant?"

"Hell no," I said. There went her tip. "I just have a stomach bug."

"Mhhm." She grunted.

I re-entered the restaurant trying not to breathe too deeply. I wandered through the busy dining room until I found our table. The only open seat was between Bernie and the man from the tombstone company. As I pulled out my chair and sat down I mouthed the word "thanks" at Alexis and Ronnie. Then I scanned the menu and tried not to breathe in Bernie's strong smell. He'd used a new cologne ever since his vacation, a mixture of cactus and dragon breath. It smelled horrible. It didn't help that he doused himself with it in massive amounts. I felt like I might faint.

The waiter came over to take our drink order. I ordered a ginger ale.

Bernie looked at me with a quizzical expression. "I thought you preferred Diet Coke."

"I do, but my tummy is a little crazy today."

"Don't be nervous your first time in a fancy restaurant," Bernie said with a grin.

"What?" I said, "This is not my first time in a fancy restaurant." But Bernie wasn't listening. I was really annoyed.

I decided to get the filet mignon. I also wanted to get an order of hash browns; I thought they would help settle my stomach.

The waiter came back with our beverages. He was ready to take our order. Bernie ordered prime bone in ribeye steak, twenty four ounces of it, and a bunch of sides. "They're for the table," he claimed. Then he went around the table and ordered for everyone else.

When he came to me, I interrupted. "I can order for myself."

"She'll have the prime New York strip, sixteen ounces."

Oy vey.

I tugged at the waiters sleeve and said, "I don't want that. I would like to have-"

Bernie yelled at the waiter, "Take the order I gave you." The waiter gave me a frightened look and backed away.

I sipped my soda and sulked. I felt like a child. How much more of this shit could I stand? The man from the tombstone company pitched a lot of products to Bernie, who worked him on the price. The rest of us just sat there like lumps, not saying a word. Why were we even there? I started to fidget. Adam was right, these were the most uncomfortable seats. The chairs were old, wooden, with stiff upright backs and no cushion at all.

Our waiter came back with steaming plates of food. The table was filled with different kinds of sides including potatoes, spinach, and mushrooms. All the steaks were bloody rare.

Everyone started to dig in. I managed to force down three bites, and a few more got smuggled into my napkin. The creative disposal made a small dent in the sixteen ounce serving of meat.

Bernie's plate was almost clean. He had devoured his twenty-four ounces in two minutes flat, and was mopping up the leftover juices with a piece of bread. His napkin was tucked into the neck of his shirt. He looked like such a loser.

Bernie elbowed me in the ribs. "Are you going to eat that?" I shook my head and handed him my plate. He stacked my plate on top of his empty one and started to eat.

The waiter came back to clear the plates and hand out dessert menus. "Key lime pie for everyone," Bernie announced.

"I'll just have some tea," I said to the waiter.

Everyone else ordered coffee. Soon we all had hot cups steaming in front of us. When the pie was served, I slid my slice over to Bernie. He looked confused, then shrugged his shoulders. He was delighted to have two pieces of pie.

The waiter came over with the bill and handed it to the tombstone guy. He slipped his credit card inside without even looking at the total. "Did everyone enjoy lunch?" he asked.

In unison, as if we'd practiced, we said, "Yes, thank you."

I couldn't wait to get out of there. The bright orange walls and all the dumb pictures were making me woozy.

Finally, the waiter came back and the tombstone guy signed the check. Everyone stood up and made a beeline for the door.

While Bernie waited for the valet, Ronnie, Alexis, Matt, and I walked to the garage. I was grateful for the fresh air. Matt tried to make conversation about the lunch, but no one wanted to talk to him. He brought up the new products the guy was pitching. Did we think they were good ones? "What did we learn from lunch?" Matt asked. None of us said a word. I wanted to go back to work. This whole excursion had been a waste of my time. I was still irritated that I'd had to sit next to Bernie.

When we got to the car, I nudged Ronnie and said, "What's up with making me sit next to him?"

Ronnie said, "I'm sorry. Bernie picked the seats." Why should this surprise me?

The ride back to the cemetery was silent. I looked out the window and watched the city scenery zip past. By the time we got back to Rosemonte my stomach, had started to calm down. Maybe my nerves were all wound up with the stress of work and the stupid lunch. Whatever it was, I didn't care. I was starting to feel better.

At my desk I worked on my schedule for the week. I had an appointment later, another one tomorrow. My phone rang, startling me. I answered and tried to sound professional. It was Tatyana. She wanted to know what had happened at lunch. Bernie wouldn't let her attend.

"Oh, Tatyana, it was so bad," I said. I filled her in on all the details. She laughed when I told her Bernie ordered for everyone.

"He has such a small dick, he is afraid everyone knows it. Do not let Bernie get to you. Bernie is a big bully and he will pray on any weakness you have. Julia, he is not worth it."

I trusted her. Her words struck a chord. She was so right. We gabbed for a few more minutes before I went back to my work.

I was downstairs making photocopies. Bernie was in the little office with the door closed and Matt was inside with him. They were having another secret meeting. I still couldn't quite put my finger on it, but something was off. I finished up my copies and headed back upstairs. When I was halfway up, my name crackled from the speakerphone.

I turned around and walked down to the little office. I knocked on the door and opened it before he could say "come in." Matt sat like an obedient dog next to Bernie.

I stood in the doorway. "Yes?"

"Come, sit," Bernie boomed. I slumped into a chair. "Did you enjoy the lunch?"

"Yes, thanks," I lied.

"It has come to my attention that you didn't pitch in for gas and parking."

Matt was too much of a wimp to meet my gaze. "I didn't pay Matt."

"You need to give him five dollars," Bernie said. "Do you have five dollars?"

"You're kidding me."

"Well, if it's not a stretch, then pay Matt the five dollars," Bernie ordered.

I stood up and announced, "My purse is at my desk. I'll be back."

A few moments later, I was back in the little office with the two schmucks. As I took out my wallet I heard Bernie murmur, "Louis."

I glanced at his bulbous head. He looked impressed. I rolled my eyes and asked Matt, "Can you break a hundred?"

"A hundred?" he shouted. He opened his wallet, a brown Velcro mess. A look of hatred appeared on Bernie's face. "I can't," Matt whimpered in a small voice.

"How 'bout you?" I nodded at Bernie.

Bernie grunted as he lifted his massive leg to grab his money clip from his pants' pocket. "Here," he said, thrusting five twenties at me.

"Is this better for you?" I asked Matt in a baby voice. "Can you handle this?"

Matt gave me my change.

"Is that all?" I asked them.

"Yes, you are dismissed," Bernie said.

I gave Matt some shade as I exited the little office. Matt closed and locked the door behind me. I stood outside and tried to listen, but I couldn't hear what they were saying. They were plotting something, I just knew it.

❧❦❧

My mind was clouded with the mishegas of Bernie and Matt as I drove to my evening appointment. I couldn't shake them from my mind. The whispers, the glances back and forth, and the secret meetings. It all added up to some kind of plot. The first week of the month had just ended and, I was determined to keep Matt a loser. The taste of victory over him was too sweet to lose out to him and Bernie.

I was in the Frankford neighborhood of the city. When I'd made the appointment, I was alarmed to learn Jews still lived there. Frankford wasn't the safest place to live. The aboveground El train ran twenty hours a day. The nasty thing about the El was the drip, a mysterious, possibly toxic liquid that would randomly spatter down from the above-ground tracks.

I found the house and drove a little farther down the street to park. I'd seen a BEWARE OF DOG sign posted in the yard. Awesome. Just what I needed. A trick I'd picked up from Tatyana was to always have a doggie treat just in case. I'd need the luck of the Irish to make this sale, I thought as I gathered my things and headed to the house.

Mr. Sideman's row house was in piss-poor shape. Newspapers lined the inside of the windows. The front steps had separated away from foundation. Paint peeled from the exterior walls. A chain link fence with a few broken spots framed the property.

I rang a doorbell that sounded like a sad version of a once healthy happy tweeting bird.

"Hi, Mr. Sideman," I said, with a friendly smile on my face.

He stood behind the screen door in an undershirt with armpit stains and a pair of pilled sweatpants. "You see that sign?" he yelled, pointing at the door with one dirty fingernail. I nodded, still smiling. "Well, I'm the dog," he said, exposing teeth that had been ignored for decades.

The smile vanished from my face. I felt very stupid holding a Milk-Bone in my hand.

"What the hell do you want?" Mr. Sideman chided.

I explained about the appointment, just as I had earlier on the phone. I tossed the doggie treat behind me and hoped he didn't see me do it.

"What the hell?" he peered past me to see what had landed in his yard.

"Maybe a bird?" I suggested. "How about a free jar of honey for the New Year?" I held it up for him to see.

"You're wasting your time, hon. I'm not buying anything from that dirt hole you work at."

"So, you're not going to let me in to discuss your options?" I asked.

"Hell to that. What part of the N. O. do you not understand? Are you dense? Thick in the head?"

I was close to losing my patience.

"Well, what is it? Dense or thick in the head or just plain old shit for brains?" Mr. Sideman laughed at his own joke.

I'd had enough. I was not going to take any more crap. Not from this guy, not from anyone else.

"Look here, Mr. Sideman, I made this appointment with you

over the telephone, you accepted, and now I'm here to help you," I said. When he didn't budge an inch from behind the safety of his screen door, I kept going. "You've been nothing but a rude old man. You can let me in now and we can deliberate, or I'm going to be on my merry way. What's it going to be?"

Mr. Sideman called my bluff. "Get the hell off my property before I call the cops."

"Fine. You've made the wrong decision," I yelled. I placed the jar of honey on the top step and walked off.

"Hey, come back here and give me my honey," Mr. Sideman yelled. "If I open the screen door, it'll push off my stoop and break. That's gonna be a huge sticky mess."

I turned around and grinned. "Listen, this jar of honey breaking and making a mess will be the least of your problems. Especially if you don't take care of your cemetery needs."

I walked to my car, trying to avoid the drip from the El. Mr. Sideman yelled at me the whole way down the block. He was like Bernie, and this gave my stomach a bad vibe. When I got to my car, I popped a Pepto. Then I started the engine, and cruised out of Frankford.

That hadn't gone as planned. I'd lost the sale. Mr. Sideman would probably call Rosemonte and complain about me. He was a cranky old man who'd just wanted to waste my time. Why did I let people like Matt, Bernie and Mr. Sideman screw with my head? I needed a cocktail.

The rum went down silky smooth, as usual. I sat on my couch drinking and going over how I'd let my life get out of control. I used to have fun. Now all I did was work. When I wasn't working, I was thinking about work or the people at work. This wasn't where I wanted to be in my life.

I poured myself another rum and Diet Coke. Was this drink number three? Or four? All I wanted was to go to sleep and forget about the whole screwed up day.

Chapter 27

When I woke up right before my alarm was set to go off, my head was pounding. The sharp piercing buzzer wouldn't be pleasant. My house was quiet and calm. I looked out my bedroom window. The sun had just risen and the sky was a lovely shade of baby blue. As I stood up, my body said no, not yet, and I fell back onto my bed. I rubbed my sore head, and reached for the pills on my bedside table. I popped three Advil.

On my way to the closet I passed the desk where I kept my schedule. The Weinsteins were on deck today. I needed to be in tiptop shape for them. They were a huge fish and all mine. The only thing I had to do was reel them in. I flung open my closet doors, perplexed about what to wear. I was looking for a power outfit, but something preppy that would amuse Kristen. Tiger Woods always wore red on his last day of a golf tournament. Red was his power color. I decided to borrow that good luck charm from him.

On my bed I laid out a red suit, after I looked at it carefully, I hung it back up. Too fancy. I flipped through the hangers. Perfect! I'd pair black tartan pants with a red blazer and a white shirt. You could never go wrong with a classic white shirt. Thanks, Carolina Herrera.

As I merged onto I-95, Ronnie called. "I heard you went to see Mr. Sideman last night."

"Oh no. How did you know that?"

"He called and left an angry message for Bernie."

"Fuck!" I shouted. "That's not how I wanted to start the day."

Ronnie tried to console me. "Don't worry, everyone has been out there to sell him. He's a crusty old guy who enjoys being nasty."

"So you've been there?" I asked.

He sighed. "Yes, twice."

"What's up with the newspapers on the windows?"

"I don't know," he said.

"Am I going to get into trouble with Bernie?"

Ronnie laughed. "Aren't we always in trouble with him?"

"True," I said, and laughed.

"Do you want anything from Dunkin' Donuts? It sounds like you could use a muffin."

"No thanks, I'll see you in a bit."

I felt a smidge better that no one had been able to sell Mr. Sideman. Had he let anyone into his house? He was a nutcase, for sure. I mentally prepared answers for my upcoming grilling session with Bernie. Maybe I'd let him yell and get it over with so I could save my energy for the Weinsteins.

I pulled into the parking lot and walked up the hill. I hesitated outside for a moment. My surroundings were very serene. Wishful thoughts about an alien invasion danced in my head.

At my desk sat a chocolate chip muffin, courtesy of Ronnie. He was a sweet guy. I wrote him thank you on a Post-It with a funny face drawing, and stuck it on his desk lamp. I popped the muffin top off and ate it. The stump got buried in the trash. I downed half my coffee, and listened to the familiar round-up of counselors for the morning meeting.

As usual, I was the last to arrive at the little office. Bernie perched in his chair, a dozen doughnuts in front of him. He was drooling, deciding which kind to devour first. Matt sat next to him, his hands folded like a girl's. His nails needed to be trimmed. Ugh. My nose wrinkled up. I guessed he knew what I was thinking because he unclasped his hands and slid them under the table top.

Alexis had just finished putting on her makeup. Her slinky purple low-cut dress showed off a tan still vibrant from the summer sun. Hmm. Did she go to a tanning salon? Ronnie had on a brown suit with a tan shirt. He grinned as I took the seat next to him.

"By a show of hands, who here has been out to sell Mr. Sideman?" Bernie asked. Four arms shot up. Bernie posed another question, "Why have none of you sold to him?" Everyone was silent. I wasn't going to volunteer any information. "Well, I'm waiting," Bernie said in between doughnut chomps. Still, none of us spoke up. Bernie played the message Mr. Sideman had left on the voicemail. He ranted about me leaving a jar of honey on his stoop, then he yelled about me trying to sell him a bunch of shit he didn't need.

Bernie belched. "What happened with this guy?" Bernie asked me.

I told him Mr. Sideman had been nasty, and accusing me of things that weren't true. "I put the honey down on the top step because he wouldn't open the screen door for me. I didn't want to open the door and go in uninvited. That's rude."

Bernie calmly clapped his hands. "Very good."

Huh? I was totally confused.

"Mr. Sideman has had everyone out to his dump of a hellhole because he wants a free jar of honey. He never buys, he just wants a visitor that he can fuck around with and cause drama. You figured out how to outsmart him at his own game. That's why I'm clapping for you. As your reward, how about a doughnut?"

"No. Thanks. So you're not mad that a potential customer called up and said I was annoying him?"

"Not in the least, you did a great job," he said, smiling at me. Bernie rarely smiled.

"But I didn't sell him." Suddenly I had a flashback to the old woman who'd called and complained about me and Ronnie. I had forgotten how much Bernie had loved that.

"You outsmarted him, kid." Bernie patted me on the arm. I made sure he didn't get any doughnut dust on me. He turned to the rest of the counselors and boomed, "What does everybody have for the rest of the week?"

The meeting went on forever. I kept checking my watch. The Weinsteins were due after lunch. I wanted to meet them on arrival and keep them away from Bernie and Matt. That was imperative.

Eventually, the meeting ended and we were all excused. Except for Matt the Puppet, who probably had to stay after to clean the doughnut crumbs off Bernie's pants.

I was back at my desk when Kristen called. "My husband had a small schedule change so we will be arriving separately."

"That's no problem," I said. I'd wait for both of them to arrive before I started the tour of Rosemonte.

Kristen sounded excited. A normal person would probably think she was acting fake, but I knew how invested she was in this project. "Guess what? I'm bringing along a student filmmaker. He's going to capture the moment."

"I can't wait," I said, trying to sound as excited as she was. But I didn't like having my picture taken. Now I was going to be in a home movie? Oy vey.

I sat at my desk and waited. I was so nervous my feet started tapping and didn't listen when I told them to stop. At one o'clock I decided to wait downstairs. I gathered up the folder with their family heritage information and made myself comfortable in the main office. The thought of being filmed was making me crazy. I distracted myself by thumbing through a newspaper.

Kristen came bursting through the front doors. She looked like a lady who lunched. She was dressed in a bone-colored suit, her jacket tailored perfectly. In her hands she held what some consider to be the trophy of all that was holy: a Birkin bag!

A tall gangly guy followed her in, filming the surroundings. He looked as awkward as I felt.

Kristen gave me a double air kiss. "Hello, my dear," she exclaimed. "I'm so excited about today!"

"I know, me too." What a lie.

"My husband will be here shortly," Kristen explained. "I figured he could drive us around and you can direct him."

"I direct," said the camera man.

"Oh, darling," she laughed. "I meant direction as in driving directions."

"Right." The camera man pushed his glasses up on his nose. The lenses seemed too thick for the thin wire frames, hence the slippage. His name was Randy; it was embroidered on his camera bag. He was quiet and shy at least in the presence of Kristen.

Bernie called to me from the little office. I popped my head in and tried to give him as little detail as possible. That didn't work. He wanted to meet Kristen. Shit.

When I pulled her into the little office, Bernie stuck out his nail bitten hairy mitt for her to shake.

Kristen didn't blink, she shook it like a pro and said, "Julia's uncovering many great discoveries for my family tree." Then she cut off Bernie when her cell phone rang. "Oh, excuse me," she said in the most polite voice.

Kristen took the call. Then she said to me, "My husband's waiting outside. We should go and start the tour now." She turned to Bernie. "It was lovely to meet you."

He answered, "Likewise." This wouldn't be the last of it with him. He'd be waiting for us when we got back, no matter how long the tour took us.

I opened the door for Kristen and Randy. Out front a dark green Range Rover waited for us, the engine running.

"You sit in the front, Julia." Kristen ordered.

It was going to be a long day.

I slid into the front seat and introduced myself to Mr. Weinstein. I didn't know his first name because Kristen always referred to him as her husband. "Hello," he said. Maybe his first name was Mister, his last name Weinstein.

An older man, he had at least twenty five years on Kristen. He looked smart. His hair had some gray, and he had a close shaved beard. His clothes reflected his demeanor: astute and traditional. Slacks, a button down shirt, and new looking Ferragamo loafers. The car smelled of leather, cologne, and old money.

I directed Mr. Weinstein to a section of Rosemonte where his distant relatives had been buried. As we drove, I pointed out some factoids about Rosemonte. At our first stop, we all got out and looked at the stones of Minnie and Max Weinstein. Randy asked a few questions of Kristen and Mr. Weinstein. Apparently, Randy had to call him Mr. Weinstein too.

We got back into the car and I directed them to the next stop. This time we went to see the gravestones of Rhoda and Sydney Lifshitz. Again, Randy took the lead once I brought them to the spot.

We danced this same dance for the rest of the afternoon. After we'd visited every stone on my list, Kristen was over the moon.

She told me with tears in her eyes, "I can't thank you enough, Julia. You have no idea what this means to me."

We got back in the Range Rover and I asked if they wanted to come in for a cup of coffee.

Kristen and Mr. Weinstein agreed and Randy declined. Perfect.

Randy said he'd edit the footage and get us all a copy soon. Oh goody. Did I really need a copy? After he left, we went inside and I got the Weinsteins settled in the lobby. I left to brew a fresh pot of coffee.

They were only out there alone for two minutes. Apparently, that was too long. The diseases known as Bernie and Matt infected them. I heard footsteps as I came back to the lobby. I called out, but Kristen didn't respond. The door was closed.

No fucking way was I going to let this happen! Not after all the time I'd invested in the Weinsteins.

Suddenly, I knew. The scam became crystal clear. All the private meetings. The whispers. The numbers on the white board. *They were stealing sales.* Bernie was helping Matt snake sales away from other Family Services counselors! That's how Matt always ended up in first place.

What slimy rats. Both of them. I fumed. I was not going to let it happen to me. Those scumbags were not going to steal my sale away!

I ran back to the kitchen and grabbed the almost full pot of fresh coffee. I placed it on a tray with cups, sugar and creamer. I rushed to the little office and called out, "My hands are full. I have the coffee. Please open the door."

Kristen opened the door. "That smells absolutely divine," she said.

I unloaded the tray and served the coffee. I only poured a cup for Bernie so I could give him a dirty look. I stared directly into his evil eyes.

"Whoops, we ran out." I said. "Not enough coffee for Matt. Looks like you'll have to go make your own cup." I was seething, yet calm. I was trying to keep my cool.

"I'm not in the mood for coffee," Matt announced. He placed his presentation book on the table and clasped his hands. His nails had been trimmed since our last encounter. He looked directly at me, his eyes cold. I stared right back. How dumb, I thought. Did he think I would sit there and let him steal my sale? I wasn't going to let him win. I stared until he looked away. Loser.

Matt didn't care that he'd lost the staring contest; he opened his presentation book and jumped right in. As he talked about the history of Rosemonte, Kristen gave me a look like, "What's going on?" I rolled my eyes. Inside I felt panicked. I didn't know what to do. The Weinsteins were big money. I couldn't sling any more mud that would make me look bad so I just sat there frozen in place. I needed to take control of the situation. But how?

Finally, Mr. Weinstein raised a hand to quiet Matt. "I don't understand. We've been working exclusively with Julia. Why are you stepping in now, Bob?" he asked Matt.

"My name is Matt, sir. We work as a team at Rosemonte."

Such a liar. No way would I ever be on a team with him. He was an unethical thief. Right in front of my eyes, this was how it would go down. Why hadn't Ronnie or Alexis warned me? Tatyana's hints made total sense to me now.

"Well, if you work as a team, then Julia will continue this business with us," Mr. Weinstein said.

Score! Take that, Matt the Puppet!

Matt looked at Bernie, desperate. "Actually," Bernie said, "Matt's better at giving the presentation than Julia. Julia's great at giving tours, making coffee, and looking cute." He winked.

"Well, this will be a wonderful opportunity for Julia to practice her presentation," Mr. Weinstein slid the presentation book in my direction. In a war of words, Bernie had just been shot down.

I took a deep breath and continued where Matt had left off. I added, "Most of what's in these pages we actually saw on our tour."

While Matt and Bernie fumed, Mr. Weinstein kept acting as my defender, an awesome bonus. Kristen sat next to him and played with her triple strand of pearls.

Bernie tried to take over again. "Mr. Weinstein, I can see that you're not ready to buy today. Why don't you come back tomorrow? Or Matt can come out to your home later this evening."

"I've been to their home. Everything is fine. I don't need any help from you two," I said in a steely tone.

Kristen stood up, Birkin in hand. "Matt would you be so kind as to show me where the ladies room is?"

"Julia will show you," Matt said rudely.

"You're closer to the door, dear," Kristen said in a not so nice voice. Matt stood up and she followed him out of the little office. Thank you, Kristen.

Mr. Weinstein pulled out a checkbook. "Look, Bernie. Julia has done a fantastic job of making my wife happy. She automatically gets my sale because of that. Do you have a wife?"

"Yes, I do," Bernie groaned.

"You're the breadwinner?" Mr. Weinstein asked.

Bernie bobbed his giant head.

"Then, man to man, you'll understand when I say happy wife, happy life. I don't care much for you, or your lapdog Matt."

I stifled a laugh. I was impressed Mr. Weinstein could throw down like that.

"Julia's a good girl and she's getting my sale. Now, no offense, but Julia and I can handle it from here," he said.

Mr. Weinstein was so in love with Kristen, he was willing to go through all this bullshit just to make her happy. The two of them had an electric connection. I couldn't help but grin.

Bernie grunted. "I'm sure you'll want a price reduction and only I can give those. So I need to be involved."

Since when? Bernie couldn't change the rule any time he felt like it. Could he?

"Do I look like I need a price reduction?" Mr. Weinstein chuckled. Then he leaned forward in his chair. "Are you this rude to all of your potential customers? Look, this is what I want, and whatever the price is will be okay. Do you understand?" He turned to face me. "As we discussed, Julia, I want the full setup for Kristen and me. In addition, I want spaces for my children and their spouses." He drew on a piece of paper. "Let my kids handle their arrangements when it's their time. This is for me and my wife. Now, how much for something like this?" He showed me his rough sketch.

Bernie picked up a calculator from the side table and punched the keys. "$51,995. You don't have that kind of cash," Bernie blurted. "If you did, you'd have on better clothes."

"I like my clothes. However, I don't like you," Mr. Weinstein said in a cool voice.

Matt and Kristen came back in. "Are we done, honey?" she asked. She hooked an arm through his.

"Almost," he said. He turned back to Bernie. "49 even and Julia gets the full commission."

How could Bernie say no to that? Sales had been bad lately and Bernie needed whatever he could get. His eye began to twitch. A sale like this did not come in the door every day. The sale was too much money to give up, even if his ego had been stomped on.

The energy in the little office was indescribable. My stomach was going crazy. Matt looked sick and sad. Bernie appeared to be mortified. Kristen was giddy. Mr. Weinstein was resolute.

"Do we have a deal?" Mr. Weinstein broke the silence.

"Yeah, okay," Bernie muttered.

Mr. Weinstein wrote a check and slid it across the table to me. Hurray. "You can bring the paperwork to my house, Julia. Tonight or tomorrow, whatever works best for you."

I smiled, and said, "Thank you. I'll bring the papers over tonight on my way home."

"Very well then," he said and shook my hand. Kristen gave me a hug and two more air kisses. They both walked out of the little office hand in hand.

Matt, Bernie and I sat there waiting to launch what would be a fight to the death. The car engines started out front. From the window I saw the Range Rover and Kristen's Bentley roll down the hill. They were gone.

Go time.

"What the hell is wrong with the two of you?" I yelled. "Why did you try to steal *my* sale?"

"This does not concern you," Matt said in a wimpy voice.

"I'm afraid it does, Matt." I paced in the little office. "How long has this been going on, Bernie? Why do you do this kind of shit? What secrets does Matt have on you that you cave to him and help him steal? Why do the others let you get away with it? Do you enjoy acting like a fraud? How do you feel, knowing you're stealing money from your co-workers?" I sat down and silenced myself. I needed a drink. Maybe a whole bottle of rum.

"I don't know what you're blathering about, Julia. Matt was just trying to assist you in a sale. What's the problem?" Bernie asked.

"Are you really trying to flip the script on me? Do you think I'm that stupid?" I knew they were shady. But for some reason I thought I'd be exempt from their woven web of lies. I was wrong.

"Why are you so upset? Is it your time of the month? Jesus, you and Alexis. Both ragging at the same time." Bernie frowned in disgust.

"You are such an asshole!" My rage was boiling over. How much more abuse could I take?

"Yes or no? Got your period? That's got to be it. You do look a little bloated." Bernie said.

Matt agreed, "Yeah, bloated. Do you want some Tylenol?"

"No, but you're gonna need it when I'm done with you." I balled my hands into fists, ready to punch Matt the Puppet right in his big fat mouth.

Matt scooted his chair closer to Bernie's.

"Move over. She's not going to hit you, and if she does, she'll go to jail," Bernie said.

"Me, go to jail? How about you go to jail for all the unethical sales tactics, theft, and con artistry? Or just for being a dickhead?" I was screaming.

"You stole them from me," Matt whined.

"Who? What?" I sputtered.

"The Fishmans," Matt wimpered.

"We've been over this. Mrs. Fishman was my teacher in high school. She never told me she was working with you. Plus, you never said you were trying to sell them. In fact, she told me she didn't care to work with you because of how you treated her daughter."

"You're spewing lies," Matt yelled. "The Fishmans were mine.

Mine!" He pointed a finger to his chest. His face was pale.

"Look," I said. "We're in sales. Whoever sells the most is the top dog. You need help selling and Bernie fixes it for you and that's not fair. Plain and simple, not fair." I paused for effect. "Both of you are cheaters."

"What are you talking about? You have no proof of that," Bernie yelled.

"If I have no proof, why are you yelling? I can practically see your heart beating out of your chest." How many times had he screwed over Ronnie and the others?

"Look, Julia, it's been a long day." Bernie scooped the sweat from his face and wiped it on his pant leg. "Sometimes things get complicated. You see a situation one way and it appears different to someone else."

"What's up with these bullshit riddles? Just tell me why you and Matt steal sales. Why you think it's okay to take from someone else when they do all the work."

Bernie let out a sigh. "Julia, you're a good salesperson, but you could use a little work. You tend to sell to old men."

"So what? Most of the people buying here are old men. Just answer my question, Fuckface."

"What I'm trying to say is that you have... Daddy issues."

I felt like I'd been sucker punched in the gut. I knew Bernie was upsetting me on purpose. He wanted to show me that he was in charge and I'd have to take whatever he dished out. I'd witnessed this behavior one too many times with all the other Family Service counselors. It wouldn't work on me.

"Excuse me? You think I have daddy issues? Why, because my father died when I was a kid so that automatically means I have to be fucked up emotionally? I have news for the both of you," I said, my confidence building inside me. "My father taught me lots of things before his untimely death. He taught me to have a strong work ethic. Respect, honesty. But most of all, he taught me to stand up for myself and not take shit from anyone. And that includes the two of you."

I stood up and leaned over the table. I meant business. "The two of you have some serious issues. *I'm fine.* Actually, I'm more than fine. I'm fucking fantastic. Your lives are on the downward slope, I'm young and full of life. I'm on the upward slope. And I'm outta here. I quit."

I grabbed Mr. Weinstein's check off the table. "You want this?" I asked my hands at the ready to tear it up.

"Just calm down," Bernie said. "No need to act rash."

"Me, rash? Like the one in between your legs when you pissed yourself? I'm not acting rash. I'm acting like you do. Like a fuckface."

I *was* acting like he did. I sickened myself. I'd never gone ballistic on anyone like this before. Still, it felt necessary.

"What do you want? More vacation time? Take a deep breath and try to relax," Bernie said.

"I want the both of you to know how much I hate your fucking guts! You are horrible human beings. I can't stand the sight of either of you. It amazes me that you two ass clowns found women to marry. You should go home tonight and literary kiss the ground they walk on. You are not deserving of them."

I sat down and crossed my legs. "As for this check, I want Ronnie to handle them. Not Matt. Or else I'll tear it up right now. What's your move, Bernie?"

"Fine, Ronnie will take it," Bernie answered without looking in Matt's direction.

"I'm going to call them right now. You two zip it up. Or else I'll tell them what's going on," I ordered.

Bernie pushed the phone towards me. I dialed Kristen's cell.

"Hi, Julia." She'd answered on the first ring.

"Hi, Kristen. Listen, I have a situation going on over here. Everything's fine and I'll explain later. As far as the paperwork tonight, I'm going to send over my associate, Ronnie. Is that okay with you?"

"Sure," Kristen answered. "Just as long as it's not that slimy Matt."

"No worries, he won't be there," I said, and we hung up.

"So this is the deal, take it or leave it. Ronnie goes over to the Weinsteins with the paperwork and he gets a cut of the action. I, of course, get the rest. If I were you, I'd cut out this shit. The next person you try to screw over might not be as nice as me. Who knows what they could do to a couple of chumps like you?"

Bernie rung out his pocket square, it was drenched in sweat. "Fine. Whatever."

I took my tacky blue plastic name tag and threw it at Matt. "I'm going to clean out my desk. Then I'll be leaving. There's no need for me to stay here a minute longer than that."

I marched out of the little office and up the stairs. I grabbed a box from the bathroom for my personal items. Right away, my stomach felt better. I didn't have a hankering for Pepto-Bismal. I felt strong.

 Ronnie was waiting for me at my desk. He looked sad. "You're leaving us?"

"I'm sorry, Ronnie. I can't stay here. This place is the worst."

"I know." He twiddled his thumbs. "I'll take care of whoever you need me to."

"I know you will. It'll just be the Weinsteins." I handed him their file. "The contract is filled out, you just have to go over there tonight for signatures."

"Wow, that's the easiest commission I've ever made. Thanks," he said, looking me in the eye. "Why me? Why not Alexis?"

"Because you trained me, Ronnie, and we're friends. Why didn't you tell me about what Matt and Bernie were up to?"

Ronnie stared out the window. "This has been going on for a long time. Even before I started working here. It's not fair, it's just how things go around here. You're young and have a different view. I'm old and need job security."

"Ronnie, that's not true. It's never too late to change anything, including how this shithole is run."

I looked in my box. There wasn't much in there; my cemetery flats, a six-pack of Diet Coke, my datebook, and some Pepto-Bismol. "I guess I'm done."

Ronnie and I hugged, and I started my last walk down the hall.

"Word travels fast," Alexis called out. "I wish I had the balls you have."

I laughed, "They're not that big."

"Come on, your balls are the size of your boobs. They're huge." She made an obscene hand gesture.

"Well, I guess your theory could have some truth to it." I giggled as I made my way down the stairs for the final time. In the lobby, I bellowed, "Goodbye, Rosemonte."

Outside, the air was fresh and clean. I felt alive again.

I got in my car and started the engine. I had no idea where I was headed or what I was going to do next. My bank account was fat, so at least I was financially prepared.

As my car passed through the black wrought iron gates for the last time, I took a look over my shoulder. Mr. Sideman was right. The place was a dirt hole.

Chapter 28

On my way home, I called Adam.

"Hey," he answered.

"Hi. Look, I'll explain everything later, but here's the short story. I quit Rosemonte."

"Okay," Adam said. "Bernie's an asshole. I know how the stress has been getting to you. Look, I'm about to pull in for a funeral, but how about dinner tonight? I'll scoop you up at eight."

"Perfect." I was relieved. I didn't want him to scold me about quitting the job he helped me to land. "I'll wait for your call."

I got home a half-hour earlier than if I'd worked a full day. I plunked the box from my office on my dining room table, went upstairs and started the shower. I shed my clothes and hopped in. The hot water rejuvenated me.

I thought about the cemetery. I'd met so many strange people. Now I had some really great stories to tell at cocktail parties. In a relatively short time, I had learned so much about myself, like how low I'd go to make a sale. That was an unpleasant lesson. But I'd also honed my people skills. I'd learned about communication. And love. The best part of the whole experience was what strangers had taught me about love. Real love. I'd heard so many romantic stories, and I'd seen so much devotion! This gave me hope. That one day I'd find my one true love and be forever smitten with him. 'Til death—and after. Forever. I'd seen that kind of love now and I knew what it looked like. I wouldn't settle for anything else.

I didn't want to leave the shower, but when my fingers started to look like raisins, it's time exit. I wrapped myself in a towel and headed to my bedroom. Looking through my closet, I realized I was tired of suits. Going to dinner in a Juicy track set and flip-flops would be pure enjoyment. My hair air-drying and my face makeup free, I felt clean and effortless. Rosh Hashanah was around the corner, the Jewish New Year. What better time to start fresh?

I went downstairs to chill and wait for Adam to call from the corner. I turned on the television and played along with the contestants' on *Jeopardy*.

The knock at my door startled me. I looked through the peephole. Adam?

I opened the door. "Sorry. I didn't hear the phone? Did you call my house or my cell?" I went to grab my purse.

"Come back here," Adam shouted.

"I'm sorry, did I leave the lock on the screen door?" I walked back. Adam was holding a bouquet of Gerber Daisies, my favorite flower. The arrangement was a rainbow of colors.

"These are for you," he said, tilting his head to the side.

OMG. "Thanks, these are gorgeous." I exclaimed. "Is this because I quit today? I don't want any pity. Rosemonte sucks."

Adam chuckled.

"I want to put them in a vase with water." I walked into the kitchen. "Adam, this arrangement is so massive; it takes up my whole kitchen." I was expecting him to say something like that's because you live in the ghetto and have a shitty house. But he was silent. I gave him a hug and said, "Thanks for the flowers, man. You ready to go to dinner?" My tummy was chanting, feed me, feed me.

Adam pulled me closer for another hug. "You're so dumb."

Here we go. I thought and waited to hear how stupid I'd been to leave Rosemonte.

"Things are going to change between me and you," he said. "I need to treat you the way you should be treated. I can't fight my feelings any longer. I want to date you, Julia."

"Come again? Whoa. I sure didn't see *this* coming."

Adam laughed. "I know. That's why I said you're so dumb. You're my best friend. You're also beautiful and so awesome. I want us to be together. A couple."

He pulled me in tight for a kiss. His lips were smooth with freshly applied ChapStick. He had just the right amount of five o'clock shadow.

The kiss, our first ever, would be make it or break it. Were we well matched as a couple or just friends? I'd wrestled with my feelings about Adam for years. Finally I had the chance to see if he was the man I wanted.

His waxy lips surrounded mine. I tasted Altoids. I felt submerged. He darted his tongue around my mouth. Somehow my tongue chose not to mingle with his. Our teeth rubbed. Gross. I wasn't feeling him. I wasn't into it. The long awaited kiss was anything but good.

He drew away, his eyes dreamy. "Come on, I've waited a long time for this moment." He put his arm around me and led me towards the staircase.

What moment? The kiss had been horrible. But I was glad it had happened. My on again off again feelings were no more. Adam was not for me. That kind of relationship wouldn't work. We were friends, not lovers.

I shrugged his arm off my shoulder and went over to stand by the couch. "Adam, this isn't going to work for me. I've been confused for a long time about you and me, but this isn't going to happen. You and me isn't a good idea. I'm sorry, but I think we should stay friends."

Adam looked stoic and grand in his fancy suit. Not a hair out of place. "Are you sure? I thought this, us, you and me?" The color drained from his face. "I don't understand."

"If working at Rosemonte taught me one thing, it's not to fuck around. Life is only so long. I don't want to waste any more of it. I need to get my life together. For real this time."

"So…let's discuss your plans over dinner. I've got some ideas for you. I can make a few phone calls. I can set you up." Adam jingled his car keys in his pants pocket.

"No. From now on, I'm going to make my own ideas click. I have connections too, ya know." I remembered Mr. Fishman's interest in investing in young entrepreneurs. My heart pulsed in my ears. I stood tall and sucked in my stomach. "In fact, I got a lead I'm working on right now."

"Okay. If this is what you really want, don't call me when you've run out of options."

Ouch. Harsh. I got it, I'd just shot him down. Still, that had hurt.

"That was mean of me. I'm sorry, kid." He walked to the door, then turned around before leaving. "Call me soon, let me know what your next move is. Okay?"

"Sure." I smiled at him and he nodded sadly, then let himself out.

I rummaged through the box on the table. My datebook was on the bottom, the leather edges rounded and tattered. I found the number for the Fishmans and dialed.

"Fishman residence, this is Cecilia."

"Hi, Cecilia. Is Mr. Fishman home?" My voice quivered.

"Yes ma'am. Who's calling, please?"

"Julia. Julia Daniels," I said.

My heart beat a little faster in my chest. I knew it had been there all along, but now it was ready to soar with passion for the next adventure life would bring me. A new bakery? A man to share it with?

I knew what I wanted. I wanted both.

Acknowledgments

My dearest Nicole, you and I have been through it all, bad boyfriends, bosses, and blue jeans. I appreciate your support for *all* my ventures. Thanks Mrs. B.!

Virginia Aronson, from Write By The Beach, my editor and so much more. Thank you for taking me under your wing, and showing me the way. You rock!

A huge heartfelt thank you and round of applause to Scarlett Rugers from Chick Lit Book Covers Company. Australia is far away but I've always felt that you were right next to me in Florida.

Saving the very best for last, to my husband, my Lane, you are a man of many talents, from web design to technical support and contract negotiations. I would be so lost without you by my side. Thank you for believing in me always. I love you!